Gustave Aimard

The Buccaneer Chief

Gustave Aimard

The Buccaneer Chief

1st Edition | ISBN: 978-3-73407-919-1

Place of Publication: Frankfurt am Main, Germany

Year of Publication: 2019

Outlook Verlag GmbH, Germany.

Reproduction of the original.

THE BUCCANEER CHIEF

A Romance of the Spanish Main

BY

GUSTAVE AIMARD

AUTHOR OF SMUGGLER CHIEF, STRONG HAND, ETC.

LONDON

WARD AND LOCK, 158, FLEET STREET

MDCCCLXIV

CHAPTER I.

THE HOSTELRY OF THE COURT OF FRANCE.

Although the Seine, from Chanceaux, its fountainhead, to Havre, where it falls into the sea, is not more than four hundred miles in length, still, in spite of this comparatively limited course, this river is one of the most important in the world; for, from the days of Cæsar up to the present, it has seen all the great social questions which have agitated modern times decided on its banks.

Tourists, artists, and travellers, who go a long distance in search of scenery, could not find anything more picturesque or more capriciously diversified than the winding banks of this river, which is skirted by commercial towns and pretty villages, coquettishly arranged on the sides of verdant valleys, or half disappearing in the midst of dense clumps of trees.

It is in one of these villages, situated but a few leagues from Paris, that our story began, on March 26th, 1641.

This village, whose origin dates back to the earliest period of the French Monarchy, was at that time pretty nearly what it is now; differing in this respect from all the hamlets that surround it, it has remained stationary; on seeing it you might fancy that centuries have not passed as far as it is concerned. When the neighbouring hamlets became villages, and were finally transformed into large towns, it continually decreased, so that its population at the present day scarce attains the amount of four hundred inhabitants.

And yet its situation is most happy: traversed by a stream and bordered by a river, possessing an historic castle, and forming an important station on one of the railway lines, it seemed destined to become an industrial centre, the more so because its inhabitants are industrious and intelligent.

But there is a spell upon the place. The great landowners who have succeeded each other in the country, and who mostly grew rich in the political commotions, or by risky speculations, have tacitly agreed to impede in every possible way the industrial aspirations of the population—have ever egotistically sacrificed public interest to their private advantage.

Thus the historic castle to which we alluded has fallen into the hands of a man who, sprung from nothing, and feeling himself stifled within its walls, allows them to crumble away before the effects of time, and, to save the expense of a gardener, sows oats in the majestic alleys of a park, designed by Le Nôtre, whose grand appearance strikes with admiration the traveller, who sees it at a distance as he is borne past in the train.

The same thing is going on in the whole of this unhappy hamlet, which is condemned to die of inanition in the midst of the abundance of its neighbours.

This village was composed at the period of our narrative of a single long narrow street, which ran down from the top of a scarped hill, crossed a small rivulet, and terminated only a few yards from the Seine.

This street, through its entire length, was bordered by low, ugly tenements, pressing closely together, as if for mutual support, and mostly serving as pothouses for the waggoners and other people who at this period, when the great network of the French royal roads had not yet been made, continually passed through this village, and sought shelter there for the night.

The top of the street was occupied by a very wealthy, religious community, next to which stood a large building hidden at the end of a spacious garden, and serving as hostelry for the wealthy personages whom their business or pleasure brought to this place, which was surrounded for ten leagues round by sumptuous seigneurial mansions.

There was nothing externally to cause this building to be recognized as an inn; a low gateway gave access to the garden, and it was not till the traveller had gone along the whole of the latter that he found himself in front of the house.

It had, however, another entrance, looking out on a road but little frequented at the time, and which was employed by horses and coaches, when the traveller had succeeded in obtaining the landlord's leave to put up there.

Although this house, as we said, was a hostelry, its owner did not admit everybody who proposed to lodge there; on the contrary, he was very difficult in the choice of his guests, asserting, rightly or wrongly, that a hostelry, which had been honoured on several occasions by the presence of the King and the Cardinal Minister, must not serve as an asylum either for vagabonds or nightbirds.

In order to justify the right he claimed, the landlord had, a few months previously, had the arms of France daubed on a metal plate by a strolling painter, and inscribed under it in golden letters—"*The Court of France.*" This sign he put up over his door.

This inn enjoyed a great reputation, not only in the country, but in all the surrounding provinces, and even as far as Paris—a reputation, we are bound to add, well deserved, for if mine host was particular in the choice of his lodgers, when the latter had succeeded in gaining admission he treated them, men and beasts, with a peculiar care, that had something paternal about it.

Although it was getting on for the end of March, and, according to the almanac, 'Spring had begun some days previously,' the cold was nipping, the rime-laden trees stood out sadly against the leaden sky, and a thick, hardened layer of snow covered the ground for some depth.

Although it was about ten o'clock at night, it was light, and the moon, floating in russet clouds, profusely shed her sickly beams, which rendered it almost as light as day.

All were asleep in the village, or, at least, seemed to be so; the *Court of France* alone emitted a light through its ground floor barred windows, which proved that somebody was still up there.

Still, the inn did not offer shelter to any traveller.

All those who during the day, and since nightfall, had presented themselves, had been mercilessly turned away by the landlord, a stout man, with a rubicund face, intelligent features, and a crafty smile, who was walking at this moment with an air of preoccupation up and down his immense kitchen, every now and then casting an absent glance at the preparations for supper, one portion of which was roasting before a colossal fireplace, whilst the rest was being got ready by a master cook and several assistants.

A middle-aged, short, plump woman, suddenly burst into the kitchen, and addressed the landlord, who had turned round at the noise.

"Is it true," she asked, "Master Pivois, that you have ordered the dais room to be got ready, as Mariette declares?"

Master Pivois drew himself up.

"What did Mariette tell you?" he enquired, sternly.

"Well, she told me to prepare the best bedroom."

"Which is the best bedroom, Dame Tiphaine?"

"The dais room, master, since it is the one in which His Majesty—"

"In that case," mine host interrupted her, in a peremptory tone, "prepare the dais room."

"Still, master," Dame Tiphaine ventured—who possessed a certain amount of credit in the house, in the first place, as legitimate spouse of the landlord himself, and then, again, through sundry very marked traits of character—"with all the respect I owe you, it seems to me—"

"With all the respect I owe you," he exclaimed, stamping his foot passionately, "you're a fool, my good creature, obey my orders, and do not trouble me further!"

Dame Tiphaine comprehended that her lord and master was not in a humour that evening for being contradicted. Like a prudent woman, she bowed her head and withdrew, reserving to herself the right of taking a startling revenge at a future date for the sharp reprimand she had received.

Doubtless satisfied with his display of authority, Master Pivois, after taking a triumphant glance at his subordinates, who were surprised at this unusual act of vigour, though they did not dare show it, walked toward a door that led into the garden; but at the moment when he laid his hand on the key, this door, vigorously thrust from the outside, opened right in the face of the startled landlord, who tottered back to the middle of the room, and a man entered the kitchen.

"At last!" the stranger said, joyously, as he threw his plumed hat on a table and took off his cloak. "By heaven! I almost found myself in a desert."

And before mine host, who was growing more and more astounded at his cool behaviour, had the time to oppose it, he took a chair, and comfortably installed himself in the chimney corner.

The newcomer appeared to be not more than twenty-five years of age; long black curls fell in disorder on his shoulders; his marked features were noble and intelligent; his black eyes, full of fire, announced courage, and the habit of commanding; his countenance had a certain stamp of grandeur, tempered by the cordial smile that played round his wide mouth, full of brilliantly white teeth; his red, and rather swollen lips, were adorned, according to the fashion of the day, with a most carefully waxed moustache, while his square chin, indicative of obstinacy, was covered by a long royale.

His dress, while not rich, was, however, becoming—cut with taste, and affected a certain military air, which was rendered more marked by the brace of pistols the stranger carried in his belt, and the long iron-handled sword that hung at his side.

Altogether, his lofty stature, and muscular, well-developed person, and the air of audacity spread all over him, rendered him one of those men, the breed of whom was so common at the period, and who at the first glance contrived to claim from people with whom accident brought them in contact that respect to which, whether justly or unjustly, they believed they had a right.

In the meanwhile, the landlord, who had slightly recovered from the emotion and surprise he had experienced at what he almost regarded as a violation of his domicile, advanced a few steps toward the stranger, and while bowing lower than he had intended, and doffing his cotton nightcap before the flashing glance the other bent on him, he stammered, in anything but a steady voice—

"My lord—"

But the latter interrupted him without ceremony.

"Are you the landlord?" he asked, sharply.

"Yes," Master Pivois grunted, as he drew himself up, feeling quite constrained at answering when he was preparing to question.

"Very good," the stranger continued; "look after my horse, which I left I know not where in your garden; have him put in the stable, and tell the ostler to wash his withers with a little vinegar and water, for I am afraid he has hurt himself a little."

These words were uttered so carelessly, that the landlord stood utterly confounded, unable to utter a syllable.

"Well," the stranger continued, at the expiration of a moment, with a slight frown, "what are you doing here, ass, instead of obeying my orders?"

Master Pivois, completely subdued, turned on his heels, and left the room, tottering like a drunken man.

The stranger looked after him with a smile, and then turned to the waiting-men, who were whispering together, and taking side-glances at him.

"Come and wait on me," he said; "place a table here before me near the fire, and bring me some supper—make haste, s'death, or I shall die of hunger!"

The waiting-men, delighted in their hearts at playing their master a trick, did not let the order be repeated; in a second a table was brought up, the cloth laid, and, on re-entering the room, the landlord found the stranger in the act of carving a magnificent partridge.

Master Pivois assumed at the sight all the colours of the rainbow—at first pale, he turned so red that a fit of apoplexy might be apprehended, so vivid was his emotion.

"By Heaven," he exclaimed, stamping his foot angrily, "that is too much."

"What?" the stranger asked, as he raised his head and wiped his moustache; "What is the matter with you, my good man?"

"Matter, indeed!" mine host growled.

"By the way, is my horse in the stable?"

"Your horse, your horse," the other grumbled, "as if that is troubling me."

"What is it then, if you please, master mine?" the stranger asked, as he poured out a bumper which he conscientiously drained to the last drop. "Ah," he said, "it is Jurançon; I recognise it."

This indifference and this coolness raised the landlord's anger to the highest pitch, and caused him to forget all prudence.

"Cogswounds," he said, boldly seizing the bottle, "it is a strange piece of impudence thus to enter an honest house without the owner's permission; decamp at once, my fine gentleman, unless you wish harm to befall you, and seek a lodging elsewhere, for, as far as I am concerned, I cannot and will not give you one."

The stranger had not moved a feature during this harangue; he had listened to Master Pivois without displaying the slightest impatience: when the landlord at length held his tongue, he threw himself back in his chair, and looked him fixedly in the face.

"Listen to me in your turn, master," he said to him, "and engrave these words deeply on your narrow brain: this house is an inn, is it not? Hence it must be open without hesitation to every stranger who comes here for food and lodging with money in his pocket. I am aware that you claim the right of only receiving such persons as you think proper; if there are people who put up with that, it is their business, but for my part, I do not intend to do so. I feel comfortable here, so I remain, and shall remain as long as I think proper; I do not prevent you from swindling me, for that is your duty as a landlord, and I have no right to object; but, if I am not served politely and dexterously—if you do not give me a proper bedroom to spend the night in—in a word, if you do not perform the duties of hospitality toward me in the way I expect, I promise to pull down your signboard, and hang you up in its place, on the slightest infraction you are guilty of. And now I suppose you understand me?" he added, squeezing the other's hand so hard that the poor fellow uttered a yell of agony, and went tottering against the kitchen wall: "Serve me, then, and let us have no more argument, for you would not get the best of the quarrel if you picked one with me."

And without paying further attention to the landlord, the traveller continued his interrupted supper.

It was all over with the landlord's attempted resistance; he felt himself vanquished, and did not attempt a struggle which had now become impossible. Confused and humiliated, he only thought of satisfying this strange guest who had installed himself by main force in the house.

The traveller did not in any way abuse his victory; satisfied with having obtained the result he desired, he did not take the slightest liberty.

The result was that gradually, from one concession to another—the one offering, the other not refusing—they became on the best possible terms; and toward the end of the supper, mine host and the traveller found themselves, without knowing how, the most affectionate friends in the world.

They were talking together. First of the rain and fine weather, the dearness of provisions, the king's illness, and that of his Eminence the Cardinal; then, growing gradually bolder, Master Pivois poured out a huge bumper of wine for his improvised guest, and collected all his courage.

"Do you know, my good gentleman," he said to him suddenly, shaking his head with an air of contrition, "that you are fearfully in my way?"

"Stuff!" the stranger answered, as he tossed off the contents of his glass, and shrugged his shoulders, "Are we coming back to the old story of just now? I thought that settled long ago."

"Alas! I would it were so for everybody as it is for me."

"What do you mean?"

"Pray do not get into a passion, sir," the landlord continued timidly; "I have not the slightest intention of insulting you."

"In that case explain yourself in the Fiend's name, my master, and come frankly to the point; I do not understand what others beside yourself have to do in the matter."

"That is just the difficulty," said Master Pivois, scratching his head.

"Speak, zounds! I am not an ogre; what is it that causes you such anxiety?"

The landlord saw that he must out with it, and fear giving him courage, he bravely made up his mind.

"Monseigneur," he said, honestly, "believe me that I am too much the man of the world to venture to act with rudeness to a gentleman of your importance —"

"Enough of that," the stranger interrupted, with a smile.

"But—" the host continued.

"Ah! There is a *but*."

"Alas! Monseigneur, there always is one, and today a bigger one than ever."

"Hang it all, you terrify me, master," the stranger remarked, with a laugh; "tell me quickly, I beg of you, what this terrible but is."

"Alas! Monseigneur, it is this: my entire hostelry was engaged a week ago by a party of gentlemen; I expect them to arrive in an hour—half an hour, perhaps, and—"

"And?" the stranger asked, in an enquiring tone, which caused the host to shudder.

"Well, Monseigneur," he resumed in a choking voice, "these gentlemen insist on having the hostelry to themselves, and made me swear not to receive any other traveller but themselves, and paid me to that effect."

"Very good," said the stranger, with an air of indifference.

"What do you say; very good? Monseigneur," Master Pivois exclaimed.

"Hang it! What else would you have me say? You have strictly fulfilled your engagement, and no one has the right to reproach you."

"How so, sir?"

"Unless you have someone concealed here," the stranger answered, imperturbably, "which, I confess, would not be at all honourable on your part."

"I have nobody."

"Well, then?"

"But you, monseigneur?" he hazarded timidly.

"Oh, I," the stranger replied laughingly, "that is another affair; let us make a distinction, if you please, master; you did not receive me, far from it; I pressed my company on you, as I think you will allow."

"It is only too true."

"Do you regret it?"

"Far from it, monseigneur," he exclaimed eagerly, for he was not at all desirous of re-arousing the slumbering wrath of the irascible stranger; "I am only stating a fact."

"Very good, I see with pleasure, Master Pivois, that you are a very serious man; you are stating a fact, you say?"

"Alas! yes," the luckless host sighed.

"Very good; now follow my reasoning closely."

"I am doing so."

"When these gentlemen arrive, which according to your statement, will be soon, you will only have one thing to do."

"What is it, monseigneur?"

"Tell them exactly what has passed between us. If I am not greatly mistaken this honest explanation will satisfy them; if it be otherwise—"

"Well, if it be so, what am I to do, sir?"

"Refer them to me, Master Pivois, and I will undertake in my turn to convince them; gentlemen of good birth perfectly understand each other."

"Still, monseigneur—"

"Not a word more on this subject, I must request; but stay," he added, and listened, "I believe your company are arriving."

And he carelessly threw himself back in his chair.

Outside, the trampling of horses on the hardened snow could be distinctly heard, and then several blows were dealt on the door.

"It is they," the host muttered.

"A further reason not to keep them waiting; go and open the door, master, for it is very cold outside."

The landlord hesitated for a moment and then left the room without replying.

The stranger carefully folded himself in his mantle, pulled the brim of his beaver over his eyes, and awaited the entrance of the newcomers, while affecting an air of indifference.

The waiting-men, who had sought shelter in the most remote corner of the room, were trembling in the prevision of a disturbance.

CHAPTER II.

A FAMILY SCENE.

In the meanwhile the new arrivals were making a great noise in the road, and seemed to be growing impatient at the delay in letting them into the hostelry.

Master Pivois at length decided to open to them, though he was suffering from a secret apprehension as to the consequences which the presence of a stranger in the house might have for him.

As soon as a stable-lad had by his orders, drawn back the bolts, and opened the carriage-gates, several horsemen entered the yard, accompanied by a coach drawn by four horses.

By the light of the lanthorn held by his lad the landlord perceived that the travellers were seven in number; three masters, three servants, and the coachman on the box. All were wrapped up in thick cloaks, and armed to the teeth.

So soon as the coach had entered the yard, the horsemen dismounted; one of them, who appeared to exercise a certain authority over his companions, walked up to the landlord, while the others brought the coach up to the main entrance of the house, and closed the gates.

"Well, master," said the traveller to whom we allude, with a very marked foreign accent, although he expressed himself very purely in French; "have my orders been punctually executed?"

At this question, which was very embarrassing to him, Master Pivois scratched his head, and then replied like the cunning peasant he was—

"As far as possibly, yes, my lord."

"What do you mean, scoundrel?" the traveller resumed roughly; "Your instructions were precise enough."

"Yes, my lord," the landlord said humbly; "and I will even add that I was liberally paid beforehand."

"In that case, what have you to say?"

"That I have done the best I could," Master Pivois replied in growing confusion.

"Ah! I suppose you mean that you have someone in the house?"

"Alas! yes, my lord," the landlord answered, hanging his head.

The traveller stamped his foot passionately.

"S'blood!" he exclaimed; then, at once resuming an apparent calmness, he continued, "Who are the persons?"

"There is only one."

"Ah!" said the traveller, with satisfaction, "If there be only one, nothing is more easy than to dislodge him."

"I fear not," the landlord ventured timidly, "for this traveller, who is a stranger to me, I swear, looks to me like a rude gentleman, and not at all inclined to surrender his place."

"Well, well, I will take it on myself," the traveller remarked carelessly, "where is he?"

"There, in the kitchen, my lord, warming himself at the fire."

"That will do; is the room ready?"

"Yes, my lord."

"Rejoin those gentlemen, and show them the way yourself; none of your people must know what takes place here."

The landlord, delighted at having got off so cheaply, bowed respectfully, and hastily retired in the direction of the garden; as for the traveller, after exchanging a few whispered words with a footman, who remained with him, he pulled his hat over his eyes, opened the door, and boldly entered the kitchen.

It was deserted: the stranger had disappeared.

The traveller looked anxiously around him; the waiting men, probably in obedience to orders previously received from their master, had withdrawn to their attics.

After a few seconds' hesitation, the traveller returned to the garden.

"Well," the landlord asked, "have you seen him, my lord?"

"No," he replied, "but it is of no consequence; not a word about him to the persons who accompany me; he has doubtless left, but if that be not the case, be careful that he does not approach the apartments you have reserved for us."

"Hum," the landlord muttered to himself, "all this is not clear;" and he withdrew very pensively.

Truth to tell, the worthy man was frightened. His new customers had unpleasant faces, and a rough manner, which reassured him but slightly; and then again he fancied he had seen alarming shadows gliding about among the trees in his garden, a fact which he had carefully avoided verifying, but which heightened his secret apprehensions.

Dame Tiphaine, torch in hand, was waiting at the house door, in readiness to light the travellers, and conduct them to their apartments. When the coach had been turned and stopped, one of the travellers went up to it, opened the door, and assisted a lady in getting out.

This lady, who was magnificently dressed, appeared to be suffering, and she walked with difficulty. Still, in spite of her weakness, she declined the arm of one of the travellers offered her in support, and approached Dame Tiphaine, who, compassionate like all women, hastened to offer her the service she seemed to request of her, and helped her to ascend the rather steep staircase that led to the dais room.

The travellers left the driver and a lackey to guard the coach, which remained horsed, and silently followed the sick lady.

The dais room, the finest in the inn, was spacious and furnished with a certain amount of luxury; a large fire crackled on the hearth, and several candles, placed on the furniture, diffused a rather bright light.

A door half hidden by tapestry communicated with a bedroom, that had a door opening on the passage, for the convenience of the attendants.

When the lady had entered the room, she sank into a chair, and thanked the landlady with a bow.

The latter discreetly withdrew, astonished and almost terrified by the gloomy faces which surrounded her.

"Holy Virgin!" she said to Master Pivois, whom she found walking in great anxiety along the passage, "What's going to happen here? These men frighten me; that poor lady is all of a tremble, and the little I saw of her face behind her mask, is as white as a sheet."

"Alas!" Master Pivois said with a sigh, "I am as frightened as you, my dear, but we can do nothing; they are too great people for us—friends of his Eminence. They would crush us without pity; we have only one thing to do, and that is to retire to our room, as we received orders to do, and to keep quiet till our services are required; the house is theirs, at this moment they are the masters."

The landlord and his wife went into their room, and not satisfied with double locking their door, barricaded it with everything that came to hand.

As Master Pivois had said to his wife, the travellers were certainly masters of the inn, or at least believed themselves so.

The stranger, while feigning the deepest indifference, had watched the landlord's every movement: as soon as the latter left the kitchen to open the door for the newcomers, he rose, threw a purse of gold to the scullions, while putting his finger on his lips to recommend silence to them, and carefully wrapping himself in his mantle, left the kitchen.

The scullions, with the intelligence characteristic of the class, comprehended that this action of the stranger concealed some plans in the execution of which it was to their interest not to interfere; they divided the money so generously given them, and remembering the orders they had received from their master, they hastily decamped, and went off to hide themselves.

The stranger, while the landlord was receiving the travellers, had proceeded to the thickest part of the garden.

On reaching the little gate to which we have referred, he whistled gently.

Almost immediately two men seemed to rise from the midst of the darkness, and came up to him.

Each of these men had a long rapier at his side, pistols in his girdle, and a musketoon in his hand.

"What is there new?" the stranger asked; "Have you seen anything, Michael?"

"Captain," the man answered, to whom the question was addressed, "I have seen nothing, but still I fear a trap."

"A trap?" the stranger repeated.

"Yes," Michael continued, "Bowline has taken bearings of several ill-looking fellows who seem desirous of boarding us."

"Stuff! You are mad, Michael. You have seen the travellers who have just arrived at the inn."

"No, captain; on the contrary, they exactly resemble the fellows who have been chasing us ever since the day before yesterday, regular Cardinal's bloodhounds, I'll wager."

The stranger appeared to reflect. "Are they far off?" he at length asked.

"Speak, Bowline, my boy," said Michael, turning to his comrade, "and don't shiver your sails, the captain is hailing you."

"Well, then, Captain," said Bowline, a sturdy Breton, with a crafty look, "I sighted them over the starboard quarter at about four o'clock; I spread all my canvas to distance them, and I fancy I have left them four or five cables length in the rear."

"In that case we have about an hour before us?"

"Yes, about, Captain," Bowline replied.

"That is more than we want; listen, my lads, and swear on your honour as sailors to obey me."

"You may be quite sure we shan't fail, Captain," they answered.

"I reckon on you."

"Shiver my topsails, we know that," Michael replied.

"Whatever may happen to me," the stranger continued, "leave me to act alone, unless I give you express orders to come to my assistance. If the Cardinal's bloodhounds were to arrive while we are up aloft, you will bolt."

"We bolt!" the two sailors exclaimed.

"You must, lads! Who would deliver me if we were all three prisoners?" the stranger asked.

"That's true," Michael answered.

"Well then, that's settled, is it not?"

"Yes, Captain."

"Ah! By the way, if I am arrested you will want money to liberate me; take this."

He placed in their hands a heavy purse, which the sailors accepted without any remark.

"Now follow me, and keep your weather eye open, my lads."

"All right, Captain," Michael answered, "we are on watch."

The stranger then proceeded towards the house, closely followed by the two sailors. He reached the passage, at the end of which the travellers' room was, at the moment when Master Pivois and his wife were locking themselves in their bedroom.

The coach, guarded by the driver and a footman, was still standing in front of the principal entrance, but the three men passed unnoticed.

So soon as the landlady had left the room, the traveller who appeared to have a certain degree of authority over his companions, opened the bedroom door, doubtless to make certain there was no spy listening; then he took a chair, sat down by the fire, and made a sign to his companions to imitate him; the two lackeys alone remained standing near the door, with their hands resting on the muzzles of their carbines, butts of which were on the ground.

For some moments there was a funereal silence in this room, although six persons were assembled in it.

At length the traveller made up his mind to speak, and addressed the young lady, who was reclining in her chair, with her head bent on her breast and pendant arms.

"My daughter," he said, in a grave voice, and speaking in Spanish, "the moment has arrived for a clear and distinct explanation between us, for we have only four leagues to travel ere we reach the end of our long journey. I intend to remain twenty-four hours in this hostelry, in order to give you time to repair your strength, and allow you to appear in a proper state before the man for whom I destine you."

The young lady only replied to this dry address by a hollow groan.

Her father continued, without appearing to notice the utter state of prostration in which she was—

"Remember, my daughter, that if, on the entreaty of your brothers here present, I consented to pardon the fault you have committed, it is on the express condition that you will obey my orders without hesitation, and do all I wish."

"My child?" she murmured, in a voice choked by grief—"What have you done with my child?"

The traveller frowned, and a livid pallor covered his face; but he immediately recovered himself.

"That question again, unhappy girl?" he said, in a gloomy voice; "Do not trifle with my wrath by reminding me of your crime, and the dishonour of my house."

At these words the girl drew herself up suddenly, and with a hurried gesture pulled off the velvet mask that covered her face.

"I am not guilty," she said, in a haughty voice, and looking her father in the face; "and you are perfectly aware of it, for it was you who introduced the

Count de Barmont to me. You encouraged our love, and it was by your orders that we were secretly married. You dare not assert the contrary."

"Silence, wretch!" the traveller exclaimed, and rose passionately.

"Father!" the two gentlemen, who had hitherto remained motionless and as if strangers to this stormy interview, exclaimed, as they threw themselves before him.

"Well," he said, as he resumed his seat, "I will restrain myself: I will only ask you one further question, Doña Clara—will you obey me?"

She hesitated for a moment, and then appeared to form a supreme resolution.

"Listen to me, my father," she replied, in a hurried though firm voice; "you told me yourself that the moment for an explanation between us had arrived; very well, let us have this explanation. I, too, am your daughter, and jealous of the honour of our house; that is why I insist on your answering me without equivocation or deception."

While speaking thus, the young lady, who was only sustained by the factitious strength sorrow imparted to her, for she was frail and delicate, was supremely beautiful; with her body bent back, her head haughtily raised, her long and silky black hair falling in disorder on her shoulders, and contrasting with the marble pallor of her face; with her large eyes, inflamed by fever and inundated with tears, that slowly coursed down her cheeks, and with her bosom heaving from the emotion that held mastery over her—there was about her whole person something deathly, which seemed no longer to belong to the earth.

Her father felt involuntarily affected, in spite of his ferocious pride; and it was with a less rough voice he replied—

"I am listening to you."

"Father," she resumed, leaning her hand on the back of her chair in order to support herself, "I told you that I am not guilty, and I repeat that the Count de Barmont and myself were secretly united in the church of la Merced at Cadiz, and were so by your orders. As you know it, I will not dwell further on this point; my child is, therefore legitimate, and I have a right to be proud of it. How is it, then, that you, the Duke de Peñaflor, belonging to the highest class in Spain, not satisfied with tearing me on the very day of marriage from the husband yourself selected, and depriving me of my infant on the day of its birth, accused me of committing a horrible crime, and insisted on enchaining me to another husband, while my first is still living? Answer me, my father, so that I may know the nature of that honour about which you so often speak to me, and what is the motive that renders you so cruel to an unfortunate girl, who owes her life to you, and who, ever since she has been in this world, has only felt love and respect for you."

"This is too much, unnatural daughter!" the Duke shouted, as he rose wrathfully—"And as you are not afraid of braving me so unworthily—"

But he suddenly checked himself, and stood motionless, trembling with fury and horror; the bedroom door had suddenly opened, and a man appeared in it, upright, haughty, with flashing eye, and hand on his sword hilt.

"Ludovic, at last!" the young lady shrieked, as she rushed towards him.

But her brothers caught her by the arms, and constrained her to sit down again.

"The Count de Barmont!" the Duke muttered.

"Myself, my lord Duke de Peñaflor," the stranger replied, with exquisite politeness—"you did not expect me, it appears to me?"

And, walking a few paces into the room, while the two sailors who had followed him guarded the door, he proudly put his hat on again, and folded his arms.

"What is going on here?" he asked, in a haughty voice; "And who dares to use violence to the Countess de Barmont?"

"The Countess de Barmont?" the Duke repeated, contemptuously.

"It is true," the other remarked, ironically; "I forget that you expect at any moment a dispensation from the Court of Home, which will declare my marriage null and void, and allow you to give your daughter to the man whose credit has caused you to be nominated Viceroy of New Spain."

"Sir!" the Duke exclaimed.

"What, do you pretend I am in error? No, no, my lord Duke, my spies are as good as yours—I am well served, believe me: thank heaven I have arrived in time to prevent it. Make way there!" he said, repulsing by a gesture the two gentlemen who opposed his passage—"I am your husband, madam; follow me, I shall be able to protect you."

The two young men, leaving their sister, who was in a semi-fainting state, rushed on the Count, and both buffeted him in the face with their gloves, while drawing their swords.

The Count turned fearfully pale at this cruel insult; he uttered a wild beast yell, and unsheathed.

The valets, held in check by the two sailors, had not made a movement.

The Duke rushed between the three men, who were ready for the assault.

"Count," he said, coolly, to the younger of his sons, "leave to your brother the duty of chastising this man."

"Thanks, father," the elder answered, as he fell on guard, while his younger brother lowered the point of his sword, and fell back a pace.

Doña Clara was lying motionless on the floor.

At the first attack the two enemies engaged their swords up to their guard, and then, as if of common accord, each retreated a step.

There was something sinister in the appearance of this inn room at the moment.

This woman, who lay writhing on the floor, suffering from a horrible nervous crisis, and no one dreaming of succouring her.

This old man, with frowning brow, and features contracted by pain, witnessing with apparent stoicism this duel between his elder son and his son-in-law, while his younger son was biting his lips with fury because he could not assist his brother; these sailors, with pistols at the breasts of the lackeys, who were palsied with terror; and in the centre of the room, scarce lighted by a few smoking candles, these two men, sword in hand, watching like two tigers the moment to slay each other.

The combat was not long; too great a hatred animated the two adversaries for them to lose time in feeling each other's strength. The Duke's son, more impatient than the Count, made thrust on thrust, which the other had great difficulty in parrying; at length, the young man feeling himself too deeply engaged, tried to make a second backward step, but his foot slipped on the boards, and he involuntarily raised his sword; at the same moment the Count liberated his blade by a movement rapid as thought, and his sword entirely disappeared in his adversary's chest; then he leaped back to avoid the back thrust, and fell on guard again.

But it was all over with the young man; he rolled his haggard eyes twice or thrice, stretched out his arms, while letting go his sword, and fell his whole length on the floor, without uttering a word.

He was dead.

"Assassin!" his brother screamed, as he rushed sword in hand on the Count.

"Traitor!" the latter replied, as he parried the thrust, and sent the other's sword flying to the ceiling.

"Stay, stay!" the Duke cried, as he rushed half mad with grief between the two men, who had seized each other round the waist, and had both drawn their daggers.

But this tardy interference was useless; the Count, who was endowed with a far from common strength, had easily succeeded in freeing himself from the young man's grasp, and had thrown him on the ground, where he held him by placing his knee on his chest.

All at once a mighty rumour of arms and horses was heard in the house, and the hurried steps of several men hurrying up the stairs became audible.

"Ah!" the Duke exclaimed, with a ferocious joy, "I believe my vengeance is at hand, at last!"

The Count, not deigning to reply to his enemy, turned to the sailors.

"Be off, my lads!" he shouted in a voice of thunder.

They hesitated.

"He goes if you wish to save me," he added.

"Boarders away!" Michael yelled, as he dragged away his comrade; and the two men seizing their musquetoons by the barrel, as if to use them as clubs in case of need, and to clear the way, rushed into the passage when they disappeared.

The Count listened anxiously, he heard oaths and the sound of an obstinate struggle; then, at the expiration of a moment, a distant cry, that summons which sailors know so well, reached him.

Then his face grew calmer, he returned his sword to its sheath and coolly awaited the newcomers, muttering to himself—

"They have escaped, one chance is left me."

CHAPTER III.

THE ARREST.

Almost at the same moment ten or twelve men burst into the room rather than entered it, the noise that continued outside let it be guessed that a great number of others was standing on the stairs and in the passages, ready, were it required, to come to the assistance of the others.

All these men were armed, and it was easy to recognise them at once as guards of the King, or rather of His Eminence the Cardinal.

Only two of them, with crafty looks and squinting eyes, dressed in black like ushers, had no visible weapons; these, in all probability were more to be feared than the others, for beneath their feline obsequiousness they doubtless concealed an implacable will to do evil.

One of these two men held some papers in his right hand, he advanced two or three paces, cast a suspicious glance around him, and then took off his cap with a courteous bow.

"In the King's name! gentleman," he said in a quick sharp voice.

"What do you want?" the Count de Barmont asked, advancing resolutely towards him.

At this movement, which he took for a hostile demonstration, the man in black recoiled with an ill-disguised start of terror, but feeling himself backed up by his acolytes, he at once resumed his coolness, and answered with a smile of evil augury—

"Ah! Ah! The Count Ludovic de Barmont, I believe," he remarked with an ironical bow.

"Yes, sir," the gentleman replied haughtily, "I am the Count de Barmont."

"Captain in the navy," the man in black imperturbably added, "at present, commanding His Majesty's, frigate The Erigone."

"As I told you, sir, I am the person you are in search of," the Count added.

"It is really with you that I have to deal, my lord," he replied, as he drew himself up. "S'death, my good gentleman, you are not easy to catch up; I have been running after you for a week, and was almost despairing about having the honour of a meeting."

All this was said with an obsequious air, a honeyed voice, and with a sweet smile, sufficient to exasperate a saint, and much more the person whom the strange man was addressing, and who was endowed with anything but a placable character.

"By Heaven!" he exclaimed, stamping his foot passionately; "Are we to have much more of this?"

"Patience, my good sir," he replied in the same placid tone; "patience, good Heaven, how quick you are!" then after taking a glance at the papers he held in his hand, "Since by your own confession you allow yourself to be really Count Ludovic de Barmont, captain commanding His Majesty's frigate

Erigone, by virtue of the orders I bear, I arrest you in the King's name, for the crime of desertion; for having without authorization abandoned your vessel in a foreign country, that is to say, at the Port of Lisbon, in Portugal." Then raising his head and fixing his squinting eyes on the gentleman, he added, "Surrender your sword to me, my lord."

M. de Barmont shrugged his shoulders disdainfully.

"The sword of a gentleman of my race shall never be placed in the hands of a scoundrel of your stamp," he said, with contempt; and drawing his sword, he coldly broke the blade across his knee, and threw the fragments through the window panes, which they broke.

Then he drew his pistols from his belt and cocked them.

"Sir, sir!" the myrmidon exclaimed, recoiling in terror, "This is rebellion, remember, rebellion against the express orders of His Majesty and His Eminence the Cardinal Minister."

The Count smiled disdainfully, and raising his pistols in the air, fired them, the bullets being buried in the ceiling; then clasping them by the barrel he threw them also out of the window; after which he crossed his hands on his chest, and said coolly—

"Now do with me what you please."

"Have you surrendered, my lord?" the fellow asked with ill-disguised alarm.

"Yes, from this moment I am your prisoner."

The man in black breathed again; although he was unarmed, the haughty gentleman still made him feel uncomfortable.

"Still," the latter added, "allow me to say a couple of words to this lady;" and he pointed to Doña Clara, who, waited upon by Dame Tiphaine, who had hurried in at the disturbance in spite of her husband's entreaties and orders, was beginning to regain her senses.

"No, not a word, not a syllable," the Duke exclaimed, as he threw himself between his daughter and the Count; "remove the villain, remove him."

But the bailiff, pleased with the facility the Count had displayed in surrendering to him, and not wishing to excite his anger, pleased above all at being able to show his authority without incurring resistance, bravely interposed.

"Pray, sir, allow the gentleman to speak to the lady," he said, "and to unburden his heart."

"But this man is an assassin," the Duke shouted violently, "before us is still lying the corpse of my unhappy son, killed by him."

"I pity you, sir," the myrmidon said without being at all affected; "I cannot offer any remedy for that; and you must make application in the proper quarter. Still, if it can be of any comfort to you, be convinced that I shall make a careful note of the accusation you bring, and will recall it to mind at the right time and place. But you must be equally eager to get rid of us, as we are to get away from here: hence allow this gentleman to bid farewell to the lady quietly, and I am convinced it will not take long."

The Duke darted a ferocious glance at the bailiff; but, not wishing to compromise himself with such a fellow, he did not answer, and fell back with a gloomy air.

The Count had watched this altercation without displaying either impatience or anger; with pale forehead and frowning brow, he waited, doubtless ready to break into some terrible extremity if his request were not granted.

The bailiff only required to take one look at him to guess what was passing in his heart; and, not feeling at all anxious for a fresh contest to begin, he had prudently manoeuvred to avoid it.

"Come," he said, "speak, my worthy gentleman, no one will oppose it."

"Thanks," the Count answered hoarsely and approached Doña Clara, who watched him advance with an ardent gaze fixed on him.

"Clara," he said to her in a firm and deeply marked voice, "do you love me?"

She hesitated for a moment and bowed her head while heaving a profound sigh.

"Do you love me?" he repeated.

"I do love you, Ludovic," she replied in a faint and trembling voice.

"Do you love me, as your husband before God and man, as the father of your child?"

The young lady rose, her black eyes flashed fire, and stretching out her hands before her, she said in a voice choked by emotion—

"In the presence of my father, who is ready to curse me, before the body of my dead brother and in the face of the men who are listening to me, I swear, Ludovic, that I love you as the father of my child, and that I shall remain faithful to you, whatever may happen."

"Very good, Clara," he answered, "God has received your oath and will help you to keep it; remember that, whether dead or alive, you belong to me as I belong to you, and that no person on earth shall break the ties that unite us.

Now farewell, and keep your courage."

"Farewell!" she muttered, as she fell back in her chair and buried her face in her hands.

"Let us go, gentlemen! Do with me what you please," the Count said as he turned to the exempt and the guards, who were involuntarily affected by this scene.

The Duke bounded with a tiger leap on his daughter, and seizing her right arm with a frenzied gesture, he forced her to raise her tear-swollen face to his, and fixing on her a glance loaded with all the rage that swelled his heart, he said in a voice which fury rendered sibilant—

"Daughter, prepare to marry within two days, the man I destine for you. As for your child, you will never see it again; it no longer exists for you."

The young lady uttered a cry of despair and fell back deprived of her senses in the arms of Dame Tiphaine.

The Count, who at this moment was leaving the room, stopped short and turned round to the Duke with his arm stretched out toward him:

"Hangman," he shouted in a hoarse voice which chilled his auditors with horror, "I curse you, I swear on my honor as a gentlemen to take on you and yours so terrible a vengeance, that the memory of it shall remain eternal; and if I cannot reach you, you and the whole nation to which you belong shall be buried beneath the implacable weight of my hatred. Between us henceforth there is a war of savages and wild beasts, without truce or mercy; farewell."

And leaving the proud Spaniard horrified by this fearful anathema, the gentleman quitted the room with a firm step, and taking a last loving glance at the woman he adored, from whom he was perhaps eternally separated.

The passages, stairs, and inn garden were filled with armed men; it was evidently a miracle that the two sailors had succeeded in escaping and getting away safe and sound; this gave the Count, hope and he went down the stairs with an assured step, carefully watched by his escort who did not let him out of sight.

The guards had been long before warned that they would have to do with a naval officer possessing an inordinate violence of character, prodigious vigour and indomitable courage; hence the resignation of the prisoner, which they believed to be assumed, only inspired them with very slight confidence, and they were continually on the defensive.

When they came out into the garden the chief of the exempts noticed the coach, which was still standing at the door.

"Why," he said with a grin and rubbing his hands, "here's the very thing we want. In our hurry to get here, we forgot to provide ourselves with a coach; be good enough to get in, my lord," he said as he opened the door.

The Count got in without any further hesitation; and the exempts then addressed the driver who was sitting motionless on his box.

"Come down, scamp," he said in a tone of authority; "I require the use of this coach for an affair of state. Give up your place to one of my men. Wideawake," he added, turning to a tall impudent looking fellow standing by his side, "get up on the box in that man's place—let us be off."

The driver did not attempt to resist this peremptory order; he descended and his place was immediately taken by Wideawake; the exempt then entered the carriage, seated himself facing his prisoner, closed the door, and the steeds, aroused by a vigorous, lash, dashed forward dragging after them the heavy vehicle round which the twenty odd soldiers were collected.

For a considerable period the coach rolled along without a word being exchanged between the prisoner and his guard.

The Count was thinking, the exempt sleeping, or, to speak more correctly, pretending to sleep.

In the month of March the nights are beginning to shorten; daylight soon appeared, and broad white stripes were beginning to cross the sky.

The Count, who up to this moment had remained motionless, gave a slight start.

"Are you suffering, my lord?" the exempt inquired. This question was addressed to him with an intonation so different from that hitherto employed by the man who had made him prisoner; there was in the sound of his voice an accent so really gentle and sympathizing, that the Count involuntarily started, and took a fixed look at his singular companion: but so far as he could see by the faint light of coming dawn, the man in front of him still had the same crafty face and the same ironical smile stereotyped on his lips. The Count found himself in error, and throwing himself back, merely uttered one word, "No," in a tone intended to break off any attempt at conversation between his guardian and himself.

But the former was probably in a humour for talking, for he would not be checked; and pretending not to remark the manner in which his advances had been received, he continued—

"The nights are still chill, the breeze enters this coach on all sides, and I feared lest the cold had struck you."

"I am habituated to suffer heat and cold," the Count answered; "besides, it is probable that if I have not yet made my apprenticeship, I am about to undergo one which will accustom me to endure everything without complaining."

"Who knows, my lord?" the exempt said, with a shake of the head.

"What?" the other objected, "Am I not condemned to a lengthened captivity in a fortress?"

"Yes, according to the terms of the order, which it is my duty to carry out."

There was a momentary silence. The Count gazed absently at the country which the first beams of day were beginning to illumine. At length he turned to the exempt.

"May I ask whither you are taking me?" he said.

"I see no objection to your doing so."

"And you will answer my question?"

"Why not? There is nothing to prevent it."

"Then we are going?"

"To the isles of St. Marguerite, my lord."

The Count trembled inwardly. The islands of Lerins, or Sainte Marguerite, enjoyed at that time, even, a reputation almost as terrible as the one they acquired at a later date, when they served as a prison to the mysterious iron mask, whom it was forbidden to take even a glance at under penalty of death.

The exempt looked at him fixedly without speaking.

It was the Count who again resumed the conversation.

"Where are we now?" he asked.

The exempt bent out of the window, and then resumed his seat.

"We are just arriving at Corbeil, where we shall change horses."

"Ah!" said the Count.

"If you wish to rest, I can give orders for an hour's stay. Perhaps you feel a want of some refreshment?"

This singular man was gradually acquiring in the Count's eyes all the interest of an enigma.

"Very good," he said.

Without replying the exempt let down the window.

"Wideawake!" he shouted.

"What is the matter?" the latter asked.

"Pull up at the Golden Lion."

"All right."

Ten minutes later the coach halted in the Rue St. Spire, in front of a door over which creaked a sign representing an enormous gilt cat, with one of its paws on a ball. They had arrived.

The exempt got out, followed by the Count, and both entered the inn: one portion of the escort remained in the saddle in the street, while the others dismounted and installed themselves in the common room.

The Count had mechanically followed the exempt, and on reaching the room, seated himself in a chair by the fire, in a first floor decently furnished room. He was too busy with his own thoughts to attach any great attention to what was going on around him.

When the landlord had left them alone, the exempt bolted the door inside, and then placed himself in front of his prisoner.

"Now," he said, "let us speak frankly, my lord."

The latter, astonished at this sudden address, quickly raised his head.

"We have no time to lose in coming to an understanding, sir; so please to listen without interrupting me," the exempt continued. "I am François Bouillot, the younger brother of your foster father. Do you recognise me?"

"No," the Count replied, after examining him attentively for a moment.

"That does not surprise me, for you were only eight years old the last time I had the honor of seeing you at Barmont Castle: but that is of no consequence; I am devoted to you, and wish to save you."

"What assures me that you are really François Bouillot, the brother of my foster father, and that you are not attempting to deceive me?" the Count answered, in a suspicious accent.

The exempt felt in his pocket, pulled out several papers, which he unfolded, and presented them open to the Count.

The latter looked at them mechanically: they consisted of a baptismal certificate, a commission, and several letters proving his identity. The Count handed him the letters back.

"How is it that you should have been the man to arrest me, and arrived so opportunely to aid me?" he asked.

"In a very simple way, my lord: your order of arrest was obtained from the Cardinal Minister by the Dutch Embassy. I was present when M. de Laffemas, a familiar of his Eminence, who is kind to me, left the Palais Cardinal order in hand: I was there, and he chose me. Still, as I was able to decline, I should have done so, had I not seen your name on the paper, and remembered the kindness your family had shown to me and my brother. Taking advantage of the opportunity my profession of exempt offered me, I resolved to repay you what your friends have done for mine, by attempting to save you."

"That does not seem to me very easy, my poor friend."

"More so than you may fancy, my lord: I will leave here one-half our escort, and then only ten will remain with us."

"Hum! That is a very decent number," the Count replied, involuntarily interested.

"They would be too many if there were not among the ten men seven of whom I am certain, which reduces the number of those we have to fear to three. I have been running after you for a long time, my lord," he added, with a laugh, "and all my precautions are taken: through some excuse, easy to be found, we will pass through Toulon, and on arriving there, we will stop for an hour or two at a hostelry I know. You will disguise yourself as a mendicant monk, and leave the inn unnoticed. I will take care to get rid of the guards I am not certain of. You will proceed to the port furnished with papers I will hand you; you will go on board a charming chasse-marée, called the *Seamew*, which I have freighted on your account, and which is waiting for you. The master will recognise you by a password I will tell you, and you will be at liberty to go whither-soever you please. Is not this plan extremely simple, my lord?" he asked, rubbing his hands joyously, "And have I not foreseen everything?"

"No, my friend," the Count answered with emotion, as he offered him his hand; "there is one more thing you have not foreseen."

"What is that, my lord?" he asked, in surprise.

"That I do not wish to fly," the young man answered, with a melancholy shake of the head.

CHAPTER IV.

THE ISLE OF SAINTE MARGUERITE.

At this answer, which he was so far from anticipating, the exempt gave a start of surprise, and looked at the Count as if he had not exactly understood him.

The gentleman smiled gently.

"That surprises you, does it not?" he said.

"I confess it, my lord," the other stammered, with embarrassment.

The Count went on:

"Yes," he said, "I can understand your surprise at my refusal to accept your generous proposition. It is not often you find a prisoner to whom liberty is offered, and who insists on remaining a captive. I owe you an explanation of this extraordinary conduct; this explanation I will give you at once, so that you may no longer press me, but leave me to act as I think proper."

"I am only the most humble, of your servants, my lord Count. You doubtless know better than I what your conduct should be under the circumstances, you have therefore no occasion to explain it to me."

"It is precisely because you are an old servant of my family, François Bouillot, and because you are giving me at this moment a proof of unbounded devotion, that I believe myself obliged to tell you the motives for this refusal, which has so many reasons to surprise you. Listen to me, then."

"As you insist, my lord, I obey you."

"Very good, take a chair, and place yourself here by my side, as it is unnecessary for others beside yourself to hear what I am going to say."

The exempt took a stool and seated himself by his master's side, exactly as the latter had ordered, while still keeping up a respectful distance between himself and the gentleman.

"In the first place," the Count resumed, "be thoroughly convinced that if I refuse your offer, it is not through any motive of a personal nature as regards yourself. I have full confidence in you, for nearly 200 years your family has been attached to mine, and we have ever had reason to praise their devotion to our interest. This important point being settled, I will go on. I will suppose for a moment that the plan you have formed is successful, a plan which I will not discuss, although it appears to me very difficult to execute, and the slightest accident might, at the last moment, compromise its issue. What will happen? Forced to fly without resources, without friends, I should not only be unable to take the revenge I meditate upon my enemies, but surrendered, so to speak, to their mercy, I should speedily fall into their hands again, and thus become the laughing stock of those whom I hate. I should be dishonoured; they will despise me, and I shall have but one way of escape from a life henceforth rendered useless, as all my plans would be overthrown, and that is blowing out my brains."

"Oh! my lord!" Bouillot exclaimed, clasping his hands.

"I do not wish to fall," the Count continued imperturbably, "in the terrible struggle which has this day begun between my enemies and myself. I have taken an oath, and that oath I will keep, regardless of the consequences. I am young, hardly twenty-five years of age; up to the present, life has only been one long joy for me, and I have succeeded in everything, plans of ambition, fortune and love. Today misfortune has come to lay its hand on me, and it is welcome; for the man who has not suffered is not a perfect man; grief purifies the mind and tempers the heart. Solitude is a good councillor; it makes a man comprehend the nothingness of small things, expands the ideas, and prepares grand conceptions. I require to steel myself through sorrow, in order to be able one day to repay my enemies a hundredfold all that I have suffered at their hands. It is by thinking over my broken career and my ruined future, that I shall find the necessary strength to accomplish my vengeance. When my heart is dead to every other feeling but that of the hatred which will entirely occupy it, I shall be able pitilessly to trample underfoot all those who today laugh at me and believe they have crushed me, because they have hurled me down; and then I shall be really a man, and woe to those who try to measure their strength with mine. You tremble at what I am saying to you at this moment, my old servant," he added more gently, "what would it be were you able to read in my heart all the hatred, auger, and rage it contains against those who have mercilessly ground me beneath their heel, and who have eternally deprived me of happiness, in order to satisfy the paltry calculations of a narrow and criminal ambition?"

"Oh, my lord Count! Permit an old servant of your family, a man who is entirely devoted to you, to implore you to resign these fearful schemes of vengeance. Alas! You will be the first victim of your hatred."

"Have you forgotten, Bouillot," the Count replied ironically, "what is said in our country, about the members of the family to which I have the honor of belonging?"

"Yes, yes, my lord," he said with a melancholy shake of the head; "I remember it, and will repeat it if you wish."

"Do so."

"Well, my lord, the distich is as follows—"

"'The Counts of Barmont Senectaire, Demon-hate and heart of stone.'"

The Count smiled.

"Well do you fancy that I have degenerated from my ancestors?"

"I suppose nothing, sir, Heaven forbid!" he answered humbly, "I only see with terror that you are preparing a hideous future for yourself."

"Be it so! I accept it in all its rigor, if God will permit me to accomplish my oath."

"Alas! My lord, you know that man proposes; you are at this moment a prisoner of the Cardinal; reflect, I implore you, who knows whether you will ever leave the prison to which I am conducting you? Consent to be free."

"No; cease your entreaties! The Cardinal is not immortal. If not before, my liberty will be restored me on his death, which cannot be long deferred, I hope. And now carefully bear this in mind, my resolution is so fixed, that if in spite of my orders you abandon me here, at the inn where we now are, the first use I should make of the liberty you have given me back, would be to go at once and surrender myself into the hands of his Eminence; you understand me thoroughly, I suppose?"

The old servant bowed his head without answering, and two tears slowly ran down his cheeks.

This dumb grief, so true and so touching, affected the Count more than he would have supposed; he rose, took the poor fellow's hand and shook it several times.

"Let us say no more about this, Bouillot," he remarked to him affectionately, "although I will not profit by it, your devotion has deeply affected me, and I will ever feel eternally grateful to you for it. Come, my old friend, let us not grow foolish; we are men and not childish poltroons, confound it."

"Well, no matter, my lord, I do not consider myself beaten," the exempt replied, as he threw himself into the arms open to receive him; "you cannot prevent me from watching over you, whether near or afar."

"That I do not oppose, my friend," the Count replied with a laugh; "do as you please; besides," he added seriously, "I confess that I shall not be sorry when I am sequestered from the world to know what is going on, and to be kept informed, of passing events; some unforeseen fact might occur which would modify my intentions and make me desire the recovery of my liberty."

"Oh, be sure of that, my lord," he exclaimed, pleased at this quasi victory and conditional promise, "I will arrange so that you shall not be at a loss for news; I have not served his Eminence for six years for nothing; the Cardinal is a good master, I have profited by his teaching, and know several tricks; you shall see me at work."

"Well, that is agreed, and we understand each other now. I think it would be wise to breakfast before continuing our journey, for I feel an appetite that greatly requires appeasing."

"I will give the landlord orders to serve you at once, my lord."

"You will breakfast with me, Bouillot," he said as he gave him a friendly tap on the shoulder; "and I hope it will be always so, until our arrival at the Isle of St. Marguerite."

"It is certainly a great honour for me, sir, but—"

"I expect it; besides are you not almost a member of my family?"

François Bouillot bowed and left the room; after ordering a copious breakfast, he commanded one part of the escort back to Paris; then he returned to the room, followed by the landlord, who, in a second, covered the table with all that was wanted to make a good meal, and withdrew discreetly, leaving his guests to attack the dishes placed before them.

The journey was continued without any incident worthy of note.

The prisoner's conversation with his keeper had been decisive; the latter was too well acquainted with the character of the man with whom he had to deal to attempt to revert to a subject which had been so distinctly disposed of on the first occasion.

At the period when our history takes place, France was not as now intersected by magnificent roads, and the shortest journey demanded an enormous expenditure of time; the coaches, heavy vehicles badly built and worse horsed, had great difficulty in resisting the numerous joltings and the ruts in which they were for the greater portion of the time buried up to the axletree, and hence, in spite of the speed employed, seventeen days elapsed ere the prisoner and his escort arrived at Toulon.

This town was even at that early period one of the principal military ports of France, and the Count felt an indescribable pang at heart when he entered it.

It was in this town that his naval career had begun, here for the first time he had set foot aboard a vessel with the rank of midshipman, and had undergone the preparatory trials of that rude naval profession, in which, in spite of his youth, he soon attained a great reputation and almost celebrity.

The coach stopped in the Haymarket, in front of the "Cross of Malta," probably the oldest inn in France, for it is still in existence, although it has undergone many indispensable changes both internally and externally.

So soon as he had installed his prisoner comfortably in the Inn, François Bouillot went out.

If he placed a sentry before the Count's door, it was rather in obedience to his duty, than through any fear of escape, for he had not even taken the trouble to lock the door, so convinced was he beforehand that unfortunately his prisoner would not attempt to pass out of it.

He remained away for about two hours.

"You have been absent a long time," the Count remarked on his return.

"I had some important business to settle," he replied.

The Count, without adding a word, resumed his walk up and down the room which Bouillot's return had interrupted.

There was a momentary silence, Bouillot was evidently embarrassed, he went about the room, pretending to arrange sundry articles of furniture, and disarranging everything; at last seeing that the Count obstinately remained silent and would not perceive that he was in the room, he placed himself in front of him so as to bar his passage, and looked at him intently as he whispered with a stress on the words.

"You do not ask where I have been."

"What is the use?" the Count replied carelessly; "About your own business, of course."

"No, my lord, about yours."

"Ah!" he said.

"Yes, the *Seamew* awaits you."

The Count smiled and slightly shrugged his shoulders.

"Ah, ah, you are still thinking of that; I believed, my dear Bouillot, that it was arranged between us that we should not return to this subject. That was the reason, then, that you lengthened our journey, by making us pass through Toulon, at which I felt surprised. I could not account for the strange itinerary you were following."

"My lord," he muttered, clasping his hands imploringly.

"Come, you are mad, my dear Bouillot, you ought to know by this time, though, that when I have formed a resolution, good or bad, I never alter it; so no more of this, I beg, it would be quite useless. I pledge you my word as a gentleman."

The old servant uttered a groan that resembled a death rattle.

"Your will be done, my lord," he stammered. "When do we start for Antibes?"

"At once, if you wish it."

"Very good, the sooner the better."

After bowing, the exempt left the room to make all preparations for departure.

As we see, the parts were completely introverted, it was the prisoner who gave orders to his keeper.

One hour later, in fact, the Count quitted Toulon. All along the road the two men, constantly companions, and eating and drinking together, conversed about indifferent matters. Bouillot had at last recognized the fact that it was useless to make any further effort to induce the Count to escape; still he had not given up his scheme, but merely deferred it till a more distant period, reckoning as an ally the annoyance of a prolonged detention, and an inactive and useless life upon an organization so impetuous as that of the prisoner.

So soon as he arrived at Antibes, by the express command of the Count, who seemed to take a certain pleasure in tormenting him, he set out in search of some boat to carry them across to Sainte Marguerite.

His search was neither long nor difficult; as bearer of a Cardinal's order, he laid an embargo on the first fishing boat he came across, and embarked aboard it with all his people.

On leaving the mainland, the Count turned, and a smile of peculiar meaning played round his lips.

Bouillot, deceived by this smile, whose secret intention he did not penetrate, bent down to the Count's ear.

"If you like, there is still time," he whispered.

The Count looked at him, shrugged his shoulders, and without replying, sat down in the stern of the boat.

"Push off," Bouillot then shouted to the master.

The latter seized his boathook, and they were soon under weigh.

The Lerins islands form a group composed of several rocks, and two islands surrounded by shoals; the first known as Isle Sainte Marguerite, the second as Saint Honorat.

At the period of our narration only the first was fortified; the other, inhabited by a few fishermen, merely contained the still considerable ruins of the monastery founded by Saint Honorat circa the year 400.

The Sainte Marguerite island was uninhabited, flat, and only offering along its entire coast, one very unsafe creek for vessels. Although it is extremely fertile, and pomegranates, orange and fig trees, grow there in the open air, no one had thought of taking up his abode there, and we are not aware whether a change has since taken place.

A very important fortress, which, at a later date, attained a melancholy reputation as a state prison, was erected on the island, the greater portion of which it occupied.

This fort was composed of three towers, connected together by terraces, which time had covered with a yellowish moss, while a wide deep moat surrounded the walls.

A few years prior to the beginning of our story, in 1635, the Spaniards had seized it by surprise.

The Cardinal, in order to prevent the repetition of such a calamity, had judged it advisable to protect the fort from a *coup de main*, by placing there a garrison of fifty picked soldiers, commanded by a major performing the duties of governor. He was an old officer of fortune, whom this post served as a retreat, and who, far from the cares of the world, led a perfect canonical life, thanks to a tacit understanding with the smugglers, who alone cast anchor in these parts.

The officer who commanded the fort at this moment was an old gentleman, tall, thin, and wizened, with harsh features, who had had a leg and arm cut off. His name was Monsieur de l'Oursière; he was constantly scolding and abusing his subordinates, and the day when he left the Crown regiment, in which he held the rank of major, was kept as a holiday by the whole regiment, officers and men; so cordially was the worthy man detested.

Cardinal de Richelieu was a good judge of men; in selecting Major de l'Oursière to make him governor of Sainte Marguerite, and metamorphose him into a gaoler, he had found the exact post which suited his quarrelsome temper, and his cruel instincts.

It was on this amiable personage that the Count de Barmont would have to be dependant for doubtless a considerable period; for, if the Cardinal Minister easily shut the gate of a state prison on a gentleman, to make up for it, he was never in a hurry to open it again, and a prisoner, unless something extraordinary occurred, was almost safe to die forgotten in his dungeon, except when his Eminence had a whim to have his head cut off in broad daylight.

After a number of countersigns had been exchanged with a profuseness of caution which bore witness to the good guard and strict discipline maintained by the governor, the prisoner and his escort were at length introduced into the fortress, and admitted to the Major's presence.

The Major was just finishing his breakfast, when a Cardinal's messenger was announced to him: he buttoned his uniform, put on his sword and hat, and ordered the messenger to be shown in.

François Bouillot entered, followed by the Count, bowed, and presented the order of which he was the bearer.

The governor took it, and read it through; then he turned to the Count, who was standing motionless a few paces in the rear, made him a slight bow, and addressed him in a dry voice, and with a rough accent.

"Your servant, sir," he said to him: "are you the Count de Barmont, whose name is written on this paper?"

"Yes, sir," the Count answered, bowing in his turn.

"I am sorry, sir, truly sorry," the Major resumed; "but I have strict orders with reference to you, and a soldier only knows his duty; still, believe me, sir, hum, hum, that I shall try to reconcile my natural humanity with the rigour that is recommended to me, hum, hum, I know how gentlemen ought to behave to each other, sir; be assured of that."

And the governor, doubtless satisfied at the speech he had just uttered, smiled, and drew himself gracefully up.

The Count bowed, but made no answer.

"You shall be conducted to your apartment at once, sir," the Major went on; "hum, hum! I wish it was handsomer, but I did not expect you; hum, hum, and you know how things are—hum, hum, we will manage to lodge you more comfortably hereafter; la Berloque," he added, turning to a soldier standing near the door, "conduct this gentleman, hum, hum, to room No. 8, in the second turret; hum, hum, I believe it is the most habitable one; your servant, sir, your servant, hum, hum!"

And after having thus unceremoniously dismissed the Count, the Major went into another room.

M. de Barmont, accompanied by Bouillot and the guards, who had brought him, followed the soldier.

The latter led them through several passages, and up various stairs, and then stopped before a door, garnished with formidable bolts.

"It is here," he said.

The Count then turned to Bouillot, and affectionately offered him his hand.

"Farewell, my old friend," he said to him in a gentle but firm voice, while a vague smile played round his lips.

"Farewell, till we meet again," Bouillot said, with a stress on the words. Then he took leave of him, and withdrew, with his eyes full of tears.

The door closed with a mournful sound on the prisoner.

"Oh!" the old servant muttered, as he pensively went down the turret stairs, "Woe to those who venture to oppose the Count, if ever he leaves his prison again! And he shall do so, I swear it, even if I must risk my life in securing his escape."

CHAPTER V.

A BACKWARD GLANCE.

The family of the Count de Barmont Senectaire was one of the most ancient and noble in Languedoc; their origin went back to an antiquity so remote, that we may declare without fear of contradiction that it was lost in the mist of ages.

A Barmont Senectaire fought at Bouvines by the side of Philip Augustus.

The chronicle of Joinville mentions a Barmont Senectaire, knight banneret, who died of the plague at Tunis, in 1270, during the second crusade of King Louis IX.

Francis I. on the evening of the battle of Marignano, gave the rank of Count on the battlefield itself to Euguerrand de Barmont Senectaire, captain of one hundred men at arms, to reward him for his grand conduct and the sturdy blows he had seen him deal during the whole period of that combat of giants.

Few noble families have such splendid title deeds among their archives.

The Counts de Barmont were always military nobles, and they gave France several celebrated generals.

But in the course of time, the power and fortune of this family gradually diminished: during the reign of Henri III. it was reduced to a condition bordering on poverty. Still, justly proud of a stainless past, they continued to carry their heads high in the province, and if the Count de Barmont endured hard privations in order to support his name worthily, nothing of this was visible externally, and everybody was ignorant of the fact.

The Count had attached himself to the fortunes of the King of Navarre as much through the hope of regaining a position through the war, as through admiration of this prince, whose genius he had probably divined. A brave soldier, but young, impetuous, and handsome, the Count had several affairs of gallantry. One among others with a lady of the Town of Cahors, affianced to a very rich Spanish noble, whom he succeeded in carrying off on the very day before that appointed for the marriage. The Spaniard, who was very strict in matters affecting his honour, considered this joke in bad taste, and demanded satisfaction of the Count; the latter gave him two sword thrusts, and left him dead on the ground. This affair attracted great attention, and gained the Count much honor among people of refinement; but the Spaniard, contrary to expectation, recovered from his wounds. The two gentlemen fought again, and this time the Count so ill treated his adversary that the latter was constrained to give up all thoughts of a new meeting. This adventure disgusted the Count with gallantry, not that he personally feared the results of the hatred which the Duke of Peñaflor had sworn against him, for he never heard of him again, but because his conscience reproached him with having, for the satisfaction of a caprice which passed away so soon as it was satisfied, destroyed the happiness of an honourable man, and he felt remorse for his conduct in the affair.

After bravely fighting by the side of the King during all his wars, the Count finally retired to his estates, about the year 1610, after the death of that Prince, disgusted with the Court, and feeling the necessity of repose after such an amount of fatigue.

Here, four or five years later, wearied with the solitude in which he lived, and, perhaps, in the hope of expelling from his mind a troublesome recollection, which, in spite of the time that had elapsed, did not cease to torture him, the Count resolved to marry, and selected for his wife a young lady belonging to one of the best families in the province—charming and gentle, but as poor as himself; this circumstance was far from bringing ease into the family, whose position daily became more difficult.

The union, however, was a happy one; in 1616 the Countess was delivered of a son, who at once became the joy of the poor household.

This son was Count Ludovic, whose story we have undertaken to tell.

In spite of his fondness for the boy, the Count, however, brought him up strictly, wishing to make of him a rude, brave, and loyal gentleman, like himself.

Young Ludovic felt at an early hour, on discovering what misery was concealed behind the apparent splendour of his family, the necessity of creating for himself an independent position, which would allow him not only to be no longer a burden to parents whom he loved, and who sacrificed to him the greater portion of their income, but to restore also the eclipsed lustre of the name he bore.

Contrary to the custom followed by his ancestors, who had all served the king or his armies, his tastes led him to the navy.

Owing to the assiduous care of an old and worthy priest, who had become his tutor through attachment to his family, he had received a solid education, by which he had profited; accounts of voyages, which constituted his principal reading, inflamed his imagination; all his thoughts were turned to America, where, according to the statements of sailors, gold abounded, and he had but one desire—to land himself in this mysterious country, and take his part of the rich crop which everybody garnered there.

His father, and his mother even more, for a long time resisted his entreaties. The old man, who had fought during so many years, could not understand why his son should not do the same, or prefer the navy to a commission in the army. The Countess, in her heart, did not wish to see her son either soldier or sailor, for both professions terrified her; she feared for her son the unknown perils of distant excursions, and her tenderness was alarmed by the thought of what might be an eternal separation.

Still, something must be done, and as the young man obstinately adhered to his resolution, his parents were compelled to yield and consent to what he desired, whatever might be the future consequences of this determination.

The Count still had some old friends at Court, among them being the Duke de Bellegarde, who stood on terms of great intimacy with King Louis XIII., surnamed the "*Just*" during his lifetime, because he was born under the sign of Libra.

Monsieur de Barmont had also been connected at an earlier date with the Duke d'Epernon, created Admiral of France in 1587; but he had a repugnance in applying to him, owing to the rumours that were spread at the time of the assassination of Henri IV. Still, in a case so urgent as the present one, the Count comprehended that for the sake of his son he must silence his private feelings, and at the same time as he addressed a letter to the Duke de Bellegarde, he sent another to Epernon, who at this period was Governor of Guyenne.

The double answer the Count expected was not long deferred; M. de Barmont's two old friends had not forgotten him, and hastened to employ their credit on his behalf.

The Duke d'Epernon especially, better situated through his title of Admiral to be useful to the young man, wrote that he would gladly undertake the duty of pushing him on in the world.

This took place at the beginning of 1631, when Ludovic de Barmont had reached his sixteenth year.

Being very tall, with a proud and haughty air, and endowed with rare vigour and great agility, the young man seemed older than he in reality was. It was with the liveliest joy that he learned how his wishes had been fulfilled, and that nothing prevented him from embracing a maritime career.

The Duke d'Epernon's letter requested the Count de Barmont to send his son as speedily as possible to Bordeaux, so that he might at once place him aboard a man-of-war, to commence his apprenticeship.

Two days after the receipt of this letter the young man tore himself with difficulty from the embraces of his mother, bade his father a respectful farewell, and took the road to Bordeaux, mounted on a good horse, and followed by a confidential valet.

The navy had for a long time been neglected in France; and left during the middle ages in the hands of private persons, as the government, following the example of the other continental powers, did not deign to try and secure a respectable position on the seas, much less a supremacy; thus we see during the reign of Francis I., who was, however, one of the warlike Kings of France, Ango, a ship broker of Dieppe, from whom the Portuguese had taken a vessel during a profound peace, authorized by the King, who was unable to procure him justice, to equip a fleet at his own expense. With this fleet Ango, we may remark incidentally, blockaded the port of Lisbon, and did not cease hostilities until he had forced the Portuguese to send to France ambassadors humbly to ask peace of the King.

The discovery of the New World, however, and the no less important one of the Cape of Good Hope, by giving navigation a greater activity and a more extended sphere, at the same time as they widened the limits of commerce, caused the necessity to be felt of creating a navy, intended to protect merchant vessels against the attacks of corsairs.

It was not till the reign of Louis XIII. that the idea of creating a navy began to be carried into execution. Cardinal de Richelieu, whose vast genius embraced everything, and whom the English fleets had caused several times to tremble during the long and wearying siege of Rochelle, passed several decrees relating to the navy, and founded a school of navigation, intended to educate those young gentlemen who desired to serve the King aboard his vessels.

It is to this great minister, then, that France is indebted for the first thought of a navy; this navy was destined to contend against the Spanish and Dutch fleets, and during the reign of Louis XIV., to acquire so great an importance, and momentarily hold in check the power of England.

It was this school of navigation created by Richelieu that the Viscount de Barmont entered, thanks to the influence of the Duke d'Epernon.

The old gentleman strictly kept the pledge he had given his former comrade in arms; he did not cease to protect the young man, which, however, was an easy task, for the latter displayed an extraordinary aptitude, and a talent very rare at that date in the profession he had embraced.

Hence, in 1641, he was already a captain in the navy, and had the command of a twenty-six gun frigate.

Unfortunately, neither the old Count de Barmont nor his wife was able to enjoy the success of their son or the new era opening for their house; they both died a few days apart from each other, leaving the young man an orphan at the age of two-and-twenty.

As a pious son, Ludovic, who really loved his parents, lamented and regretted them, especially his mother, who had always been so kind and tender to him; but, as he had been accustomed for so many years to live alone during his long voyages, and only to trust to himself, he did not feel the loss so painfully as he would have done had he never left the paternal roof.

Henceforth the sole representative of his house, he regarded life more seriously than he had hitherto done, and redoubled his efforts to restore to his name its almost eclipsed lustre, which, thanks to his exertions, was beginning to shine again with renewed brilliancy.

The Duke d'Epernon still lived, but a forgotten relic of an almost entirely departed generation—a sickly octogenarian, who had quarrelled long ago with Cardinal de Richelieu, his influence was null, and he could do nothing for the man he had so warmly protected a few years previously.

But the Count did not allow this to prey on his mind; the naval service was not envied by the nobility, good officers were rare, and he believed that if he cautiously avoided mixing himself up in any political intrigue, he might have a brilliant career.

An accident, impossible to foresee, was fated to destroy all his ambitious plans, and ruin his career forever.

This is how the affair occurred:—The Count de Barmont, at the time commanding the Erigone, twenty-six gun frigate, after a lengthened cruise in the Algerian waters to protect French merchant vessels against the Barbary pirates, steered for the states of Gibraltar, in order to reach the Atlantic, and return to Brest, whither he had orders to proceed at the end of his cruise; but just as he was about to pass through the Straits, he was caught by a squall, and after extraordinary efforts to continue his course, which almost cast him on to the coast of Africa, owing to the strength of the wind and the rough, chopping sea, he was obliged to stand off and on for several hours, and finally take refuge in the port of Algeciras, which was to windward of him, on the Spanish coast.

So soon as he had anchored, and made all snug, the commandant, who knew from experience that two or three days would elapse ere the wind veered, and allowed him to pass the Straits, ordered his boat, and went ashore.

Although the town of Algeciras is very old, it is very small, badly built, and scantily populated; at this period, more especially, it only formed, as it were, a poor market town. It was not till after the English had seized Gibraltar, situated on the other side of the bay, that the Spaniards comprehended the importance of Algeciras to them, and have converted it into a regular port.

The Captain had no other motive for landing at Algeciras, than the restlessness natural to sailors, which impels them to leave their vessel as soon as they have cast anchor.

Commercial relations were not established at that time, as they now are. The government had not yet fallen into the custom of sending to foreign ports residents ordered to watch over their countrymen, and protect their transactions—in a word, consulates had not yet been created: only those ships of war, which accident might lead to any port, now and then undertook to procure justice for those of their countrymen, whose interests had been encroached on.

After landing, and giving orders to his coxswain to come and fetch him at sunset, the Captain, merely followed by a sailor, of the name of Michael, to whom he was greatly attached, and who accompanied him everywhere, turned into the winding streets of Algeciras, curiously examining everything that offered itself to view.

This Michael, to whom we shall have several occasions to refer, was a tall fellow, with an intelligent face, about thirty years of age, and who had vowed an eternal devotion to his captain since the day when the latter had risked his life in saving his, by jumping into a boat during a terrible storm four years before, to help him when he had fallen into the sea while going up the shrouds to ease the mainsail.

Since that day Michael had never left the Count, and had always contrived to sail with him. Born in the vicinity of Pau, the country of Henri IV., he was like the king, his fellow countryman, gay, mocking, and even sceptical. An excellent sailor, endowed with tried bravery, and far from ordinary vigour, Michael offered in his person the perfect type of the Béarnaise Basque, a strong and rough, though loyal and faithful race.

Only one individual shared in Michael's heart the unbounded friendship he felt for his chief. This privileged being was a Breton sailor, gloomy and taciturn, who formed a complete antithesis to him, and whom, owing to his slowness, the crew had favoured with the characteristic name of Bowline, which he had accepted, and was so accustomed to answer to it, that he had almost forgotten the name he previously bore.

The service the Count had done Michael, the latter had rendered to Bowline: hence he was attached to the Breton through this very service, and while mocking and teasing him from morning till night, he had a sincere friendship for him.

The Breton understood Michael, and so far as his reserved and slightly demonstrative nature permitted, he testified on every occasion his gratitude to the Basque, by letting himself be completely directed and governed by him in all the actions of his life, without ever attempting to revolt against the frequent exorbitant demands of his mentor.

If we have dwelt so long on the character of these two men, it is because they are destined in the course of this work to play an important part; and the reader must be acquainted with them, in order to understand the facts we shall have to record.

The Count and his sailor continued to advance along the streets, the one reflecting and amusing himself the other remaining, through respect, a few paces in the rear, and desperately smoking a pipe, whose stem was so short that the bowl almost touched his lips.

While walking thus straight before them, the promenaders soon reached the end of the town, and turned into a lane bordered by aloes, which led, with a rather steep incline, to the top of a hill, whence could be enjoyed the entire panorama of the bay of Algeciras, which, we may remark in a parenthesis, is the finest in the world.

It was about two in the afternoon, the hottest moment of the day. The sun profusely poured down its torrid beams, which made the pebbles in the road sparkle like diamonds.

Hence everybody had gone within doors to enjoy the siesta, so that, since landing, the two sailors had not met a living creature; and if the Arabian Nights, which were not translated till a century later, had been known at the time, the Count, without any great effort of the imagination, might have believed himself transported to that city where all the inhabitants had been sent to sleep by a wicked impostor, so complete was the silence around him, while the landscape had the aspect of a desert. To complete the illusion, the breeze had fallen, there was not a breath of air, and the vast expanse of water stretched out at their feet was as motionless as if composed of ice.

The Count stopped, pensively gazing with an absent eye at his frigate, which at this distance was scarce as large as a skiff.

Michael smoked more than ever, and admired the country with straddling legs, and his arm behind his back, in that position so liked by sailors.

"Hilloh!" he said suddenly.

"What is the matter with you?" the Count asked him, as he turned round.

"Nothing the matter with me, Captain," he replied, "I am only looking at a lady who is coming up here at a gallop. What a fancy to go at that pace in such a heat as this."

"Where is she?" asked the Count.

"Why, there, Captain," he said, stretching out his hand to larboard.

The Count turned his eyes in the direction which Michael indicated to him.

"Why, that horse has bolted," he exclaimed, a moment later.

"Do you think so, Captain?" the sailor remarked, calmly.

"Zounds! I am certain of it. Look, now that she is nearer to us. The rider is clinging despairingly to the mane. The unhappy girl is lost!"

"Very possibly," Michael said, philosophically.

"Quick, quick, my lad!" the Captain shouted, as he rushed to the side where the horse was coming up. "We must save the lady, even if we perish!"

The sailor made no answer; he merely took the precaution of withdrawing his pipe from his mouth and placing it in his pocket, and then he set out at a run behind his captain.

The horse came on like a whirlwind. It was a barb of the purest Arab race, with a small head, and legs fine as spindles. It bounded furiously with all four legs on the narrow path it was following, with eyes full of flashes, and apparently snorting fire through its dilated nostrils. The lady on its back, half reclining on its neck, had seized its long mane with both hands, and, half insane with terror, as she felt herself lost, she uttered stifled cries at intervals.

Very far in the rear, several horsemen, who formed almost imperceptible dots on the horizon, were coming up at full speed.

The track on which the horse was engaged, was narrow and rocky, and led to a precipice of frightful depth, toward which the animal was dashing with a headlong speed.

A man must either be mad, or endowed with a lion's courage, to try and save this unhappy woman under such conditions, when he had ninety-nine chances in a hundred of being crushed, without succeeding in rescuing her from death.

The two sailors, however, made no reflections of this nature, and without hesitation resolved to make a supreme effort. They stood facing each other on either side of the track, and waited without exchanging a word. They understood one another.

Two or three minutes elapsed, and then the horse passed like a tornado; but with the speed of thought the two men dashed forward, seized it by the bridle, and, hanging their whole weight on it, allowed themselves to be dragged onward by the furious animal.

There was for a moment a terrible struggle between intelligence and brute strength. At length the brute was conquered. The horse stumbled, and fell panting on the ground.

At the moment of its fall, the Count removed in his arms, the lady so miraculously saved, and he bore her to the side of the road, where he respectfully laid her down.

Terror had certainly deprived her of consciousness.

The Count guessing that the horsemen coming up, were relations or friends of her to whom he had just rendered so great a service, repaired the disorder in his clothes and awaited their arrival, while gazing admiringly at the young lady lying at his feet.

She was a charming young creature, scarce seventeen years of age, with a delicate waist, and marked and adorably beautiful features; her long black silky hair had escaped from the comb that confined it and fell in perfumed curls over her face, on which a slight flush presaged a speedy return to life.

The young lady's dress, which was very rich and remarkably elegant, would have led to the supposition that she was of high rank, had not the stamp of aristocracy, spread over her entire person, removed all doubts on that score.

Michael, with his characteristic coolness which nothing ever upset, had remained by the side of the horse which, calmed by the fall and trembling in all its limbs, had allowed itself to be raised without offering the slightest resistance; the Basque after removing the saddle, had plucked a wisp of grass, and began rubbing the horse down, while admiring it, and muttering every now and then.

"I don't care, it's a noble and beautiful animal! It would have been a pity had it rolled over that frightful precipice; I am glad it is saved."

The worthy sailor did not think the least bit in the world of the young lady, for his entire interest was concentrated on the horse.

When he had finished rubbing down, he put the saddle and bridle on again and led the horse up to the Count.

"There," he said with an air of satisfaction, "now the horse is calm; poor creature, a child could guide it with a thread."

In the meanwhile the horsemen rapidly approached, and soon came up to the two French sailors.

CHAPTER VI.

LOVE AT FIRST SIGHT.

These horsemen were four in number. Two of them appeared to be persons of importance, the other two were domestics.

On coming within a few steps of the Count, the first two dismounted, threw their bridles to the footman and advanced, hat in hand, towards the gentleman, whom they saluted with exquisite politeness.

The Count courteously returned their greeting, while taking a side-glance at them.

The first was a man of about sixty; he was tall, his demeanour was graceful and his face appeared handsome at the first glance, for the expression was imposing, although gentle and even kind. Still, on examining it with greater attention, it was possible to see from the gloomy fire of his glance, which seemed at times to emit magnetic flashes, that this gentleness was merely a mask intended to deceive the vulgar; his projecting cheek bones, his wide retiring forehead, his nose bent like a bird's beak and his square chin denoted a cold cruelty blended with a strong dose of obstinacy and pride.

This man wore a handsome hunting dress covered with lace, and a heavy gold chain, called a *fanfaronne*, was passed several times round his ostrich plumed hat.

This fanfaronne had been brought into fashion by the adventurers who returned from New Spain; and though very ridiculous, it had been enthusiastically adopted by the haughty Castilians.

This gentleman's companion, much younger than he, but dressed quite as richly, had one of those faces whose features at the first glance appear so commonplace and insignificant, that you do not take the trouble of looking at them, and an observer might pass close by without seeing them, but his small grey eyes sparkling with cleverness, half hidden under bushy eyebrows, and the curl of his thin sarcastic lip, would have completely contradicted any physiognomist, who might take this person for a man of common intellect and ordinary capacity.

The elder of the two riders bowed a second time.

"Sir," he said, "I am the Duc de Peñaflor; the person whose life you have saved by running such a risk of losing your own, is my daughter, Doña Clara de Peñaflor."

As the Count came from Languedoc, he spoke Spanish as purely as his mother tongue.

"I am delighted, sir," he replied with a graceful bow, "at having served as the instrument of providence to preserve a child for her father."

"I think," the second rider observed, "that it would be as well to offer Doña Clara some succour; my dear cousin seems to be seriously indisposed."

"It is only emotion," the young man replied; "that caused this fainting fit, which, if I am not mistaken, is beginning to wear off."

"Yes indeed," said the Duke, "I think I saw her make a slight movement, it will be better not to trouble her, but let her regain her senses quietly; in that way, we shall avoid a shock whose results are sometimes very dangerous to delicate and nervous organisations, like that of my dear child."

All this was spoken with a cold, dry, steady voice, very different to what a father ought to have employed, whose daughter had just miraculously escaped death.

The young officer did not know what to think of his real or feigned indifference.

It was only Spanish hauteur. The Duke loved his daughter as much as his proud and ambitious nature allowed him to do, but he would have been ashamed to let it be seen, especially by a stranger.

"Sir," the Duke resumed a moment later, as he stepped aside to display the gentlemen who accompanied him, "I have the honour of presenting to you my cousin and friend, Count Don Stenio de Bejar y Sousa."

The two gentlemen bowed to each other.

The Count had no motive to maintain an incognito, and saw that the moment had arrived to make himself known.

"Gentlemen," he said, "I am Count Ludovic de Barmont Senectaire, Captain in the Navy, and commanding the French frigate the *Erigone*, now anchored in Algeciras Bay."

On hearing the Count's name pronounced, the Duke's face turned frightfully pale; he frowned till his eyebrows joined, and he gave him a strangely meaning glance.

But this emotion did not last longer than a flash: by a violent effort of the will the Spaniard thrust back to the bottom of his heart, the feelings that agitated him; his previous impassiveness returned to his face, and he bowed with a smile.

The ice was broken between the three gentlemen, for they saw they were equals; their manner at once changed, and they became as affable as they had at first been stiff and reserved.

The Duke was the first to renew the conversation in the most friendly voice.

"You are doubtless taking advantage of the truce made a short time back, between our two nations, my lord, to visit our country?"

"Pardon me, my lord Duke, I was not aware that hostilities had ceased between our two armies. I have been at sea for a long time, and without news of France; chance alone brought me to this coast a few hours ago, and I sought shelter in Algeciras Bay, to await a change of wind to pass the Straits."

"I bless the accident, Count, since I owe to it my daughter's safety."

Doña Clara had opened her eyes, and, though still very weak, she was beginning to account for the position in which she found herself.

"Oh," she said, in a soft and humorous voice, and with an inward shudder, "had it not been for that gentleman, I should be dead!" and she attempted to smile, while fixing on the young man her large eyes full of tears, with an expressive gratitude it is impossible to describe.

"How do you feel, my daughter?" the Duke asked. "I am quite well, now, I thank you, papa," she replied; "when I felt that Moreno no longer obeyed the bit, and was running away, I believed myself lost, and terror caused me to faint; but where is my poor Moreno?" she added a moment after, "Has any misfortune happened to him?"

"Reassure yourself, señorita," the Count replied with a smile, and pointing to the horse, "here he is, all right, and quite calmed; if you like you can ride back on him without the slightest apprehension."

"I certainly will mount my good Moreno," she said, "I bear him no ill will for his prank, although it nearly cost me dear."

"My lord," the Duke then said, "I venture to hope that we shall not part thus, and that you will deign to accept the cordial hospitality which I offer you at my castle."

"My time is not my own, unfortunately, my lord Duke, and duty demands my immediate presence on board. Be assured I deeply regret my inability to accept your kind offer."

"Do you then expect to set sail so soon?"

"No, sir; on the contrary, I hope," he replied, laying a certain stress on the words, "to remain here some time longer."

"In that case," the Duke remarked with a smile, "I do not consider myself beaten. I am certain we shall meet again soon, and become more intimate acquaintances."

"That is my most eager desire, sir," the young man said, taking a side glance at Doña Clara, who hung her head with a blush.

The Count then took leave, and proceeded in the direction of Algeciras, while the horsemen slowly retired in exactly the opposite direction.

The Captain walked on very thoughtfully, reflecting on the singular adventure of which he had so suddenly been the hero; recalling the slightest details, and admiring in memory the beauty of the young lady, whose life he had been so fortunate as to save.

Being constantly absorbed by the thousand claims of his rude profession, and nearly always at sea, the Count, though almost twenty-five years of age, had never yet loved; he had not even thought about it; the few women he had hitherto met had produced no effect on his heart, his mind had always remained free in their presence, and no serious engagement had as yet disturbed its tranquillity. Hence it was with a certain terror mingled with astonishment, that while reflecting on the meeting which had suddenly interrupted his quiet walk, he perceived that the beauty of Doña Clara and her gentle voice had left a powerful impression on his mind, that her image was ever present, and that his memory with implacable fidelity ever recalled even its apparently most indifferent details, the short interview he had had with her.

"Come, come," he said, shaking his head several times as if to drive away a troublesome thought; "I am mad."

"Well, Captain," said Michael, who took advantage of this exclamation, to give a free course to the reflections which he burned to express aloud, "I don't care, but you must confess it was very lucky all the same for that young lady, that we were there at the very nick of time."

"Very lucky, indeed, Michael," the Count replied, delighted at this diversion; "had we not been there the unhappy young lady would have been lost."

"That is true, and hopelessly so; poor little thing."

"What a frightful fate! So young, and so lovely."

"I allow that she is well built, although I fancy her lines are a little too fine, and she is a trifle too pale." The Count smiled, but made no reply to the sailor's rather venturesome opinion.

The latter, feeling himself encouraged, went on—

"Will you allow me to give you a bit of advice, Captain?"

"What is it, my lad? Speak without fear."

"As for fear, deuce take me if I feel that, but I should not like to pain you."

"Pain me, about what?"

"Well, all the worse, I must out with it. When you mentioned your name, Captain, to the old Duke—"

"Well, what happened?"

"On hearing it pronounced, he suddenly turned as pale as a corpse; he frowned upon you so terrible a look that I fancied for a moment that he wished to assassinate you; don't you consider that funny, Captain?"

"What you say is impossible; you are mistaken."

"You did not notice it, because you had your head down, but I was looking at him without seeming to do so, and am quite certain about what I say."

"But reflect, Michael, I do not know this nobleman, I never saw him before today; how can he possibly feel hatred for me; you are rambling, my good fellow."

"Not at all, Captain, I am certain of what I state; whether you know him or not is no business of mine, but as for him, I will wager that he knows you, and intimately too; the impression you produced on him was too strong for it to be otherwise."

"I will admit, if you like, that he knows me, but one thing I can certify, that I never offended him."

"That is a point on which a man can never be sure, Captain; look you, I am a Basque, and have known the Spaniards for a long time; they are a strange people—proud as cocks, and rancorous as fiends; believe me, distrust them always; that can do no harm, and especially that old gentleman, who has a crafty face I do not like at all."

"All that has no common sense, Michael, and I am as mad as yourself in listening to you."

"Very well," the sailor said with a toss of the head, "we shall see hereafter whether I am mistaken."

The conversation ended here; still Michael's remarks occupied the Captain more than he would have liked to show, and he returned on board with a very thoughtful air. On the next morning at about ten o'clock an excellent pleasure yacht hailed the frigate.

This vessel contained the Duc de Peñaflor, and his silent cousin, Count de Bejar y Sousa.

"On my faith, my dear Count," the Duke said, good-humouredly, after the first compliments, "you are going to find me very unceremonious, for I have come to carry you off."

"Carry me off?" the young man replied with a smile.

"On my word, yes. Just imagine, Count, my daughter insists on seeing you; she only speaks of you, and as she does pretty well what she pleases with me —a thing that will not surprise you greatly. She sent me to you to tell you that you must absolutely accompany me to the castle."

"So it is," Don Stenio said with a bow, "the Señorita Doña Clara insists on seeing you."

"Still—" the other objected.

"I will listen to nothing," the Duke remarked quickly, "you must make up your mind, my dear Count, you can only obey, for you are aware that ladies cannot be thwarted; so come, reassure yourself, though, I am not going to take you far, for my castle is scarce two leagues from here."

The Count, who in his heart, felt a lively desire to see Doña Clara again, did not allow himself to be pressed one bit more than was correct: then, after giving the necessary orders to his second in command, he accompanied the Duc de Peñaflor, followed by Michael, who seemed to be the Captain's shade.

This was the way in which began a connection which was soon to be changed into love, and have, at a later date, such terrible consequences for the unhappy officer.

The Duke and his eternal cousin who never quitted him, overwhelmed the Count with protestations of friendship, granted him the most perfect liberty at the castle, and appeared not at all to notice the intelligence which was soon established between Doña Clara and the young man.

The latter, completely subjugated by the passion he experienced for the young lady, yielded to his love with the confident and unreflecting abandonment of all hearts that love for the first time.

Doña Clara, a simple girl, brought up with all the rigid strictness of Spanish manners, but an Andalusian from head to foot, had listened with a quiver of delight to the confession of this love which she had shared from the first moment.

Everybody, therefore, was happy at the castle; Michael alone formed an exception, with his stolid face, which was never unwrinkled; the more rapidly he saw matters tending to the conclusion the young people desired, the more gloomy and anxious he became.

In the meanwhile the frigate had left Algeciras for Cadiz.

The Duke, his daughter, and Don Stenio had made the passage on board; the Duc de Peñaflor wanted to go to Seville, where he had large estates, hence he accepted with eager demonstrations of joy the proposal the Count made him, of conveying him on board his frigate to Cadiz, which is only some twenty leagues from Seville.

On the day after the frigate's arrival at Cadiz, the Captain put on his full uniform, went ashore, and proceeded to the Duke's palace.

The Duke, doubtless warned of his visit, received him with a smile on his lips, and with a most affectionate air.

Emboldened by this reception, the Count, overcoming his timidity, requested leave to marry Doña Clara.

The Duke received it favourably; said that he had expected this request, and that it satisfied all his wishes, since it caused the happiness of a daughter he loved.

"Still," he remarked to the Count, "although there was a truce between the two countries, a peace was not yet signed. Though, according to all appearance it would be soon carried out, for all that, he feared lest the news of this marriage might injure the Count's future, by rendering the Cardinal ill disposed toward him."

This reflection had several times offered itself to the young officer's mind; hence he hung his head, not daring to reply, because, unluckily, he had no valid reason to offer, that would remove the Duke's objections.

The latter came to his assistance by saying that there was a very simple way of arranging matters to the general satisfaction, and removing this apparently insurmountable difficulty.

The Count quivering with fear and pleasure, asked what this method was.

The Duke then explained to him that he meant a secret marriage. As long as the war lasted, silence would be maintained, but once peace was concluded and an ambassador sent to Paris, the marriage should be publicly announced to the Cardinal, who then would probably not feel offended by the union.

The young man had been too near seeing his dream of bliss eternally destroyed to raise the slightest objection to this proposition; secret or not, the marriage would not be the less valid and he cared little for the rest. Hence he consented to all the conditions imposed on him by the Duke, who insisted that the marriage might be effected in such a way as to keep him in ignorance of it, so that in the event of his Eminence attempting to turn the King against him, he might employ this pretended ignorance in foiling the ill will of those who might attempt to ruin him.

The Count did not exactly understand what the King of Spain had to do with his marriage; but as the Duke spoke with an air of conviction, and seemed to be greatly alarmed about the King's displeasure, he consented to everything.

Two days later at nightfall, the young couple were married at the Church of la Merced, by a priest, who consented for a heavy sum to lend his ministration to this illegal act.

Michael the Basque and Bowline served as witnesses of the captain, who, on the pressing recommendation of the Duke, was unwilling to let any of his officers into his secrets, while he was sure of the silence of the two sailors.

Immediately after the ceremony, the new bride was taken off on one side by her witnesses, while her husband withdrew greatly annoyed on the other, and went aboard the frigate.

When the Count on the next morning presented himself at the Duke's palace, the latter informed him that, in order to remove any pretext for malevolence, he had thought it advisable to send away his daughter for a while, and she had gone to stay with a relation residing at Grenada.

The Count did not allow his disappointment to be seen; he withdrew, pretending to accept as gospel the somewhat specious reasoning of the Duke.

Still, he was beginning to find the Duke's conduct towards him very extraordinary, and he resolved to clear up the doubts that arose in his mind.

Michael and Bowline were sent into the country to reconnoitre.

The Count learned from them, not without surprise, at the end of two days' researches that Doña Clara was not at Grenada, but merely at Puerto Santa Maria, a charming little town facing Cadiz on the opposite side of the road.

The Captain, so soon as he possessed the information for the success of the plan he meditated, managed by the intervention of Michael, who spoke Spanish like an Andalusian, to send a note to Doña Clara, and at nightfall, followed by his two faithful sailors, he landed at Santa Maria.

The house inhabited by the young lady was rather isolated; he set the two sailors on sentry to watch over her safety, and walked straight up to the house.

Doña Clara herself opened the door for him. The joy of the couple was immense, and the Count retired shortly before sunrise; at about ten o'clock, he went as usual to pay a visit to his father-in-law, in whose presence he continued to feign the most complete ignorance as to Doña Clara's abode, and was most kindly welcomed.

This state of things went on for nearly a month. One day the Count suddenly received information of the resumption of the hostilities between Spain and France; he was himself forced to quit Cadiz, but wished to have a final interview with the Duke, in order to ask him for a frank explanation of his conduct; in the event of this explanation not satisfying him, he was resolved to carry his wife off.

When he arrived at the Duke's palace, a confidential servant informed him that his master, suddenly summoned by the king, had started an hour previously to Madrid, without, to his great regret, having had time to take leave of him.

On hearing this, the Count had a presentiment of evil; he turned pale, but succeeded in overcoming his emotion, and calmly asked the valet whether his master had not left a letter for him; the servant answered in the affirmative and handed him a sealed note.

The Count broke the seal with a trembling hand and ran through the letter, but his emotion was so great on perusing the contents that he tottered, and had not the valet sprang forward to support him, he would have fallen to the ground.

"Ah!" he muttered, "Michael was right," and he crumpled the paper savagely.

But suddenly recovering himself, he overcame his grief and, after giving the valet several louis, hurried away.

"Poor young man!" the valet muttered with a sorrowful shake of the head and re-entered the palace, the gates of which he closed after him.

CHAPTER VII.

DESPAIR.

A few yards from the palace the Count met Michael, who was coming towards him.

"A boat, quick, quick, my good Michael," he shouted, "'tis a matter of life and death."

The sailor, terrified at the condition in which he saw his commandant, wished to ask him what the matter was, but the Count roughly imposed silence on him by repeating his order to procure a boat at once.

Michael bowed his head.

"Woe is me. I foresaw this," he muttered, with mingled grief and anger, and he ran off towards the port.

It is not a difficult task to find a boat at Cadiz, and Michael had only to choose; comprehending that the Count was in a hurry, he selected one pulled by ten oars.

The Count arrived at the same moment.

"Twenty louis for you and your crew if you are at Puerto in twenty minutes," he shouted, as he leaped into the boat, which was almost capsized by the violence of the shock.

The boat started, the sailors bent over their oars, and made her fly through the water.

The captain with his eyes obstinately fixed on Santa Maria, and striking his clenched fist on the boat's gunwale, in spite of the excessive speed at which it was going, incessantly repeated in a choking voice—

"Quicker, quicker, muchachos."

He passed like an arrow across the bows of the frigate, whose crew were preparing to weigh anchor. At length they reached Puerto.

"No one is to follow me," the captain cried, as he leaped ashore.

But Michael did not heed this order, and at the risk of what might happen to him, he set out in pursuit of the Count, whom he would not abandon in his present frightful condition.

It was fortunate he did so, for when he reached the house Doña Clara had inhabited, he saw the young man lying senseless on the ground.

The house was deserted, and Doña Clara had disappeared.

The sailor took his captain on his shoulders and conveyed him to the boat, where he laid him as comfortably as he could in the stem sheets.

"Where are we going?" the master asked.

"To the French frigate; and make haste," Michael replied.

When the boat was alongside the frigate, Michael paid the master the promised reward, and then aided by several of the crew, conveyed the captain to his cabin. As it was eminently necessary to keep the Count's secret, and avoid arousing suspicions, the sailor in his report to the first commandant, ascribed to a violent fall from a horse, the condition in which the captain was; then, after making a signal to Bowline to follow him, he returned to the cabin.

M. de Barmont was still as motionless as if he were dead; the chief surgeon of the frigate in vain bestowed the greatest care on him without succeeding in recalling life, which seemed to have fled forever.

"Send away your assistants; Bowline and myself will suffice," Michael said to the doctor, with a meaning glance.

The surgeon comprehended, and dismissed the mates. When the door had closed on them the sailor drew the doctor into a gun berth, and said to him, in so low a voice as to be scarce audible—

"Major, the Commandant has just experienced a great sorrow, which produced the terrible crisis he is suffering from at this moment. I confide this to you because a surgeon is like a confessor."

"All right, my lad," the surgeon replied; "the Captain's secret has been trusted to sure ears."

"I am convinced of that, Major; the officers and crew must suppose that the Captain has been thrown from his horse, you understand. I have already told the lieutenant so in making the report."

"Very good; I will corroborate your statement, my lad."

"Thanks, Major; now I have another thing to ask of you."

"Speak."

"You must obtain the lieutenant's leave that no one but Bowline and myself may wait on the Captain. Look you, Major, we are old sailors of his, he can say what he likes before us; and then, too, he will be glad to have us near him; will you get this leave from the lieutenant?"

"Yes, my lad; I know that you are a good fellow, sincerely attached to the Captain, and that he places entire confidence in you; hence, do not feel alarmed—I will settle that with the lieutenant, and you and your companion shall alone come in here with me so long as the Captain is ill."

"Thanks, Major; if an opportunity offers itself I will repay you this; on the faith of a Basque, you are a worthy man."

The surgeon began laughing.

"Let us return to our patient," he said, in order to cut short the conversation.

In spite of the intelligent care the doctor paid him the Count's fainting fit lasted the whole day.

"The shock was frightful," he said—"it was almost a congestion."

It was not till night, when the frigate had been for a long time at sea, and had left Cadiz roads far behind it, that a favourable crisis set in, and the Captain became slightly better.

"He is about to regain his senses," the doctor said.

In fact, a few convulsive movements agitated the Count's body, and he half-opened his eyes; but his glances were wild and absent; he looked all around him, as if trying to discover where he was, and why he was thus lying on his bed.

The three men, with their eyes fixed on him, anxiously watched this return to life, whose appearance was anything but reassuring to them.

The surgeon, more especially, seemed restless; big forehead was wrinkled, and his eyebrows met, through the effort of some internal emotion.

All at once the Count hurriedly sat up, and addressed Michael, who was standing by his side.

"Lieutenant," he said to him, in a quick, sharp voice, "let her fall off a point, or else the Spanish vessel will escape—why have you not beat to quarters, sir?"

The surgeon gave Michael a sign.

"Pardon, Commandant," the latter replied, humouring the sick man's fancy, "we have beaten to quarters, and the tops are all manned."

"Very good," he answered; then suddenly changing his ideas, he muttered—"She will come, she promised it me. But no, she will not come; she is dead to me henceforth—dead! dead!" he repeated, in a hollow voice, with different intonations; then he uttered a piercing cry—"Oh, heaven! How I suffer!" he exclaimed, bursting into sobs, while a torrent of tears inundated his face.

He buried his head in his hands, and fell back on his bed.

The two sailors anxiously examined the surgeon's impassive face, trying to read in his features what they had to hope or fear.

The latter uttered a deep sigh of relief, passed his hand over his damp forehead, and turning to Michael, said—

"Heaven be praised! He sheds tears—he is saved."

"Heaven be praised!" the sailors repeated, crossing themselves devoutly.

"Do you think he is mad, Major?" Michael asked, in a trembling voice.

"No, it is not madness, but delirium; he will soon fall asleep—do not leave him; when he awakes he will remember nothing. If he ask for drink give him the potion I have prepared, and which is on that table."

"Yes, Major."

"Now I am going to retire; if any unforeseen accident occur, warn me at once; but, in any case, I shall look in again tonight."

The surgeon left the cabin; his previsions were soon realised, M. de Barmont gradually fell into a calm and peaceful sleep.

The two sailors stood motionless by his bedside; no nurse could have watched a patient with greater care and more delicate attention than did these two men, whose exterior seemed so hard, but whose hearts were really so kind.

The whole night passed away thus; the surgeon had come in several times, but after a few minutes' examination he withdrew with an air of satisfaction, and laying a finger on his lips.

About morning, at the first sunbeam that entered the cabin, the Count made a slight movement, opened his eyes, and slightly turned his head.

"My good Michael, give me some drink," he said, in a feeble voice.

The sailor handed him a glass.

"I feel crushed," he muttered; "have I been ill?"

"Yes, a little," the sailor replied; "but now it is all over, thank heaven! You need only have patience."

"I feel the motion of the frigate—are we under weigh?"

"Yes, Commandant."

"And who gave the orders?"

"Yourself, last night."

"Ah!" he remarked, as he handed back the glass. His head fell heavily on the pillow again, and he was silent.

Still, he did not sleep; his eyes were opened, and gazed anxiously all around.

"I remember," he murmured, while two tears welled in his eyes; then he suddenly addressed Michael.

"It was you who picked me up and brought me aboard?"

"Yes, Captain, 'twas."

"Thanks! and yet it would have perhaps been better to leave me to die."

The sailor shrugged his shoulders disdainfully.

"That is a fine idea, strike me!" he grumbled.

"Oh, if you only knew," he said, sorrowfully.

"I knew all; did I not warn you of it the first day?"

"That is true; I ought to have believed you—but, alas! I already loved her."

"Zounds! I knew that, and she deserved it."

"Does she still love me?"

"Who can doubt it, poor dear creature?"

"You are a good man, Michael."

"I am just."

There was another silence.

At the expiration of a few minutes the Count renewed the conversation.

"Did you find the letter?" he asked. "Where is it?"

"Here," he said, as he handed it to him.

The Count eagerly clutched it.

"Have you read it?" he asked.

"For what purpose?" said Michael. "Zounds, it must be a tissue of lies and infamies! And I am not curious about reading such things."

"There, take it," said the Count.

"To tear it up?"

"No, to read it."

"What's the good?"

"You must know the contents of the letter—I order it."

"That is different—give it here."

He took the letter, opened, and ran through it.

"Read it aloud," said the Count.

"That is a pretty job you give me, Commandant. Still, as you wish it, I must obey you."

"I implore you, Michael."

"Enough, Captain."

And he began reading the strange missive aloud.

It was short and laconic, but on that very account it necessarily produced a more terrible effect, because every word was carefully chosen to go straight home.

The following was its tenor:—

MY LORD,

You have not married my daughter: I defrauded you by a false marriage. You shall never see her again—she is dead to you. For many years there has been an implacable hatred between your family and mine. I should not have gone to seek you, but Heaven itself brought you in my way. I understood that it was desired I should avenge myself, and I obeyed. I believe that I have succeeded in breaking your heart forever. The love you have for my daughter is sincere and deep. All the better, for you will suffer the more cruelly. Farewell, my lord. Believe me, you had better not try to find me, for, if you succeed, my vengeance will be even more terrible. My daughter will marry in a month the man she loves, and whom alone she has ever loved.

"Don Estevan de Sylva, Duc de Peñaflor."

When the sailor had finished reading he turned an enquiring glance to his chief. The latter shook his head several times, but made no other reply.

Michael handed back the letter, which the Captain at once concealed beneath his pillow.

"What do you intend to do?" the sailor asked him, a moment after.

"You shall know hereafter," the Count answered, in a hollow voice. "I could not form a determination now, for my head is still heavy, and I require to reflect."

Michael gave a nod of assent.

At this moment the doctor came in. He appeared delighted at seeing his patient in so good a state, and with a joyous rubbing of his hands, promised that he should leave his bed in a week at the latest.

In fact, the surgeon was not mistaken, for the Count rapidly recovered; ere long he was able to rise, and at the end of a few days, were it not for a cadaverous pallor spread over his face, and which he ever retained, his strength seemed to have entirely come back to him.

M. de Barmont steered his frigate up the Tagus, and anchored before Lisbon. So soon as the vessel was moored the Captain summoned the second in command to his cabin, and had a long conversation with him, after which he went ashore with Michael and Bowline.

The frigate remained under the command of the first lieutenant: the Count had abandoned it for ever.

This deed almost constituted a desertion; but M. de Barmont was resolved on returning to Cadiz at all hazards.

During the few days that had elapsed since his conference with Michael, the Count had reflected, as he promised the sailor.

The result of his reflections was, that Doña Clara had been deceived by the Duke like himself, and believed herself really married—indeed, the whole of the young lady's behaviour to him proved the fact. In desiring to insure his vengeance too thoroughly, the Duke had gone beyond his object: Doña Clara loved him, he felt certain of that. She had only obeyed her father under the constraint of force.

This admitted, only one thing was left the Count to do; to return to Cadiz, collect information, find the Duke, and have a solemn explanation with him in his daughter's presence.

This plan drawn up in his mind, the young man immediately set, about carrying it out, leaving the command of his vessel to the lieutenant, at the risk of destroying his career and being pursued as a traitor, as the war was raging between France and Spain. He freighted a coaster; and, followed by his two sailors, to whom he had frankly explained his intention, but who would not leave him, he returned to Cadiz.

Thanks to the thorough knowledge of Spanish he possessed, the Count did not arouse any suspicions in that city, where it was easy for him to obtain the information he desired.

The Duke had really set out for Madrid. The Count at once proceeded to that city. A gentleman of the importance of the Duc de Peñaflor, a grandee of Spain of the first class, a *caballero cubierto*, could not travel without leaving traces, especially when nothing led him to suspect that he was followed. Hence the Count had not the slightest difficulty in discovering the route he had taken, and he arrived at Madrid, persuaded that he should soon have with the Duke the explanation he so ardently desired.

But his hopes were foiled. The Duke, after being honored with a private audience by the King, had set out for Barcelona.

Fatality interfered, but the Count would not be baffled: he mounted his horse, crossed Spain, and arrived at Barcelona.

The Duke had embarked for Naples on the previous day.

This pursuit was assuming the proportions of an Odyssey: it seemed as if the Duke felt that he was being pursued.

It was not so, however. He was carrying out a mission with which his sovereign had entrusted him.

The Count made enquiries, and learnt that the Duc de Peñaflor was accompanied by his daughter, and two sons.

Two days later, M. de Barmont was sailing to Naples, on board a smuggling vessel.

We will not enter into all the details of this obstinate pursuit, which lasted for several months.

We will confine ourselves to saying that the Count missed the Duke at Naples, as he had missed him at Madrid and Barcelona, and that he traversed the whole of Italy, and entered France, still in chase of his intangible enemy, who seemed to fly before him.

But during the interval, although the Count did not suspect, the parts had been greatly modified, if not completely changed.

In this way.

The Duke had a great interest in knowing what the Count would do. Though it was certain that the war would compel him to leave Spain, still he was too well acquainted with the young man's resolute and determined character to suppose for a moment that he would accept the insult offered him, without trying to take a startling revenge.

In consequence, he had left at Cadiz a confidential man with orders to watch the Count's movements with the greatest care, in the event of his reappearing, and to warn the Duke of what steps he might take.

The man had conscientiously and most skilfully discharged the delicate duty entrusted to him, and while the Count was pursuing the Duke, he pursued the

Count, never letting him out of sight, stopping when he stopped, and setting out behind him directly he saw him start.

When at last he felt assured that the Count was really after his master, he got ahead of him, rejoined the Duke, whom he came up with in the neighbourhood of Pignerol, and reported to him all that he had learned.

The Duke, though internally terrified by the hateful persistency of his enemy, pretended to attach but very slight importance to this communication, and smiled contemptuously on listening to his servant's report.

But, for all this, he did not neglect to take his precautions; and, as peace was on the point of being signed, and a Spanish plenipotentiary was in Paris, he sent off the same valet to him at full speed, with a pressing letter.

This letter was a formal denunciation of the Count de Barmont Senectaire.

Cardinal de Richelieu raised no difficulty about granting an order to arrest the Count, and police agents of his Eminence, commanded by François Bouillot, left Paris in pursuit of the unhappy officer.

The latter, completely ignorant of what was going on, had continued his journey, and even gained ground on the Duke, who, persuaded that henceforth he would have nothing to fear from his enemy, as the latter would be arrested before he could come up with him, now travelled by easy stages.

The Duke's calculations were false, however. He had not reflected that the Cardinal's guards, not knowing where to find the man whom they had orders to arrest, and obliged to feel their way, would be compelled to almost double their journey: and this really occurred.

Moreover, as, with the exception of Bouillot, not one of them was personally acquainted with the Count, and he, as we now know, desired nothing so much as the Count's escape, he passed through the midst of them unsuspected, which occasioned them a great loss of time, by compelling them to turn back.

We have already narrated how, after the stormy explanation which took place between father-in-law and son-in-law, the latter was arrested, taken by Bouillot to the Isle St. Marguerite, and delivered over to Major de l'Oursière. And now that we have fully explained the respective positions of each of our characters, we will resume our narrative at the point where we left it.

CHAPTER VIII.

THE PRISONER.

We have mentioned that after proof of identity, and perusal of the order of arrest, Major de l'Oursière, governor of the fortress of St. Marguerite, had the Count conducted to the room which was to serve as his prison, until the day when it might please the Cardinal to restore him to liberty.

This room, very spacious and lofty, of an octagonal shape, and with whitewashed walls, fifteen feet thick, was only lighted by two narrow loopholes, covered with an under and outer iron trelliswork, which completely prevented any looking out.

A large chimney, with a wide mantelpiece, occupied one corner of the room: facing was a bed, composed of a thin palliasse and a narrow mattress laid on a deal bedstead, formerly painted yellow, though time had completely removed the colour.

A rickety table, a stool, a chair, a night commode, and an iron candlestick, completed the furniture, which was more than modest.

This room was situated on the highest floor of the tower, the platform of which, where a sentry tramped day and night, served as the ceiling.

The soldier drew the bolts that garnished the iron-lined door of this room. The Count entered, with a firm step.

After taking a glance at these cold, sad walls, destined henceforward to serve him as a habitation, he sat down on a chair, crossed his arms on his breast, hung his head, and began to reflect.

The soldier, or rather gaoler, who had gone out, returned an hour later, and found him in the same position.

He brought with him sheets, blankets, and wood to light a fire. Behind him two soldiers carried the portmanteau containing the prisoner's clothes and linen, which they placed in a corner, and retired.

The gaoler at once set to work making the bed. Then he swept the room and lit the fire. When these different duties were accomplished, he approached the prisoner.

"My lord?" he said to him politely.

"What do you want with me, my friend?" the Count answered, raising his head and looking at him gently.

"The governor of the castle desires the honour of an interview with you, as he says he has an important communication to make."

"I am at the governor's orders," the Count said laconically.

The gaoler bowed and went out.

"What can the man want with me?" the Count muttered, so soon as he was alone.

He had not long to wait, for the door opened again and the governor made his appearance.

The prisoner rose to receive him, bowed, and then silently waited for him to speak.

The Major made the gaoler a sign to withdraw, and then, after a fresh bow, he said with cold politeness,—

"My lord Count, gentlemen should respect each other. Although the orders I have received on your account from the Cardinal are very strict, I still desire to shew you any attention that is not incompatible with my duty. I have, therefore, come to you frankly in order to have an understanding on the subject."

The Count guessed to what this speech tended, but did not let it be seen, and answered,—

"Mr. Governor, I am grateful, as I ought to be, for the steps you have been kind enough to take; may I ask you, therefore, to have the goodness to explain to me the nature of your orders, and what the favours are by which you can alleviate their severity. But, in the first place, as I am at home here," he added, with a melancholy smile; "do me the honour of seating yourself."

The Major bowed, but remained standing.

"It is unnecessary, my lord," he remarked, "as what I have to say to you is very short; in the first place, you will observe that I have had the delicacy to send you the trunk containing your effects unexamined as I had the right to do."

"I allow the fact, Major, and feel obliged; to you for it."

The Major bowed.

"As you are an officer, my lord," he said, "you are aware that his Eminence the Cardinal, although he is a great man, is not very liberal to officers whose infirmity or wounds compel them to quit the service."

"That is true."

"The governors of fortresses more especially, although nominated by the

King, being obliged to pay a long price to their predecessors for the office, are reduced to a perfect state of want, if they have not saved up some money."

"I was not aware of that circumstance, sir, and fancied that the governorship of a fortress was a reward."

"So it is, my lord, but we have to pay for the command of fortresses like this, which are employed as state prisons."

"Ah! Very good."

"You understand, it is supposed that the governor makes a profit by the prisoners intrusted to his keeping."

"Of course, sir; are there at present many unhappy men who have incurred the displeasure of His Eminence detained in this castle?"

"Alas, sir, you are the only one, and that is exactly the reason why I desire to have an amicable settlement with you."

"For my part, be assured, sir, that I desire nothing more earnestly."

"I am convinced of that, and hence will discuss the question frankly."

"Do so, sir, do so; I am listening to you with the most serious attention."

"I have orders, sir, not to let you communicate with anyone but your gaoler, to give you neither books, papers, pens, or ink, and never to allow you to quit this room; it appears there is great fear of your escape from here, and his Eminence is anxious to keep you."

"I am extremely obliged to his Eminence, but luckily for me," the Count answered with a smile, "instead of having to deal with a gaoler, I am dependent on a true soldier, who, while strictly obeying his orders, considers it unnecessary to torture a prisoner already so unhappy as to have fallen into disgrace with the King and the Cardinal minister."

"You have judged me correctly, my lord, though the orders are so strict. I command alone in this castle, where I have no control to fear. Hence I hope to have it in my power to relax the rigor I am commanded to show you."

"Whatever may be your intention in that respect, allow me, sir, in my turn to speak like a frank and loyal sailor. As prisoner of your King, doubtless for a very long time, money is perfectly useless to me; though not rich, I enjoy a certain ease, on which I congratulate myself, as this ease permits me to requite any polite attentions you may show me; service for service, sir, I will give you every year 10,000 livres, paid in advance; and, on your side, will you allow me to procure, at my own charges of course, all the objects susceptible of alleviating my captivity."

The Major felt as if about to faint. The old officer of fortune had never in his whole life possessed so large a sum.

The Count continued without seeming to notice the effect his words produced on the governor.

"Well then, that is quite understood. To the sum the King pays you for my board, we will add 200 livres a month, or 2,400 per annum, for papers, pens, ink, &c., suppose we say the round sum of 3,000 livres, does that suit you?"

"Ah, Sir, it is too much, a great deal too much."

"No, Sir, since I assist an honourable man, who will owe me thanks for it."

"Ah! I shall be eternally grateful, sir; but, do not be angry with my frankness, you will oblige me to offer up vows to keep you as long as possible."

"Who knows, sir, whether my departure will not some day be more advantageous than my stay here?" he said with a meaning smile; "be good enough to lend me your tablets."

The Major offered them to him.

The Count tore out a leaf, with a few pencilled words on it, and handed it back to him.

"Here," he said, "is a draught for 16,000 livres, which you can receive at sight from Messrs. Dubois, Loustal, and Co., of Toulon, whenever you have leisure."

The governor clutched the paper with a start of joy.

"But it seems to me that this draft is 800 livres in excess of the sum agreed on between us?" he said.

"That is correct, sir, but the 800 livres are for the purchase of different articles, of which here is the list, and which I must ask you to procure for me."

"You shall have them tomorrow, my lord," and after bowing very low the governor walked backwards out of the room.

"Come," the Count muttered gaily, when the heavy door had closed on the Major; "I was not deceived, I judged that man correctly, and his is really perfect, but his most thoroughly developed vice is decidedly avarice; I can make something of it, I fancy, when I like, but I must not go ahead too fast, but act with the greatest prudence."

Certain of not being disturbed, at least for some hours, the Count opened the trunk brought in by the two soldiers, in order to convince himself whether the governor had told him the truth, and the contents were really intact.

The trunk had not been examined.

In the foresight of a probable arrest, the Count when he started in pursuit of the Duc de Peñaflor, had purchased several objects which he found again with the most lively satisfaction.

In addition to a certain quantity of clothes and linen, the trunk contained a very fine and strong silk cord, nearly one hundred fathoms in length, two pairs of pistols, a dagger, a sword, powder and bullets, objects which the governor would have confiscated without any scruple, had he seen them, and which the Count had laid in at all risks, trusting to chance.

There were also several iron and steel tools, and concealed in a double bottom, a very heavy purse containing the sum of 25,000 livres in gold, in addition to another almost equally large amount in Spanish quadruples sewn into a wide leathern belt.

So soon as the Count was certain that the Major had told him the truth, he carefully locked the trunk again, hung the key round his neck by a steel chain, and sat down quietly in the chimney corner.

His meditations were interrupted by the gaoler. This time the man not only brought him bed furniture, far superior to what he had given him before, but he had added a carpet, a mirror, and even toilet utensils.

A cloth was spread on a table, upon which he placed in a moment a very appetising dinner.

"The Major begs me to apologize, sir," he said; "tomorrow he will send you what you asked for. In the meanwhile he has forwarded you some books."

"Very good, my friend," the Count replied.

"What is your name?"

"La Grenade, sir."

"Has the Governor selected you to wait on me?"

"Yes, sir."

"My friend, you appear to me a good fellow, here are three louis for you. I will give you the same amount every month if I am satisfied with your attention."

"Had you given me nothing, sir," La Grenade replied, as he took the money, "it would not have prevented me from serving you with all the zeal of which I am capable, and if I receive these three louis, it is only because a poor devil like me has no right to refuse a present from so generous a gentleman as you. But, I repeat, sir, I am quite at your service, and you can employ me in whatever way you please."

"Goodness!" the Count said, in surprise; "and yet I do not know you, as far as I am aware, La Grenade—whence, may I ask, comes this great devotion to my person?"

"I am most willing to tell you, sir, if it interests you. I am a friend of M. François Bouillot, to whom I am under certain obligations; he ordered me to serve and obey you in everything."

"That good Bouillot," said the Count. "Very well, my friend, I shall not be ungrateful. I do not want you anymore at present."

The gaoler put some logs on the fire, lit the lamp, and withdrew.

"Well," said the Count, with a laugh, "Heaven forgive me! I believe that, though a prisoner in appearance, I am as much master of this castle as the governor, and that I can leave it without opposition on any day I like. What would the Cardinal think if he knew how his orders were executed?"

He sat down to table, unfolded his napkin, and began dining with a good appetite.

Things went on thus, in the way agreed on between the Governor and his prisoner.

The arrival of Count de Barmont at the fortress had been a windfall for the Major, who, since he had received from the royal munificence the command of this castle as retiring pension, had not once before had an opportunity to derive any profit from the position that had been given him. Hence he promised to make a gold mine of his solitary prisoner; for the Isle of St. Marguerite, as we have already remarked, had not yet acquired the reputation which it merited at a later date as a State prison.

The Count's room was furnished as well as it could be; everything he demanded in the shape of books was procured him, though he had to pay dearly for them, and he was even allowed to walk on the towers.

The Count was happy—so far, at least, as the circumstances in which he found himself allowed him to be so: no one would have supposed, on seeing him work so assiduously at mathematics and navigation, for he applied himself most seriously to the completion of his maritime education, that this man nourished in his heart a thought of implacable vengeance, and that this thought was ever present to him.

At the first blush, the resolution formed by the Count to allow himself to be incarcerated, while it was easy for him to remain free, may seem strange: but the Count was one of those men of granite whose thoughts are immutable, and who, when they have once formed a resolution, after calculating with the utmost coolness all the chances for and against, follow the road they have laid down for themselves, ever marching in a straight line without caring for the obstacles that arise at each step on their path and surmounting them, because they decided from the first that they would do so—characters that grow and are perfected in the struggle, and sooner or later reach the goal they have designed.

The Count understood that any resistance to the Cardinal would result in his own utter ruin; and there was no lack of proofs to support this reasoning: by escaping from the guards who were taking him to prison, he would remain at liberty, it is true, but he would be exiled, obliged to quit France, and wander about in foreign parts alone, isolated, without resources, ever on the watch, forced to hide himself, and reduced to the impossibility of asking, that is to say, of obtaining the necessary information he required to avenge himself on the man who, by robbing him of the wife he loved, had at the same blow not only destroyed his career and fortune, but also eternally ruined his happiness.

He was young, and could wait; vengeance is eaten cold, say the southerners—and the Count came from Languedoc. Besides, as he had said to Bouillot, in a moment of expansiveness, he wished to suffer, in order to kill within him every human feeling that still existed, and to find himself one day armed *cap-à-pie* to face his enemy.

Cardinal Richelieu and Louis XIII. were both seriously ill. Their death would not fail to produce a change of reign in two, three, or four years at the most, and that catastrophe would arrive, one of whose consequences it is to produce a reaction, and consequently, to open to all the prisoners of the defunct Cardinal the dungeons to which he had condemned them.

The Count was twenty-five years of age: hence time was his own, and the more so because, when restored to liberty, he would enter on all his rights, and as an enemy of Richelieu, be favourably regarded at Court, and, through the temporary credit he would enjoy, be in a condition to regain all the advantage he had lost as concerned his foe.

Only energetically endowed men, who are sure of themselves, are capable of making such calculations, and obstinately pursuing a line of conduct so opposed to all logical combinations; but these men who thus resolutely enlist chance on their side, and reckon on it as a partner, always succeed in what they purpose doing, unless death suddenly cuts them short.

Through the intercession of La Grenade, and the tacit connivance of the

Governor, who closed his eyes with a charming inattention, the Count was not only cognizant with all that was going on outside, but also received letters from his friends, which he answered.

One day, after reading a letter which la Grenade had given him when bringing in breakfast, a letter from the Duc de Bellegarde, which had reached him through Michael, for the worthy sailor had refused to leave his Commandant, and had turned fisherman at Antibes, with Bowline as his assistant, the Count sent a message to the Governor, requesting a few minutes' conversation with him.

The Major knew that every visit he paid his prisoner was a profit to him, hence he hastened to his room.

"Have you heard the news, sir?" the Count said at once on seeing him.

"What news, my lord?" the Major asked, in amazement, for he knew nothing.

In fact, placed as he was at the extreme frontier of the kingdom, news, no matter its importance, only reached him, so to speak, by accident.

"The Cardinal Minister is dead, sir. I have just learned it from a sure hand."

"Oh!" said the Major, clasping his hands, for this death might cause him the loss of his place.

"And," the Count added, coldly, "His Majesty King Louis XIII. is at death's door."

"Great heaven, what a misfortune!" exclaimed the Governor.

"This misfortune may be fortunate for you, sir," the Count resumed.

"Fortunate! When I am menaced with the loss of my command! Alas, my lord, what will become of me if I am turned out of here?"

"That might easily, happen," said the Count. "You have, sir, always been a great friend of the defunct Cardinal, and known as such."

"That is, unhappily, too true," the Major muttered, quite out of countenance, and recognizing the truth of this affirmation.

"There is, I think, an advantageous mode of arranging matters."

"What is it, my lord? Speak, I implore you!"

"It is this: listen to me carefully—what I am going to say is very serious for you."

"I am listening, my lord."

"Here is a letter all ready written for the Duc de Bellegarde. You will start at once for Paris, passing through Toulon, where you will cash this draft for 2000 livres, to cover your expenses. The Duke is sincerely attached to me. For my sake he will receive you kindly: you will come to an understanding with him, and obey him in everything he orders."

"Yes, yes, my lord."

"And if within a month from this time at the latest—"

"From this time at the latest—" the Governor repeated, panting with impatience.

"You bring me here my full and entire—pardon, signed by H. M. Louis XIII.—"

"What?" the Governor exclaimed, with a start of surprise.

"I will at once pay you," the Count continued, coldly, "the sum of 50,000 livres, to indemnify you for the loss my liberation must entail on you."

"Fifty thousand livres!" the Major exclaimed, his eyes sparkling with greed.

"Fifty thousand! yes, sir," the Count replied. "And, besides, I pledge myself, if you wish it, to get you confirmed in your command. Is this matter settled?"

"But, my lord, how am I to manage at Paris?"

"Follow the instructions the Duc de Bellegarde will give you."

"What you ask of me is very difficult."

"Not so difficult as you pretend to believe, sir; however, if this mission does not suit you—"

"I did not say that, sir."

"In a word, you can take it or leave it."

"I take it, my lord—I take it. Great heaven!—fifty thousand livres!"

"And you start?"

"Tomorrow."

"No, tonight."

"Very good—tonight."

"All right! Here are the letter and the draft. Oh! by the way, try to put yourself in communication with a fisherman at Antibes of the name of Michael."

"I know him," the Major said, with a smile.

"Indeed!" said the Count. "There would be no harm, either, in your trying to find the exempt who brought me here, one François Bouillot."

"I know where to find him," the Major replied, with the same meaning smile.

"Very good! in that case, my dear Governor, I have nothing more to add, or any recommendations to make to you, beyond wishing you a pleasant journey."

"It will be so, my lord, I pledge you my word."

"It is true that it is a round sum—fifty thousand livres!"

"I shall not forget the amount."

After saying this the Major took leave of his prisoner, and retired, with a profusion of bows.

"I believe that I am going to be free this time!" the Count exclaimed, so soon as he was alone—"Ah! my lord Duke, we are now about to fight with equal weapons!"

CHAPTER IX.

MAJOR DE L'OURSIÈRE.

Had it been possible for Count de Barmont to notice through the thick oak planks, lined with iron, that formed the door of his prison, the face of the governor on leaving him, he would not have chanted victory so loudly, or believed himself so near his deliverance.

In fact, so soon as the Major had no longer cause to dread his prisoner's clear-sighted glance, his features immediately assumed an expression of cynical malice impossible to render; his half-closed eyes flashed with a gloomy fire beneath his grey eyelids and an ironical smile raised the corners of his pale thin lips.

It was twilight; night was beginning to fall, and confound all objects, by burying them in a dark pall, which momentarily grew denser.

The Major returned to his apartments, put a heavy cloak on his shoulders, pulled his hat over his eyes, and sent for his lieutenant.

The latter presented himself at once.

He was a man of about forty, with a delicate and intelligent face, whose features were imprinted with gentleness and even kindness.

"I am starting this moment, sir," the governor said to him, "for Antibes, whither important business summons me; my absence will probably be prolonged for several days. While I remain absent from the castle, I invest you with the command; watch over its safety, and guard against any attempted escape on the part of the prisoner, though I doubt his making it. Such attempts, though they do not succeed, injure the reputation of a fortress, and the character of its governor."

"I will watch with the greatest care, sir!"

"I am certain of that, sir. Is there any fishing boat in the roads? I should prefer not using the boat belonging to the fortress, as the garrison is so weak."

"The fishing boat you generally use, sir, and which is commanded by one Michael, I think, was alongside the quay hardly an hour ago, but he has probably started to fish outside the reef, as he usually does."

"Hum," said the Major, "even were he still there, I should scruple at making the poor fellow lose so much time in putting me ashore. These fishermen are not rich, and every minute you take from them makes them lose a part of the trifling profit of a long and hard night's work."

The officer bowed, apparently sharing his chief's philanthropic ideas, although his face evidenced the surprise which the expression of such sentiments by a man like the Major caused him.

"Are there no other boats here?" the Major asked, affecting an air of indifference.

"I beg your pardon, sir, a smuggling lugger is just about putting out to sea."

"Very good; warn the master that I wish him to take me on board. Be good enough to make haste, sir, for I am in a hurry."

The officer withdrew to carry out the order given him; the Major took some papers, doubtless important, from an iron casket, hid them under his coat, wrapped himself in his cloak, and left the castle, under the salute of the sentries who presented arms as he passed.

"Well?" he asked the officer who came to meet him.

"I have spoken to the master, sir, he awaits you," the other replied.

"I thank you, sir; now, return to the castle, and watch carefully over its safety till my return."

The officer took leave, and the Major proceeded toward a sort of small quay, where the lugger's yawl was waiting for him.

So soon as the governor was aboard, the smuggler let go the hawser, and set sail.

When the light vessel was well under weigh, the master respectfully walked up to the Major.

"Where are we to steer?" he asked, as he doffed his woollen nightcap.

"Ah, ah! is it you, Master Nicaud?" the governor said; for, accustomed to have dealings with the smugglers, he knew most of them by their names.

"Myself, at your service, if I can do anything, Mr. Governor," the master answered politely.

"Tell me," said the Major, "would you like to earn ten louis?"

The sailor burst into a hearty laugh.

"You are joking with me, of course, Mr. Governor," he said.

"Not at all," the Major went on, "and the proof is, here they are," he added, as he drew from his pocket a handful of gold, which he carelessly tossed in his hand; "I am therefore awaiting your answer."

"Hang it, Mr. Governor, you are well aware that ten louis forms a very fine lump of money for a poor fellow like me; I am most willing to earn the canaries, what must I do for them?"

"Well, a very simple thing! take me to St. Honorat, where I feel inclined for a stroll."

"At this time of night?" the master remarked in surprise.

The Major bit his lips on perceiving that he had made a foolish remark.

"I am very fond of the picturesque, and wish to enjoy the effect of the convent ruins in the moonlight."

"That is an idea like any other," the skipper answered; "and as you pay me, Mr. Governor, I can have no objection."

"That is true. Then you will take me to Saint Honorat, land me in your boat, and stand off and on while waiting for me. Is that agreed?"

"Perfectly."

"Ah! I have a decided taste for solitude, and hence I must insist on none of your men landing on the island while I am there."

"The whole crew shall remain on board, I promise you."

"All right, I trust to you, here is the money."

"Thanks," said the skipper, pocketing it; then he said to the steerer, "down with the helm," and added, "Hilloh, my lads, brace the sheets to larboard."

The vessel quickly came up to the wind, and leaped over the waves in the direction of Saint Honorat, whose black outlines stood out on the horizon.

It is but a short passage between Saint Marguerite and Saint Honorat, especially for such a clipper as the smuggling lugger.

The vessel was soon off the island.

The master lay to, and ordered a boat to be let down.

"Mr. Governor," he said respectfully, doffing his cap, and stopping the governor, who was walking up and down in the stern; "we are all ready, and the boat waits for you."

"Already! All the better," the latter answered.

At the moment when he was going to get into the boat, the skipper arrested him.

"Have you pistols?" he asked him.

"Pistols?" he said as he turned round; "What for? is not this island deserted?"

"Entirely."

"Hence I can run no risk."

"Not the slightest; hence that is not the reason why I asked you the question."

"What is it then?"

"Hang it, it is as black as in the fiend's oven; there is no moon, you cannot distinguish an object ten yards from you. How shall I know when you want to come on board again, unless you warn me by a signal?"

"That is true; what had I better do?"

"Here is a pistol, it is not loaded, but there is powder in the pan, and you can squib it."

"Thanks," said the Major, taking the pistol, and thrusting it through his girdle.

He got into the boat, which was dancing on the waves, and sat down in the stern sheets; four vigorous sailors bending over the oars made her fly through the water.

"A pleasant trip," the skipper shouted.

It appeared to the Major as if this wish had been uttered with a very marked ironical tone by Master Nicaud, but he attached no further importance to it, and turned his eyes toward land, which was gradually looming larger.

Ere long the boat's bows grated on the sand; they had arrived.

The Major went ashore, and after ordering the sailors to return aboard, he drew his cloak over his face, went off with long steps, and soon disappeared in the darkness.

However, instead of obeying the injunction given them, three of the sailors landed in their turn, and followed the Major at a distance, while careful to keep themselves out of sight. The fourth, who remained to keep the boat, hid the latter behind a point, secured it to a projecting rock, and leaping ashore, fusil in hand, he remained on the watch with his eyes fixed on the interior of the island.

The Major, in the meanwhile, continued to advance hurriedly in the direction of the ruins, whose imposing outline was already beginning to present itself to his eyes, borrowing from the surrounding gloom a still more imposing aspect.

The Major, convinced that his orders had been punctually carried out, for he had no motive to distrust Master Nicaud, whom he had ever and under all circumstances found willing and faithful, walked on without turning his head, or even taking precautions, which he considered unnecessary, as he was far from suspecting that several men were following his footsteps, and watching his movements.

It was easy to see from the deliberate manner in which he walked, and the facility with which he evaded obstacles and found his way in the darkness, that this was not the first time the Major had come to this spot, though it appeared so solitary and deserted.

After entering the ruins, M. de l'Oursière passed through a cloister, encumbered with shapeless fragments, and forcing his way between stones and brambles, he entered the chapel, a magnificent specimen of the purest Roman style, whose crumbling roof had fallen in under the incessant efforts of time, and only the choir and apse still remained intact amid broken columns and desecrated altars.

The Major passed through the choir, and reached the apse, where he halted.

After carefully examining for a moment the surrounding objects, as if he expected to find someone or something he did not perceive, he at length resolved to clap his hands thrice.

At the same moment a man rose scarce two paces from him.

This sudden apparition, though he fully expected it, made the Major start, and he fell back a step, laying his hand on his sword.

"Ah, ah, my master," the stranger said, in a mocking voice, "pray do you take me for a spectre, that I cause you such terror?"

The man was wrapped up in a thick cloak, whose folds concealed his shape, while a broad leafed plumed hat entirely covered his face and rendered him completely unrecognizable. Only the end of his cloak raised by the scabbard of a long rapier, proved that whoever the man might be, he had not come unarmed to this gloomy rendezvous.

"I am at your orders, sir," the Major said, raising his hand to his hat, but without removing it.

"And ready to serve me, no doubt," the stranger resumed.

"That depends," the Major remarked roughly, "times are no longer the same."

"Ah, ah," the stranger continued still sarcastically, "what news is there? I shall be delighted to learn it of you."

"You know it as well as I do, sir."

"No matter, tell me all the same what the great news is, that thus produces modifications in our relations which have hitherto been so amicable?"

"It is useless to jeer thus, sir; I have served you, you have paid me, and we are quits."

"Perhaps so, but go on. I presume you wish to propose a new bargain to me?"

"I have nothing to propose; I have merely come because you expressed a desire to see me, that is all."

"And your prisoner, are you still satisfied with him?"

"More than ever. He is a charming gentleman, who does not at all deserve the melancholy fate thrust on him; I really feel an interest in him."

"Confound it, that comes expensive, I did not take that interest into account, and I was wrong, I see."

"What do you mean, sir?" the Major protested with an indignant air.

"Nothing but what I say to you, my dear sir. Hang it, you amuse me with your scruples, after taking money from all parties during the last eighteen months; the Cardinal is dead and the King is on the point of following him, that is what you wished to tell me, is it not? A new reign is preparing, and it is probable that, if only through a spirit of contradiction, the new government will upset everything done by the one that preceded it, and that its first care will be to open the prison doors; you also wished to tell me that Count de

Barmont, who possesses warm friends at court, who will not fail to employ their influence on his behalf, cannot fail to be set at liberty ere long. Confusion, I knew all that as well and even better than you, but what matter?"

"How, what matter?"

"Certainly, if Count de Barmont has devoted friends, he has implacable enemies; bear that in mind."

"And the result will be?"

"That in four days at the latest, you will receive an order signed by Louis XIII. himself."

"To what effect?"

"Oh! Good heaven, no great thing, except that Count de Barmont will be immediately transferred from St. Marguerite to the Bastille; and once there," he added in a hollow voice, which made the Major shudder involuntarily, "a man is eternally erased from the number of the living or only leaves it a corpse or a maniac. Do you comprehend me now?"

"Yes, I understand you, sir; but who guarantees that the Count will not have escaped before the four days to which you refer?"

"Oh! With a governor like yourself, Major, such an eventuality seems to me highly improbable."

"Well, well," the Major observed, "very extraordinary tales are told about the escape of prisoners."

"That is true; but another thing reassures me against this escape."

"And what is that, sir?"

"Merely that the Count himself declared that he would never consent to escape, and was not at all anxious about liberty."

"Well, sir, that is the very thing that deceives you; it seems that he has now changed his opinion, and is eagerly soliciting through his friends to obtain his liberty."

"Ah! Have we come to that point?" the stranger said, fixing on the Major a glance which flashed through the gloom.

The governor bowed.

There was a silence, during which no other sound was audible, save that of the heavy flight of the nocturnal birds in the ruins.

"A truce to further chattering," the stranger resumed in a fierce voice; "how much do you ask to prevent the prisoner escaping until the king's order reaches you?"

"Two hundred thousand livres," the Major answered roughly.

"Was I not right in telling you that it would be expensive?" the stranger said with a grin.

"Dear or not, that is my price, and I shall not bate it."

"Very good, you shall have it."

"When?"

"Tomorrow."

"That will be too late."

"What?" the stranger asked haughtily.

"I said it would be too late," the Major repeated imperturbably.

"In that case, when must you have it?"

"At once."

"Do you fancy I carry 200,000 livres about me?"

"I do not say that, but I can accompany you where you are going, and on reaching Antibes, we will say, you can pay me the amount."

"That is a good plan."

"Is it not?"

"Yes, only there is an obstacle to its success."

"I do not see one."

"But I do."

"What is it, sir?"

"That, if I give you a meeting here, and come disguised and alone, I have probably an object."

"Of course! You wish to remain incog."

"You are full of penetration, my dear sir; and yet we can come to an understanding."

"I do not see how, unless you consent to what I ask."

"You are a judge of diamonds, since we have hitherto only bargained in them."

"That is true, I am a tolerable judge of them."

"Here is one that is worth 100,000 crowns, take it."

And he offered a small case of black shagreen.

The Major eagerly seized it.

"But," he objected, "how can I be certain that you are not deceiving me?"

"An affecting confession," the stranger observed laughingly.

"Business is business, I risk my soul in serving you."

"As for your soul, my dear sir, reassure yourself; in that quarter you have nothing to risk. But I will give you the satisfaction you desire."

And taking a dark lanthorn from under his cloak, he let the light play on the diamond.

The Major only required one glance to assure himself of the value of the rich reward offered him.

"Are you satisfied?" the stranger asked, as he placed the lanthorn again under his cloak.

"Here is the proof," the Major answered, as he concealed the box, and handed him a bundle of papers.

"What is this?" the stranger inquired.

"Papers of great importance for you, in the sense that they will tell you who the Count's friends are, and the means they can employ to restore him to liberty."

"Bravo!" the stranger exclaimed, as he eagerly took the bundle of papers; "I no longer regret having paid so heavy a price for your assistance. Now we have discussed every point, I think?"

"I think so too."

"In that case, farewell! When I want you, I will let you know."

"Are you going already?"

"What the deuce would you have me do longer in this owl's nest? It is time for each of us to rejoin the persons waiting for us."

And after giving the Major a slight wave of the hand, he turned away and disappeared behind the ruins of the high altar.

At the same moment the stranger was suddenly seized by several men, so that not only was he unable to offer a useless resistance, but found himself bound and gagged before he had recovered from the surprise this attack had caused him.

His silent aggressors then left him rolling on the ground with convulsive bounds of impotent rage, and disappeared in the darkness without paying any further attention to him.

The Major, after a momentary hesitation, also resolved to leave the place, and slowly proceeded in the direction of the shore. On arriving within a certain distance, in obedience to skipper Nicaud's hint, he cocked his pistol and flashed the powder in the pan; then he continued to advance slowly.

The boat had doubtless made haste to meet him, for at the same moment as the Major reached the shore, its bows ran into the sand.

The governor stepped silently into it; twenty minutes after he found himself on board the lugger, where master Nicaud received him respectfully cap in hand.

The boat was hauled up to the davits, sail was set on the lugger, and she stood out to sea before a fresh breeze.

CHAPTER X.

THE SEAGULL LUGGER.

A lugger is a three mast vessel, with narrow lines aft and bulging bows; it has a foremast, mainmast, and a driver greatly inclined over the stern; its bowsprit is short; it carries large sails and at times topsails.

From this description it is easy to see that luggers have the same rig, on a larger scale, as chasse-marées.

Although the draft on water of these vessels is rather great aft, as they are generally quick and good sea boats, they are largely employed for smuggling purposes, in spite of the inconvenience of the large sails which have to be shifted with each tack.

The Seagull was a vessel of ninety tons, neatly fitted up, and carrying four small iron guns of eight to the pound, which caused her to bear a greater resemblance with a corsair than a peaceful coaster.

Still, in spite of a rather numerous crew, and her rakish appearance, during about a year since this vessel began frequenting the coast of Provence and the Lerins islands, not a word of harm had been said against her. Skipper Nicaud passed for an honest worthy man, although a little rough and quarrelsome,— faults, by the way, peculiar to nearly all sailors, and which in no way diminished the excellent reputation which the master of the Seagull enjoyed.

So soon as Major de l'Oursière had regained the lugger's deck, and the vessel had stood off, after taking a parting glance at St. Honorat, whose outline was gradually disappearing in the mist, he walked aft, seized the manrope and went down into the cabin.

But on entering the cabin, which he supposed to be unoccupied, as the skipper was on deck, the Major with difficulty restrained an exclamation of surprise.

There was a man in the cabin, seated at a table, and contently imbibing rum and water, while smoking an enormous pipe, and forming an aureole around him of bluish smoke.

In this man the Major recognised Michael the Basque, the fisherman.

After a moment's hesitation, the Major walked in, although the presence of this individual aboard the lugger was rather singular. Still there was nothing in the thing that should terrify the Major, who had no reason to suppose that Michael was hostile to him, or that he had anything to apprehend from him.

At the noise made by the Major on entering the cabin, the sailor half turned to him, though without removing the pipe from his lips. After taking a pull at the glass he held in his right hand, he said in a bantering tone,—

"Why, if I am not mistaken, it is our estimable governor of St. Marguerite; delighted to see you, I am sure, Major."

"Why," the Major replied, in the same key, "it's that worthy fellow, Michael. By what chance do I find you here, when I had a right to suppose you engaged fishing, at this moment, Lord knows where?"

"Ah!" said Michael, with a laugh; "There's as good fishing here as anywhere. Won't you take a seat, Major, or are you afraid of compromising your dignity by sitting down by the side of a poor fellow like me?"

"You do not think that," the Major answered, as he seated himself.

"Don't you smoke, eh?" Michael asked him.

"No; that is a sailor's amusement."

"It is so, Major. But I suppose you drink?"

The Major held out a glass, which the sailor liberally filled.

"Here's your health, Major. If I expected to meet anyone, it wasn't you, I assure you."

"I thought so."

"Indeed I didn't."

"Well, to tell you the truth, I did not expect to meet you, either."

"I am aware of that. You have come from St. Honorat."

"Hang it all! You cannot be ignorant of that fact, since I find you here."

"It was on your account, then, that we lost two hours in tacking between the islands, at the risk of running on to a reef, instead of attending to our business?"

"What do you mean by business? Are you a smuggler at present?"

"I am everything," Michael replied, laconically, emptying his glass.

"But what the deuce are you doing here?" asked the Major.

"What are you?" the sailor said, answering one question by another.

"I—I?" the Major began, in embarrassment.

"You hesitate!" Michael continued, banteringly. "Well, I will tell you, if you like."

"You, Michael?"

"Why not? You went to St. Honorat to admire the beauties of nature," and he burst into a hearty laugh. "Is it not so?"

"Yes. I have always passionately admired the picturesque. But that reminds me. I have forgotten to tell skipper Nicaud where I wish him to land me."

And he made a movement, as if to rise.

"It is unnecessary," the sailor said, obliging him to sit down again.

"How? Unnecessary! On the contrary, I must do it, without further delay."

"Still you have time, Major," the sailor said, peremptorily; "besides, I must speak with you first."

"You speak with me?" the Major exclaimed, in stupefaction.

"So it is, Major," the other replied, sarcastically. "I have very important matters to tell you. In your devil of a castle that is impossible, because you have there a number of soldiers and gaolers, who, at your slightest frown, interrupt the person addressing you, and throw him without ceremony into some hole, where they unscrupulously leave him to rot. That is discouraging, on my honour. But here it is far more agreeable, as I am not afraid that you will have me locked up —at least, not for the present. Hence, as the opportunity offers, I wish to take advantage of it to empty my budget, and tell you what I have on my heart."

The Major felt internally anxious, without yet knowing positively what he had to fear, so extraordinary to him seemed this way of speaking on the part of a sailor, who had hitherto always displayed a servile politeness toward him. Still, he did not allow anything of this to be seen, but leaned carelessly over the table.

"Very good, let us talk, since you feel so great an inclination for it, my good Michael; for I have time, as I am in no hurry."

The sailor made his chair turn half round on its hind legs, and finding himself by this movement right facing M. de l'Oursière, he examined him cunningly, for an instant, then drained the contents of his glass; and, after banging the empty glass on the table, he said,—

"It is really a charming passion of yours, Major, to go thus at night to admire the ruins of the convent of St. Honorat in the darkness. It is, really, a charming passion, and a very profitable one, from what I have been able to learn."

"What do you mean?" the Major asked, turning pale.

"I mean what I say, nothing else! Do you believe in hazard, Major?"

"Why—"

"No more, I fancy, in that which makes me meet you here, than in the chance that makes you find on a desert island diamonds worth three hundred thousand livres; because the one thing is as impossible as the other?"

This time the Major did not attempt to reply, for he felt he was caught out.

Michael continued in the same sneering and bantering tone—

"It is certainly ingenious to act as you do. A man soon grows rich by taking with both hands, but like all trades that are too good, this one is rather risky."

"You insult me, scoundrel!" the Major stammered. "Take care what you say. If I call—"

"Come, come," the sailor interrupted, with a coarse laugh; "I do not intend to notice the insult you cast in my teeth, for I have something else to do. As for calling out, just try it, and you will see what will happen."

"That—that is treachery!"

"Hang it! Are we not all more or less traitors? You are one—I am one; that is allowed: hence, believe me, it is useless to dwell any longer on this subject, and we had better revert to our business."

"Speak," the Major muttered in a gloomy voice.

"But, stay. I wish to give you a proof of frankness, and show you once for all how wrong you would be in keeping up, I will not say the least hope, but the slightest illusion as to what is going on here."

Then, tapping the table smartly with the heel of his glass, he shouted,—

"Come here, Nicaud, I want you."

A heavy step resounded on the cabin stairs, and almost immediately Skipper Nicaud's cunning face was framed by the doorway.

"What do you want, Michael?" he asked, without seeming even to notice the Major's presence.

"Only a trifle, my lad," the sailor replied, pointing to the officer, who had turned pale, through the emotion he felt. "Only a simple question for the personal satisfaction of this gentleman."

"Speak."

"Who is the present commander of the Seagull lugger, in whose cabin we are now seated?"

"Why, you, of course."

"Then everyone aboard, yourself included, must obey me?"

"Certainly; and without the slightest observation."

"Very good. Then supposing, Nicaud, I were to order you to take the Major here present, fasten a couple of round shot to his feet, and throw him overboard, what would you do, my lad?"

"What would I do?"

"Yes."

"Obey."

"Without any observation?"

Skipper Nicaud shrugged his shoulders.

"Shall I do it?" he asked, stretching out his huge fist towards the Major, who shuddered.

"Not yet," Michael answered. "Go back on deck, but do not go far, as I shall probably want you soon."

"Very good," said the master, and disappeared.

"Are you now edified, Major?" Michael asked, turning carelessly to the horrified governor; "And are you not beginning to understand that I, poor chap as I am, compared with you, have you, temporarily, at any rate, completely in my power?"

"I allow it," the Major stammered, in a faint and choking voice.

"In that case, I believe we shall come to an understanding."

"Come to the facts, sir, without further circumlocution."

"Good!" Michael exclaimed, coarsely; "That's how I like to see you. In the first place, hand me the diamond which your accomplice gave you in the ruins."

"Then you mean robbery. I had hoped better things of you," the Major answered, disdainfully.

"Call it what you like, Major," the sailor said imperturbably; "the name does not alter the thing—give me the diamond."

"No," the Major answered coldly, "the diamond is my fortune, and you shall only have it with my life."

"That condition, illogical though it is, will not check me, I assure you, for I will kill you, if necessary, and then take the diamond," and he cocked a pistol.

There was a silence.

"Well, then, it is really this diamond you want?"

"That and something else," said Michael.

"I do not understand you."

The sailor rose, placed the pistol to his chest, and said frowningly—

"I will make you understand me."

The Major felt he was lost, and that this man would kill him.

"Stop!" he said.

"Have you decided?"

"Yes," he answered, in a voice choked with rage, and drawing the box from his bosom, he muttered, "Curse you, take it!"

Michael returned the pistol to his belt, opened the box, and attentively examined the diamond.

"It is the one," he said, as he closed the box again, and stowed it away.

The unlucky officer followed all these movements with a lack-lustre eye.

Michael resumed his seat, poured himself out a glass of rum, swallowed it at a draught, and then bending forward as he filled his pipe, said—

"Now, let us talk."

"What, talk?" asked the Major; "Have we not finished yet?"

"Not yet—what a hurry you are in. At present we have said nothing."

"What more do you want of me?"

"That is meant for a reproach; but I allow for your ill temper, and owe you no grudge for it. It is a sad thing for a man who has been poor all his life to see himself robbed in a moment of a fortune which he had only just secured. Well, then, listen to me, Major," he said, assuming a consolatory air, and putting his elbows on the table, "it is easy for you to regain the fortune you have lost, and it only depends on yourself."

The Major opened his eyes widely, not knowing whether to take what the sailor said to him seriously; but as he risked nothing by permitting an explanation, he prepared to give him the most earnest attention.

The other continued—

"No matter how I learned the fact—I know for certain, and the affair of the diamond is an undeniable proof of it—that, while on one hand, you feigned to feel the greatest interest for Count de Barmont, from whom you have drawn large sums, though I don't say it in reproach, by means of this feigned pity; on the other, you betray him without shame to his enemies, whom you make pay for it heavily. I merely mention this as a fact, and it is unnecessary to discuss it," Michael said, checking the Major, who was about to speak. "Now, I have made up my mind that, against wind and tide, and in spite of all the intrigues of his enemies to prevent it, the Count shall be free, and free through me. This is my plan: listen attentively to this, Mr. Governor, for the affair concerns you' more nearly than you seem to suppose. The Count has learnt the death of Cardinal de Richelieu, and I sent him the news in a letter from the Duc de Bellegarde. You see that I know everything, or nearly so: he at once requested to see you, and you granted his wish. What took place at your interview? Speak, and before all, be frank: in my turn, I will listen to you."

"Of what use is it to repeat our conversation?" the Major asked, ironically.

"For my private satisfaction," Michael answered, "and your special interest: do not be in too great a hurry to rejoice, Major, for you are not out of my hands yet. Believe me, you had better yield with a good grace, for your interest demands it."

"My interest?" he repeated, in amazement.

"Go on, Major; when the time arrives, be assured, I shall give you the explanation you desire."

The old officer reflected for a moment: at last he decided to speak, resolved, if the opportunity offered itself hereafter, to make the sailor pay dearly for all his agony and humiliation.

"The Count," he said, "engaged me to go to Paris, and negotiate with the Duc de Bellegarde, in order to bring him back his order of release, which the duke is certain to obtain from the king."

"That is good. And when do you intend to start for Paris?"

"I have started."

"Ah! Ah!" said Michael, with a laugh. "It appears that you have stopped on the road, but that has nothing to do with the affair. Is that all?"

"Nearly so."

"Hum! then there is something else?"

"Less than nothing."

"No matter—out with it, for I am very curious. Did not the Count promise you something?"

"Yes."

"How much?"

"Fifty thousand livres," the Major said, with repugnance.

"Ah, ah, that is a tidy sum! And you were setting about earning it in a strange fashion; but I do not wish to refer to that any more. Do you wish to recover your diamond, and at the same time gain the fifty thousand livres promised by the Count? Speak, it depends on yourself."

"You are jesting with me, and not speaking seriously."

"Never, on the contrary, have I been more serious. On the Count's arrival at the castle you command, you were only a poor scrub of an officer of fortune, who, during his whole life, had been struggling against odds, and perched like an owl on an old wall, you were exposed on your isle to die as you had lived; that is to say, without a rap. During the last fifteen or eighteen months, things have completely changed with you. With what you have extorted from the Count, and what his enemies have given you, you have succeeded in getting together a very decent sum. Admitting that you were to receive the Count's fifty thousand livres, and I were to give you back the diamond, it would produce you a perfectly independent fortune, enabling you to retire when you pleased, and end your days in joy and abundance. Is not that your opinion?"

"Certainly, but I shall not touch the 50,000 livres, and the diamond you have taken from me."

"That is true, but," he added, "it is only dependent on yourself, Major, to have it again in your possession."

"What must I do for that?"

"That is what I was waiting for, Major; you consent then, to enter into an arrangement?"

"I must; have I my free will at this moment?"

"A man always has it when he likes, Major, you know that as well as I do; the only thing is, that as you are a man endowed with a strong dose of intelligence, and understand, that when a person has made a fortune by means more or less honourable, he must keep it at all hazards, you are beginning to lend a more attentive ear to the propositions which you guess I am preparing to make you, for you are at length convinced that it is to your interest to come to an understanding with me."

"Suppose what you like, I do not care; but tell me your propositions, so that I may know whether my honour allows me to accept them or forces me to refuse them."

Michael began laughing unceremoniously at this outburst, by which the Major sought to mask his capitulation.

"Instead of going to Paris," he said, "you will simply return to Sainte Marguerite. You will go to the Count, tell him he is free, and then return with him on board the lugger, which will wait for you. When the Count and yourself are on board, the lugger will stand out to sea. Then I will restore you your diamond and pay you the amount agreed on; and as probably you will not care to resume the command of your castle after such a frolic, I will convey you, and your wealth wherever you like, in order to enjoy it without fear of being disturbed."

"But," the Major observed, "what shall I tell the Count to persuade him that he is free by the King's orders?"

"That does not concern me, it is your affair; but hang it all, my dear Major, you are unjust to yourself in raising any doubts as to the power of your imagination. Now what do you think of my proposition, and do you accept it?"

"What security have I that you are not deceiving me, and that when I have fulfilled the conditions of the bargain you impose on me, you keep yours as strictly?"

"The word of a honest man, sir, a word, which though that of a plain sailor, is worth that of a gentleman."

"I believe you, sir," the Major answered, lowering his eyes before Michael's flashing glance.

"Then, that is settled?"

"Yes, it is."

"All right. Hallo! Nicaud!" Michael shouted.

The skipper arrived with a speed that proved he had not been far from the two speakers.

"Here I am, Michael, what do you want?"

"Where are we at this moment?" the sailor asked.

"About five leagues to windward of Sainte Marguerite."

"Very good! Keep on the same course till daybreak; at sunrise we will stand for the island, and anchor off it."

"Very good, I understand."

"Ah! Here is Mr. Governor, who I think, has great want of a little rest; can't you put him up somewhere where he will be able to sleep for two or three hours?"

"Nothing easier, as I shall not turn in tonight, nor you, I suppose, my cabin is at the Major's service, if he will do me the honour of accepting it."

The old officer was really worn out, not only by the fatigue of a long watch, but also by the emotions he had suffered from during the night. Certain that he had now no apprehensions about his safety, he heartily accepted the skipper's offer, and withdrew into the cabin, the door of which the other politely opened for him.

The two sailors went up on deck again.

"This time," said Michael, "I believe that we have manoeuvred cleverly, and that our plan will succeed."

"I am beginning to be of your opinion; but I say, wasn't that old cormorant of a governor tough?"

"Not very," Michael replied with a laugh, "besides, he had no choice; he was obliged to give in, whether he liked it or not."

As had been arranged, the lugger stood off and on from the island during the whole night, at a distance of from four to five leagues from the coast.

At sunrise, they steered directly for St. Marguerite.

The breeze had lulled nearer shore, so that it occupied some time ere the light vessel reached the species of port serving as a landing place in front of the castle.

The lugger drew too much water for it to be possible to run alongside the quay; hence it lay to a short distance off; and Nicaud had a boat lowered, while Michael went down into the cabin to warn the Major.

The latter was awake; refreshed and rested by sleep, he was no longer the same man, he now regarded his position in its true light, and understood that the means offered him to escape from the disagreeable position in which he was placed by his double treachery, was more advantageous than otherwise for him.

It was almost with a smile that he wished Michael good day, and he made no difficulty about accepting the hand the sailor offered to him.

"Well," he asked him, "whereabouts are we, Michael?"

"We have arrived, Major."

"Already? Are you not afraid it is too early to go ashore?"

"Not at all; it is nine o'clock."

"So late? Hang it, it seems that I have slept soundly; in truth, I feel quite jolly this morning."

"All the better, Major, that is a good sign; I suppose you remember our arrangements?"

"Perfectly."

"And you will play fairly with us?"

"In my turn I pledge my honour to it, and I will keep it, whatever may happen."

"Come, I am glad to hear you talk like that; I am beginning to alter my opinion about you."

"Stuff," the Major remarked laughingly, "you do not know me yet."

"You are aware that the boat is ready, it is only waiting for you to go ashore."

"If that is the case, I will follow you, Michael; I am now as eager as you are to finish the affair."

The Major went on deck and got into the boat, which was at once pushed off, and set out for the landing place.

Michael's heart beat ready to burst, while he followed with an anxious eye, the light yawl which was rapidly leaving the lugger, and was already close in shore.

CHAPTER XI.

FRANCE, FAREWELL!

The Major had scarce landed at Sainte Marguerite, ere everything were in commotion in the fort.

On leaving the isle on the previous evening, the governor had stated that he was going on a journey, and would be absent a week, perhaps two.

The Lieutenant, intrusted with the command of the fort during his absence, eagerly hastened to meet him, curious to learn the motive for such a speedy return.

The Major at first replied evasively, that news he had received on landing on the mainland, had necessitated the immediate interruption of his journey; and, while conversing thus, he entered the fort and proceeded to his apartments, followed by the Lieutenant whom he had invited to accompany him.

"Sir," he said to him so soon as they were alone, "you will immediately choose from the garrison ten resolute men; and proceed with them on board the fishing vessel I noticed at anchor when I entered the fort. The missive I entrust to you is most important, and if you carry it out thoroughly, may have important results for you; it must be managed with the most profound secrecy, however, for it is a secret of state."

The Lieutenant bowed gratefully, evidently flattered at the confidence his chief placed in him.

The Major continued.

"You will land on the coast a little below Antibes, and keep the boat, which you will use for your return; you will manage so as not to enter the town till nightfall, without attracting any attention, you will lodge your men as best you can without arousing suspicions, but so as to have them under hand at any moment. Tomorrow morning at ten o'clock, you will present yourself to the town commandant, hand him a letter I shall give you, and place yourself at his disposal. Have you understood me thoroughly, sir?"

"Perfectly, Mr. Governor."

"Before all, I recommend you the most utter discretion; remember that your fortune probably depends on the success of the mission."

"I will obey you, Major, and I hope that you will only have compliments to pay me on my return."

"I trust so too, sir, but make haste, for you must be gone in half an hour. During your preparations I will write the letter; it will be ready when you come to take leave again."

The lieutenant, after bowing respectfully, retired with a joyous heart, not having the slightest suspicion of the treachery meditated by his chief, and went off at full speed to make all the preparations for his departure.

The Major had under his orders a garrison of fifty men, commanded by three officers, a captain and two lieutenants.

This captain, the next in rank to him, would doubtless have greatly impeded the success of the bold stroke he meditated, owing to the pretext he would have been obliged to invent, in order to account for the want of a release in writing for the Count.

By sending him away, the Major had only to deal with two subalterns, ranking too low in the military scale to venture to make observations, or hesitate to accomplish his orders, the more so, because during the ten or twelve years M. de l'Oursière had commanded Fort Sainte Marguerite, nothing in his conduct had led to the slightest painful suspicions about his honour.

Forced by circumstances to betray his duty and quit his native land forever, which he knew he should never see again after this audacious scheme, the Major wished to leave nothing to chance, but turn his lost position to the greatest possible advantage. He hoped that the measures he had taken would protect him from any danger, when his treachery was eventually discovered.

But, through a very laudable feeling of justice, especially on the part of such a man and under such circumstances, the Major desired alone to bear the burden of his infamous conduct and not to attract suspicion of complicity on his poor officers, whom duty compelled to obey him, in what they considered a portion of their military service.

Hence he wrote to the governor of Antibes a very circumstantial letter, in which he narrated, without the slightest omission, the treason he meditated, and which would be carried out at the time when the governor read the strange missive; he explained the motives that obliged him to act as he was doing, while taking on himself all the responsibility of such a deed, and acquitting his officers and soldiers, not only of all co-operation, but of all cognisance, even indirect, of his project.

These duties scrupulously accomplished—for it was impossible for the governor to be deceived as to the frankness of his confession, or to doubt them for a moment—the Major folded the letter, sealed it carefully, and laid it on the table while awaiting the return of his second in command.

Now, as his vessels were burnt, M. de l'Oursière could no longer retreat; he must push on and succeed; the certainty of certain ruin if his scheme were foiled, removed his last doubts, and restored him all the necessary calmness to act with the coolness demanded by the strange circumstances in which he found himself placed.

The Captain entered.

"Well?" the Major asked him.

"I am ready to start, Mr. Governor; my soldiers are already on board the fishing boat, and we shall have left the island in ten minutes."

"Here is the letter you have to deliver into the hands of the Governor of Antibes, sir; remember my instructions."

"I will obey them in every point."

"In that case, Heaven guard you! and good-bye," the Major said, as he rose.

The officer saluted, and left the room.

The Major watched through the open window of his room; he saw him leave the fort, go down to the shore, and on board the fishing vessel; the sail was hoisted, and ere long the boat started, slightly heeling over under the power of the breeze.

"Ough!" said the Major, closing the window, with a sigh of relief—"that's one, now for the other."

But, before aught else, the old officer shut himself up in his room, burnt certain papers, pocketed others, put some clothes in a small valise, as he did not wish to take all belonging to him, through fear of arousing suspicions, and carefully wrapping up in his cloak a small and very heavy iron casket, which, doubtless, contained his ready money, he assured himself by a glance around that everything was in order, opened the door again, and called.

A soldier appeared.

"Beg Mess. de Castaix and de Mircey to come here," he said, "as I wish to speak to them."

They speedily arrived, greatly puzzled at this unexpected interview, for usually the Governor talked but little with his officers.

"Gentlemen," he said to them, after returning their salute, "an order from the King caused me to return here in all haste. I have to take our prisoner, M. de Barmont, to Antibes, where your Captain has preceded me with a sufficient escort to prevent any attempt at escape on the part of the prisoner. I have acted thus because it is the King's good pleasure that this transference of the Count from one prison to another may have the appearance of a liberation, and I shall explain it in that sense to the prisoner, in order that he may have no suspicion of the new orders I have received. Until my return, which will be in two days at the least, you, Monsieur de Castaix, as senior officer, will assume the command of the fortress. I am pleased to believe, gentlemen, that I shall only have to praise the aptitude you will display in performing your duties during my absence."

The two officers bowed: accustomed to the Cardinal's tortuous and mysterious policy, the Major's remarks did not at all surprise them, for, although His Eminence was dead, the event had not occurred so long that the King should have in any way modified his sullen mode of governing.

"Be kind enough to give orders for the prisoner to be brought into my presence, while I inform him of his liberation," he added, with a mocking smile, whose strange meaning the officers did not comprehend. "You will have all the effects belonging to him placed in the boat of the smuggling lugger on board which I came back. Go, gentlemen."

The officers withdrew.

The Count was greatly surprised when La Grenade opened the door of his cell, and begged him to follow him, as the Governor wished to speak with the prisoner.

He fancied the Major on the road to Paris, as had been arranged between them on the previous evening, and did not at all understand his presence at the fort after the solemn promise he had made.

Another thing also caused him great surprise—ever since he had been a prisoner at Saint Marguerite the Governor had not once sent for him; on the contrary, he had always put himself out of the way by visiting his cell.

But the thing that completely routed his ideas was La Grenade's recommendation to him, to place all his belongings in a trunk, and take the key.

"Why this most unnecessary precaution?" the Count asked him.

"No one ever knows what may happen, sir," the gaoler replied, cunningly; "it is as well to take precautions; and stay, if I were you I would put on my hat and take my cloak."

And while speaking thus, the soldier actively helped him to pack his trunk.

"There, that's done," he said, with a grin of satisfaction, when the Count had taken out the key; "here are your hat and cloak."

"My hat, if you like," the young man remarked, laughingly, "but why my cloak? I run no risk of catching a pleurisy in my short walk to the Governor's presence."

"Will you not take it?"

"Certainly not."

"Then I will; you'll see you will want it."

The young gentleman shrugged his shoulders, without replying, and they left the room, the door of which the gaoler did not take the trouble to lock after him.

The Major was walking up and down his room while awaiting the prisoner. La Grenade showed him in, laid the cloak on a chair, and withdrew.

"Ah, ah!" said the Major, with a laugh—"I see that you suspected something."

"I, Mr. Governor? What was it, if you please?"

"Zounds! you appear to be dressed as if for a journey."

"It is that ass of La Grenade, who, I know not for what reason, obliged me to put on my hat, and insisted on bringing my cloak here."

"He was right."

"How so?"

"My lord, I have the honour to inform you that you are a free man."

"I free!" the Count exclaimed, turning pale with joy and emotion.

"The King has deigned to sign your liberation, and I received the orders on landing at Antibes."

"At last!" the Count burst forth, but then immediately recovered himself. "Can you show me the order, sir?"

"Excuse me, my lord, that is forbidden."

"Ah! For what reason?"

"It is a general precaution, sir."

"In that case I will not press it: at least, you are permitted to tell me at whose request my liberty was granted me?"

"I see no objection to that, sir—it was at the request of the Duc de Bellegarde."

"The dear Duke!—a real friend!" the Count cried, in great emotion.

The Major, with the utmost coolness, handed him a pen, and pointed to a blank space in the register.

"Will you be kind enough, sir, to sign this register?"

The Count hurriedly perused it, and saw that it was a species of certificate of the honourable way he had been treated during the period of his detention. He signed.

"Now, sir, as I am free, for I presume I am so—" "Free as a bird, my lord."

"In that case I can retire. I know not why, but during the last instant these thick, gloomy walls, seem to stifle me, and I shall not breathe at my ease till I feel myself in the open air."

"I understand that, sir. I have made every preparation, and we will embark whenever you please."

"*We?*" the Count asked, in surprise.

"Yes, my lord, I shall accompany you."

"For what reason, may I ask?"

"To do you honour, sir—for no other reason."

"Very good," he said, thoughtfully; "let us go, then; but I have some traps here."

"They are already on board: come, sir."

The Major took up his valise and casket, and left the room, followed by the Count.

"Did I not tell you you would want your cloak?"

La Grenade said to M. de Barmont, with a bow, as he passed—"Pleasant voyage to you, sir, and good luck."

They went down to the waterside. During the walk, which was not very long, the Count's brow became more and more clouded; he fancied he could notice a certain sorrow on the faces of the officers and soldiers who were watching his departure—they whispered together, and pointed to the Count in anything but a reassuring way, and it gave him much cause for anxiety.

Every now and then he took a side-glance at the Major, but he appeared calm, and had a smile on his face.

They at length reached the boat, and the Major stepped aside to let the Count get into it first.

As soon as they were both in, the boat was pushed off. During the whole passage from the shore to the lugger the Count and the Major remained silent.

At length they came along side the little vessel, a rope was thrown to them, and they went up the side.

The yawl was immediately hauled up, all sail was set, and the lugger stood out to sea.

"Ah!" the Count exclaimed on perceiving Michael, "You are here, then I am saved!"

"I hope so," the latter replied; "but come, my lord, we have matters to discuss."

They went down into the cabin, followed by the Major.

"There, now we can talk, Captain—the first thing is to settle our accounts."

"Our accounts?" M. de Barmont repeated, in surprise.

"Yes, let us proceed regularly. You promised this gentleman 50,000 livres?"

"Yes, I did."

"And you authorize me to give them to him?"

"Certainly."

"Good; in that case he shall have them." Then, turning to the Major—"You have scrupulously kept your promises, and we will keep ours as loyally. Here, in the first place, is your diamond, which I give you back: I will hand you over the money in a moment. I suppose you no more wish to remain in France than we do—eh?"

"I do not wish it the least in the world," the Major replied, delighted at having regained possession of his diamond.

"Where would you like to be landed? Will England suit you, or do you prefer Italy?"

"Well, I do not exactly know."

"Do you like Spain better? 'Tis all the same to me."

"Why not Portugal?"

"Done for Portugal. We will drop you there in passing."

The Count had listened with growing surprise to this conversation, which was incomprehensible to him.

"What is the meaning of all this?" he at length asked.

"It means, Captain," Michael distinctly answered, "that the King has not signed the pardon—that you are a prisoner, and would probably have remained so all your life had not this gentleman, luckily for you, consented to open the door."

"Sir!" the Count exclaimed, making a movement toward the Major.

Michael stopped him.

"Do not be in a hurry to thank him," he said—"wait till he has told you what has occurred, and in what way he found himself obliged to set you at liberty, when he would probably have preferred not to do so."

"Come, come!" said the Count, stamping his foot passionately—"Explain yourself! I understand nothing of all this. I wish to know everything—everything, I tell you!"

"This man will tell you it, Captain; but he is afraid at present of the consequences of his confession, and that is why he hesitates to make it."

M. de Barmont smiled disdainfully.

"This man is beneath my contempt," he said; "whatever he may say I will not take the slightest vengeance on him—he is pardoned beforehand, I pledge him my word as a gentleman."

"Now speak, Major," said Michael; "during that time I will go on deck again with Skipper Nicaud, or, if you prefer it, Bowline, who has played his part remarkably well throughout the affair."

Michael left the cabin, and the two men remained alone.

The Major understood that it was better to make a clean breast of it: hence he told the Count, without any equivocation, the full details of his treachery, and in what manner Michael had compelled him to save him, when, on the contrary, he was paid to ruin him.

Although the name of the Duc de Peñaflor had not once been mentioned during the Major's narration, the Count divined that it was he alone who had dealt him all the blows he had felt so severely during the last eighteen months; however great his resolution might be, this depth of hatred, this Machiavellian vengeance terrified him; but in this extremely detailed narrative one point seemed to him obscure, and that was, how Michael had discovered the final machinations of his enemies, and done so opportunely enough to be able to foil them.

All the questions the Count asked on this head the Major was unable to answer, for he was ignorant.

"Well," asked the sailor, suddenly entering the cabin, "are you now informed, Captain?"

"Yes," the latter replied, with a certain tinge of sadness, "except on one point."

"What is it, Captain?"

"I should like to know in what manner you detected this cleverly contrived plot."

"Very simply, Captain, and I will tell you the whole affair in a couple of words. Bowline and I, without the Major suspecting it, followed him carefully into the ruins, while cautiously avoiding being seen; in this way no part of his conversation with the stranger escaped us. When the Major handed him the papers, and the stranger retired, I jumped at his throat, and, with Bowline's help, took the papers from him—"

"Where are these papers?" the Count interrupted him eagerly.

"I will give them to you, Captain."

"Thanks, Michael; now go on."

"Well, my story's finished; I gagged him to prevent him calling out, and after tying him up like a plug of tobacco to stop him running after us, I left him there and went away."

"What, you went away, Michael, leaving the man thus gagged and bound on a desert isle?"

"What would you have had me do with him, Captain?"

"Oh, perhaps it would have been better to kill him, than leave him exposed to such a horrible punishment."

"He had been so precious tender to you, hadn't he, Captain? Stuff! Pity for such a ferocious brute would be madness on your part; besides, the fiend always protects his creatures, you may be sure, and I am certain that he has escaped."

"How so?"

"Hang it, he didn't swim off to Saint Honorat; his people were probably concealed somewhere: tired of not seeing him return, they will have set out to seek him, and picked him up where I put him to bed; he will probably have got off with gnawing the bit for two or three hours."

"Well, that is possible, Michael, and even probable. Where are you taking us?"

"Zounds, you are the commander here, Captain; we will go wherever you please."

"I will tell you, but first let us land the Major, for I fancy he wishes to be free of our company as much as we do of his."

At this moment Bowline's voice was heard.

"Hilloh, Michael," he shouted, "we have a large vessel to windward."

"Confusion!" said the sailor, "Has she hoisted her colours?"

"Yes; she is a Norwegian."

"That will be a good opportunity for you, Major," said the Count.

"Eh, helmsman," Michael shouted, without awaiting the Major's answer, "steer down to the Norwegian."

The Major considered it useless to protest.

Two hours later the vessels were within speaking distance: the stranger was bound for Helsingfors, and the captain consented to take the passenger offered him.

The Major was consequently transported on board, with everything belonging to him.

"Now, Captain," said Michael, when the boat had returned, "where shall we steer?"

"Let us go to the islands," the Count answered sadly, "henceforth we shall only find a shelter there and taking a last glance at the coast of France, whose outline was beginning to fade away in the distant horizon," he muttered, with a sigh, and concealing his face sorrowfully in his hands, "Farewell, France!"

In these two words was exhaled the last human feeling that remained at the bottom of the heart of this man who had been so tried by adversity, and who, vanquished by despair, was going to ask of the new world the vengeance which the old world so obstinately refused him.

CHAPTER XII.

THE BEGINNING OF THE ADVENTURE.

The seventeenth century was a period of transition between the middle ages, that were exhaling their last sigh, and the modern era, which the great thinkers of the eighteenth century were destined to constitute so splendidly.

Under the repeated blows of the implacable Cardinal de Richelieu, that gloomy filler of the unity of the despotic power of kings, an immense reaction had been effected in ideas. It was a silent reaction, that from the outset sapped the minister's work, and he was far from suspecting its causes or power. It was more especially in the latter half of the seventeenth century that the world offered a strange spectacle.

At that period, the Spaniards, who were possessors, by the right of force, of the greater part of America, where they had multiplied colonies, were masters of the sea which the celebrated "broom of Holland" had not yet swept. The English navy was only beginning to be formed, and, in spite of the continuous efforts of Richelieu, the French navy was not in existence.

Suddenly several adventurers sprang up, no one knew whence, who, alone, castaways of civilization, men of all classes, from the highest to the most humble, belonging to all nations, but chiefly to the French, perched themselves like vultures on an imperceptible islet in the Atlantic, and undertook to contend against the Spanish power, after declaring a merciless war on their private authority. Attacking the Spanish fleet with unheard-of audacity, and, like a gadfly fastened to a lion's flank, holding in check the Spanish Colossus, they compelled it to treat with them on equal terms, with no other help but their courage and their energetic will.

In a few years their incredible exploits and audacious coups de main inspired the Spaniards with such terror, and acquired for themselves such a great and merited reputation, that the disinherited of fortune, the seekers of adventures, flocked from all parts of the world to the island that served them as a refuge, and their number was so enormously augmented, that they almost succeeded in forming themselves into a nationality by the sole force of their will, and their boldness. Let us say in a few words, who these men were, and what was the origin of their strange fortune.

For this purpose we must return to the Spaniards.

The latter, after their immense discoveries in the New World, had obtained from Pope Alexander VI. a bull which conceded to them the exclusive possession of the two Americas.

Supported by this bull, and considering themselves the sole owners of the New World, the Spaniards tried to keep all other nations away from it, and began to treat as corsairs all the vessels they came across between the two tropics.

Their maritime power, and the important part they played at that time on the American continent did not leave the governments the power of protesting, as they would have desired, against this odious tyranny.

Then it happened that English and French outfitters, excited by the thirst of gain, and paying no heed to the Spanish pretensions, equipped vessels which they dispatched to the so-coveted rich regions, to cut off the Spanish transports, plunder the American coast, and fire the town.

Treated as pirates, these bold sailors frankly accepted the position offered them, committed awful excesses wherever they landed, carried off rich spoil, and despising the law of nations, and not caring whether the Spaniards were at war or not with the countries to which they belonged, they attacked them wherever they met them.

The Spaniards, entirely engaged with rich possessions in Mexico, Peru, and generally on the Continent, which were mines of inexhaustible wealth for them, had committed the fault of neglecting the Antilles, which stretch from the Gulf of Mexico to the Gulf of Maracaibo, and only established colonies in the four large islands of that archipelago.

Hidden in bays behind the windings of the coast, the adventurers dashed suddenly at the Spanish vessels, carried them by boarding, and then returned ashore to share the plunder.

The Spaniards, in spite of the great number of their vessels, and the active watch they kept up, could no longer traverse the Caribbean Sea, which the adventurers had selected as the scene of their exploits, without running the risk of obstinate engagements with men, whom the smallness and lightness of their vessels rendered almost intangible.

This wandering life possessed such charms for the adventurers, who had assumed the characteristic name of filibusters or freebooters, that for a long time the idea did not occur to them of forming a permanent settlement among the islands, which they employed as a temporary retreat.

Things were in this state when, in 1625, a cadet of Normandy, of the name of d'Esnambuc, to whom the law of entail left no hope of fortune, except what he could acquire by his industry or courage, fitted out at Dieppe a brigantine of about seventy tons, on board which he placed four guns and forty resolute men, and set out to chase the Spaniards and try to enrich himself by some good prize.

On arriving at the Caymans, small islands situated between Cuba and Jamaica, he suddenly came across the track of a Spanish vessel bearing thirty-five guns and a crew of three hundred and fifty men; it was a critical situation for the corsair.

D'Esnambuc, without giving the Spaniards time to look about them, steered down and attacked them. The action lasted for three hours with extraordinary obstinacy; the Dieppois defended themselves so well, that the Spaniards despairing of conquest and having lost one-half their crew, were the first to decline fighting, and shamefully fled from the small vessel.

Still, the latter had suffered severely, and could be hardly kept above water, ten men had been killed, and the rest of the crew, being covered with wounds, were not worth much more.

As the isle of Saint Kitts was no great distance off, d'Esnambuc reached it with much difficulty, and took refuge there to careen his vessel, and cure his wounded. Then calculating, that, for the success of his future expeditions, he required a sure retreat, he resolved to establish himself on this island.

St. Kitts, which the Caribs called Liamuiga, is situated in 17 to 18 degrees N. latitude and 65 W. longitude. It is 23 leagues W.N.W. of Antigua, and about 3 leagues to the N.W. of Guadeloupe, and is one of the Caribbean Islands.

The general aspect of this island is remarkably beautiful, it is commanded by Mount Misery, an extinct volcano, three thousand five hundred feet high, which occupies the whole northwest part, and gradually descends in lower ranges, till it dies away on the South in the plains of the Basse terre.

The barrenness of the mountains forms a striking contrast with the fertility of the plains.

The valleys display a really extraordinary wealth of vegetation, while the mountains only offer to the eye a confused chaos of broken rocks, whose interstices are filled up with a clayey matter that checks all vegetation.

Water is rare, and of a bad quality, for the few streams that descend from Mount Misery are strongly impregnated with saline particles, to which strangers find a difficulty in growing accustomed.

But a precious thing for the filibusters, Saint Kitts possesses two magnificent ports, well sheltered and easy of defence, and its coasts are serrated with deep bays, where, in case of danger, their light vessels would easily find a shelter.

D'Esnambuc, on landing, found several refugee Frenchmen who lived on good terms with the Caribs, and who not only received him with open arms, but joined him and selected him as their leader.

By a singular chance, on the same day that the Dieppois landed at St. Kitts, English freebooters commanded by Captain Warner, who had also suffered in an engagement with the Spaniards, took refuge at another point in it.

The corsairs of the two nations who could not be separated by any idea of conquest, agriculture, or commerce, and who pursued the same object, fighting the Spaniards, and establishing a refuge against the common enemy, easily came to an understanding; then, after dividing the island, they settled down side by side, and lived for a long time on excellent terms, which nothing disturbed.

On one occasion they even combined their arms against the Caribs, who, alarmed by the progress of their new settlement, attempted to expel them.

The filibusters made a horrible carnage among the Indians, and forced them to implore for mercy.

A few months after, Warner and d'Esnambuc put out to sea again; the latter proceeded to Paris, the former to London, each for the purpose of soliciting the protection of his government for the rising colony.

As usual, these men, who at the beginning had only sought a temporary refuge, now felt a desire to see the development of a settlement founded by themselves, and which in a short time had assumed a real importance.

Cardinal de Richelieu, ever disposed to favour projects tending to augment the foreign power of France, received the filibuster with the greatest distinction, entered into his views, and formed a company, called "The Company of the Islands," in order to promote the interests of the colony.

The capital was 45,000 livres, of which Richelieu subscribed for his part 10,000.

D'Esnambuc was invested with the supreme command.

Among the claims stipulated in his commission there is one which we must quote, owing to its strangeness, for it imposed on white men in America a temporary slavery harsher even than that of the Negro.

This is the clause, whose sinister consequences we shall see developed during the course of this story.

"No labourer intended for the colony will be allowed to embark, unless he engages to remain for three years in the service of the company, which will have the right to employ him on any task it thinks proper, without granting him the right to complain or break the contract entered into by him."

These labourers were called Engagés or "thirty-six monthers," a polite way of getting rid of the word slave.

Captain Warner, who had been more highly favoured, returned with a large body of colonists. Still the good understanding was kept up for some time between the two nations; but the English took advantage of the weakness of the French, who could not oppose their usurpations, to encroach on their rights, and formed a fresh settlement at Nevis, the next island to St. Kitts.

Still d'Esnambuc did not despair of the fate of the colony. He proceeded again to France, and solicited of the Cardinal help in men and money, to repulse the undertakings of his troublesome neighbours.

Richelieu granted his request.

By his orders, Rear Admiral de Cussac arrived at St. Kitts, with six heavily armed ships; he surprised ten English vessels in the roads, captured three, sank three others, and put the rest to flight.

The English made no further attempts to leave their boundaries, and peace was re-established.

M. de Cussac, after supplying the colony with rum and provisions, set sail, and went to found a settlement on St. Eustache, an island four leagues N. W. of St. Kitts.

The Spaniards, however, who, since the appearance of the filibusters in American waters, had suffered so greatly from their depredations, saw them with great alarm settling permanently on the West India islands.

They understood of what importance it was to them not to allow fixed settlements in these regions, unless they wished to see their colonies destroyed and their commerce ruined.

They consequently resolved to act vigorously against those fellows whom they regarded as pirates, and to utterly destroy their lurking places, which had already acquired formidable proportions.

In consequence Admiral don Fernando de Toledo, whom the court of Madrid had placed at the head of a powerful fleet, sent in 1630 to Brazil to fight the Dutch, received orders to destroy in passing, the viper's nest formed by the filibusters at St. Kitts.

The sudden apparition of this immense force off the island filled the inhabitants with stupor. The united resources of the English and French adventurers and their desperate courage were not sufficient to avert the danger that menaced them, and repulse so formidable an attack.

After a desperate fight, in which a great number of filibusters, especially Frenchmen, were killed, the others got into their light canoes and fled to the adjacent isles of St. Bartholomew, Antigua, St. Martin, and Montserrat, or to any place in short where they hoped to find a temporary refuge.

The English, we are unfortunately compelled to state, shamefully fled at the beginning of the action, and eventually asked leave to capitulate.

One half of them were sent to England on board Spanish ships, while the rest engaged to evacuate the island as soon as possible,—a promise which was forgotten immediately after the departure of the Spanish fleet.

This expedition was the only one that Spain seriously attempted against the filibusters.

The French soon left the islands where they had sought refuge, and returned to St. Kitts, where they re-established themselves, though not without a quarrel with the English, who had taken advantage of the opportunity to seize their land, but whom they forced again beyond their old borders.

It is a singular fact, which proves that the filibusters were not bandits and nameless men, as attempts have been made to brand them, that the inhabitants of St. Kitts were remarkable beyond all the other colonists for the gentleness and urbanity of their manners; the traditions of politeness left by the first Frenchmen who settled there, have been maintained even to the present day; in the eighteenth century it was called the Gentle Island, and there is a proverb in the Antilles to the effect, that "the nobility were at St. Kitts, the citizens at Guadeloupe, the soldiers at Martinique, and the peasants at Grenada."

Things remained for a long time in the state we have just described; the filibusters, growing bolder and bolder through the Spanish cowardice, enlarged the scene of their exploits, and retaining a bitter memory of the sack of their island, felt a double hatred for the Spaniards, who had branded them with the name of Ladrones (robbers). They no longer displayed any moderation, and seated in the light canoes that composed their entire fleet, they watched for the rich transports from Mexico, dashed boldly aboard them, carried them, and returned to St. Kitts loaded with plunder.

The colony prospered, the land was well cultivated, and the plantations were carefully made.

For these men, the majority of whom had no hope left of ever returning to their native land, had performed their work with the feverish ardor of people who are creating for themselves a new nationality and preparing a last asylum, so that only a few years after the destruction of the colony by the Spaniards, St. Kitts had again become a flourishing colony, thanks in the first instance to its fertility and the energy and intelligence of its inhabitants, but above all to the incessant toil of the engagés of the company.

We have now to explain what these poor fellows were and the fate they met with at the hands of the colonists.

We have already stated that the company sent to the islands, men whom they had engaged for three years.

They accepted anybody, workmen belonging to all trades, even surgeons who, persuading themselves that they were destined to carry on their own profession in the colonies, allowed themselves to be seduced by the fair promises which the company did not hesitate to lavish.

But once their consent was given, that is to say, signed, the company regarded them as men belonging to it body and soul; and when they reached the colonies, agents *sold* then for three years to the planters, at the rate of thirty or forty crowns a head, and did so in the broad daylight and in the governor's presence.

They thus became real slaves, subject to the adventurers of the colony, and condemned to the rudest tasks.

Hence, the poor wretches, so unworthily abused, beaten terribly and worn out by a fatigue under a deadly climate, generally succumbed ere they had attained the third year, which was to set them at liberty.

This was carried so far that the masters at last attempted to prolong the stipulated slavery beyond three years. Toward the end of 1632, the colony of St. Kitts incurred great dangers, for the engagés whose time was up and whom their masters refused liberty, took up arms, organized a resistance, and prepared to attack the colonists with that energy of desperation which no force can resist. M. d'Esnambuc only succeeded in making them lay down their arms and arrest bloodshed by conceding their just demands.

At a later date, when the sad condition in which the company's agents placed the engagés, became known in France, it became almost impossible for the latter to find volunteers; hence they were obliged to go about the roads and highways to enlist vagabonds whom they intoxicated and induced to sign, while in that condition, an engagement which it was impossible to break.

We will dwell the more earnestly on this point, because during the course of our narrative, we shall have frequently to revert to the engagés. We will only add one word about the wretches whom England sent to the colonies under the same conditions.

If the fate of the French engagés was frightful, that of the English, history proves to us, was horrible.

They were treated with the most atrocious barbarity. They formed an engagement for seven years, and then, at the end of that time, when the moment to regain their liberty had at length arrived, they were intoxicated, and advantage was taken of their condition to make them sign a second engagement for the same period.

Cromwell, after the sack of Drogheda, sold more than 30,000 Irish for Jamaica and Barbados.

Nearly two thousand of these wretched succeeded in escaping on board a vessel, which, in their ignorance of navigation, they allowed to drift and the current cast it ashore at Saint Domingo. The poor fellows, not knowing where they were, and being without food or resources, all died of hunger. Their piled-up bones, bleached by time, remained for several years on Cape

Tiburón, at a spot which was called Irish Bay on account of the terrible catastrophe, and still bears the name.

The reader will pardon us for having entered into such lengthened details about the establishment of the filibusters of St. Kitts; but as it was on this little island that the terrible association of adventurers, whose history we have undertaken to tell, had its birth, it is necessary to make the reader fully acquainted with these facts, so that we might not be obliged to return to them hereafter. Now, we will resume our narrative to which the preceding chapters serve, so to speak, as a prologue, and leaping at one bound across the space that separates Sainte Marguerite from the Caribbean islands, we will proceed to St. Kitts a few months after the escape, for we dare not say the liberation, of Count Ludovic de Barmont Senectaire.

CHAPTER XIII.

THE COUNCIL OF THE FILIBUSTERS.

Several years elapsed without producing any notable changes in the colony.

The adventurers still continued, with the same obstinacy, their expeditions against the Spaniards; but as their expeditions were isolated, and had no sort of organization, the losses experienced by the Spaniards, though very great, were much less considerable than might be anticipated.

About this time, a lugger manned by forty resolute men, and armed with four iron guns, anchored off St. Kitts, proudly displaying the French flag at its stern.

This vessel brought to the colony a fresh contingent of brave adventurers.

Immediately after their arrival, they landed, formed the acquaintance of the inhabitants, and testified a desire to settle on the island.

The chief, to whom his comrades gave the name of Montbarts, and for whom they appeared to have an unbounded devotion, informed the colonists, that like them, he professed a profound hatred for the Spaniards, and that he was followed by two ships of that nation, which he had captured, and had given the prize masters orders to steer for St. Kitts.

These good men were received with shouts of joy by the inhabitants, and Montbarts had a narrow escape from being carried in triumph.

As he had announced, three or four days later two Spanish vessels anchored at St. Kitts. They bore at their stern the Castilian flag reversed, in sign of humiliation, while above it proudly fluttered the French ensign.

There was one horrible circumstance, however, which chilled even the bravest with horror. These vessels bore at their bowsprit, and at their cross-jack, as well as at the main and foreyard, groups of corpses. By Montbarts order, the crews of the two vessels had been hung, without showing mercy even to a boy.

The chief of the adventurers generously gave the cargo of the two ships to the colonists, only asking for sufficient land in return, on which to build a house.

This request was at once granted; the newcomers then disarmed their lugger, came ashore, and began their installation.

Montbarts was a young man of about seven or eight-and-twenty, with manly and marked features, and a fixed and piercing eye. The expression of his face was essentially sad, mocking, and cruel: a dead pallor; spread over his face, added, were it possible, a strangeness to his whole person. Tall and powerfully built, though supple and graceful, his gestures were elegant and noble, while his speech was soft, and the terms he employed were carefully chosen. He exercised a singular fascination over those who approached him, or whom accident brought into relation with him. They felt at once repulsed and attracted by this singular man, who seemed the only one of his species on the earth, and who, without appearing to be anxious for it, imposed his will upon all, gained obedience by a sign or a frown, and who only seemed to live when he was in the thick of a fight, when fires crossed above his head, forming him an aureole of flame, when corpses were piled up around him, when blood flowed beneath his feet, and when bullets whistled in his ears, and when he rushed drunk with powder and carnage upon the deck of a Spanish ship.

Such was what was said of him by his comrades, and by those who had been struck by his singular countenance, and wished to know him: but beyond this moral and physical portrait of the man, it was impossible to obtain the slightest information as to his past life. Not one of the sailors who came with him knew the slightest episode of it, or, as was probable, refused to discover anything.

Hence, when the colonists perceived that all their questions would remain unanswered, they gave up the useless task of asking them. They accepted Montbarts for what it pleased him to be, the more so, as his, former life not only did not concern them, but also interested them very slightly.

The adventurer only remained ashore for the period strictly necessary to establish his household comfortably; then, one day, without warning anybody, he went on board his lugger with the crew he had brought with him, only leaving five or six men at St. Kitts to manage his plantation, and set sail. A month after, he returned, having in tow a richly laden Spanish vessel, with the crew hanging to the yards as before.

Montbarts went on thus for a whole year, never remaining more than two or three days ashore, then going off, and returning with a prize with its entire crew suspended from the yards.

Matters attained such a pitch, the audacity of the daring corsair was crowned with such success, that the rumour of it reached France. Then, the Dieppe adventurers, comprehending all the profit they might derive from this interloping war, fitted out vessels, and went to join the colonists of St. Kitts, for the purpose of organising a hunt of the Spaniards, and carrying it out on a grand scale.

Filibusterism was about to enter on its second phase, and become a regular association.

Montbarts had built his hatto, or principal residence, at the spot where the English afterwards formed Sandy-point battery.

It was an excellently chosen position, militarily speaking, where, in case of attack, it was easy not only to act on the defensive, but also to repulse the enemy with serious loss.

This hatto, built of trunks of trees, and covered with palm leaves, stood nearly at the extremity of a cape, whence the greater part of the island and the sea for a considerable distance on the right and left could be commanded. This cape, which was nearly precipitous, and one hundred and fifty feet high seawards, could only be reached by a narrow, rough path, intersected at regular distances by strong palisades, and wide, deep ditches, which had to be crossed on planks, that were easy to remove. Two four-pounder guns, placed in position at the head of the path guarded the approaches.

This hatto was divided into four rather large rooms, furnished with a luxury and comfort rather singular in an out-of-the-way island like St. Kitts, but which was fully justified by the usual occupation of the owner, who merely required to take any furniture that suited him out of his prizes.

A long pole, serving as a flagstaff, planted in front of the door of the hatto, displayed in the breeze a white ensign with a red jack in the right hand top corner. This flag was that of the corsairs, which Montbarts sometimes changed for one all black, having in its centre a death's head and crossbones, all white. This was an ill-omened flag, which, when hoisted at the peak, signified that the conquered had no hope of mercy to expect.

It was a warm day towards the end of May, about eighteen months after Montbarts' arrival at St. Kitts. Several persons, stern looking and rough mannered, almost armed to the teeth, were conversing together as they followed the path that led from the plain to the platform on which Montbarts' hatto stood.

It was nearly ten o'clock at night, and the sky was transparent and clear. Thousands of stars sparkled in the heavens, the moon profusely shed her white light, and the atmosphere was so pellucid, that the smallest objects were visible at a long distance. There was not a breath in the air, or a rustle among the leaves; the sea, calm as a mirror, died away with a soft and mysterious murmur on the sandy beach; the fireflies buzzed noisily, and at times dashed against the pedestrians, who contented themselves with driving them away with their hands, without, on that account, interrupting a conversation which seemed greatly to interest them.

These men were five in number, and all in the prime of life. Their features were energetically marked, and their faces revealed audacity and resolution carried to the highest pitch. Their slightly curved shoulders, and the way in which they straddled their legs in walking, while swaying their arms, would have caused them to be recognised as sailors at the first glance, had not their dress sufficiently proved the fact.

They were talking in English.

"Stuff!" one of them was saying at the moment when we join in their conversation; "We must see. All that glistens is not gold, as they say down there. Besides, I wish for nothing better than to be mistaken, after all."

"No matter," another replied; "in accordance with your laudable custom, you begin by expressing a doubt."

"Not at all," the first speaker sharply interposed; "a fear, at the most."

"Well," a third said; "we shall soon know what we have to expect, for here we are halfway up the path, thank Heaven!"

"That demon of a Montbarts," the first went on, "has famously chosen his position. His hatto is impregnable, on my word as a man."

"Yes. I do not think that the *gavachos*[1] will ever venture to attempt an escalade. But, by the way," he added suddenly, and halted; "suppose we are taking a useless walk, and Montbarts is not at home?"

"I will answer for your finding him at home, Red Stocking, so set your mind at rest."

"How do you know?" asked the man addressed by this singular name.

"My God! Don't you see his flag hoisted at the masthead?"

"That is true. I had not noticed it."

"But now you see it, I suppose?"

"I should be blind if I didn't."

"Well," one of the filibusters said, who had hitherto maintained silence; "all this does not tell us why the meeting is to be held. Do you know anything about it, brother?"

"No more than you," Red Stocking replied. "It is probably some daring project which Montbarts is meditating, and wishes us to take a part in."

"But you know that he has not only summoned us, but also the principal French filibusters?"

"In that case I am quite at sea," Red Stocking remarked. "However, it is of little consequence at present, as I presume we shall soon know what is wanted of us."

"That is true, because we have arrived."

In fact, they reached at this moment the head of the path, and found themselves on the platform exactly facing the hatto, whose door was open as if inviting them to enter.

A very bright light poured through the doorway, and the sound of loud talking testified that there was a rather large gathering inside the hatto.

The Englishmen continued to advance, and soon found themselves on the threshold.

"Come in, brothers," Montbarts' harmonious voice was heard saying from the interior; "come in, we are waiting for you."

They entered.

Six or seven persons were assembled in the room, which they entered: they were the most renowned chiefs of the filibusters. Among them were Belle Tête (handsome head), the ferocious native of Dieppe, who had murdered more than three hundred of his engagés, whom he accused of dying of indolence; Pierre le Grand, the Breton, who always boarded the Spanish galleons in the disguise of a female; Alexandre Bras de fer (iron arm), a young and apparently frail and delicate man, with effeminate features, but in reality endowed with a prodigious and herculean vigour, and destined hereafter to become one of the heroes of the buccaneering trade; Roc, surnamed the Brazilian, although born at Groningen, a town in East Friesland; and lastly, two old acquaintances of ours, Bowline and Michael the Basque, who both arrived at St. Kitts at the same time as Montbarts, and whose reputation as filibusters was already great.

As for the English, who had just entered the hatto, five in number; they were Red Stocking, whose name was mentioned in the preceding conversation; Morgan, a young man hardly eighteen years of age, with a haughty face and aristocratic manners; Jean David, a Dutch sailor, settled in the eastern part of the island; Bartholomew, a Portuguese, also settled in the English colony; and lastly, William Drake, who had taken an oath never to attack the Spaniards, unless they were in the proportion of fifteen to one, so great was the contempt he professed for the proud nation.

It was, as we see, a select gathering of all the great filibusters of the day.

"You are welcome, brothers," said Montbarts; "I am glad to see you, for I was awaiting you impatiently. Here are pipes, tobacco, and spirits; smoke and drink," he added, pointing to a table placed in the centre of the room.

The filibusters sat down, lighted pipes, and filled glasses.

"Brothers," Montbarts resumed a moment later, "I have requested you to come to my hatto for two reasons of great importance, and of which the second necessarily depends on the first: are you prepared to listen to me?"

"Speak, Montbarts," William Drake answered in the name of all; "you, whom the gavachos have surnamed the Exterminator, a name I envy you, brother, for you can only wish the good of filibustering."

"That is the very subject," Montbarts answered.

"I was sure of it, brother. Speak, we will listen to you religiously."

They prepared to listen attentively. All these energetic men, who recognised no laws but those themselves had made, knew not what envy was, and were ready to discuss with the most entire good faith the proposals which they foresaw Montbarts desired to make to them.

The latter reflected for a moment, and then spoke in a gentle voice, whose sympathetic accent soon captivated his audience.

"Brothers," he said, "I will be brief, for you are picked men, with warm hearts and firm hands, with whom a long speech is not only useless, but also ridiculous Since my arrival at St. Kitts, I have been studying filibustering, its life, manners, and aspirations, and I have recognised with sorrow that the results do not justify its efforts. What are we doing? Nothing, or almost nothing. In spite of our indomitable courage, the Spaniards laugh at us; too weak, owing to our isolation, to inflict serious losses on them, we expend our energy in vain; we shed our blood, to take from them a few wretched vessels.

It is not thus that matters ought to go on; this is not the vengeance which each of us dreamed of. What is the cause of our relative weakness toward our formidable enemy? The isolation, to which I alluded just now, and which will forever paralyze our efforts."

"That is true," Red Stocking muttered.

"But how can we alter it?" David asked.

"Alas!" William Drake added, "The remedy is unfortunately impossible."

"We are adventurers merely, and not a power," said Belle Tête.

Montbarts smiled—that pale, peculiar smile of his, which turned the heart cold.

"You are mistaken, brothers," he said, "the remedy is found; if we like, we shall soon be a power."

"Speak, speak, brother," all the adventurers exclaimed, springing up.

"This is my plan, brothers," he continued; "we are here twelve, of all nations, but with one heart; the flower of filibusterism, I declare loudly; without fear of contradiction, for each of us has furnished proofs of it, and what proofs! Well, let us join and form a family; from our share of the prizes let us set aside a sum intended to form the common treasury, and while remaining at liberty to organize private expeditions, let us swear never to injure or thwart one another, to offer mutual help when needed, to labour with all our power to the ruin of Spain, and while keeping our association secret from our comrades and brothers, to combine our forces when the moment arrives to crush our implacable enemy at one blow. Such, brothers, is the first proposal I have to make to you. I await your answer."

There was a momentary silence; the filibusters understood the importance of their brother's proposal, and the strength it would give them in the future. They exchanged glances, whispered together, and at length William Drake replied in the name of all—

"Brother," he said, "you have just elucidated in a few words a question which has hitherto remained in obscurity. You have perfectly defined the cause of our weakness, by finding at the same time, as you promised us, not the remedy, but the means to render an association hitherto due to accident and almost useless, really formidable and useful: but this is not all. This association, to which you allude, requires a head to direct it, and ensure the success of its efforts at the right moment. It is therefore necessary that while our association remains secret, and, as it were, not in existence at all, in every point that does not affect its object, one of us should be appointed chief; a chief, the more powerful, because we shall be devoted to him, and aid him in working for the general good."

"Is this really your opinion, brothers?" Montbarts asked. "Do you accept my proposal such as I made it, and as William Drake has modified it?"

"We accept it so," the filibusters replied with one voice.

"Very good. Still I think that this chief, to whom you refer, should be unanimously elected by us; that his authority may be taken from him at a meeting of the assembly by a majority of voices, if he do not strictly fulfil the conditions he has accepted; that, as guardian of the treasury, he must always be ready to furnish his accounts, and that his appointment should not exceed five years, unless renewed."

"All that is fair," said Red Stocking; "no one can understand the general good better than you, brother."

"Hence," David remarked, "we shall be partners; no quarrel, no dissension can well be possible among us."

"While ostensibly retaining our free will and most complete independence," Belle Tête reminded.

"Yes," Montbarts replied.

"Now, brothers," said Drake, rising, and doffing his cap, "listen to me: I, William Drake, swear on my faith and honour, the most complete devotion to the association of the Twelve, submitting myself beforehand to undergo the punishment my brothers may please to inflict on me, even death, if I were to betray the secret of the Association, and break my oath. Heaven help me!"

After Drake each filibuster uttered the same oath in a firm voice, and with a solemn accent.

They resumed their seats.

"Brothers," said Montbarts, "what we have hitherto done is nothing; it is only the dawn of the new era which is about to open, for the glorious days of filibustering are beginning—twelve men like us, united by the same thought, must perform miracles."

"We will do so, be assured, brother," Morgan said, as he carelessly picked his teeth with a gold pin.

"Now, brothers, before I submit my second proposal to you, I believe we had better elect a president."

"That is true," said David; "as the company is formed, let us elect the president."

"One word first," said Michael the Basque, stepping into the centre of the circle.

"Speak, brother."

"I wish to add this: every member of the Association who falls into the hands of the gavachos shall be delivered by the other members, whatever perils they may have to incur in doing so."

"We swear it!" the filibusters shouted enthusiastically.

"Unless it is impossible," Morgan said.

"Nothing is impossible for us," William Drake remarked, rudely.

"That is true, brother. You are right, I was mistaken," Morgan replied, with a smile.

"The society will be called that of The Twelve; only the death of a member will allow another to be admitted, and he must be chosen unanimously," Michael continued.

"We swear it!" the filibusters exclaimed once more.

"Now, brothers," said Bartholomew, "let us proceed to the election, by ballot, in order to protect the liberty of the vote."

"There are pens, ink, and paper on that table, brothers," Montbarts remarked.

"And here is my cap," Red Stocking said, with a laugh; "throw your votes into it."

And, removing his beaver skin cap, the filibuster laid it on the ground in the middle of the room.

Then the adventurers, with perfect order, rose one after the other, and in turn went to write their vote, which they deposited, after rolling up the paper, in Red Stocking's cap.

Then all the adventurers returned to their seats:

"Have we all voted?" David asked.

"All!" the filibusters replied, in chorus.

"Now, brother," Drake said to David, "since you hold the cap, proclaim the result."

David questioned his comrades with a glance, and they bowed their heads in affirmation; then he took up the first roll that came to hand, opened it, and read—

"Montbarts, the Exterminator."

And passed on to a second.

"Montbarts, the Exterminator," he read again.

It was the same with the third, fourth, and so on up to the twelfth and last—all bore the words—

"Montbarts, the Exterminator."

It was a sinister challenge given to the Spanish nation, of whom this man was the most obstinate enemy.

Montbarts rose, took off his hat, and bowed gracefully to his comrades.

"Brothers," he said, "I thank you—the confidence you place in me shall not be disappointed."

"Long live Montbarts, the Exterminator!" all the filibusters shouted, impulsively.

The terrible company of The Twelve was created. Filibusterism then really became a formidable power.

[1] Term of contempt for the Spaniards.

CHAPTER XIV.

THE SECOND PROPOSAL.

Montbarts allowed the enthusiasm of his comrades time to calm, and then spoke again.

There was no change in his appearance; nothing in his face denoted the joy of triumph or of satisfied ambition; still the vote of his companions, by nominating him Chief of the filibusters, had rendered him in a moment a man more powerful than many a prince. His face was just as impassive, his voice equally firm.

"Brothers," he said, "do you remember that I had a second proposal to make to you?"

"That is true," William Drake replied—"speak, brother, we are listening to you."

"The second proposal is as follows: still, I must request you before answering me to reflect fully on it. Your opinion must not be lightly expressed, for, I repeat to you, and dwell on it in order that you may thoroughly understand me, this proposition is most serious and grave. In a word, it is this:—I propose to you to abandon the island of St. Kitts, and choose another place of refuge, more convenient, and, above all, safer for you."

The filibusters gazed at him in amazement.

"I will explain," he said, stretching out his arms as if to request silence; "listen to me carefully, brothers, for what you are going to hear interests you all. Our refuge is badly chosen, and too remote from the centre of our expeditions; the difficulties we have to surmount in returning to it, in consequence of the currents that make our ships drift, and the contrary winds that oppose their speed, make us lose precious time. Now, the Caribbean archipelago is composed, of more than thirty islands, among which it is easy for us, it seems to me, to choose the one that suits us best. This idea which I bring before you today I have been revolving in my mind for a long time. I have not limited my expeditions to the pursuit of the gavachos. I have also made a voyage of discovery, and believe that I have found the spot suited for us."

"Whereabouts is it, brother?" David asked, making himself spokesman for his companions.

"I mean the island which the Spaniards call Hispaniola, and you know as St. Domingo."

"But, brother," Bartholomew here interposed, "that island, which, I allow, is immense, and covered with magnificent forests, is inhabited by the Spaniards; if we went there it would be really placing ourselves in the wolf's throat."

"I thought as you do before I had assured myself of the reality of the fact, but now I am certain of the contrary; not alone is the island only partially occupied by the gavachos, but we shall also find allies in the parties they have despised."

"Allies!" the filibusters exclaimed, in surprise.

"Yes, brothers, and in this wise.—When Don Fernando de Toledo attacked St. Kitts, the French who succeeded in escaping from the massacre took refuge on the adjacent islands, as you are aware; many of them went further, and reached St. Domingo, where they found a refuge. That was bold, was it not? But, I repeat to you, the Spaniards occupy scarce one-half of it. At the period of the discovery they left some horned cattle on the island; these beasts have propagated, and now exist in herds. The immense savannahs of St. Domingo are covered with innumerable herds of wild oxen which graze on all the uninhabited part; these herds, as you are aware, are a certain resource for revictualling our ships, and, moreover, the vicinity of the Spanish colonists offers us the means to satiate our hatred upon them; besides, our companions who have been established on the island for some years past wage an incessant and obstinate war upon them."

"Yes, yes," said Belle Tête, pensively; "I understand what you are saying to us, brother. You are right up to a certain point; but let us discuss the matter quietly and coolly, like serious men."

"Speak," Montbarts replied; "each of us has the right to express his opinion when the common interest is concerned."

"Brave though we are, and we may boast of it frankly, for, thank heaven, our courage is well known, we are not strong enough for all that—at present at least—to measure ourselves against the Spanish power on land; there is a difference between capturing a ship and facing an entire population. You allow that, I suppose, brother?"

"Certainly I do."

"Very good, I will go on. It is evident that the Spaniards, who up to the present have probably not noticed them, or, at any rate, owing to their small number and slight importance, have disdained the adventurers established on the desert part of the island; when they see that this establishment, which they supposed to be temporary, and due to the caprice of our brothers, is becoming permanent, and assuming the menacing proportions of a colony, they will refuse to permit it—what will happen then? This: they will collect all their forces, assail us suddenly, destroy us after a desperate resistance, and ruin at one blow, not only our new colony, but also our hopes of vengeance."

These remarks of Belle Tête, which displayed close logic, produced a certain effect on the filibusters, who began exchanging meaning looks; but Montbarts did not allow the spirit of opposition time to spread, and at once went on to say—

"You would be right, brother, if, as you suppose, we were to place our principal establishment on St. Domingo; it is evident that we should be crushed by numbers, and forced to retire disgracefully; but a man would know me badly if he supposed that I, who have an implacable hatred of these infamous gavachos, could possibly conceive such a plan for a moment, if I had not previously assured myself about its success, and the profit we shall derive from it."

"Come, brother," Drake said, "explain yourself clearly; we are listening to you with the most earnest attention."

"To the northwest of St. Domingo, and only separated from it by a narrow channel, there is an island about eight leagues long, surrounded by rocks called the iron coast, which render any landing impossible, except at the south, where there is a fine port, whose bottom is composed of sand, and where vessels are sheltered from all winds, which, besides, are not violent in those parts; there are also a few sandy bays scattered along the coast, but they are only approachable by canoes. This island is called Tortuga or Tortoise Island, owing to its shape, which slightly resembles that animal. Here it is, brothers, I propose that we should form our principal establishment, or, if you prefer it, our headquarters. The Port of Peace, and Port Margot, situated facing Tortoise Isle, will enable us to keep up an easy communication with St. Domingo: sheltered in our island, as in an impregnable fortress, we shall brave the efforts of the whole Spanish power. But I do not wish to deceive you, and must tell you everything; the Spaniards are on their guard; they have foreseen that if buccaneering goes on, that is to say, if they do not succeed in destroying us, the excellent position of that island would not escape our notice, and that we should probably attempt to seize on it: hence they have had it occupied by twenty-five soldiers, commanded by an alférez. Do not smile, brothers; although the garrison is small, it is sufficient, owing to the manner in which it is entrenched, and the difficulties a landing offers; and then, too, it can easily obtain reinforcements from the Grande Terre in a very short time. I have often landed in disguise on Tortoise Isle. I have inspected it with the greatest care, and hence you can attach the most entire confidence to the information I am giving you."

"Montbarts is right," Yoc, the Brazilian, said at this moment; "I know Tortoise Isle, and, like him, I am persuaded that island will offer us a far surer and more advantageous shelter than St. Kitts."

"Now, brothers," Montbarts resumed, "reflect, and answer yes or no. If you accept my offer I will prepare to realize my plan by seizing the island; if you refuse, I will never mention it again."

And, in order by his absence to give more liberty for discussion, the adventurer left the room, and proceeded to the terrace in front of the hatto, where he began walking up and down, apparently indifferent to what was going on, but in his heart very anxious as to the result of the deliberation.

He had only been walking up and down for a few minutes, when a slight whistle was audible a short distance off, so gently modulated, that it needed all the sharpness of hearing with which the filibuster was endowed, to catch it.

He walked rapidly in the direction where this species of signal had been heard. At the same moment, a man lying on the ground, and so thoroughly concealed by the gloom that it was impossible to perceive him unless he was known to be there, raised his head, and displayed in the white moonbeams the copper face, and delicate and intelligent features of a Carib.

"Omopoua?" the filibuster said.

"I am waiting!" the Indian laconically answered, as he sprang up at one bound, and stood erect before him.

Omopoua, that is to say, the leaper, was a young man of twenty-five years of age at the most, of a tall and admirably proportioned stature, whose skin had the gilded shade of Florentine bronze. He was naked, with the exception of thin canvas drawers, fastening round his hips, and falling nearly to his knees. His long, black hair, parted in the centre of his head, fell on his shoulders on either side. He had no other weapons but a long knife, and a bayonet passed through a cowhide belt.

"Has the man arrived?" Montbarts asked.

"He has."

"Has Omopoua seen him?"

"Yes."

"Does he fancy himself recognised?"

"Only the eye of a determined foe could guess him beneath his disguise."

"That is well! My brother will conduct me to him?"

"I will lead the pale chief."

"Good! Where shall I find Omopoua an hour after sunrise?"

"Omopoua will be in his hut."

"I will come there;" and, hearing several voices calling him from the interior of the hatto, he said, "I reckon on the Indian's promise."

"Yes, if the chief keeps his."

"I shall keep it."

After exchanging a last meaning look with the filibuster, the Carib glided down the face of the cliff, and disappeared almost instantaneously.

Montbarts remained for a moment motionless, plunged in deep thought; then, giving a sudden start, and passing his hand over his forehead, as if to efface any sign of emotion, he hastily re-entered the hatto.

The deliberation was ended. The filibusters had returned to their seats, and Montbarts went back to his, and waited with affected indifference, till one of his comrades thought proper to speak.

"Brother," David then said, "we have thoroughly discussed your proposal. My comrades authorize me to tell you that they accept it, but they merely desire to know what means you intend to employ in carrying out your plan, and insuring its success?"

"Brothers, I thank you," Montbarts replied, "for giving me your consent. As to the means I intend to employ in seizing Tortoise Isle, permit me, for the present, to keep them secret, as the success of the expedition depends on it. You need only be told that I do not wish to compromise the interests of anyone, and that I intend to run all the risk alone."

"You do not understand me, brother, or else I have explained myself badly," David replied. "If I asked you in what way you proposed to act, I was not at all impelled by a puerile curiosity, but because, in so serious a question, which interests the entire association, we have resolved to accompany you, and to die or conquer with you. We wish to share the honour of the triumph, or assume a part of the defeat." Montbarts felt involuntarily affected by these generous words, so nobly pronounced; and by a spontaneous movement he held out his hands to the filibusters, who pressed them energetically, and said, —

"You are right, brothers. We must all share in the great work which, I hope, will at length place us in the position to achieve great things. We will all go to Tortoise Island. But I will ask you—and believe me that I am not speaking thus through any ambitious motive—to let me conduct the expedition."

"Are you not our chief?" the filibusters exclaimed.

"We will obey you according to the laws of buccaneering," David added. "The man who conceives an expedition has alone the right to command. We will be your soldiers."

"That is settled, brothers. Tomorrow morning, at eleven, after attending the sale of the new engagés, who arrived from France the day before yesterday, I will go to the governor, and tell him I am preparing a fresh expedition, and enlistment can begin at once."

"Not one of us will be missing at the rendezvous," said Belle Tête. "I must buy two engagés to fill the places of two idlers, who have just died of sheer idleness."

"That is settled," said Bartholomew. "At eleven o'clock we will all be at Basse Terre."

They then rose and prepared to retire: for the whole night had passed away in these discussions, and the sun, although still beneath the horizon, was already beginning to tinge it with a purple hue, that testified it would soon appear.

"By the way," Montbarts said, with an indifferent air to Morgan, whom with the rest he accompanied to the head of the path; "if you are not greatly attached to your Carib—I forget how you call him—"

"Omopoua?"

"Ah! yes. Well, I was saying that if you were not indisposed to part with him, I should feel obliged by your letting me have him."

"Do you want him?"

"Yes. I think he will be useful to me."

"In that case, take him, brother. I yield him to you, although he is a good workman, and I am satisfied with him."

"Thanks, brother. What value do you set on him?"

"Well, I will not bargain with you, brother. I saw a rather handsome fusil in your house. Give it to me, and take the Indian, and we shall be quits."

"Wait a minute, then."

"Why?"

"Because I will give you the fusil at once. You will send me the Indian; or, if I have time, I will call and fetch him during the day."

The filibuster returned to the hatto, took down the fusil, and carried it to Morgan, who threw it on his shoulder with a movement of joy.

"Well, that is settled," he said. "Good-bye, for the present."

"We shall meet again soon," Montbarts answered, and they separated.

Montbarts threw a thick cloak over his shoulders, put on a broad brimmed hat, whose brim fell over his face, and concealed his features, and then turning to Michael, said:

"Mate, an important matter obliges me to go to Basse Terre; you will go to our governor, the Chevalier de Fontenay, and without entering into any details, and being very careful not to betray our secret, you will simply warn him that I am preparing a fresh expedition."

"Very good, mate, I will go," Michael answered.

"You will then examine the lugger, and occupy yourself with Bowline, in getting her ready to put to sea."

After giving these instructions to the two sailors, Montbarts left the house, and descended the cliff.

The Chevalier de Fontenay, like M. d'Esnambuc, whom he had succeeded two years before as governor of St. Kitts, was a cadet of Normandy, who had come to the isles to try his fortune, and before becoming governor had joined in many buccaneering expeditions. He was exactly the man they wanted; he left them at liberty to act as they pleased, never asked them for any accounts, understood at half a word, and contented himself with raising a tithe on the prizes—a voluntary tribute which the adventurers paid him in return for the protection he was supposed to give them in the king's name by legitimating their position.

The sun had risen, a fresh sea breeze caused the leaves to rustle, and the birds were singing on the branches. Montbarts walked on hurriedly, looking neither to the right nor left, and apparently plunged in deep thought.

On reaching the entrance of the village of Basse Terre, instead of entering it, he skirted it, and going along a narrow path that crossed a tobacco plantation, he went toward the interior of the island, proceeding in the direction of Mount Misery, whose rise was already perceptible beneath his feet.

After a very long walk, the filibuster at length stopped at the entrance of a dry gorge, on one of the slopes of which stood a wretched hut of tree trunks, poorly covered with palm leaves. A man was standing in the doorway of this cabin: on perceiving Montbarts he uttered a cry of joy and rushed toward him, running over the rocks with the rapidity and lightness of a deer.

This man was Omopoua, the Carib; on coming up to the filibuster, he fell on his knees.

"Rise," the adventurer said to him, "what have you to thank me for?"

"My master told me an hour ago that I no longer belonged to him, but to you."

"Well, did I not promise it to you?"

"That is true, but the white men always promise, and never keep their word."

"You see a proof of the contrary; come, get up, your master has sold you to me, it is true, but I give you your liberty; you have now but one master, God."

The Indian rose, laid his hand on his chest, tottered, his features were contracted, and for a moment he seemed suffering from a violent internal emotion, which in spite of all the power he had over himself, he could not succeed in mastering.

Montbarts, calm and gloomy, examined him attentively, while fixing a scrutinizing glance upon him.

At length the Indian succeeded in speaking, though his voice issued from his throat like a whistle.

"Omopoua was a renowned chief among his people," he said; "a Spaniard had degraded him by making him a slave, through treachery, and selling him like a beast of burden: you restore Omopoua to the rank from which he ought never to have descended. It is well, you lose a bad slave, but gain a devoted friend; were it not for you I should be dead—my life belongs to you."

Montbarts offered the Carib his hand, which he kissed respectfully.

"Do you intend to remain at Saint Kitts, or would you like to return to Haiti?"

"The family of Omopoua," the Indian replied, "and what remains of his people, are wandering about the savannahs of Bohis, but where you go, I will go."

"Very good, you shall follow me; now lead me to the man, you know whom."

"At once."

"Are you certain he is a Spaniard?"

"I am."

"You do not know for what motives he has entered the island?"

"I do not."

"And at what place has he sought shelter?"

"With an Englishman."

"In the English colony there?"

"No; at Basse Terre."

"All the better. What is the Englishman's name?"

"Captain William Drake."

"Captain Drake!" Montbarts exclaimed with surprise, "It is impossible."

"It is so."

"In that case, the Captain does not know him."

"No; the man entered his house and asked for hospitality, and the Captain could not refuse it to him."

"That is true; go up to my hatto, take clothes, a fusil—in short, what weapons you like, and come to me at Captain Drake's; if I am no longer there, you will find me on the port; begone."

Montbarts then turned back, and proceeded toward Basse Terre, while the Carib went towards the hatto as the bird flies, according to Indian custom.

Basse Terre was the entrepôt, or to speak more correctly, the headquarters of the French colony: at the period when our story is laid it was only a miserable township, built without order, according to the caprice or convenience of each owner, an agglomeration of huts, rather than a town, but producing at a distance a most picturesque effect through this very chaos of houses of all shapes and sizes, thus grouped along the seashore, in front of magnificent roads, filled with vessels swinging at their anchors, and constantly furrowed by an infinite number of canoes.

A battery of six guns, built on an advanced point, defended the entrance of the roads.

But in this town, apparently so mean, dirty, and wretched, it was possible to watch the circulation of the life full of sap, vigour, and violence belonging to the strange inhabitants, unique in the world, who formed its heterogeneous population. The narrow gloomy streets were crowded with people of every description and colour, who came and went with a busy air.

There were pothouses at the corner of all the streets and squares, perambulating dealers shouted their goods in a ropy voice, and public criers, followed by a crowd which was swelled at every step by all the idlers, announced with a mighty noise of trumpets and drums, the sale on that very day of the engagés, who had just arrived in a Company's vessel.

Montbarts passed unnoticed through the crowd, and reached the door of Captain Drake's house—a rather handsome looking and cleanly kept house, which stood on the seashore at no great distance from the governor's residence.

The filibuster pushed the door, which, according to the custom of the country, was not locked, and entered the house.

CHAPTER XV.

THE SPY.

Montbarts, as we said, walked into the house.

There were two persons in the first room, which was contrived a double debt to pay, as half sitting room, half kitchen.

These two persons were an engagé of Captain Drake and a stranger.

As for the Captain, he was absent at the moment.

The filibuster's eye flashed at the sight of the stranger, and an ill-omened smile curled his pale lips.

As for the latter, he was seated at a table in the middle of the room, and quietly breakfasting on a piece of cold bacon, washed down by a bottle of Bordeaux,—a wine, let us remark, parenthetically, which, though unknown in Paris till the reign of Louis XV., when the Duc de Richelieu brought it into fashion on his return from the government of Guyenne—had been for a long time appreciated in America.

The stranger was of rather tall stature, with a pale face, and ascetic features, thin, bony, and angular; but his noble manners indicated a high rank in society, which rank his simple and even more than modest costume tried in vain to conceal.

On the filibuster's entrance, the stranger, without raising his head, took a side-glance at him from under his long velvety eyelashes, and again became absorbed or appeared to be so, in the contemplation of the capital breakfast set before him.

Everything was in common among the filibusters, everyone took from the other, whether he was at home or not, anything he wanted, arms, gunpowder, clothes or food, and the person from whom it was taken had no right to protest or make the slightest observation; this was not merely admitted and tolerated, but was regarded as a right which all took advantage of without the slightest scruple.

Montbarts, after looking round the room, took a chair, seated himself unceremoniously opposite the stranger, and turning to the engagé, said—

"Bring me some breakfast—I am hungry."

The other, without venturing the slightest remark, immediately prepared to obey.

In a very short time he had served up an excellent breakfast for the filibuster, and then took his place behind his chair to wait on him.

"My friend," the filibuster said, carelessly, "I thank you; but when I take my meals I do not like to have anybody behind me. Leave the room, but remain in front of the house door;" and he added, with a singularly meaning glance, "let no one enter here without my orders: no one—you understand me?" he said, laying a stress on the words; "Not even your master, were he to come. Can I depend on you?"

"Yes, Montbarts," said the engagé, and left the room.

At the name of Montbarts, uttered by the servant, the stranger gave an almost imperceptible start, and fixed an anxious glance on the filibuster; but immediately recovering himself, he began eating again in the most perfect tranquillity, or at least apparently so.

For his part, Montbarts went on eating without troubling himself, or seeming to trouble himself, about the guest seated just opposite to him.

This performance went on for some minutes; no other sound was heard in the room, where such violent passions were smouldering, but that produced by the knives and forks scratching on the platters.

At length Montbarts raised his head and looked at the stranger.

"You are very taciturn, sir," he said to him, with the simple air of a man who is wearied at a lengthened silence, and wishes to get up a conversation.

"I, sir?" the stranger replied, as he looked up in his turn with the calmest air; "Not that I am aware of."

"Still, sir," the filibuster resumed, "I would remark, that during the quarter of an hour I have had the honour of passing in your company, you have not once addressed a syllable to me, not even in greeting."

"Pray excuse me, sir," the stranger said, with a slight bow; "the fault is entirely involuntary: besides, as I have not the advantage of knowing you—?

"Are you quite sure of that, sir?" the adventurer interrupted, ironically.

"At least, I think so; hence, having nothing to say to you, I suppose that it would be useless to begin a conversation which would have no object."

"Who knows, sir?" the filibuster remarked, jeeringly; "Conversations the most frivolous at the outset, frequently become very interesting at the expiration of a few minutes."

"I doubt whether that would be the case with ours, sir. Permit me, therefore, to break it off at once. Besides, I have finished my meal," the stranger said, rising; "and some serious business claims my attention. Pray forgive me, therefore, for parting company so hurriedly, and believe in the sincerity of my regret."

The adventurer did not leave his seat, but throwing himself back in it with a graceful nonchalance, while playing with the knife he held in his hand, he said in his gentle insinuating voice—

"Pardon me, my dear sir; only one word, pray."

"In that case make haste, sir," the stranger replied, as he stopped, "for I am greatly pressed for time, I assure you."

"Oh! You will certainly grant me a few minutes," the adventurer remarked, with the old sarcasm.

"As you desire it so eagerly, I will not refuse it you, sir. But I really am in a hurry."

"I have no doubt on that point, sir; more especially hurried to leave this house —is it not so?"

"What do you mean, sir?" the stranger asked, haughtily.

"I mean," the adventurer replied, as he rose and placed himself between the stranger and the door, "that it is useless to feign any longer, and that you are recognized."

"I recognized? I do not understand you. What does this language mean?"

"It means," Montbarts said brutally, "that you are a spy and a traitor, and that you will be hanged within ten minutes."

"I?" the stranger replied, with very cleverly assumed surprise; "Why, you must be mad, sir, or suffering under a strange mistake. Let me pass, I request."

"I am not mad or mistaken, Señor Don Antonio de la Ronda."

The stranger started, a livid pallor covered his face, but he immediately recovered himself.

"Why, this is madness!" he said.

"Sir," Montbarts remarked, still calm, but remaining in front of the door, "when I affirm, you deny. It is evident that one of us lies, or is mistaken. Now I declare that it is not I, hence it must be you; and to remove your last doubts on this point, listen to this, but first be good enough to resume your seat. We shall have, however much it may annoy you, to converse for some time and I will remark, that it is a very bad taste to talk standing face to face like two gamecocks ready to fly at each other's combs, when it is possible to act otherwise."

Mastered, in spite of himself, by the adventurer's flashing glance obstinately fixed on him, and by his sharp, imperative accent, the stranger returned to his seat, and fell into it rather than sat down.

"Now, sir," the filibuster continued, in the same calm voice, as he reseated himself and placed his elbows on the table, "in order at once to dissipate all the doubts you may have, and to prove to you that I know more about you than you will doubtless like, let me tell you your history in a couple of words."

"Sir!" the stranger interrupted.

"Oh, fear nothing," he added, with studied sarcasm, "I shall be brief: I no more like than you do to waste my time in idle discourses; but just notice, by the bye, that, as I prophesied, our conversation, at first frivolous, has suddenly grown interesting. Is not this singular, I ask you?"

"I am awaiting your explanation, sir," the stranger replied, coolly; "for, up to the present, whatever you may say, I do not comprehend a word of all that it pleases you to say to me."

"By Heavens! You are a man after my heart. I was not mistaken about you. Brave, cold, and crafty, you are worthy to be a filibuster, and to lead an adventurous life with us."

"You do me a great honour, sir; but all this does not tell me—"

"Zounds! I am coming to it, sir—a little patience. How quick you are! Take care: in your profession a man must be cool before all else, and you are not so at this moment."

"You are very witty, sir," the stranger said, bowing ironically to his opponent.

The latter was offended by this sudden attack, and smote the table with his fist.

"Here is your history in two words, sir," he said. "You are an Andalusian, born at Malaga, a younger son, and consequently destined to take orders. One fine day, not feeling any liking for the tonsure, you fled from the paternal roof and embarked on a Spanish vessel bound for Hispaniola. Your name is Don Antonio de la Ronda. You see, sir, that up to this point I am well informed, am I not?"

"Pray go on, sir," the stranger replied, with perfect coolness; "your remarks are most interesting." Montbarts shrugged his shoulders, and went on.

"On arriving at Hispaniola, you contrived, in a short time, thanks to your good looks and polished manners, to secure powerful protectors; and thus, though you only left Europe three years ago, you have made such rapid progress, that you are at present one of the most influential men in the colony. Unluckily—"

"Do you say unluckily?" the stranger interrupted with a jeering smile.

"Yes, sir," the adventurer replied imperturbably; "unluckily your fortune turned your head so thoroughly—"

"So thoroughly?"

"That in defiance of your friends, you were arrested and threatened with a trial for embezzling a sum of nearly two million piastres; a noble amount, on which I compliment you. Any other man but you, sir, I feel a pleasure in allowing the fact, would have been ruined, or nearly so, as the case was very serious; and the Council of the Indies does not joke on money matters."

"Permit me to interrupt you, my dear sir," the stranger said with the most perfect ease; "you are telling this story in a very talented manner, but if you go on so, it threatens to last indefinitely. If you permit it, I will finish it in a few words."

"Ah! Ah! Then you allow its truth now?"

"Of course," the stranger said with admirable coolness.

"You acknowledge yourself to be Don Antonio de la Ronda?"

"Why should I deny it longer, when you are so well informed?"

"Better still; so that you confess to fraudulently entering the colony for the object of—"

"I confess anything you like," the Spaniard said quickly.

"Well, that being well established, you deserve to be hung, and you will be so in a few minutes."

"Well, no," he replied without losing any of his coolness; "that is where we differ essentially in opinion, sir, your conclusion is not in the least logical."

"What?" the adventurer exclaimed, surprised at this sudden change of humour which he did not expect.

"I said that your conclusion was not logical."

"I heard you perfectly."

"And I am going to prove it," he continued; "grant me in your turn a few moments' attention."

"Very good; we must be merciful to those who are about to die."

"You are very kind; but thank Heaven I am not there yet. There's many a slip between the cup and the lip, as a very sensible proverb says."

"Go on," the filibuster said with an ominous smile.

But the Spaniard was not affected.

"It is evident to me, sir, that you have some business or bargain to propose to me."

"I?"

"Certainly, and for this reason; having recognized me as a spy, for I must allow that I am really one (you see that I am frank in my confession), nothing was easier for you than to have me strung up to the nearest tree, without any form of trial."

"Yes, but I am going to do so."

"No, you will not do it now, and for this reason. You believe for reasons I am ignorant of, for I will not insult you by supposing that you had a feeling of pity for me, you who are so justly called by my countrymen the Exterminator —you believe, I say, that I can serve you, be useful to you in the success of one of your plans; consequently instead of having me hanged, as you would have done under any other circumstances, you came straight to find me here, where I fancied myself well hidden, in order to converse with me, like one friend with another. Well, I ask for nothing better, come, speak, I am listening; what do you want of me?"

And after uttering these words with the most easy air he could assume, Don Antonio threw himself back in his chair delicately rolling a cigarette between his fingers.

The filibuster gazed for a moment at the Spaniard with a surprise which he did not attempt to conceal, and then burst into a laugh.

"That will do," he said, "I prefer that; at least there will be no misunderstanding between us. Yes, you have guessed correctly, I have a proposal to make to you."

"That was not difficult to discover, sir; and pray what is the nature of the proposal?"

"Well, it is very simple, I only require you to act exactly in the opposite way to what you intended, to change sides, in short."

"Very good, I understand, that is to say, instead of betraying you for the advantage of Spain, I am to betray Spain for your profit."

"Yes, you see it is easy."

"Very easy, in fact, but decidedly shabby; and supposing that I consent to your request, what advantage shall I derive from it?"

"In the first place I need hardly say that you will not be hung."

"Pooh! To die by hanging, drowning, or a musket ball, is always much the same thing. I should desire a more distinct benefit, with your leave."

"Confound it, you are difficult to satisfy, then it is nothing to save one's neck from a slip knot?"

"My dear sir, when, as in my case, a man has nothing to lose and consequently everything to gain by any change in his position, death is rather a comfort than a calamity."

"You are a philosopher, so it seems."

"No, confound it! such absurdity never troubled me, I am merely a desperate man."

"That is often the same thing; but let us return to our matter."

"Yes, that will be better."

"Well! I offer you my whole share of the first ship I take; does that suit you?"

"That is something better; but unluckily the ship to which you refer is like the bear in the fable, not caught yet; I should prefer something more substantial."

"Well, I see I must yield to you; serve me well and I will reward you so generously that the King of Spain himself could not do more."

"Well, that is agreed, I'll run the risk; now be kind enough to tell me the nature of the service you expect from me?"

"I wish you to help me in taking by surprise Tortoise Island, where you lived for a long time, and where, if I do not err, you still have friends."

"I see no inconvenience in trying that, although I will begin by making my reservations."

"What are they?"

"That I do not pledge myself to insure the success of your hazardous undertaking."

"That remark is fair, but do not alarm yourself, if the Island is well defended, it shall be well attacked."

"I am convinced; now for the next matter."

"I will let you know it when the time arrives, señor; for the present, other business engages our attention."

"As you please, sir, you will be the best judge of the opportunity."

"Now, sir, as I had the honour of telling you at the outset, since I know you to be a very sharp hand, and very capable of slipping through my fingers like an eel, without the slightest scruple, and as I wish to avoid that eventuality, and save you any notion of the sort, you will do me the pleasure of going at once aboard my lugger."

"A prisoner!" the Spaniard said with a gesture of ill humour.

"Not as a prisoner, my dear Don Antonio, but regarded as a hostage, and treated as such, that is to say, with all the attention compatible with our common security."

"Still, the word of a gentleman—"

"Is valued between gentlemen, I allow, but with us *Ladrones*, as you call us, it has no value in my opinion; you hidalgos of old Spain, even make it a case of conscience to violate it without the slightest scruple, when your interest invites you to do so."

Don Antonio hung his head; recognizing in his heart, though unwilling to allow it, the exact truth, of the filibuster's words.

The latter enjoyed for a moment the Spaniard's discomfiture, and then rapped the table twice or thrice with the handle of his knife.

The captain's engagé at once entered the room.

"What do you want of me, Montbarts?" he asked.

"Tell me, my good fellow," the adventurer asked, "have you not seen a red Carib prowling round this house?"

"Pardon me, Montbarts, a Carib asked me only a moment ago, whether you were here, and I answered in the affirmative, but I did not like to transgress the orders I had received from you, and allow him to enter as he desired."

"Very good. Did not the man mention his name?"

"On the contrary, that was the very first thing he did; it is Omopoua."

"The very man I was expecting; tell him to come in, pray, for he is sure to be hanging about the door; and come with him."

The engagé went out.

"What do you want with this man?" the Spaniard asked with a shade of anxiety, which did not escape the adventurer's sharp eye.

"This Indian is simply intended to be your guard of honour," he said.

"Hum! It really seems as if you are anxious to keep me."

"Extremely so, señor."

At this moment, the engagé returned followed by the Carib, who had made no change in his primitive costume; but had taken advantage of Montbarts' permission to arm himself to the teeth.

"Omopoua and you, my friend, listen attentively to what I am going to say to you; you see this man?" he said pointing to the Spaniard who was still perfectly impassive.

"We see him," they answered.

"You will take him on board the lugger and hand him over to my mate, Michael the Basque, recommending him to watch over his guest most attentively! If, during the passage from here to the vessel, this man attempts to take to flight, blow out his brains without mercy. Have you understood me thoroughly?"

"Yes," said the engagé, "trust to us, we answer for him with our heads."

"That is well, I accept your word; and now, sir," he added, addressing Don Antonio, "be good enough to follow these two men."

"I yield to force, sir."

"Very good, that is how I regard the matter, but reassure yourself, your captivity will be neither harsh nor long, and I shall keep the promises I have made you, if you keep yours. Now, go and farewell for the present."

The Spaniard, without replying, placed himself between his two keepers voluntarily and left the room.

Montbarts remained alone.

CHAPTER XVI.

THE SLAVE SALE.

A moment after Montbarts rose, put on his cloak, which he had thrown on a chair when he came in, and prepared to quit the house.

On the threshold he found himself face to face with Captain Drake.

"Ah," said the latter, "here you are."

"Yes! I have been breakfasting at your house."

"You did well."

"Will you accompany me to the sale?"

"I do not want any hired man."

"Nor I, but you know the enlistment will commence immediately afterwards."

"That is true; let me say a word first to my engagé, and I will follow you."

"He has gone out."

"Why! I ordered him not to leave the house."

"I have given him a commission."

"Oh! That is different."

"You do not ask me what the commission is I have given your engagé," Montbarts remarked a moment later.

"Why should I? It does not concern me, I suppose."

"More than you imagine, brother."

"Nonsense, how so?"

"You offered hospitality to a stranger, did you not?"

"Yes, but what of that?"

"You shall see. This stranger, whom you do not know, for of course you do not—"

"No more than Adam; what do I care who he is? hospitality is one of those things which cannot be refused."

"That is true, but I recognized the man."

"Ah, ah, and who is he then?"

"Nothing less than a Spanish spy, brother."

"My God!" the captain said, stopping dead short.

"What is the matter with you now?"

"Nothing, nothing, except that I will go and blow out his brains, unless you have done so already."

"Pray, do nothing of the sort; this man, I feel convinced, brother, will prove very useful to us."

"Nonsense, how so?"

"Leave me to act; if we manage properly, we may draw profit even from a

Spanish spy; in the meanwhile, I have had him taken on board the lugger by your engagé, and a man of my own, where he will be watched so that he cannot part company."

"I trust to you for that, and thank you, brother, for having freed me from the scoundrel."

While talking thus, the two men arrived at the spot where the sale of the engagés to the colonists was to take place.

On the right of the square was a spacious shed, built of clumsily planed planks, and open to the wind and rain; in the centre of the shed was a table for the officials and secretaries of the company, who had to manage the sale and draw up the contracts; an easy chair had been set apart for the governor, by the side of a rather lofty platform, on which each engagé, male or female, mounted in turn, so that the purchasers might examine them at their ease.

These wretches, deceived by the company's agents in Europe, had contracted engagements, whose consequences they did not at all understand, and were convinced that, on their arrival in America, with the exception of a certain tax they had to pay the company for a certain period, they would be completely free to earn their livelihood as they thought proper. The majority were carpenters, masons and bricklayers, but there were also among them ruined gentlemen and libertines who detest work and who imagined that in America, the country of gold, fortune would visit them while they slept.

A company's ship had arrived a few days previously and brought one hundred and fifty engagés, among them were several young and pretty women, thoroughly vitiated, however, and who, like the Manon Lescault of the Abbé Prevost, had been picked up by the police in the streets of Paris, and shipped off without further formality.

These women were also sold to the colonists, not apparently as slaves, but as wives.

These unions contracted in the gipsy fashion, were only intended to last a settled time which must not exceed seven years, unless with the mutual consent of the couple, though the clause was hardly ever appealed to by them; at the end of that time they separated, and each was set at liberty to form a fresh union.

The engagés had been landed two days before; these two days had been granted them, that they might slightly recover from the fatigue of a long sea voyage, walk about and breathe the reviving land breeze, of which they had so long been deprived.

At the moment when the two adventurers arrived, the sale had been going on for half an hour; the shed was crowded with colonists who desired to purchase slaves, for we are compelled to use that odious term, for the poor creatures were nothing else.

At the sight of Montbarts, however, whose name was justly celebrated, a passage was opened, and he thus succeeded in reaching the side of the governor, Chevalier de Fontenay, round whom the most renowned adventurers were collected, among them being Michael the Basque.

Monsieur de Fontenay received Montbarts with distinction; he even rose from his chair and walked two or three steps to meet him, which the filibusters considered in very good taste, and felt grateful to him for it; this honour paid to the most celebrated among them cast a reflection on them all.

After exchanging a few compliments with the governor, Montbarts bent down to Michael's ear.

"Well, mate?" he said to him.

"The Spaniard is aboard," Michael replied, "and carefully watched by Bowline."

"In that case I can be at my ease?"

"Perfectly."

During this aside, the sale had been going on.

All the male engagés had been sold, with the exception of one who was standing at this moment on the platform, by the side of a company's agent, who acted as auctioneer, and praised the qualities of the human merchandise he offered.

This engagé was a short, stout, powerfully built man, from twenty-five to twenty-six years of age, with harsh, energetic, but intelligent features, whose grey eyes sparkled with audacity and good humour.

"Pierre Nau, native of the sands of Olonne," said the company's agent, "twenty-five years of age, powerful and in good health, a sailor. Who'll say forty crowns for the Olonnais, forty crowns for three years, gentlemen."

"Come, come," said the engagé, "if the person who buys me is a man, he will have a good bargain."

"Going for forty crowns," the company's agent repeated, "forty crowns, gentlemen."

Montbarts turned to the engagé.

"What, you scoundrel," he said to him, "you a sailor and sell yourself instead of joining us? You have no pluck."

The Olonnais began laughing.

"You know nothing about it. I have sold myself, because I must do so," he answered, "so that my mother may be able to live during my absence."

"How so?"

"How does it concern you? You are not my master, and even if you were, you would have no right to inquire into my private affairs."

"You seem to me a bold fellow," Montbarts remarked.

"Indeed, I believe I am; besides, I wish to become an adventurer like you fellows, and for that purpose I must serve my apprenticeship to the trade."

"Going for forty crowns," cried the agent.

Montbarts examined with the most serious attention the engagé, whose firm glance he could hardly manage to quell; then, doubtless satisfied with his triumph, he turned to the agent.

"That will do," he said, "hold your row: I buy this man."

"The Olonnais is adjudged to Montbarts the exterminator, for forty crowns," the agent said.

"Here they are," the adventurer answered as he threw a handful of silver on the table; "now come," he ordered the Olonnais, "you are now my engagé."

The latter leapt joyously off the platform and ran up to him.

"So you are Montbarts the exterminator?" he asked him curiously.

"I think you are questioning me," the adventurer said with a laugh, "still, as your question appears to me very natural, I will answer it this time; yes, I am Montbarts."

"In that case I thank you for buying me, Montbarts; with you I am certain soon to become a man."

And at a sign from his new master, he respectfully placed himself behind him.

The most curious part of the sale for the adventurers then began, that is to say, the sale of the women.

The poor wretches, mostly young and pretty, mounted the platform trembling, and in spite of their efforts to keep a good countenance, they blushed with shame, and burning tears ran down their cheeks on seeing themselves thus exposed before all these men, whose flashing eyes were fixed upon them.

The company made its greatest profit by the women, and it was the more easy to realise, because they were got for nothing, and sold at the highest possible figure.

The men were generally knocked down at a price varying from thirty to forty dollars, but never went beyond that; with the women it was different, they were put up to auction, and the governor alone had the right to stop the sale, when the price appeared to him sufficiently high. These women were always sold amid cries, shouts and coarse jests, generally addressed to the adventurers who did not fear running the risk of venturing on the shoal-beset ocean of marriage.

Belle Tête, that furious adventurer to whom we have already referred, and whom we saw at the meeting at the hatto, had, as he had resolved, purchased two engagés to take the place of the two who had died, so he said, of indolence, but, in reality of the blows he dealt them; then, instead of returning home he had confided the engagés to his overseer; for the adventurers, like the slave owners, had overseers, whose duty it was to make the white slaves toil; and the adventurer remained in the shed watching the sale of the women with the most lively interest.

His friends did not fail to cut jokes at his expense, but he contented himself with shrugging his shoulders disdainfully, and stood with his hands crossed on the muzzle of his long fusil, and with his eyes obstinately fixed on the platform.

A young woman had just taken her place there in her turn; she was a frail delicate girl, with light curling hair that fell on her white rather thin chest. Her smooth and pensive forehead, her large blue eyes full of tears, her fresh cheeks, her little mouth, made her appear much younger than she in reality was; she was eighteen years of age, and her delicate waist, her well-turned lips, her decent appearance, in short everything about her delicious person had a seductive charm, which formed a complete contrast with the decided air and vulgar manners of the women who had preceded her on the platform, and those who would follow her.

"Louise, born at Montmartre, aged eighteen years; who will marry her for three years, at the price of fifteen crowns?" the company's agent asked in his sarcastic voice.

The poor girl buried her face in her hands and wept bitterly.

"Twenty crowns for Louise," an adventurer shouted, drawing nearer.

"Twenty-five," another said immediately.

"Make her hold her head up so that we can have a look at her," a third cried brutally.

"Come, little one," the agent said, as he obliged her to remove her hands from her face; "be polite and let them look at you, it is for your own good, hang it all! Twenty-five crowns."

"Fifty," said Belle Tête, without moving from the spot.

All eyes were turned to him; up to this moment Belle Tête had professed a profound hatred for marriage.

"Sixty," shouted an adventurer who did not desire to buy the girl, but wished to annoy his comrade.

"Seventy," said another with the same charitable intention.

"One hundred," Belle Tête shouted angrily.

"One hundred crowns, gentlemen, one hundred for Louise for three years," the stoical agent said.

"One hundred and fifty."

"Two hundred."

"Two hundred and fifty."

"Three hundred," several adventurers shouted, almost simultaneously, as they drew nearer to the platform.

Belle Tête was pale with rage, for he feared lest she might escape him.

The adventurer had persuaded himself, rightly or wrongly, that he wanted a wife to manage his household; now he had seen Louise, Louise pleased him, she was for sale, and he resolved to buy her.

"Four hundred crowns!" he said with an air of defiance.

"Four hundred crowns," the company's agent repeated in his monotonous voice.

There was a silence.

Four hundred crowns is a large sum; Belle Tête triumphed.

"Five hundred!" a sharp shrill voice suddenly shouted.

The contest was beginning again; the adversaries had only stopped to regain their strength.

The company's agent rubbed his hands with a jubilant air, while repeating,—

"Six hundred, seven, eight, nine hundred crowns!"

A species of frenzy had seized on the spectators, and all bid furiously; the girl was still weeping.

Belle Tête was in a state of fury which approached to madness; clutching his fusil frenziedly in his clinched hand, he felt a wild temptation to send a bullet into the most determined of his competitors. Only the presence of M. de Fontenay restrained him.

"A thousand," he shouted in a hoarse voice.

"One thousand two hundred!" the most obstinate competitor immediately yelled.

Belle Tête stamped savagely, threw his fusil on his shoulder, drew his cap on to his head with a blow of his fist, and then with a step as slow and solemn as that of a statue would be, if a statue could walk, he went to place himself by the side of his unendurable rival, and letting the butt of his fusil fall heavily on the ground, scarce an inch from the man's foot, he looked him in the face for a moment with a defiant air, and shouted in a voice choked by emotion,—

"Fifteen hundred!"

The adventurer regarded him in his turn fiercely, fell back a step, and, after renewing the powder in the pan of his fusil, said, in a calm voice—

"Two thousand!"

Before these two obstinate adversaries the other bidders had prudently withdrawn; the competition was turning into a quarrel, and threatened to become sanguinary.

A deadly silence brooded over the shed; the over-excited passions of these two men had spoiled all the pleasures of the spectators, and silenced all their jokes.

The Governor followed with interest the different incidents of this struggle, ready to interfere at any moment.

The adventurers had gradually fallen back, and left a large free space between the two men.

Belle Tête recoiled a few paces in his turn, suddenly examined the priming of his fusil, and then, pointing the latter at his adversary, shouted—

"Three thousand!"

The other raised his fusil at the same moment to his shoulder.

"Three thousand five hundred crowns!" he shouted, as he pulled the trigger—the fusil was discharged.

But the Governor, with a movement rapid as thought, threw up the barrel with the end of his cane, and the ball lodged in the roof.

Belle Tête remained motionless, though, on hearing the shot, he lowered his fusil.

"Sir," the Governor exclaimed, indignantly, addressing the adventurer who had fired, "You have acted in a dishonourable way, and almost committed a murder."

"Governor," the adventurer coolly replied, "when I fired he had his gun pointed at me, and hence it is a duel."

The Governor hesitated, for the answer was specious.

"No matter, sir," he continued, a moment later, "the laws of duelling were not respected; to punish you I put you out of the bidding. Sir," he said, addressing the company's agent, "I order that the woman, who was the cause of this deplorable aggression, be knocked down to Señor Belle Tête for three thousand crowns."

The agent bowed with rather an angry look, for the worthy man had hoped, from the way things were going on, to reach a much higher figure; but he dared not make any observations to Chevalier de Fontenay; he must yield, and so he did.

"Louise is adjudged for three thousand crowns," he said, with a sigh of regret —not for the woman, but for the money—"to M. Belle Tête."

"Very good, Governor," the baffled adventurer said, with an ugly smile, "I must bow to your final sentence; but Belle Tête and I will meet again."

"I hope so, too, Picard," Belle Tête answered, coldly; "there must be bloodshed between us now." During this time Louise had come down from the platform, when another woman took her place, and had stationed herself, still weeping, by the side of Belle Tête, who was henceforth her lord and master.

M. de Fontenay gave a commiserating glance at the poor girl, who was about, in all probability, to endure such a cruel existence with so harsh a man, and then gently said to her—

"Madame, from this day you are for three years the legitimate wife of M. Belle Tête, and owe him obedience, affection, and fidelity; such are the laws of the colony: in three years you will be your own mistress, at liberty to leave him or to continue to live with him, if he desire it; be good enough to sign this paper."

The unhappy woman, blinded by her tears, and crushed by despair, signed, without looking at it, the paper which the Governor offered her; then she cast a heart-broken glance at this silent and indifferent crowd, in which she knew that she could not find a friend.

"Now, sir," she asked, in a gentle and trembling voice, "what must I do?"

"You must follow this man, who will be your husband for three years," M. de Fontenay answered, with a touch of pity, which he could not overcome.

At this moment Belle Tête laid his hand on the girl's shoulder; she shuddered all over, and looked wildly at him.

"Yes," he said, "my girl, you must follow me; for, as the Governor has told you, I am your husband for three years, and till the expiration of that time, you will have no other master but me. Now, listen to this, my darling, and engrave it carefully on your mind, so as to remember it at the right moment: what you have done, what you have been, until now, does not concern me, and I care little about it; but," he added, in a hollow, ferocious voice, which chilled the poor girl with horror, "from this day, from this moment, you belong to me—to me alone: I intrust to you my honour, which becomes yours, and if you compromise that honour—if you forget your duties," he said, as he dashed the butt end of his musket on the ground, so harshly, that the hammer rattled with an ill-omened sound, "this will remind you of them; now, follow me."

"Be gentle to her, Belle Tête," M. de Fontenay could not help saying—"she is so young."

"I shall be just, Governor: now, thanks for your impartiality, it is time for me to retire. Picard, my old friend, you know where to find me."

"I shall not fail to come and see you, but I do not, wish to trouble your honeymoon," Picard replied, with a growl.

Belle Tête withdrew, followed by his wife.

The sale henceforth offered nothing of interest; the few women remaining were sold at prices far inferior to that which Louise had fetched, to the great regret, we are bound to add, of the Company's agent.

The adventurers were preparing to leave the shed where they imagined there was nothing more to see; but at this moment Montbarts mounted the platform, and addressed the crowd in a sonorous voice—

"Brothers," he said, "stay, I have an important communication to make to you."

The adventurers remained motionless.

CHAPTER XVII.

THE ENLISTMENT.

All the adventurers assembled round the platform, anxiously awaiting what Montbarts had to tell them.

"Brothers," he said, a moment after, "I am preparing a new expedition, for which I require three hundred resolute men; who among you will follow Montbarts the Exterminator?"

"All, all!" the adventurers shouted, enthusiastically.

The Governor prepared to withdraw.

"Pardon me, Chevalier de Fontenay," Montbarts said, "be kind enough to remain a few minutes longer; the expedition I have projected is most serious: I am about to dictate a charter party, to which I will ask you, as Governor of the colony, to append your signature before that of our companions—moreover, I have a bargain to propose to you."

"I will remain, since you desire it, Montbarts," the Governor replied, as he returned to his seat; "now be kind enough to inform me of the bargain you wish to propose."

"You are the owner, sir, I think, of two brigantines of eighty tons each?"

"I am."

"These brigantines are useless to you at this moment, as you appear, at least until fresh orders, to have given up cruising, while they will be very useful to me."

"In that case, sir, they are at your service from this moment," the Governor replied, gallantly.

"I thank you, as I ought, for your politeness, sir, but that is not my meaning; in an expedition like the one I meditate, no one can foresee what may happen, hence I propose to buy your two ships for four thousand crowns cash."

"Very good, sir, since you wish it; I am delighted to be of service to you; the two ships are yours."

"I shall have the honour of handing you the four thousand crowns within an hour."

The two men bowed; and then the filibuster turned to the adventurers, who were waiting, panting with, impatience, and whose curiosity had been heightened by the purchase of the two vessels.

"Brothers," he said, in his sonorous and sympathetic voice, "for two months past no expedition has been attempted, and no ship has put to sea; are you not beginning to grow tired of this idle life which you and I are leading? Are you not beginning to run short of money, and are not your purses light? Zounds, comrades, come with me, and within a fortnight your pockets shall be full of Spanish doubloons, and the pretty girls, who today are so coy, will then lavish their most charming smiles on you—down with the Spaniards, brothers!

Those of you who are willing to follow me can give their names to Michael the Basque, my mate. Still, as the shares will be large, the danger will be great; to obtain them I only want men resolved to conquer or to die bravely, without asking quarter of the enemy or granting it; I am Montbarts the Exterminator—I grant no mercy to the Spaniards, nor do I ask it of them."

Enthusiastic shouts greeted these words, uttered with that accent which the celebrated filibuster knew so well how to assume when he wished to seduce the individuals he was addressing.

The enlistment began; Michael the Basque had seated himself at the table previously occupied by the Company's agent, and wrote down the names of the adventurers, who pressed round him in a crowd, and who all wished to join in an expedition which they foresaw would be most lucrative.

But Michael had received strict instructions from his master: convinced that he should not want for men, and that more would offer than he needed, he carefully selected those whose names he took, and pitilessly rejected those adventurers whose reputation for, we will not say bravery, for all were brave as lions, but for reckless daring, was not thoroughly established.

Still in spite of Michael's intended strictness, the number of three hundred was soon complete. We need scarce say they were the flower of the filibusters, all adventurers, the least renowned of whom had performed deeds of incredible daring, men with whom attempting impossibilities and achieving them had become but mere child's play.

The first inserted were, as had been agreed on the preceding night, the members of the society of the Twelve.

Hence M. de Fontenay, who, an old filibuster himself, knew all these men, not only by reputation, but from having seen them at work, could not recover from his surprise, and incessantly repeated to Montbarts, who was standing, calm and smiling at his side, "What can you be after? Do you mean to seize on Hispaniola?"

"Who knows?" the filibuster replied sportively.

"Still, I think I have a right to your confidence," the governor said in an offended tone.

"The most entire, Sir; still, you are aware that the first condition of security in an expedition is secrecy."

"That is true."

"I cannot tell you anything, but do not prevent you from guessing."

"Guessing! But how?"

"Well, perhaps the charter party will set you on the right track."

"Well, let me hear it."

"A little patience still; but stay, here is Michael coming toward me. Well," he asked him, "have you completed our number?"

"I should think so; I have three hundred and fifty men."

"Hang it, that is a great number."

"I could not do otherwise than accept them; when it is a question about going with Montbarts, it is impossible to keep them back."

"Well, we will take them, if it must be so," Montbarts said with a smile, "give me your list."

Michael handed it to him; the filibuster looked round him, and perceived an agent of the Company, whom curiosity had kept back, and who had remained in the shed to witness the enlistment.

"You are a Company's agent, I think, sir?" he said to him, politely.

"Yes, sir," the agent replied with a bow, "I have that honour."

"In that case, may I ask you to do me a service?"

"Speak, sir, I shall be only too glad to oblige you."

"My companions and myself are no great clerks, and we can use a hatchet better than a pen; would it be presuming too much on your kindness to ask you to be good enough to serve as my secretary for a few minutes, and write down the charter party I shall dictate to you, and which my comrades will sign, after having it read to them?"

"I am only too happy, sir, that you deign to honour me with your confidence," the agent said with a bow.

Then he seated himself at the table, selected some paper, mended a pen and waited.

"Silence, if you please, gentlemen," said the Chevalier de Fontenay, who had exchanged a few words in a low voice with Montbarts.

The private conversations were checked, and a profound silence was established almost instantaneously. M. de Fontenay continued.

"A filibustering expedition, composed of three ships, two brigantines and a lugger, is about to leave St. Kitts, under the command of Montbarts, whom I appoint, in the name of His most Christian Majesty, Louis, fourteenth of that name, admiral of the fleet. This expedition, whose object remains secret, has been joined by 350 men, the flower of the filibusters. The three captains chosen to command the ships are, Michael the Basque, William Drake, and John David. They are ordered to obey in every point the commands they will receive from the admiral, and each captain will himself appoint his officers." Then, turning to Montbarts, he added, "Now admiral, dictate the charter party."

The adventurer bowed, and addressing the Company's agent, who was watching with head and pen erect, he said to him—

"Are you ready, sir?"

"I await your orders."

"In that case write as I dictate."

No expedition ever left port without having previously proclaimed the charter party: this document, in which the rights of each man were rigorously stipulated, served as the supreme law for these men, who, undisciplined though they were ashore, bowed without a murmur to the strictest decrees of the naval code: so soon as they had set foot on the vessel for which they were engaged, the captain of yesterday became a sailor today, accepted without grumbling the eventual inferiority which the duration of the cruise alone maintained, and which ended on the return to port, by placing each member of the expedition on the same level, and on a footing of the most perfect equality.

We quote literally the charter party our readers are about to peruse, because from this authentic act they will understand more easily the range and power of this strange association, and the manner in which the filibusters treated each other.

Montbarts dictated what follows in a calm voice amid the religious silence of his auditors, who only interrupted him at intervals, by shouts of approbation.

"Charter party decreed by Admiral Montbarts, Captains Michael the Basque, William Drake, John David, and the Brethren of the Coast, who have voluntarily placed themselves under their orders, and which is fully consented to by them."

"The admiral will have a right, in addition to his share, to one man per hundred."

"Each captain will receive twelve shares."

"Each brother four shares."

"These shares will only be counted after the king's part has been deducted from all the shares."

"The surgeons will receive, in addition to their share, two hundred dollars each, as payment for their medicaments."

"The carpenters, in addition to their share, will each, have a claim for one hundred dollars, in remuneration of their labours."

"Any disobedience will be punished by death, whatever be the name or rank of the culprit."

"The brothers who distinguish themselves in the expedition will be rewarded in the following manner—The man who pulls down the enemy's flag from a fortress, and hoists the French one, will have a claim, in addition to his share, to fifty piastres."

"The man who takes a prisoner, when out in search of news of the enemy, will have, in addition to his share, one hundred piastres."

"The grenadiers, for each grenade thrown into a fort, five piastres."

"Any man, who in action captures a high officer of the enemy, will be rewarded by the admiral, if he has risked his life, in a generous way."

"Rewards offered, in addition to their share, to the wounded and mutilated."

"For the loss of both legs, fifteen hundred crowns, or fifteen slaves, at the choice of the recipient: if there are enough slaves."

"For the loss of both arms, eighteen hundred piastres or eighteen slaves, at choice."

"For a leg, no distinction between right and left, five hundred piastres or five slaves."

"For an eye, one hundred piastres or a slave; for an arm or a hand, no distinction between right and left, four hundred piastres or four slaves."

"For both eyes, two thousand piastres, or twenty slaves."

"For a finger, one hundred piastres or one slave: if any man be dangerously wounded in the body he will have five hundred piastres or five slaves."

"It is already understood, that, in the same way, as with the king's part, all these rewards will be raised on the whole of the booty, before dividing the shares."

"Any enemy's vessel captured either at sea or at anchor, will be divided between all the members of the expedition, unless it be valued at more than ten thousand crowns, in which case one thousand crowns will be set apart for the first ship's crew that boarded: the expedition will hoist the royal flag of France, and the admiral bear in addition the *red, white, and blue* flag."

"No officer or sailor of the expedition will be allowed to remain ashore anywhere unless he has previously obtained the admiral's permission, under penalty of being declared a maroon, and prosecuted as such."

When this last paragraph which, like all that preceded it, had been listened to in the most profound silence, had been recorded by the Company's agent, Montbarts took the charter party, and read it through in a loud clear voice—

"Does this charter party suit you, brethren?" he then asked the filibusters.

"Yes, yes," they shouted, waving their caps, "long live Montbarts! Long live Montbarts!"

"And you swear, as my officers and myself swear, to obey without a murmur, and strictly carry out all the clauses of this charter party?"

"We swear it," they repeated.

"Very good," Montbarts continued; "the embarkation will commence at sunrise tomorrow, and all the crews must be on board the fleet before ten o'clock."

"We will be there."

"Now, brethren, let me remind you that each of you must be armed with a fusil, and a cutlass, have a bag of bullets, and at least three pounds of gunpowder: I repeat that the expedition we are about to undertake is most serious, so that you may not forget to choose your chums, that they may aid you in the case of illness or wounds, and make your wills, as otherwise your shares would lapse to the king. You have understood me, brothers? Employ as you please the few hours' liberty left you, but do not forget that I expect you on board at day break tomorrow."

The filibusters replied by shouts, and left the shed, where there only remained the governor, Montbarts, his captains, and the new engagé called the Olonnais, whom the adventurer had bought by auction a few hours previously, and who, far from being sad, seemed, on the contrary, extremely pleased at all that was going on in his presence.

"As for you, gentlemen," Montbarts said, "I have no orders to give you, for you know as well as I what you have to do. Draw lots for your commands, then go on board, inspect the masts and rigging, and get ready to sail at the first signal. These are the only recommendations, I think, I need make you. Good-bye."

The three captains bowed, and at once withdrew.

"Ah!" Chevalier de Fontenay said, with an accent of regret, "My dear Montbarts, I never see an expedition preparing without having a lively feeling of sorrow, and almost of envy."

"Do you regret your adventurous life, sir? I understand that feeling, although each expedition brings you an augmentation of wealth."

"What do I care for that? Do not believe that I make an avaricious calculation. No! My thoughts are of a higher order. But the moment is badly chosen to chatter with you. Go, sir! And if you succeed, as I do not doubt—and yet, who knows? On your return we shall perhaps be able to come to an understanding; and then we will attempt an expedition together, which I hope will be talked about for a long time."

"I shall be glad," the filibuster replied, politely, "to have you as a partner. Your brilliant courage, and far from ordinary merit, are to me certain guarantees of success. I shall therefore have the honour to hold myself at your orders, if it please Heaven that I succeed this time, and return safe and sound from the expedition I meditate."

"Good luck, sir; and let us hope to meet again soon."

"Thank you, sir."

They shook hands; and as, while conversing, they had left the shed, they went different roads, after a parting bow.

The filibuster, followed by the engagé, proceeded slowly towards his house.

At the moment when he left the town, a man placed himself before him, and bowed.

"What do you want with me?" the adventurer asked, giving him a scrutinizing glance.

"To say a word to you."

"Say on."

"Are you Captain Montbarts?"

"You must be a stranger, to ask that question."

"No matter. Answer."

"I am Captain Montbarts."

"In that case, this letter is for you."

"A letter for me!" he exclaimed, in surprise.

"Here it is," the stranger said, as he presented it.

"Give it to me."

And he took it from him.

"Now my commission is performed, farewell."

"A word, in your turn."

"Speak."

"From whom comes this letter?"

"I do not know; but you will probably learn by reading the contents."

"That is true."

"Then I may retire?"

"Nothing prevents you."

The stranger bowed, and went away.

Montbarts opened the letter, hurriedly perused it, and turned pale. Then he re-read it; but this time slowly, and as if he wished to dwell on each sentence.

A moment later he seemed to form a resolution, and turned to his engagé, who was standing a few paces from him.

"Come here," he said to him.

"Here I am," said the other.

"You are a sailor?"

"A 1, I fancy."

"That is well. Follow me."

The filibuster turned back, hastily re-entered the town, and proceeded toward the sea.

He seemed to be seeking something. A moment later, his gloomy face grew brighter.

He had just seen a light canoe pulled up on the beach.

"Help me to float this canoe," he said to the engagé.

The latter obeyed.

So soon as the canoe was afloat, Montbarts leaped in, closely followed by his engagé; and seizing the paddles, they put off from the shore.

"Step the mast, so that we may hoist a sail so soon as we are free of the ships."

The Olonnais, without answering, did as he was ordered.

"Good!" Montbarts continued. "Now haul the sheets aft, and hand them to me, my lad."

In a second the sail was hoisted, set, and the light canoe bounded like a petrel over the crest of the waves.

They ran thus for some time without exchanging a word. They had left the ships far behind them, and passed out of the roads.

"Do you speak Spanish?" Montbarts suddenly asked the engagé.

"Like a native of Old Castile," the other answered.

"Ah! Ah!" said Montbarts.

"It is easy to understand," the Olonnais continued. "I went whaling with the Basques and Bayonnese, and for several years smuggled along the Spanish coast."

"And do you like the Spaniards?"

"No!" the other answered, with a frown.

"You have a motive, of course?"

"I have one."

"Will you tell it me?"

"Why not?"

"Out with it, then."

"I had a boat of my own, in which, as I told you, I smuggled. I worked six years to save up the money to buy this boat. One day, while seeking to land prohibited goods in a bay to windward of Portugalete, I was surprised by a Spanish revenue lugger. My boat was sunk, my brother killed, myself dangerously wounded, and I fell into the hands of the Gavachos. The first bandage they placed on my wounds was a bastinado, which left me for dead on the ground. Believing, doubtless, that they had killed me, they abandoned me then, and paid no further attention to me. I succeeded by boldness and cunning, after enduring indescribable tortures from hunger, cold, fatigue, &c., too lengthy to enumerate, in at length leaping across the frontier, and finding myself once again on French soil. I was free, but my brother was dead. I was ruined, and my old father ran a risk of dying of hunger—thanks to the Spaniards. Such is my history. It is not long.—How do you like it?"

"It is a sad one, my good fellow; but it is as much hatred as the desire of growing rich which has brought you among us?"

"It is hatred, before everything."

"Good! Take the helm in my place, while I reflect. We are going to Nevis. Steer to windward of that point which juts out down there to the southeast."

The engagé seized the helm. Montbarts wrapped himself in his cloak, pulled his hat over his eyes, let his head sink on his chest, and remained motionless as a statue. The canoe still advanced, vigorously impelled by the breeze.

CHAPTER XVIII.

NEVIS.

Nevis is only separated from St. Kitts by a channel half a league in width at the most.

This charming little island, whose fertility is remarkable, is, according to all probability, the result of a volcanic explosion; and this assertion is nearly proved by a crater containing a spring of hot water strongly impregnated with sulphur.

Seen from a distance, it offers the appearance of a vast cone; it is, in fact, only a very lofty mountain, whose base is watered by the sea; its sides at first offering an easy incline, become, at a certain height, excessively abrupt; all vegetation ceases, and its snow covered peak is lost in the clouds.

During the attack of the Spaniards on St. Kitts, several adventurers had sought shelter on this isle. Some of them, seduced by attractive sites, permanently settled there, and commenced forming plantations; few in number, it is true, and too far apart for the inhabitants to aid each other in the event of an attack from an external foe, but which prospered, and promised, ere long, to acquire a certain amount of importance.

The filibuster, although his little skiff was impelled by a good breeze, took some time in reaching the island, because he was obliged to go along the entire length of the channel ere he reached the spot where he wished to go.

The sun was already beginning to decline, when the canoe at length put into a small sandy creek.

"Pull up the canoe, hide the paddles among the reeds," said Montbarts, "and follow me."

The Olonnais obeyed with the punctuality and intelligent vivacity which he displayed in everything, and then said to his master—

"Shall I take my fusil?"

"There is no harm in doing so," the latter replied; "an adventurer should never go unarmed."

"Very good; I will remember that."

They proceeded inland, following a scarce-traced path, which ran with a gentle incline from the beech, wound round a rather steep hill, and after passing through a leafy mahogany forest, led to a narrow esplanade, in the centre of which a light canvas tent had been pitched, not far from a rock.

A man, seated before the entrance of the tent, was reading a Breviary. He was dressed in the strict attire of the Franciscans, and seemed to have passed middle life. He was pale and thin, his features were ascetic and stern, his countenance was intelligent, and a marked expression of gentleness was spread over it. At the sound of the adventurers' footsteps he raised his head quickly, turned towards them, and a melancholy smile played round his lips.

Hurriedly closing his book, he rose and walked a few steps toward the newcomers.

"Heaven be with you, brothers!" he said in Spanish, "If you come with pure intentions; if not, may it inspire you with better thoughts."

"My father," the filibuster said, returning his salutation, "I am the man whom the adventurers of St. Kitts call Montbarts, and my intentions are pure, for in coming here I have only yielded to the desire you expressed to see me, if you are really Fray Arsenio Mendoza, from whom I received a letter a few hours ago."

"I am the person who wish to see you, brother; and that is really my name."

"In that case speak, I am ready to hear you."

"Brother," the monk answered, "the things I have to communicate to you are of the highest importance, and concern you alone. Perhaps it would be better that you alone should hear them."

"I do not know what important matters you can have to tell me, father; but in any case, learn that this man is my engagé, and, as such, it is his duty to be deaf and dumb when I order him."

"Very good, I will speak in his presence, since you demand it; still, I repeat to you, that it would be better for us to be alone."

"I will act in accordance with your wish. Retire out of hearing, but keep in sight," he said to his engagé.

The latter retired about one hundred yards down the path, and leant on his fusil.

"Do you fear any treachery on the part of a poor monk like me?" the Franciscan asked, with a sad smile; "That would be very gratuitously imputing to me intentions very remote from my thoughts."

"I suppose nothing, father; still, I am accustomed," the filibuster coarsely answered, "always to be on my guard when I am in the presence of a man of your nation, whether he be priest or layman."

"Yes, yes," he said, in a sorrowful voice, "you profess an implacable hatred for my unhappy country, and for that reason are called the Exterminator."

"Whatever be the feelings I profess for your countrymen and the name it has pleased them to give me, it is not, I suppose, to discuss this point with me that you have come here at a serious risk, and requested me to meet you."

"Indeed, it was not for that motive, you are right, my son, though, personally, I might have a good deal to say on that subject."

"I would observe, father, that the hour is advancing—I have but little time at your service, and if you do not hasten to explain yourself, I shall be, to my great regret, constrained to leave you."

"You would regret it for your whole life, brother, were it as long as a patriarch's."

"That is possible, though I greatly doubt it. I can only receive bad news from Spain."

"Perhaps so; in any case, these are the news of which I am the bearer."

"I am listening to you."

"I am, as my gown shows you, a monk of the order of San Francisco de Asís."

"At least, you have the look of one," the adventurer remarked, with an ironical smile.

"Do you doubt it?"

"Why not? Would you be the first Spaniard who was not afraid to profane a sacred dress, in order to spy our movements the more easily?"

"Unfortunately what you say is true, and it has happened only too often; but I am merely a monk."

"I believe you, till I have proof of the contrary; so go on."

"Very good. I am the spiritual director of several ladies of quality in the island of Hispaniola: one among them, young and beautiful, who only arrived in the West Indies a short time ago with her husband, appears to be devoured by an incurable grief."

"Indeed! And what can I do to prevent it, father?"

"I know not: still, this is what took place between this lady and myself. The lady, who, as I told you, is young and fair, and whose charity and goodness are inexhaustible, spends the greater part of her days in her oratory, kneeling before a picture representing our Lady of Mercy, imploring her with tears and sobs. Interested, in spite of myself, by this so true and so profound grief, I have on several occasions employed the right which my sacred office gives me, to try and penetrate into this ulcerated heart, and obtain from my penitent a confession, which would permit me to give her some consolation."

"And I presume that you have not succeeded, father?"

"Alas! No, I have not."

"Allow me to repeat to you, that, up to the present I do not see in this very sad story, which is to some extent, however, that of most women, anything very interesting to me."

"Wait, brother, I am coming to that."

"In that case, proceed."

"One day, when this lady appeared to me to be more sad than usual, and I redoubled my efforts to induce her to open her heart to me—doubtless overcome by my solicitations, she said these words to me, which I repeat to you exactly:—'My father, I am an unhappy, cowardly, and infamous creature, and a terrible malediction weighs on me. Only one man has the right to know the secret which I try, in vain, to stifle in my heart. Upon this man depends my salvation. He can condemn or acquit me: but whatever be the sentence he may pronounce, I will bow without a murmur beneath his will, too happy to expiate at this price the crime of which I have been guilty.'"

While the monk was pronouncing these words, the usually pale face of the adventurer had turned livid, a convulsive trembling agitated his limbs, and, in spite of his efforts to appear calm, he was constrained to lean against one of the tent pickets, lest he should fall on the ground.

"Go on!" he said, in a hoarse voice. "Did this woman tell you the man's name?"

"She did, brother. 'Alas!' she said to me, 'Unfortunately the man on whom my destiny depends is the most implacable enemy of our nation. He is one of the principal chiefs of those ferocious adventurers who have vowed a merciless war against Spain. I shall never meet him, except in the horrors of a combat, or during the sack of a town fired by his orders. In a word, the man I am speaking to you about is no other than the terrible Montbarts the Exterminator.'"

"Ah!" the adventurer muttered, in a choking voice, as he pressed his hand forcibly against his chest, "The woman said that?"

"Yes, brother; such are the words she uttered."

"And then?"

"Then, brother, I, a poor monk, promised her to seek you, to find you, no matter where you were, and repeat her words to you. I had only death to fear in trying to see you, and I long ago offered God the sacrifice of my life."

"You have acted like a noble-hearted man, monk; and I thank you for having had confidence in me. Have you nothing to add?"

"Yes, brother, I have. When the lady saw me fully resolved to brave all perils for the sake of finding you, she added, 'Go, then, my father: it is doubtless Heaven that takes pity on me, and inspires you at this moment. If you succeed in reaching Montbarts, tell him that I have a secret to confide to him, on which the happiness of his whole life depends; but that he must make haste, if he wish to learn it, for I feel that my days are numbered, and that I shall soon die.' I promised her to accomplish her wishes faithfully, and I have come."

There was a silence for some minutes. Montbarts walked up and down with hanging head, and arms folded on his chest, stopping every now and then to stamp his foot savagely: then, resuming his hurried walk, while muttering unconnected words in a low voice.

All at once he stopped before the monk, and looked him straight in the face.

"You have not told me all," he said to him.

"Pardon me, brother; everything, word by word."

"Still there is an important detail, which you have doubtless forgotten, as you have passed it over in silence?"

"I do not understand to what you are alluding, brother," the monk replied, gravely.

"You have forgotten to reveal to me the name and position of this woman, father."

"That is true: but it is not forgetfulness on my part. In acting thus, I have obeyed the orders I received. The lady implored me to tell you nothing touching her name or position. She reserves that for herself, when you are alone together: and I swore to keep her secret."

"Ah! Ah! Señor monk," the adventurer exclaimed, with a wrath the more terrible because it was concentrated; "You have taken that oath?"

"Yes, brother, and will keep it at all risks," he answered firmly.

The adventurer burst into a hoarse laugh.

"You are doubtless ignorant," he said, in a hissing voice, "that we *ladrones*, as your countrymen call us, possess marvellous secrets to untie the most rebel tongues, and that you are in my power."

"I am in the hands of God, brother—try it. I am only a poor defenceless man, incapable of resisting you. Torture me, then, if such be your good pleasure; but know that I will die, without revealing my secret."

Montbarts bent a flashing glance on the monk who stood so calm before him; and then, a moment after, struck his forehead angrily.

"I am mad!" he exclaimed: "What do I care for this name—do I not know it already? Listen, father. Forgive me what I said to you, for passion blinded me. You came to this island freely, and shall leave it freely—in my turn I swear it to you; and I am not more accustomed to break any oaths I take—no matter their nature—than you are."

"I know it, brother. I have nothing to forgive you. I see that grief led you astray, and I pity you, for Heaven has chosen me, I feel a presentiment of it, to bring a great misfortune upon you."

"Yes, you speak truly. I did not seek this woman—I tried to forget her, and it is she who voluntarily places herself in my path. It is well, Heaven will judge between her and me. She demands that I will go and see her, and I will do so, but she must only blame herself for the terrible consequences of our interview. Still, I consent to leave her yet one chance of escape. When you return to her, urge her not to try to see me again. You see, that I have a little pity for her in my heart, in spite of all she made me suffer; but if, in spite of your entreaties, she persists in meeting me, in that case her will be done. I will go to the place of meeting she may select."

"I know where it is, brother, and am ordered to point it out to you today."

"Ah," the filibuster said, suspiciously, "she has forgotten nothing. Well, where is it?"

"The lady, you can understand, cannot quit the island, even if she wished to do so."

"That is true. So we are to meet in Hispaniola itself?"

"Yes, brother."

"And what spot has she selected?"

"The great Savannah, that separates Mirebalais from San Juan de Goava."

"Ah! The spot is famously chosen for an ambuscade," the filibuster said, with a sneering laugh, "for if I remember rightly, it is on Spanish territory."

"It forms the extreme limit, brother. Still, I will try to induce the lady to choose another spot, if you are afraid about your safety at this one."

Montbarts shrugged his shoulders with a contemptuous laugh.

"I afraid!" he said. "Nonsense, monk, you must be mad! What do I care for the Spaniards, if five hundred of them were ambushed to surprise me, I should be able to get away from them! It is settled, then, that if the lady persist in her intention of having an explanation with me, I will go to the Savannah, which extends between Mirebalais and San Juan de Goava, at the confluence of the great river and the Artibonite."

"I will do what you desire, brother; but if the lady insist, in spite of my remonstrances and entreaties, on the interview taking place, how am I to warn you?"

"As it is possible for you to come here, you will be the better able; without attracting suspicion, to enter the French part of St. Domingo."

"I will try, at any rate, brother, since it must absolutely be so."

"You will light a large fire on the coast in the vicinity of Port Margot, and I shall know what it means."

"I will obey you, brother: but when am I to light the fire?"

"How long do you propose remaining here?"

"I intend to leave immediately after our interview."

"This evening, then?"

"Yes, brother."

"Ah, ah, then there is a Spanish vessel in the neighbourhood?"

"Probably so, brother; but if you discover it and capture it, how shall I succeed in returning to Hispaniola?"

"That is true; this consideration saves the Gavachos: but believe, after due reflection, I think it my duty to give you some advice."

"Whatever it may be, brother, coming from you, I shall receive it with pleasure."

"Well, then, carry out your intention. Start at once; tomorrow it will not be pleasant for you in these waters, and I would not answer for your safety or that of your vessel. Do you comprehend me?"

"Perfectly, brother; and for the signal?"

"Light it fifteen days from today, and I will arrange so as to arrive at St. Domingo about that time."

"Very good, brother."

"And now, monk, farewell till we meet again, as it is probable we shall do."

"It is probable, indeed, brother. Farewell, and may the merciful Lord be with you!"

"So be it," the filibuster said, with an ironical laugh.

He gave a parting wave of his hand to the monk, threw his fusil on his shoulder, and went off, but a few minutes after stopped and went back.

The Franciscan had remained motionless at the same spot.

"One last word, father," he said.

"Speak, brother," he answered, gently.

"Take my advice, employ all your power over the lady to induce her to give up this meeting, whose consequences may be terrible."

"I will try impossibilities to succeed, brother," the monk replied; "I will pray to Heaven to permit me to persuade my penitent."

"Yes," Montbarts added, in a gloomy voice, "it would be better for her and for me, perhaps, if we never met again."

And roughly turning his back on the monk, he hurried along the track, where he speedily disappeared.

When Fray Arsenio felt certain that this time the adventurer had really gone, he gently raised the curtain of the tent and stepped inside.

A woman was kneeling there on the bare ground, with her head buried in her hands, and praying with stifled sobs.

"Have I punctually accomplished your orders, my daughter?" the monk said.

The woman drew herself up and turned her lovely pale and tear-swollen face toward the monk.

"Yes, padre," she murmured, in a low and trembling voice. "Bless you for not abandoning me in my distress."

"Is this really the man with whom you desire an interview?"

"Yes, it is he, father."

"And you still insist on seeing him?"

She hesitated for a moment, a shudder ran over her whole person, and then she murmured in a hardly intelligible voice—

"I must, father."

"You will reflect between this and then, I hope," he continued.

"No, no," she said, with a sorrowful shake of the head; "if that man were to plunge his dagger into my heart, I must have a final explanation with him."

"Your will be done," he said

At this moment, a slight sound was heard outside.

The monk went out, but returned almost immediately.

"Get ready, madam," he said; "our crew have come to fetch you. Remember the parting advice that *ladrón* gave me, and let us be gone as soon as possible."

Without replying, the lady rose, wrapped herself carefully in her mantilla, and went out.

An hour later, she left Nevis, accompanied by Fray Arsenio Mendoza.

Montbarts had reached St. Kitts long before.

CHAPTER XIX.

THE EXPEDITION.

During the entire passage from Nevis to St. Kitts Montbarts was in a strange state of excitement.

The interview he had held with the monk had rearoused in his heart a profound sorrow which time had deadened but not cauterized, and at the first word that fell in this hour's conversation the wound burst open again, bleeding and livid as on the day of its receipt.

How had this woman, whom he would not name, of whose presence in America he was ignorant, whom, in short, he fancied he had escaped by hiding himself among the filibusters, succeeded in so short a time, not only in learning his presence in the islands, but also in finding him again? For what object did she insist on finding him? What interest could she have in seeing him?

All these questions, which he asked himself in turn, necessarily remained unanswered, and for that very reason augmented his anxiety.

For a moment he thought of laying an ambush in the straits of Nevis and St. Eustache, the two islands between which St. Kitts is situated, capturing the Spanish vessel, and obtaining by torture the information the monk had refused to give him.

But he gave up this plan almost immediately; he had pledged his word of honour, and would not break it for anything in the world.

In the meanwhile, night had set in, and the canoe was still advancing.

Montbarts steered for the lugger, which was anchored a short distance from land.

When the light boat was under the vessel's counter, the filibuster made his engagé a sign to lay on his oars, and shouted in a loud voice—

"Lugger, ahoy!"

At once, a man whose black outline was designed on the dark blue horizon, leant over.

"Boat ahoy!" he shouted.

"Is that you, Bowline?" Montbarts continued.

"All right."

"Is Michael aboard?"

"Yes, admiral."

"Ah, you have recognised me, my lad?"

"Of course," said the Breton.

"I suppose you are watching over my prisoner?"

"I answer for him."

"But do not annoy him unnecessarily."

"All right, admiral, we will be gentle with him."

"Is Omopoua aboard at this moment?"

"Here I am, master," a second voice immediately replied.

"Ah, ah," the filibuster said with satisfaction, "all the better. I want you—come ashore."

"Are you in a hurry, master?"

"A great hurry."

"In that case, wait a moment."

And ere the filibuster could guess the Carib's intention, the noise of a body falling in the water could be heard, and two or three minutes later the Indian rested his hands on the gunwale of the canoe.

"Here I am," he said.

Montbarts could not refrain from smiling on seeing with what promptitude the savage obeyed his orders. He held out his hand, and helped him to get into the boat.

"Why such a hurry?" he said to him in a tone of friendly reproach.

The Indian shook himself like a drowned poodle.

"Nonsense," he said, "I am all right."

"Have you got the Indian?" Bowline asked.

"Yes: now good night; you will see me tomorrow."

"Tomorrow?"

"Pull," the filibuster said to the engagé.

The latter dipped his paddles, and the canoe resumed its course.

Ten minutes later, it ran aground at the very spot where Montbarts had seized it for the purpose of going to Nevis. The three men landed on the beach, pulled up the canoe, and went off in the direction of the hatto.

They passed through the town and a swarm of filibusters, who were celebrating by songs, shouts, and libations their last hours of liberty.

They went on in silence. When the three men reached the hatto, Montbarts lit a candle, and searched the house with the greatest care, to make sure that no stranger was present; then he returned to his two comrades, who were waiting for him in the Esplanade.

"Come in," he merely said to them.

They followed him.

Montbarts sat down in a chair, and then turned to the Carib.

"I have to talk with you, Omopoua," he said.

"Good," the Indian remarked, joyously; "in that case you have need of me."

"If that were true you would be satisfied, then?"

"Yes, I should be."

"For what reason?"

"Because, since I have found a white man who is good and generous, I am anxious to prove to you that all the Caribs are not ferocious and untameable, but know how to be grateful."

"I promised you, I think, to take you back to your country?"

"Yes, you made me that promise."

"Unfortunately, as I am appointed chief of an important expedition, which will probably last some time, it is impossible for me at this moment to take you back to Haiti."

The Indian's face grew dark on hearing this.

"Do not grieve, but listen to me attentively," the filibuster continued, who had noticed the change that took place in the Indian's face.

"I am listening to you."

"What I cannot do you are able to effect by yourself, if I supply you with the means."

"I do not exactly understand what the white Chief means; I am only a poor Indian, with limited ideas. I require to have things explained to me very clearly before I understand them; but it is true, that when I do understand I never forget."

"You are a Carib, hence you know how to manage a canoe?"

"Yes," the Indian answered, with a proud smile.

"Suppose I gave you a canoe, do you believe that you could fetch Haiti?"

"The great land is very far away," he said, in a sorrowful voice, "the voyage very long for a single man, however brave he may be."

"Agreed; but suppose I placed in the canoe not only provisions, but cutlasses, axes, daggers, and four fusils, with powder and ball?"

"The pale Chief would do that!" he said, with an incredulous air. "Thus armed, who could resist Omopoua?"

"Suppose I did more?" the adventurer continued, with a smile.

"The Chief is jesting; he is very gay. He says to himself, the Indians are credulous; I will have a laugh at the expense of Omopoua."

"I am not jesting, Chief—on the contrary, I am very serious; I will give you the things I have enumerated to you, and, in order that you may reach your country in safety, I will lend you a comrade, a brave man, who will be your brother, and defend you as you would defend yourself."

"And that companion?"

"Is here," said Montbarts, pointing to his engagé, who was standing calm and motionless by his side.

"Then I am not to make the expedition with you, Montbarts?" the latter said, in a sad voice, and with a reproachful accent.

"Reassure yourself," said Montbarts, tapping him gently on the shoulder; "the mission I send you on is most confidential, and even more perilous than the expedition I am undertaking. I wanted a devoted man—another self—and I have chosen you."

"You have done well, in that case; I will prove to you that you are not mistaken about me."

"I am convinced of that already, my lad. Do you accept this companion, Omopoua? He will help you to pass without being insulted through the filibusters you may meet on your route."

"Good! The pale Chief really loves Omopoua. What is the Indian to do on arriving in his country?"

"Omopoua's brothers have sought shelter, I think, in the neighbourhood of the Artibonite?"

"Yes, in the great savannahs to which the French have given the name of Mirebalais."

"Good! Omopoua will go and join his friends; he will tell them in what way the filibusters treat the Caribs: he will present his companion to them, and wait."

"I will wait: the pale Chief, then, is coming to Haiti?"

"Probably," said Montbarts, with a smile of indefinable meaning; "and the proof is, that my engagé will remain with your tribe till my arrival."

"Good! I will await the coming of the pale Chief. When am I start?"

"This very night. Go down to the beach; go in my name to the owner of the canoe which brought us ashore—here is money," and he gave him several piastres; "tell him that I buy his boat exactly as it stands. You will lay in provisions at the same time, and then wait for your comrade, to whom I have a few words to say—but he will rejoin you soon."

"I will go, then; gratitude is in my heart, and not on my lips. On the day when you ask for my life I will give it you, because it is yours, as well as that of all those who love me. Farewell!"

And he made a movement to leave the room.

"Where are you going?" Montbarts asked him.

"I am off; did you not give me leave to go?"

"Yes, but you are forgetting something."

"What is it?"

"The arms I promised you. Take from the rack a fusil for yourself, and four others, which you can dispose of as you please, six cutlasses, six daggers, and six hatchets; when you leave port, on passing the lugger, you will ask Michael the Basque, in my name, for two barrels of gunpowder and two bags of bullets—he will give them to you. Now go, and I wish you all good fortune."

The Carib, overcome by this generosity, so simple and so full of grandeur, knelt to the adventurer, and seizing his feet, which he placed on his head, he exclaimed, in a deeply affected voice—

"I pay you homage as to the best of men. I and mine are henceforth and eternally your devoted slaves." He got up, placed on his shoulder the arms which the engagé handed him, and quitted the hatto.

For some minutes his footsteps could be heard resounding on the path; but this sound gradually died away, and a complete silence returned.

"Now for us two, Olonnais!" Montbarts then said, addressing the engagé.

The latter drew nearer.

"I am listening, master," he said.

"I saw you today for the first time, and yet you pleased me at the very first glance," the adventurer continued. "I fancy myself a tolerable physiognomist. Your frank and open face, your bold-looking eyes, and the expression of audacity and intelligence spread over your features, disposed me in your favour. That is the reason why I bought you. I trust that I am not deceived about you; but I wish to make trial of you. You know that I am at liberty to shorten your engagement, or even, if I like, restore you your freedom tomorrow, so think of that, and act accordingly."

"Whether engaged or free I shall always be devoted to you, Montbarts," the Olonnais said, "hence do not speak to me of recompense, for it is useless with me: make your trial, and I hope to emerge from it with honour."

"That is speaking like a man and a frank adventurer: listen to me, then, and do not let a word of what you are about to hear escape your lips."

"I shall be dumb."

"In ten days at the most I shall anchor in Port Margot in St. Domingo; the expedition I command is intended to take Tortoise Isle by surprise; but while we are occupied on our side in surprising the Spaniards, they must not be able to attack us in the rear, and ruin our establishments at Grande Terre."

"I understand; Omopoua's Caribs are scattered along the Spanish frontier, and must be converted into allies of the expedition."

"The very thing—you have understood me perfectly. Such is your missive; but you must act with extreme cleverness and considerable prudence, in order not to give the alarm to the Gavachos on one hand, or arouse the suspicious of the Caribs on the other; the Indians are susceptible and mistrustful, especially with white men, against whom they have so many causes of complaint. The part you have to play is rather difficult, but I think you will succeed—thanks to the influence of Omopoua; besides, two days after my arrival at Port Margot, I will proceed to the savannahs of the Artibonite, in order to have an understanding, and to make the arrangements I may consider necessary. You see that I act toward you with perfect frankness, and rather as with a brother than an engagé."

"I thank you for it; you shall have no cause to repent it."

"I am glad to believe it—ah! A final recommendation, of secondary importance, but, for all that, serious."

"What is it?"

"The Spaniards frequently hunt, or make excursions in the savannahs of the Artibonite; watch them, though without letting them perceive you; let them not have the slightest suspicion of what we are meditating against them, for the least imprudence might have excessively grave consequences for the success of our plans."

"I will act with prudence, be assured."

"Now, my lad, I have only to wish you a pleasant trip, and successful result."

"Will you allow me, in my turn, to ask you a question before departing?"

"Speak, I allow it."

"For what reason have you, who possess so many brave and devoted friends, instead of applying to one of them, chosen an obscure engagé, whom you hardly know, to confide to him so difficult and so confidential a mission?"

"Are you anxious to know?" the adventurer asked, laughingly.

"Yes, if you do not consider the question indiscreet."

"Not the least in the world, and you shall be satisfied in a couple of words. Apart from the good opinion I have of you, and which is only personal, I have chosen you, because you are only a poor engagé, who arrived from France but two days ago—no one knows you, or is aware that I have purchased you: for this reason no one will dream of suspecting you, and consequently you will be a more valuable agent to me, as no one will imagine that you are my plenipotentiary, and acting under my orders. Now do you understand, my lad?"

"Perfectly, and I thank you for the explanation you have given me. Good-bye; within an hour the Carib and I will have left St. Kitts."

"Allow him to guide you during the voyage, that man is very clever, though an Indian, and he will conduct you so that you will both reach port in safety."

"I shall not fail to do so; besides, the deference I shall show him will dispose him in my favour, and further advance the success of our projects."

"Come, come," the adventurer said, with a laugh, "I see that you are a sharp lad, and I now have good hopes of the issue of your mission."

The Olonnais armed himself as the Carib had done, then took leave of his master, and went away.

"Come," Montbarts muttered, when he was alone, "I believe that my plans are beginning to assume consistency, and that I shall soon be able to deal a grand stroke."

The next morning at sunrise an unusual agitation prevailed in the township, which, however, was never very tranquil.

The filibusters, armed to the teeth, were taking leave of their friends, and preparing to proceed on board the vessels for which they had enlisted on the previous day.

The roads were cut up in all directions by a prodigious number of canoes which passed to and fro, carrying men and provisions to the departing ships.

The Chevalier de Fontenay, surrounded by a numerous staff of renowned filibusters, and having at his side Montbarts, David Drake, and Michael the Basque, was standing at the end of the wooden mole that served as a landing place, and witnessing thence the departure of the adventurers.

These men with bronzed complexion, energetic and ferocious features, and vigorous limbs, scarce clad in canvas drawers and old hats or caps, but armed with long fusils, manufactured at Dieppe expressly for them, having a heavy sharpened cutlass hanging from their belt, and carrying their stock of powder and bullets, had a strange and singularly formidable appearance, rendered even more striking by the expression of carelessness and indomitable audacity spread over their faces.

On seeing them it was easy to understand the terror with which they must inspire the Spaniards, and the incredible exploits they achieved almost as if in play, reckoning their lives as nothing, and only seeing the object, that is to say, plunder.

As they defiled before the governor and the officers elected to command them, they saluted them respectfully, because discipline demanded it, but the salute had nothing low or servile about it, it was that of men fully conscious of their value, and aware that though sailors today, they might, as they liked, be captains tomorrow.

Towards midday the crews were complete, and only the Admiral and three captains were still ashore.

"Gentlemen," Montbarts said to his officers, "so soon as we are out to sea, each of you will sail as you like; we have but a small stock of provisions on board, but the islands we pass will supply us, do not hesitate to pillage the corales of the Gavachos, for that will be so much taken from the enemy. Hence it is settled that we will each proceed separately to the general meeting place, for prudence urges us not to let the enemy suspect our strength; our meeting place is the northern island of the Grand Key; the first to arrive will await the two others, there I will give you my final instructions about the object of the expedition, of which you already know a part."

"So then," said M. de Fontenay, "you insist on keeping your secret?"

"If you absolutely demand, sir," Montbart replied, "I will—"

"No, no," he interrupted him with a laugh; "keep it, for I do not know what to do with it; besides, I have pretty nearly guessed your secret."

"Ah," Montbarts said with an air of incredulity.

"Confound it, I am greatly mistaken or you mean to make some attempt on St. Domingo."

The adventurer only answered by a crafty smile, and took leave of the governor, who rubbed his hands joyously, for he was persuaded that he had guessed the secret which it was attempted to conceal from him. An hour later the three vessels raised their anchors, set sail, and went off after giving a parting salute to the land, which was immediately answered by the battery at the point.

They soon became confounded with the white mist on the horizon, and ere long disappeared.

"Well," M. de Fontenay said to his officers as he returned to the government house, "you will see that I am not mistaken, and that this demon of a Montbarts really has a design on St. Domingo. Lord help the Spaniards!"

CHAPTER XX.

THE HATTO.

We will leave the filibustering flotilla steering through the inextricable labyrinth of the Antilles, and transport ourselves to St. Domingo, as the French call it, Hispaniola as Columbus christened it, or Haiti as the Caribs, its first and only true owners, called it.

And when we speak of the Caribs, we mean the black as well as the red, for it is a singular fact, of which many persons are ignorant, that some Caribs were black, and so thoroughly resembled the African race, that when the French planters settled at St. Vincent, and brought with them Negro slaves, the black Caribs, indignant at resembling men degraded by slavery, and fearful too lest at a later date their color might serve as a pretext to make them endure the same fate, fled into the wildest recesses of the forest, and in order to create a visible distinction between their race and the slaves brought to the island, they compressed the foreheads of their new born infants, so that they became completely flattened, which in the ensuing generation produced, as it were, a new race, and afterwards became the symbol of their independence.

Before resuming our narrative, we ask the reader's permission to indulge in a little geography: as many of the incidents of the history of filibustering will take place at St. Domingo; it is indispensable that this island should be well known.

St. Domingo, discovered on December 6, 1492, by Christopher Columbus, is, by the general verdict, the most lovely of all the Antilles. From the centre of the island rises a group of mountains, springing one from the other, from which issue three chains, running in three different directions. The longest stretches to the west, and passes through the middle of the island, dividing it into two nearly equal parts. The second chain runs north, and ends at Cape Fou. The third, less extensive than the preceding, at first follows the same direction, but ere long taking a curve to the south, terminates in Cape St. Mark.

In the interior of the island there are several other mountain ranges, though much less considerable. The result of this multiplicity of mountains is that communication, especially at the time when our story is laid, was excessively difficult between the north and south of the isle.

At the foot of all these mountains are immense plains covered with a luxurious vegetation; the mountains are intersected by ravines, which keep up a constant and beneficent humidity; they contain different metals, in addition to rock crystal, coal, sulphur, and quarries of porphyry, slate and marble, and are covered with forests of bananas, palms and mimosas of every species.

Although the rivers are numerous, the largest are unfortunately scarcely navigable, and cannot be ascended by canoes for more than a few leagues; the principal ones are the Neyva, the Macoris, the Usaque, or river of

Montecristo, the Ozama, the Juna and the Artibonite, the most extensive of all.

Seen from the offing, the appearances of this island is enchanting; it resembles an immense bouquet of flowers rising from the bosom of the sea.

We are not going to write the history of the colony of St. Domingo, but will merely say that this island so rich and fertile had, through the carelessness, cruelty and avarice of the Spaniards, fallen, one hundred and fifty years after its discovery, into such a state of wretchedness and misery, that the Spanish Government was compelled to send to this colony, which became not only unproductive but burdensome, funds to pay the troops and officials.

While St. Domingo was thus slowly decaying, new colonists, brought by accident, established themselves on the north west of the island, and took possession of it, in spite of the resistance and opposition of the Spaniards.

These new colonists were French adventurers, most of them expelled from St. Christopher on the descent of Admiral de Toledo on that colony, and who were wandering about the Antilles in search of a refuge.

At the period of the discovery, the first Spaniards had left on the island some forty head of cattle; these animals, restored to liberty, rapidly multiplied and traversed the savannahs of the interior in immense herds; the French adventurers, on their arrival, did not dream of cultivating the soil, but, seduced by the attractions of a perilous chase, they occupied themselves exclusively in pursuing the bulls and the wild boars, which were also very numerous and extremely formidable.

The sole occupation of these adventurers then was the chase; they preserved the hides of cattle and dried the meat by smoke in the Indian fashion. Hence comes the name of buccaneers, for the Caribs gave the name of *boucans* to the spot where they smoked the flesh of the prisoners taken in war, and whom they ate after fattening them.

We shall soon have occasion to return to this subject and enter into fuller details about these singular men.

Still, in spite of their love of independence, these adventurers had understood the necessity of creating outlets for the sale of their hides. Hence they established several counters at Port Margot and Port de la Paix, which they regarded as the capital of their establishments; but their position was most precarious owing to the proximity of the Spaniards, who had hitherto been sole masters of the island, and would not consent to have them as such near neighbours; hence they constantly waged a savage war, which was the more cruel because quarter was not granted on either side.

Such was the situation of St. Domingo at the time when we resume our narrative, about a fortnight after the departure of the filibustering fleet from St. Kitts under the command of Montbarts the Exterminator.

The sun, already low on the horizon, was enormously lengthening the shadows of the trees, the evening breeze was rising, gently agitating the leaves and tall grass, when a man mounted on a powerful horse, and wearing the costume of the Spanish Campesinos, followed a scarce traced path which wound through the centre of a vast plain covered with magnificent plantations of sugar cane and coffee, and led to an elegant hatto, whose pretty mirador commanded the country for a long distance.

This man appeared to be five and twenty years of age at the most; his features were handsome, but imprinted with an expression of insupportable pride and disdain; his very simple dress was only relieved by a long rapier, whose hilt of carved silver hung on his left hip and showed him to be a gentleman, as the nobility alone had the right to wear a sword.

Four black slaves, half naked, and whose bodies glistened with perspiration, ran behind his horse, one carrying a richly damascened fusil, the second a game bag, and the two others a dead boar, whose tied feet were resting on a bamboo supported by the shoulders of the poor fellows.

But the rider seemed to trouble himself but little about his companions, or rather his slaves, toward whom he did not deign to turn his head, even when speaking to them, which he did sometimes to ask them for directions in a harsh and contemptuous voice.

He held in his band an embroidered handkerchief, with which he wiped away every moment the perspiration that inundated his forehead, and looked savagely around him, while urging his horse with the spur, to the great sorrow of the slaves who were forced to double their efforts to follow him.

"Well," he at length asked in an ill-tempered tone, "shall we never arrive at this accursed hatto?"

"In half an hour at the furthest, *mi amo*," a Negro answered respectfully, "there is the mirador over there."

"What a deuce of a notion it was of my sister, to come and bury herself in this frightful hole instead of remaining quietly at her palace in St. Domingo. Women are mad, on my honour," he grumbled between his teeth.

And he spiced this most ungallant observation by furiously digging the spurs into his horse, which started at a gallop.

Still, he was rapidly approaching the hatto, all the details of which it was already easy to distinguish.

It was a pretty and rather large mansion with a terraced roof, surmounted by a mirador and with a peristyle in front formed by four columns supporting a verandah.

A thick hedge surrounded the house, which could only be reached by crossing a large garden; behind were the corrals to shut in the beasts, and the cottages of the Negroes, miserable, low and half ruined huts, built of clumsily intertwined branches and covered with palm leaves.

This hatto, tranquil and solitary, in the midst of this plain of luxuriant vegetation, and half concealed by the trees that formed a screen of foliage, had a really enchanting aspect, which, however, did not seem to produce on the traveller's mind any other effect but that of profound weariness and lively annoyance.

The arrival of the stranger had doubtless been signalled by the sentry stationed on the mirador to watch the surrounding country, for a horseman emerged at a gallop from the hatto, and came toward the small party composed of the gentleman we have described and the four slaves who still ran behind him, displaying their white, sharp teeth, and blowing like grampuses.

The newcomer was a man of short stature, but his wide shoulders and solid limbs denoted far from common muscular strength, he was about forty years of age, his features were harsh and marked, and the expression of his countenance was sombre and crafty. A broad-brimmed straw hat nearly concealed his face, a cloak called a poncho, made of one piece, and with a hole in the middle to pass his head through, covered his shoulders; the hilt of a long knife peeped out of his right boot, a sabre hung on his left side, and a long fusil was lying across the front of his saddle. When he arrived within a few paces of the gentleman, he stopped his horse short on its hind legs, uncovered, and bowed respectfully.

"*Santas tardes*, Señor Don Sancho," he said in an obsequious voice.

"Ah, ah! It is you, Birbomono," the young man said, as he carelessly touched his hat; "what the deuce are you doing here? I fancied you were hung long ago."

"Your Excellency is jesting," the other replied, with an ill-tempered grimace, "I am the Señora's Major-domo."

"I compliment her on it, and you, too."

"The Señora was very anxious about your Excellency, and I was preparing, by her orders, to make a battue in the neighbourhood. She will be delighted to see you arrive without misadventure."

"What misadventure?" the young man said, as he loosened his rein; "What do you mean, scamp? And what had I to fear on the roads?"

"Your Excellency cannot be ignorant that the ladrones infest the savannahs."

The young man burst into a laugh.

"The ladrones! What a pleasant story you are telling me, too; come, run and announce my arrival to my sister, without further chattering."

The Major-domo did not let the order be repeated, but bowed, and set off at a gallop.

Ten minutes later, Don Sancho dismounted in front of the peristyle of the hatto, where a young lady of rare beauty, but cadaverous pallor, and who appeared hardly able to keep up, as she was so weak and ill, was awaiting his arrival.

This lady was the sister of Señor Don Sancho, and the owner of the hatto.

The two young people embraced each other for a long while without exchanging a word, and then Don Sancho offered his arm to his sister, and entered the house with her, leaving the Major-domo to look after his horse and baggage.

The young gentleman led his sister to an easy chair, fetched one for himself, rolled it up to her side, and sat down.

"At last," she said a moment later, in an affectionate voice, as she took one of the young man's hands in her own, "I see you again, brother; you are here, near me—how glad I am to see you."

"My dear Clara," Don Sancho replied, as he kissed her forehead, "we have been separated for nearly a year."

"Alas!" she murmured.

"And during that year many things have doubtless happened, of which you will inform me?"

"Alas! My life during this year may be summed up in two words—I have suffered."

"Poor sister, how changed you are in so little time, I could hardly recognize you; I came to St. Domingo with such joy, and no sooner had I landed than I went to your palace; your husband, who has not altered, and whom I found as heavy and silent as usual, with an increased dose of importance, doubtless the result of his high position, told me that you were not very well, and that the physicians had ordered you country air."

"It is true," she said, with a sad smile.

"Yes; but I fancied you merely indisposed, and I find you dying."

"Let us not talk of that, Sancho, I implore you; what matter if I am ill? Did you receive my letter?"

"Had I not, should I be here? Two hours after its receipt I set out; for three days," he continued with a smile, "I have been going uphill and down dale, along frightful roads, to reach you the sooner."

"Thanks, oh thanks, Sancho; your presence renders me very happy—you will remain for a while with me, will you not?"

"As long as you like, dear sister, for I am a free man."

"Free!" she repeated, looking at him with an air of amazement.

"Well, yes; his Excellency, the Duc de Peñaflor, my illustrious father and yours, the Viceroy of New Spain, has deigned to grant me an unlimited leave."

At her father's name a slight shudder ran over the young lady's person, and her eyes became dimmed with tears.

"Ah," she said, "my father is well?"

"Better than ever."

"And has he spoken about me?"

The young man bit his lips.

"He spoke to me about you very little," he said; "but I in revenge, said a good deal about you, which re-established the balance: I even believe that he granted me the leave I asked in great measure to free himself from my chattering."

Doña Clara hung her head without replying, and her brother fixed upon her a glance full of tender pity.

"Let us talk about yourself," he said.

"No, no, Sancho; we had better talk about *him*." she replied hesitatingly.

"Of *him!*" he said in a hollow voice, and with a groan; "Alas, poor sister, what can I tell you? All my efforts have been vain; I have discovered nothing."

"Yes, yes;" she murmured, "his measures were well taken to make him disappear. Oh, Heaven! Heaven!" she exclaimed, clasping her hands wildly, "Will you not take pity on me?"

"Calm yourself, I implore you, sister; I will see, I will seek—I will redouble my efforts, and perhaps I shall at length succeed—"

"No," she interrupted him, "never, never shall we be able to effect anything; he is condemned, condemned by my father; that implacable man will never restore him to me! Oh! I know my father better than you do; you are a man, Sancho, you can try to struggle against him, but he has crushed me, crushed me at a single blow; he broke my heart by a deadly pressure in making me the innocent accomplice of an infernal vengeance! Then he coldly reproached me with a dishonour which is his work, and at the same blow eternally destroyed the happiness of three beings who would have loved him, and whose future he held in his hands."

"And you, my dear Clara, do you know nothing—have you discovered nothing?"

"Yes," she replied, looking at him fixedly, "I have made a horrible discovery."

"You terrify me, Clara; what do you mean? Explain yourself."

"Not at present, my dear Sancho, not at present, for the time has not arrived; so be patient. You know that I never had any secrets from you, for you alone have always loved me. I wrote to you to come that I might reveal this secret to you: in three days at the latest you shall know all, and then—"

"Then?" he said, looking at her intently.

"Then you shall measure, as I do, the immense depth of the gulf into which I have fallen; but enough of this subject for the present, I am suffering terribly, so let us talk of something else."

"Most willingly, my dear Clara; but what shall we talk about?"

"Well, whatever you like, dear, the rain, the fine weather, your journey, or anything of that sort."

Don Sancho understood that his sister was suffering from extreme nervous excitement, and that he would aggravate her already very serious condition by not acceding to her wishes; hence he made no objection, but readily yielded to her caprice.

"Well then," he said, "my dear Clara, since that is the case, I will take advantage of the opportunity to ask you to give me some information."

"What is it brother? I live in great seclusion as you see, and doubt whether I can satisfy you, but speak all the same."

"You know, little sister, that I am a stranger in Hispaniola, where I only arrived four days ago, and then for the first time."

"That is true; you have never visited the island; what do you think of it?"

"It is frightful, that is to say admirable; frightful as regards roads, and admirable for scenery: you see that my proposition is not so illogical as it at first appeared."

"In truth the roads are not convenient."

"Say that there are none, and you will tell the truth.";

"You are severe."

"No, I am only just; if you had seen what magnificent roads we possess in Mexico, you would be of my opinion; but that is not the point at present."

"What is it then?"

"Why, the information I want of you."

"Ah, that is true, I forgot it; but explain yourself, I am listening."

"This is it. Just imagine when I embarked at Veracruz to come here, all the persons to whom I announced my departure invariably answered me with a desperate agreement:—'Ah! you are going to Hispaniola, Señor Don Sancho de Peñaflor, hum, hum, take care.' On board the vessel I constantly heard the officers muttering among themselves 'keep a good watch, take care.' At last I reached St. Domingo; my first care was, as I told you, to go to the Count de Bejar, your husband, who received me as kindly as he is capable of doing; but when I announced my intention of coming to join you here, he frowned, and his first words were 'the deuce, Don Sancho, you want to go to the hatto, take care, take care.' It was enough to drive me mad; this sinister warning which everywhere and at all hours echoed in my ears infuriated me. I did not try to obtain any explanation from your husband, as I should not have succeeded; but I inwardly resolved to get to the bottom of this ill-omened phrase so soon as the opportunity presented itself. It did present itself soon, but I am no further advanced than I was before, and hence apply to you to solve the riddle."

"But I am waiting for your explanation, for I confess that up to the present I have not understood a word you have been saying."

"Very good, let me finish. I had scarce set out with the slaves your husband lent me, when I saw the scamps constantly turn their heads to the right and left, with a look of terror. At first I attached no great importance to this; but they ran away on seeing a magnificent wild boar. I felt a fancy to shoot it, which I did by the way, and have brought it here. When these unlucky

Negroes saw me cock my fusil they fell at my knees, clasping their hands with terror, and exclaiming in a most lamentable voice,—'Take care, Excellency, take care!' 'What must I take care of, you scoundrels?' I exclaimed in exasperation. 'The *ladrones*, Excellency, the *ladrones*!' I could obtain no other explanation from them but this; but I hope, little sister, that you will be kind enough to tell me who these formidable ladrones are."

He bent over her; but Doña Clara, with her eyes widely dilated, her arms stretched out and her features distorted, fixed upon him such an extraordinary look, that he recoiled in horror.

"The ladrones, the ladrones!" she twice repeated in a shrill voice; "Oh! have pity, brother."

She rose to her full height, advanced a few paces mechanically, and fell fainting on the floor.

"What is the meaning of this?" the young man asked himself, as he rushed forward to raise her.

CHAPTER XXI.

THE MAJOR-DOMO'S STORY.

Don Sancho, feeling very anxious about the state in which he saw his sister, hastily summoned her women who at once flocked around her. He confided her to their care, and retired to the apartment prepared for him, while ordering that he should be immediately warned so soon as Doña Clara displayed any signs of recovery.

Don Sancho de Peñaflor was a charming cavalier, gay, merry, enjoying life and repulsing with the egotism of his age and rank, every grief and even every annoyance.

Belonging to one of the first families of the Spanish aristocracy, destined to be one day immensely rich, and through his name to hold the highest offices and make one of those magnificent marriages of convenience, which render diplomatists so happy, by leaving their minds perfectly free for grand political combinations,—he strove, as far as lay in his power, to check the beating of his heart, and not to trouble by any unusual passion, the bright serenity of his existence. Captain in the army, while awaiting something better, and to have the air of doing something, he had followed his father as aide-de-camp to Mexico, when the latter was appointed viceroy of New Spain. But, being yet too young to regard life seriously and be ambitious, he had turned his attention to gambling and flirtations since his arrival in America, which greatly annoyed the Duke, for as the latter had passed the age of love, he had no mercy for young men sacrificing to the idol which he had himself worshipped for so long.

Don Sancho was generally an excellent hearted fellow and good companion, but affected, like all the Spaniards of that period, and perhaps of the present, by caste prejudices, regarding the Negroes and Indians as beasts of burden, created for his use, and disdaining to conceal the contempt and disgust he felt for these disinherited races.

In a word, Don Sancho, in accordance with the precept of his family, always looked above him and never below; he endured his equals, but established an impassable barrier of pride and disdain between himself and his inferiors.

Still, perhaps unconsciously,—for we will not give him the merit of it,—a tender feeling had glided into the cold atmosphere in which he was condemned to live, had penetrated to his heart, and at times threatened to overthrow all his transcendental theories about egotism.

This feeling was nothing else than the affection he felt for his sister,—an affection which might pass for adoration, for it was so truly devoted, respectful and disinterested; to please his sister he would have attempted impossibilities; a simple word that fell from her lips rendered him pliant and obedient as a slave; a desire she manifested became at once an order for him as serious, and perhaps more so, than if it had emanated from the King of Spain and the Indies, although that magnificent potentate haughtily flattered himself that the sun never set on his dominions.

The first words the Count uttered so soon as he found himself alone in his apartment, will show his character better than anything we can add.

"Well," he exclaimed as he sank despairingly into an easy chair, "instead of passing a few days agreeably here as I expected, I shall be obliged to listen to Clara's complaints and console her; the deuce take unhappy people, it really seems as if they had made agreement to trouble my tranquillity."

At the expiration of about three-quarters of an hour, a black slave came to inform him that Doña Clara had regained her senses, but still felt so weak and faint, that she begged him to refrain from seeing her that evening.

The young man was in his heart well pleased at the liberty granted him by his sister, and which dispensed him from recurring to a conversation which possessed no charm for him.

"Very good," he said to the slave, "give my respects to my sister, and order my supper to be served here; you will at the same time request the Major-domo to come to me as I want to speak to him. Begone!"

The slave went out and left him alone.

The young Count then threw himself back in his chair, stretched out his legs and plunged, not into any reverie, but into that state of somnolency which is neither waking or sleeping, during which the mind seems to wander in unknown regions, and which the Spaniards call a siesta.

While he was in this state, the slaves laid the table, being careful not to disturb him, and covered it with exquisite dishes.

But soon the steam of the dishes placed before him recalled the young man to the reality, he drew himself up and seated himself at the table.

"Why has not the Major-domo come," he asked, "have you neglected to tell him?"

"Pardon, Excellency, but the Major-domo is absent at this moment," a slave respectfully answered.

"Absent—for what motive?"

"He is paying his usual evening visit to the grounds, but will soon return; if your Excellency will be good enough to have a little patience, you will soon see him."

"Very good, although I do not understand the urgency of this visit. There are no wild beasts here, I suppose?"

"No, Excellency, thank heaven!"

"Then, what is the meaning of these precautions?"

"They are meant to guard the house from the attacks of the ladrones, Excellency."

"The ladrones again," he exclaimed, bounding from his seat, "why, it must be a wager! Everybody seems to have agreed to mystify me, heaven forgive me."

At this moment spurs could be heard clattering outside the room.

"Here is the Major-domo, Excellency," one of the Negroes said.

"That is lucky, let him come in."

Birbomono appeared, took off his hat, bowed respectfully to the Count, and waited to be addressed.

"Confound it," the young man said to him, "I asked for you an hour or more ago."

"I am in despair at it, Excellency, but I was only told of it this very instant."

"I know, I know. Have you dined?"

"Not yet, Excellency."

"Well then, seat yourself there, opposite to me."

The Major-domo who knew the Count's haughty character, hesitated; he did not at all understand the condescension on his part.

"Sit down, I say," the young man replied; "we are in the country, so it is of no consequence; besides, I want to talk with you."

The Major-domo then took the place pointed out to him, without further pressing.

The meal was short—for the Count ate without uttering a single word; when it was ended, he thrust away his plate, drank a glass of water after the Spanish fashion, lit an excellent cigar and gave another to the Major-domo.

"Smoke, I permit it," he said.

Birbomono gratefully accepted; but feeling more and more astonished, he could not refrain from asking himself mentally, what important motive his young master could have for treating him so condescendingly. When the table was cleared and the slaves had withdrawn, the two men remained alone. The night was magnificent and the atmosphere marvellously clear; a multitude of stars floated in æther, a sweet warm breeze penetrated through the windows, left expressly open, a profound silence lay over the landscape, and from the spot where the two men were seated, they perceived the dark mass of forest trees that closed the horizon.

"Now," said the Count, as he puffed out a cloud of bluish smoke, "let us talk."

"Very good, Excellency," the Major-domo replied.

"I have several things to ask you, Birbomono; you know me, I think, and that whether I threaten or promise, I always carry out what I say?"

"I am aware of it, Excellency!"

"Very good, that being settled, I will come to the fact without further preamble. I have certain very important information to ask of you; answering my questions is not betraying your mistress, who is my sister, and whom I love before all else; on the contrary, it is perhaps rendering her a service indirectly. Besides, if you refused to tell me what I want to know, I should learn it from another quarter, and you would forfeit any advantage to be derived from your frankness; you understand me, I suppose?"

"Perfectly, Excellency."

"Well then, what do you intend doing."

"My lord, I am devoted body and soul to your family, hence, I shall consider it a duty to answer, as best I can, all the questions you may deign to ask me, for I feel convinced that in questioning me, you have no other motive but that of being agreeable to my mistress."

"It is impossible to argue more correctly, Birbomono, I have always said that you were an intelligent man; and this answer proves to me that I was not mistaken. Now, I will begin, but let us proceed regularly, so inform me of what occurred between my sister and her husband, up to her arrival here; and the motives for her quitting St. Domingo."

"You know, Excellency, my lord Count de Bejar of Sousa, the husband of your lady sister and my master, is a gentleman not naturally given to speaking, but kind and sincerely attached to his wife, whose every wish he strives to satisfy, without even venturing a remark. At St. Domingo the Countess lived in the most absolute retirement, constantly shut up in her remotest apartments, to which only her women, her confessor and her physician had access. The Count visited her every morning and evening, remained about a quarter of an hour with her, conversing on indifferent subjects, and then withdrew."

"Hum! This mode of life of my dear sister appears to me rather monotonous; did it last long?"

"For several months, Excellency, and it would doubtless still be going on, had it not been for an event which no one but myself knows, and which induced her to come here."

"Ah, ah, and what was the event, if you please?"

"I will tell you, Excellency; one day a ship of our nation arrived at St. Domingo; during its passage through the islands, it had been attacked by the ladrones, from whom it had escaped by a miracle, capturing several of them."

"Ah! I must stop you here," the Count exclaimed suddenly sitting up; "before going further, one word about these ladrones, of whom persons are incessantly talking, and no one knows. Do you know what they are?"

"Certainly I do, Excellency."

"At last," the Count added joyously, "I have at length found what I wanted. As you know, I suppose you will tell me?"

"Most willingly, Excellency."

"Go on."

"Oh! It will not be long, Excellency."

"All the worse."

"But I believe that it will be interesting."

"All the better then, make haste."

"These ladrones are English and French adventurers, whose courage exceeds all belief; lying in ambush among the rocks in the straits through which our vessels must pass, for they have vowed a war of extermination against our nation, they dart out in wretched canoes half full of water, leap on board the ship they have surprised, capture it and carry it off. The injury done our marine by these ladrones is immense; any ship attacked by them, with but few exceptions, may be regarded as lost."

"Confusion! That is very serious; has nothing been done to clear the seas from these daring pirates?"

"Pardon me, Excellency; Don Fernando de Toledo, admiral of the fleet, sacked, by the king's orders, the island of St. Christopher, the refuge of the ladrones, carried off all he could seize, and did not leave one stone on the other in the colony they had founded."

"Ah, ah!" said the Count, rubbing his hands, "That was well done, it appears to me."

"No, Excellency, and for this reason. These ladrones, scattered but not destroyed, spread over the other islands; some of them, it is true, returned to St. Christopher, but the greater part of them had the audacity to seek a refuge in Hispaniola itself."

"Yes, but they have been expelled, I hope."

"It has been tried, at any rate, Excellency, but without success; since that period they have managed to maintain themselves in the part of the island they invaded, and have resisted all the forces sent against them. Instead of being assailed they have become assailants, and pushed on to the Spanish frontier, burning, plundering and sacking everything they met on their passage; they did this the more easily, because they inspire our soldiers with extreme terror, who as soon as they see them or even hear them, take to flight without looking behind them. This has reached such a pitch, Excellency, that the Count de Bejar, our governor, has been compelled to take their fusils from the detachments called the Fifties, ordered to protect the frontiers, and arm them with lances."

"What! Take away their fusils! And for what motive? Great heaven! this seems to me almost too incredible."

"Still, it can be easy understood, Excellency—the soldiers feel so great a terror of the ladrones, that when they found themselves in regions frequented by them, and were consequently afraid of meeting them, they discharged their fusils, expressly to warn them of their presence, and thus invite them to retire, which the ladrones never failed to do; and knowing in this way the position of the soldiers, they went off to plunder in another direction, certain of not being disturbed."

"It is almost incredible. Do you fear their visit here?"

"They have not yet come on this side; still, it is as well to be on one's guard."

"I believe so—that is excessively prudent, and I approve of it; but now let us return to the story you were telling me when I interrupted you to give me this valuable information; you were saying that a Spanish man-o'-war had arrived at Saint Domingo, having on board several ladrones as prisoners."

"Yes, Excellency. Now, you must know that the ladrones are hung so soon as they are caught."

"That measure is very wise."

"These were reserved to make an example of on the island itself, and terrify their accomplices; they were, therefore, landed, and placed in Capilla, while awaiting their execution. It was Fray Arsenio who undertook to reconcile the wretches with Heaven if it were possible."

"A rude task; but who is Fray Arsenio?"

"The confessor of my lady Countess."

"Very good; proceed."

"Just imagine, Excellency, that these ladrones are very pious men; they never attack a vessel without offering up prayers to Heaven, and sing the Magnificat and other church hymns while boarding; hence Fray Arsenio had no difficulty in making them perform their religious duties. The Governor had decided that, in order that the example should benefit the rest, these ladrones should be hung on the Spanish frontier; they were, therefore, taken out of prison, securely bound, and traversed the town in carts, guarded by a numerous escort, and passing through the crowds, who overwhelmed them with maledictions and cries of anger and threatening. But the ladrones seemed to pay no attention to this manifestation of the public hatred; they were five in number, young, and apparently very powerful. All at once, at the moment when the carts, which were going very slowly, owing to the crowd, arrived in front of the Governor's palace, the ladrones rose altogether, uttered a loud cry, and, leaping into the street, took refuge in the palace, whose guard they disarmed, and closed the gates after them; they had succeeded in cutting their bonds, no one knew how. There was at first a moment of profound stupor among the crowd on seeing such a desperate deed, but ere long the soldiers regained their courage, and marched boldly on the palace, where the ladrones received them with musket shots. The fight was bravely carried on on both sides, but all the disadvantage was on the side of our men, who were exposed to the shots of invisible enemies, and renowned marksmen, every shot from whom brought down a victim. Some twenty dead, and as many wounded, were already lying on the square; the soldiers hesitated to continue this deadly contest, when the Governor, warned of what was going on, came up at full speed, followed by his officers. Fortunately for him, the Count was not at home when the ladrones seized his palace; but the Countess was there, and the Count trembled lest she should fall into the hands of these villains. He summoned them to surrender; they only replied by a discharge, which killed several persons by the Governor's side, and slightly wounded himself."

"The daring villains!" the Count muttered—"I hope they were hung."

"No, Excellency; after holding all the forces of the town in check for two hours, they proposed a capitulation, which was accepted."

"What!" the Count exclaimed, "Accepted! Oh! This is too much."

"It is the exact truth, however, Excellency; they threatened, unless they were allowed to retire in peace, to blow themselves up with the palace, which would have entailed the general ruin of the town, and to cut the throats of the prisoners in their power—that of the Countess first of all; the Governor tore out his hair with rage, but they only laughed."

"Why they are not men!" the Count exclaimed, stamping his foot passionately.

"No, Excellency, I told you, they are demons. The Count's officers persuaded him to accept the capitulation; the bandits insisted that the streets should be cleared for their passage; they had horses brought for them, and two for the Countess and one of her servants, whom they retained as hostages till they were in safety; and they went out well armed, leading in their midst my poor mistress, trembling with terror, and more dead, than alive. The ladrones did not hurry, they went at a foot pace, laughing and talking together, turning round, and even stopping now and then to stare at the crowd, which followed them at a respectful distance. They left the town in this way, but religiously kept their promise; two hours later, my lady the Countess, to whom they had behaved with great courtesy, returned to Saint Domingo, accompanied to the palace by the acclamations and glad shouts of the populace, who fancied her lost. The next day the Count ordered me to accompany the Countess here, where the physicians recommended her to live for a while, in order to rest from the terrible emotions she had doubtless experienced while she was in the power of the bandits."

"And since your installation at the hatto I presume nothing extraordinary has occurred?"

"Yes, Excellency, something has happened, and that is why I told you at the beginning that I alone knew the event which had modified my mistress's mode of living. One of the ladrones had a very long interview with her before they left her, an interview I saw, too far off to hear what was said, it is true, but near enough to judge of the interest she felt in it, and the impression it produced on her, for I had followed my mistress, resolved not to abandon her, and help her, were it necessary, at the risk of my life."

"That is the behaviour of a good servant, Birbomono, and I thank you for it."

"I only did my duty, Excellency; so soon as the ladrones left her alone I approached my mistress, and escorted her back to the town. A few days after our arrival here my mistress dressed herself in man's clothes, left the hatto unseen, only followed by myself and Fray Arsenio, who had refused to leave her, and led us to a secluded bay on the coast, where one of the ladrones was awaiting us. This man had another long conversation with my mistress, then, bidding us get into a canoe, he took us to a Spanish brigantine, tacking in sight of the coast. I afterwards learnt that this brigantine had been freighted by Fray Arsenio by my mistress's orders. So soon as we were on board this vessel, sail was set, and we put out to sea; the *ladrón* had returned ashore in the canoe."

"Nonsense!" the young man violently interjected; "What fables are you telling me, Birbomono?"

"Excellency, I am only telling you the truth you asked of me, without adding or omitting anything."

"Well, I am willing to believe you, incredible though the whole affair appears."

"Shall I break off here, Excellency, or continue my narration?"

"Go on, in the Fiend's name! Perhaps some light will eventually issue from all this chaos."

"Our brigantine began tacking between the islands, at a great risk of being snapped up as it passed by the ladrones; but, through some incomprehensible miracle, it succeeded in passing unseen, so that in eight days it reached an island in the form of a mountain, called Nevis, I believe, and only separated by a narrow channel from St. Kitts."

"But, from what you told me yourself, St, Christopher is the den of the ladrones."

"Yes, Excellency, and so it is; the brigantine did not anchor, it merely backed sails, and lowered a boat. My mistress, the monk, and I, got into it, and we were landed on the island; but, as she put her little foot on land, the Countess turned to me, and fixing on me a glance which nailed me to the boat I was on the point of leaving, she said—'Here is a letter, which you will carry to St. Christopher, there you will inquire for a celebrated Chief of the ladrones, whose name is Montbarts: you will have him pointed out to you; follow him, and place this letter in his own hands. Go, I count on your fidelity.' What could I do? Only obey: you will agree with me, Excellency. The sailors in the boat, as if warned beforehand, conveyed me to St. Christopher, where I landed unseen: I was lucky enough to meet this Montbarts, and hand him the letter, and then I slipped away; the boat which had been waiting for me took me back to Nevis, and the Señora thanked me. At sunset Montbarts arrived at Nevis; he talked for nearly an hour with the monk, while Doña Clara was concealed in a tent, and then went away: a few minutes later, the Countess and Fray Arsenio returned aboard the brigantine, which conveyed us back to Hispaniola with the same good fortune. The monk remained in the French part of the island, for some reason I do not know, while my mistress and I, as soon as we landed, returned to the hatto, where we arrived just ten days ago."

"And then?" the Count asked, seeing that the Major-domo was silent.

"That is all, Excellency," he answered; "since then Doña Clara has remained shut up in her apartments, and nothing has happened to trouble the monotony of our existence."

The Count rose without replying, walked up and down the room in considerable agitation, and then turned to Birbomono.

"Very good, Major-domo," he said to him—"I thank you; keep your mouth shut about this, and now you can retire. Remember, that no one in the household must suspect the importance of the conversation we have had together."

"I shall be dumb, Excellency," the Major-domo answered, and retired with a respectful bow.

"It is evident," the young man muttered, so soon as he was alone, "that there is at the bottom of this affair a frightful secret, of which my sister in all probability will condemn me to take my share. I am afraid that I have fallen into a trap. Hang it all! Why could not Clara let me live at my ease in Saint Domingo?"

CHAPTER XXII.

ACROSS COUNTRY.

On the morrow, Doña Clara appeared, if not completely recovered from her previous emotion, at least in a far more satisfactory state of health than her brother had dared to hope after the fainting fit of which he had been witness.

No allusion was made, however, by one or the other to the previous evening's conversation. Doña Clara, although very pale, and excessively weak, affected gaiety and even merriment; she carried matters so far as even to take a short walk in the garden, leaning on her brother's arm.

But the latter was not deceived by this conduct; he understood that his sister, vexed at having talked to him too frankly, was trying to lead him astray as to her condition, by affecting a gaiety far from her heart. Still, he did not let anything be seen, and when the great heat of the day had passed, he pretended a desire to visit the surrounding country, in order to give his sister a little liberty: taking his fusil, he mounted his horse, and rode out, accompanied by the Major-domo, who offered to act as his guide during his excursion.

Doña Clara made but a faint effort to keep him at home; in her heart she was pleased to be alone for a few hours.

The young man galloped across country with a feverish impatience. He was in a state of excitement, for which he could not account to himself; in spite of his egotism, he felt himself interested in his sister's misfortune; so much humble resignation involuntarily affected him, and he would have been happy to infuse a little joy into this heart crushed by grief; on the other hand, the Major-domo's singular story incessantly returned to his mind, and aroused his curiosity in the highest degree. Still he would not for anything in the world have questioned his sister about the obscure parts of this narrative, or merely let her know that he was aware of her relations with the filibusters of St. Kitts.

The two men had entered the savannah territory, and talking of indifferent topics; but as the Count could not get rid of the recollection of what the

Major-domo had told him, he turned sharply toward him at a certain moment.

"By the way," he asked him sharply, "I have not yet seen my sister's confessor. How do you call him?"

"Fray Arsenio, Excellency; he is a Franciscan monk."

"Yes, that's it, Fray Arsenio. Well, why does he persist in remaining invisible?"

"For an excellent reason, Excellency; the reason I had the honour of explaining to you last evening."

"That is possible—I do not say you did not; but everything is so confused in my mind," he said, with feigned indifference, "that I no longer remember what you told me on the subject; you will therefore oblige me by repeating it."

"That is easy, Excellency. Fray Arsenio left us at the moment when we landed, and has not reappeared at the hatto since."

"That is singular: and does not Doña Clara appear alarmed and vexed at so long an absence?"

"Not at all, Excellency; the señora never speaks of Fray Arsenio, and does not inquire whether he has returned or not."

"It is strange," the young man muttered to himself; "what is the meaning of this mysterious absence?"

After this aside, the Count suddenly broke off the conversation and resumed the chase. They had been absent from the hatto for some hours, and had insensibly gone a very considerable distance; the sun was nearing the horizon, and the Count was preparing to turn back, when suddenly a great noise of breaking branches was heard at the skirt of the forest, from which they were only separated by a few shrubs, and several wild oxen dashed on to the savannah, pursued, or, to speak more correctly, hunted, by a dozen hounds, which barked furiously while snapping at them.

The oxen, seven or eight in number, passed like a tornado two horse lengths from the Count, to whom this unexpected apparition caused such a surprise, that he remained for a moment motionless, not knowing what to do.

The savage animals, still harassed by the hounds, which did not leave them, made a sudden wheel, and turning back, seemed trying to enter the forest at the spot where they had left it; but they had hardly resumed their flight in that direction, when a fusil was discharged, and a bull, struck in the head, fell dead on the ground.

At the same instant a man emerged in his turn from the forest, and walked up to the animal, which was lying motionless and nearly hidden in the tall grass, without appearing to notice the two Spaniards, and reloading as he walked along the long fusil he had, in all probability, just employed so adroitly.

This hunting episode was accomplished more quickly than it has taken us to describe it, so that Don Sancho had not quite recovered from his surprise, when the Major-domo bent down to his side and said in a low voice, half choked with terror—

"Excellency, you wanted to see a *ladrón*. Well, look carefully at that man, he is one."

Don Sancho was endowed with undaunted courage. When his first surprise had passed, he became again completely master of himself, and regained all his coolness.

After securing his seat on the saddle, he advanced slowly toward the stranger, while examining him curiously. He was a man still young, of middle height, but well and powerfully built; his regular, majestic, and rather handsome features displayed boldness and intelligence. Cold, heat, rain, and sunshine to which he had doubtless for a long time been exposed, had given his face a decided bistre hue; and although he wore his full beard, it was cut rather short.

His dress, of almost primitive simplicity, so to speak, was composed of two shirts, breeches, and jacket, all of canvas, but so covered with spots of blood and grease, that it was impossible to recognise its original colour. He wore a leathern belt, from which hung on one side a case of crocodile skin, containing four knives and a bayonet; on the other, a large calabash, stopped with wax, and a hide bag containing bullets. He wore across his shoulders a small coat of fine canvas, rolled up and reduced to its smallest compass; and in lieu of shoes, boots made of untanned oxhide. His long hair, fastened with a *víbora* skin, escaped from under a fur cap which covered his head, and was protected by a peak in front.

His fusil, whose barrel was four and a half feet in length, could be easily recognized through the strange form of its stock, as turned out by Brachie, of Dieppe, who with Gélin, of Nantes, had the monopoly of manufacturing arms for the adventurers. This fusil was of the calibre of sixteen to the pound.

The appearance of this man, thus armed and accoutred, had really something imposing and formidable about it.

You instinctively felt yourself in face of a powerful nature, of a chosen organization, accustomed only to reckon on oneself, and which no danger was great enough to astound or even affect.

While continuing to advance toward the bull, he took a side glance at the two horsemen; then, without paying any further attention to them, he whistled to his dogs, which at once gave up their pursuit of the herd, and after drawing a knife from his sheath, he began skinning the animal lying at his feet.

At this moment the Count came up to his side.

"Eh," he said to him in a sharp voice, "who are you, and what do you here?"

The buccaneer, for he was one, raised his head, looked sarcastically at the man who addressed him so peremptorily, and then shrugged his shoulders with disdain.

"Who I am?" he replied, mockingly; "You see that I am a buccaneer, and what I am doing. I am flaying a bull I have slain. What next?"

"I want to know by what right you hunt on my land?"

"Ah! This land is yours? I am very glad to hear it. Well, I am hunting here because I think proper. If that does not suit you, I feel sorry for it, my pretty gentleman."

"What do you mean?" the Count continued, haughtily; "And how do you dare to assume such a tone with me?"

"Probably, because it is the one that suits me best," the buccaneer replied, drawing himself up quickly; "go your road, my fine sir, and take some good advice; if you do not wish your handsome jerkin to be filled with broken bones within five minutes, do not trouble yourself about me more than I do about you, and leave me to attend to my business."

"I will not allow it," the young man answered, violently; "the land you are trespassing on so impertinently belongs to my sister, Doña Clara de Bejar; I will not suffer it to be invaded with impunity by vagabonds of your description. ¡Viva Dios! You will decamp at once, my master, or, if not—"

"If not?" the buccaneer asked, with eyes flashing fire, while the Major-domo, foreseeing a catastrophe, prudently glided behind his master.

As for the latter, he stood cool and impassive before the buccaneer, resolved to take the offensive vigorously, if he saw him make the slightest suspicious gesture. But, contrary to all expectation, the adventurer's menacing look became almost suddenly calm, his features resumed their usual expression of nonchalance; and it was in an almost friendly tone, in spite of its roughness, that he said—

"Halloh! What name was that you mentioned, if you please?"

"That of the owner of this savannah."

"I suppose so," the adventurer replied, laughing; "but may I ask you to repeat the name?"

"That is of no consequence, my master," the young man said disdainfully, for he fancied that his adversary was backing out of the quarrel; "the name I uttered is that of Doña Clara de Bejar of Sousa."

"Et cetera," the buccaneer said, with a laugh, "these devils of gavachos have names for every day in the year. Come, don't be angry, my young cock," he added, remarking the flush which the expression he had employed spread over the Count's face; "we are, perhaps, nearer an understanding than you imagine—what would you gain by a fight with me? Nothing; and you might, on the contrary, lose a great deal."

"I do not understand your words," the young man answered drily, "but I hope you are about to explain them."

"It will not take long, as you shall see," the other said tauntingly, and, turning to the forest, he raised his hands to his mouth in the shape of a speaking trumpet.

"Eh! L'Olonnais!" he shouted.

"Hola!" a man immediately answered, whom the denseness of the forest in which he was hidden rendered invisible.

"Come here, my son," the buccaneer continued, "I believe we have found your little matter."

"Ah, ah!" L'Olonnais, still invisible, replied, "I must have a look at it."

The young Count did not know what to think of this new incident which seemed about to change the state of affairs; he feared a coarse jest on the part of these half-savage men. He hesitated between giving way to the passion that was boiling within him, or patiently awaiting the result of the buccaneer's summons; but a secret foreboding urged him to restrain himself and act prudently with these men, who did not appear animated by an evil design against him, and whose manners, though quick and rough, were still friendly.

At this moment L'Olonnais appeared; he wore the same dress as the buccaneer: he advanced hurriedly toward the latter, and without troubling himself about the two Spaniards, asked him what he wanted, while throwing on the ground a wild bull's hide, which he was carrying on his shoulders.

"Did you not tell me something about a letter which Bowline sent you this morning by the hands of Omopoua?"

"It is true, Lepoletais. I spoke to you about it," he said, "and it was settled between us that as you know the country, you were to lead me to the person to whom I have to deliver this accursed slip of paper."

"Well, then, my son, if you like, your commission is performed," Lepoletais continued, as he pointed to Don Sancho, "he is the brother, or at least calls himself so, of the person in question."

"Stuff," L'Olonnais replied, fixing alight glance on the young man, "that gay springald?"

"Yes, he says so; for as you know, the Spaniards are such liars, that it is not possible even to trust to their word."

Don Sancho blushed with indignation.

"Who gave you the right to doubt mine?" he exclaimed.

"Nothing has done so up to the present, hence I am not addressing myself to you, but speaking generally."

"So," L'Olonnais asked him, "you are the brother of Doña Clara de Bejar, the mistress of the hatto del Rincón?"

"Once again, yes, I am her brother."

"Good! And how will you prove it to me?"

The young man shrugged his shoulders.

"What do I care whether you believe me or not?" he said.

"That is possible, but it is of great consequence to me to be certain of the fact; I am entrusted with a letter for that lady, and wish to perform my commission properly."

"In that case hand me the letter, and I will deliver it myself."

"You found that out all by yourself," the engagé said mockingly, "a likely notion that I should give you the note on your demand," and he burst into a hearty laugh, in which Lepoletais joined.

"These Spaniards doubt nothing," the buccaneer said.

"In that case go to the deuce, you and your letter," the young man exclaimed passionately, "it does not make any difference to me if you keep it."

"Come, come, don't be savage, hang it all," L'Olonnais continued in a conciliatory tone; "there is possibly a means of arranging matters to the general satisfaction; I am not so black as I look, and I have good intentions, but I do not wish to be duped, that is all."

The young man, in spite of the visible repugnance with which the adventurers inspired him did not dare to break suddenly with them; the letter might be very important, and his sister, doubtless would not pardon him if he acted petulantly in this matter.

"Come," he said, "speak, but make haste; it is late—I am far from the hatto, where I wish to return before sunset, so as not to alarm my sister unnecessarily."

"That is the conduct of a good brother," the engagé answered with an ironical smile; "this is what I propose to you: tell the little lady in question that Montbart's engagé has orders to deliver a letter to her, and that if she wishes to have it, she need only come and fetch it."

"What! Fetch it, where?"

"Here; zounds! Lepoletais and I will set up a boucan at this spot; we will wait for the lady all tomorrow here: it seems to me that what I propose is simple and easy."

"And do you believe," he answered ironically, "that my sister will consent to accept such an appointment made by a wretched adventurer? why, you must be mad!"

"I do not believe anything, I make you a proposal, which you are free to accept or refuse, that is all: as for the letter, she shall only have it by coming to fetch it herself."

"Why not accompany me to the hatto, that would be more simple, I fancy?"

"It is possible, and that was my intention at first, but I have changed my mind; so settle what you will do."

"My sister respects herself too much to take such a step, I am certain beforehand that she will indignantly refuse."

"Well, you may be mistaken, my friend," the engagé said, with a knowing smile, "who ever knows what women think!"

"Well, to cut short an interview which has already lasted too long, I will inform her of what you have said to me; still, I do not conceal from you that I shall make every effort to prevent her coming."

"You can do as you please, it does not concern me; but be assured that if it be her wish to come, as I believe, your arguments will be of no use."

"We shall see."

"Mind not to forget to tell her that the letter is from Montbarts."

During this conversation, which possessed no interest for him, Lepoletais, with the characteristic coolness and carelessness of buccaneers, was engaged in cutting down branches, and planting stakes to make the *ajoupa* under which they would camp for the night.

"You see," the engagé added, "that my comrade has already set to work; so good-bye till tomorrow, as I have no time for further talk, I must help to prepare the boucan."

"Do as you please, but I am persuaded that you are wrong in reckoning on the success of the commission I have undertaken."

"Well, you will see; at any rate mention it to the Señora. Ah! By the way, one word more, mind, no treachery."

The young man did not condescend a reply: he shrugged his shoulders disdainfully, leaped on his horse, and galloped off in the direction of the hatto, closely followed by the Major-domo.

On getting some distance away, he looked back: the ajoupa was already finished, and, as L'Olonnais had said, the two buccaneers were busily engaged in establishing their boucan, without paying any more attention to the Spaniards, who were doubtless prowling about the neighbourhood, than if they had been five hundred leagues from any habitation.

Then he continued to advance thoughtfully in the direction of the hatto.

"Well, Excellency," the Major-domo said presently, "you have seen the ladrones, what do you think of them now?"

"They are rough men," he said, shaking his head sadly, "possessing brutal and indomitable natures, but relatively frank and honest, at least from their point of view."

"Yes, yes, you are right, Excellency; and thus they gain more ground every day, and if they were left alone, I am afraid that the whole island would soon belong to them."

"Oh, we have not reached that point yet," he said with a smile.

"Pardon me, Excellency, for asking you the question, but do you intend to inform the Señora of this meeting?"

"I should like not to do so; unfortunately, after what you had told me of the things that have taken place between my sister and these men, my silence might have very serious consequences for her. Hence it is better, I believe, to tell her frankly all about it, and she will be a better judge than I of the line of conduct she should pursue."

"I believe you are right, Excellency. The Señora has perhaps a great interest in knowing the contents of that letter."

"Well, let us trust in Heaven!"

It was an hour past nightfall when they reached the hatto.

They noticed with surprise an unusual movement round the house. Several fires lighted on the plain illumined the darkness. On approaching, the Count perceived that these fires were lit by soldiers, who had established their bivouac there.

A confidential servant was watching for the Count's arrival. So soon as he saw him, he handed him several letters that had arrived for him, and begged him to go at once to the Señora, who was impatiently expecting him.

"What is there new here?" he asked.

"Two fifties arrived at sunset, Excellency," the servant answered.

"Ah!" he remarked, with a slight frown. "Very good. Inform my sister that I shall be with her in an instant."

The domestic bowed and retired. The young gentleman dismounted, and went to the apartments of Doña Clara, considerably puzzled by the unforeseen arrival of these troops at a spot which apparently enjoyed great tranquillity, and where their presence was unnecessary.

CHAPTER XXIII.

COMPLICATIONS.

We must now return to one of our characters, who up to the present has played but a secondary part in this story; but, as frequently happens, is now called on by the exigencies of our narrative to take his place in the foreground.

We refer to Count Don Stenio de Bejar y Sousa, grandee of Spain of the first class, *caballero cubierto*, governor for His Majesty Philip II. of Spain and the Indies, of the island of Hispaniola, and husband of Doña Clara de Peñaflor.

Count Don Stenio de Bejar was a true Spaniard of the age of Charles V., dry, stiff, full of pride and self-sufficiency, always with his hand on his hip, and his head thrown back when he deigned to speak, which, happened to him as rarely as possible, not through any want of sense, as he was far from being a fool; but through indolence and contempt of other men, whom he never looked at without half closing his eyes, and raising the corners of his lips disdainfully.

Tall, well built, possessed of noble manners, and a very handsome face, the Count, apart from his determined silence, was one of the most accomplished cavaliers of the Spanish court, which, however, at that period, possessed a great number of them.

His marriage with Doña Clara had been at the outset an affair of convenience and ambition, but gradually, through admiring the charming face of the woman he had married, seeing her gentle eyes fixed on him, and hearing her melodious voice resound in his ear, he had grown to love her—love her madly. Like all men accustomed to shut up and concentrate in their hearts the feelings that possessed them, the passion he experienced for Doña Clara had acquired proportions the more formidable, because the unhappy man had the desperate conviction that it would never be shared by the woman who was the object of it. All Don Stenio's advances had been so peremptorily rejected by his wife, that he at last made up his mind to abstain from them.

But, like all disappointed lovers, this gentleman, who was at the same time the husband—a very aggravating fact in the species, was naturally too infatuated with his own merit, to attribute his defeat to himself, and hence had looked around to discover the fortunate rival who had robbed him of his wife's heart.

Naturally the Count had not succeeded in finding this fancied rival, who only existed in his own imagination, and this had grown into a jealousy, the more ferocious because, as it did not know whom to settle on, it attacked everybody.

The Count was jealous, then, not like a Spaniard, for the Spaniards generally, whatever may be said to the contrary, are not affected by that stupid malady, but like an Italian; and this jealousy made him suffer the more, because, like his love, he was unable to show it; through fear of ridicule, he was compelled to lock it up carefully in his heart.

When, owing to his protection—as had been arranged on his marriage with Doña Clara, of whose previous union with the Count de Barmont he was ignorant—his father-in-law, the Duc de Peñaflor, was appointed viceroy of New Spain, and himself obtained the government of Hispaniola, the Count experienced a feeling of indescribable joy, and an immense comfort inundated his mind. He was persuaded that in America, his wife, separated from her friends and relatives, forced, to live alone, and consequently to undergo his influence, would be driven through weariness and want of something better to do, to share his love, or at least accept it: and then again, on the islands there was no rivalry to fear among a half savage population entirely absorbed by a passion far more powerful than love—a passion for money.

Alas! This time too, he was deceived. Doña Clara, it is true, gave him no more pretext for jealousy than she had done in Spain, but he did not any the more succeed in winning her affections. From the first day of her arrival at Saint Domingo, she manifested the desire to live alone and in retirement, engaged in religious practices; and the Count was constrained, in spite of his fury, to bow before a resolution which he recognised as irrevocable.

He resigned himself; his jealousy however was not extinct, it was smouldering beneath the ashes, and a spark would suffice to make it burst into a more terrible flame than before.

Still, in spite of this slight annoyance, the life the Count led at Saint Domingo was most agreeable; in the first place he ruled there in his quality of governor, saw everybody bend beneath his will, always excepting his wife, the only one perhaps he would have cared to reduce. He had his flatterers, and played the master and suzerain over all who surrounded him; moreover, a thing not to be at all despised, his position as governor secured certain imposts that rapidly augmented his fortune, which various youthful follies had considerably reduced, and he now worked hard, not only to repair the breaches, but to render them as if they had never been.

By degrees, however, the Count succeeded in lulling, if not subduing, his love; he employed one passion to uproot the other; the care of augmenting his fortune made him endure patiently the calculated indifference of the Countess. He had almost come himself to believe that he only felt for her a frank and sincere friendship; the more so because Doña Clara for her part, was charming in everything that did not touch on her husband's passion for her; she took an interest, or at least pretended to do so, in the commercial speculations which the Count did not hesitate to engage in under suppositious names, and at times she would give him, with that clear judgment so eminently possessed by women whose heart is free, excellent advice on very difficult points, by which the Count profited, and naturally took all the glory.

Things were in this state when the episode with the filibusters occurred, which the Major-domo described to Don Sancho de Peñaflor.

This mad struggle of five men against an entire town, a struggle from which they emerged victorious, had caused the Count a rage all the greater, because the filibusters, on leaving the town, had taken the Countess off with them as a hostage. He had then understood how greatly he erred, in supposing that his love and jealousy were extinguished. During the two hours that the Countess remained absent, the Count suffered a horrible torture, the more horrible because the rage he felt was impotent, and vengeance impossible, at least for the present.

Hence, from this moment, the Count vowed an implacable hatred against the adventurers, and swore to carry on a merciless war against them.

The return of the Countess safe and sound, and treated with the greatest respect by the adventurers, during the time she remained in their power, calmed the Count's wrath from a marital point of view, but the insult he had received in his quality as governor, was too grave for him to renounce his vengeance.

From this moment the most formal orders were sent to the leaders of corps to redouble their surveillance, and chase the adventurers, wherever they met them; fresh Fifties, formed of resolute men, were organized, and the few adventurers they contrived to catch, were mercilessly hung. Tranquillity was re-established in the colonies, the confidence of the colonists, momentarily disturbed, reappeared, and everything apparently returned to its accustomed state.

The Countess had expressed a desire to restore her health by a stay of several weeks at the hatto del Rincón, and the Count, to whom her physician had expressed this wish, found it only very natural; he had seen his wife go away with an easy mind, for he was convinced that at the spot whither she was going, she would have no danger to fear, and felt persuaded in his heart that this condescension on his part, would be appreciated by the Countess, and that she would feel thankful to him for it.

She had left therefore, only accompanied by a few servants and confidential slaves, delighted to escape for some time from the restraint she was obliged to impose on herself at Saint Domingo, and fostering the bold scheme which we have seen her carry out so successfully.

It was about an hour after the departure of Don Sancho de Peñaflor, to go and join his sister at the hatto; the Count was finishing his breakfast, and preparing to retire to the inner boudoir to enjoy his siesta, when an usher came into the dining room, and after apologizing for disturbing His Excellency at this moment, informed him that a man who refused to give his name, but declared that he was well known to the governor, insisted on being introduced into his presence, as he had most important communications to make to him.

The moment was badly chosen to ask for an audience, as the Count felt inclined to sleep; he answered the usher that, however important the stranger's communications might be, he did not believe them of such importance that he should sacrifice his siesta for them; he therefore Sent a message to the effect that the governor would not be at liberty till four in the afternoon, and if the stranger liked to return then he would be received.

The Count dismissed the usher, and rose, muttering to himself as he walked towards the boudoir,—

"*Dios me salve*, if I were to believe all these scamps, I should not have a moment's rest."

Whereupon he stretched himself in a large hammock, hung right across the room, closed his eyes and fell asleep.

The Count's siesta lasted three hours, and this delay was the cause of serious complications.

On waking, Don Stenio quite forgot all about the stranger; it so often happened that he was disturbed for nothing by people who declared they had urgent matters to discuss with him, that he did not attach the slightest importance to their requests for an audience, and the usher's words had completely slipped his memory.

At the time when he entered the room where he usually granted his audiences, and which at this moment was quite empty, the usher presented himself again.

"What do you want?" he asked him.

"Excellency," the usher replied with a respectful bow, "the man has returned."

"What man?"

"The man who came this morning."

"Oh yes, well, what does he want?" the Count continued, who did not know what all this was about.

"He desires, my lord, that you will do him the honour of receiving him, as he states that he has matters of the utmost gravity to tell you."

"Ah, very good, I remember now; it is the same man you announced this morning."

"Yes, Excellency, the same."

"And what is his name?"

"He will only tell it to your Excellency."

"Hum! I do not like such precautions, for they never forbode anything good; listen, José! When he arrives, tell him I never receive people who insist on keeping their incognito."

"But he is here, my lord."

"Ah! well then, it will be all the more easy, tell him so at once."

And he turned his back. The usher bowed and left the room, but returned almost immediately.

"Well! Have you sent him away?" the Count asked.

"No, my lord, he gave me this card requesting me to hand it your Excellency. He declares that, in default of his name, it will be sufficient to secure his admission to your presence."

"Oh! Oh!" said the Count, "That is curious, let me see this famous talisman."

He took the card from the usher's hand and looked at it absently; but all at once he started, frowned and said to the usher,

"Show the man into the yellow room, let him wait for me there, I will be with him in a moment. The deuce," he muttered to himself when he was alone, "it is a long time since this scoundrel let me hear anything of him, I fancied him hung or drowned; he is a clever scamp, can he really have any important information to give me? We shall see."

Then, leaving the room in which he was, he hastened to the yellow saloon where the man with the card already was.

On seeing the governor, the latter hastily rose, and made him a respectful bow.

The Count turned to the valet who had followed him to open the doors.

"I am not at home to anybody," he said; "you can go."

The valet left the room, and shut the door after him.

"Now for us two," the Count said, as he sank into his chair, and pointed to another.

"I am awaiting your lordship's orders," the stranger said respectfully.

Don Stenio remained for a moment silent, and scratching his forehead.

"You have been away for a very long time," he said at last, "well, what has become of you during the last two months?"

"I have been executing your Excellency's orders," the man answered.

"My orders? I do not remember having given you any."

"Pardon me, my lord, if I venture to remind you of certain facts, which appear to have escaped your memory."

"Do so, my good fellow, I shall be delighted at it; still, I would remark that my time is valuable, and that others besides yourself are awaiting an audience."

"I will be brief, Excellency."

"That is what I wish. Go on,"

"A few days after the affair of the ladrones, does not your Excellency remember saying to me in a moment of anger or impatience, that you would give ten thousand piastres to obtain positive information about the adventurers, their strength, plans, &c.?"

"Yes, I remember saying that; what then?"

"Well, Excellency, I was present when you made that promise. Your Excellency had deigned to employ me several times before; as you looked at me while speaking, I supposed that you were addressing me, and I have acted accordingly."

"That is to say?"

"In my devotion to your Excellency, in spite of the numberless dangers I should have to incur, I resolved to go and seek the information you appeared to desire so ardently, and—"

"And you went to seek it," the Count exclaimed with an eager start, though hitherto he had paid but very slight attention to the stranger's remarks.

"Well, yes, Excellency."

"Ah, ah," he said, stroking his chin; "and have you learnt anything?"

"An infinity of things, my lord."

"Well, let me hear some of them. But mind," he added, checking himself, "no hearsays or suppositions, for I have my ears stuffed with them."

"The information I shall have the honour of giving your Excellency, is derived from a good source, since I went to seek it in the very den of the ladrones."

The Count gazed with admiration at this man who had not feared to expose himself to so great a danger.

"If such is the case, pray continue, señor."

"My lord," the spy resumed, for we may henceforth give him that name; "I come from St. Christopher."

"Ah! Is not that the Island where the bandits take shelter?"

"Yes, my lord, and more than that, I returned in one of their vessels."

"Oh, oh," said the governor, "pray tell me all about it, my dear Don Antonio: that is your name, I believe?"

"Yes, my lord; Don Antonio de la Ronda."

"You see," the Count added with a smile; "that I have a good memory sometimes," and he laid a stress on these words, which made the spy's heart bound with joy.

The latter told him in what way he had entered the island, how he had been discovered and made prisoner by Montbarts, who put him on board one of his vessels; how a great expedition had been decided on by the adventurers against the island of Saint Domingo, in the first place, and then against Tortuga, which the ladrones had a plan for surprising, and on which they intend to establish themselves; and in what way, on reaching Port Margot, he had succeeded in escaping, and had hastened to bear the news to his Excellency the governor.

The Count listened with the most serious attention to Don Antonio's narrative, and in proportion as it progressed, the governor's brow became more anxious; in fact, the spy had not deceived him. The news was of the utmost gravity.

"Hum!" he answered; "And is it long since the ladrones arrived at Port Margot?"

"Eight days, Excellency."

"¡*Sangre de Cristo!* so long as that, and I had not been informed of it?"

"In spite of the utmost diligence, as I was constrained to take the greatest precaution lest I should fall again into the hands of the ladrones, who doubtless started in pursuit of me. I only arrived this morning, and came straight to the palace."

The Count bit his lips, several hours had been lost through his fault; still he did not notice the indirect reproach addressed to him by the spy, for he comprehended all its justice.

"You have fairly earned the ten thousand piastres promised, Don Antonio," he said.

The spy gave a start of pleasure.

"Ah, that is not all," he answered, with a meaning smile.

"What else is there?" the Count remarked; "I believed that you had nothing further to tell me."

"That depends, Excellency. I have made my official report to the Governor-General of Hispaniola, it is true—a very detailed report indeed—in which I have forgotten nothing that might help him to defend the island entrusted to his care."

"Well?"

"Well, my lord, I have now to give the Count de Bejar, of course, if he desire it, certain information which I believe will interest him."

The Count fixed on the man an investigating glance, as if he wished to read his very soul.

"The Count de Bejar?" he said with studied coldness; "What can you have to say that interests him privately, as a simple gentleman? I have not, as far as I am aware, anything to settle with the ladrones."

"Perhaps so, my lord; however, I will only speak, if your Excellency orders me, and before doing so, will beg you to forgive anything that may seem offensive to your honour in what I may say to you."

The Count turned pale and frowned portentously.

"Take care," he said to him in a threatening voice, "take care lest you go beyond your object, and in trying to prove too much, fall into the contrary excess. The honour of my name is not to be played with, and I will never allow the slightest stain to be imprinted on it."

"I have not the slightest intention to insult your Excellency; my zeal on your behalf has alone urged me to speak as I have done."

"Very good—I am willing to believe it; still, as the honour of my name regards myself alone, I do not allow any person the right to assail it, not even in a good intention."

"I ask your Excellency's pardon, but I have doubtless explained myself badly. What I have to tell you relates to a plot, formed, doubtless, without her knowledge, against the Countess."

"A plot formed against the Countess!" Don Stenio exclaimed, violently; "What do you mean, señor? Explain at once—I insist on it."

"My lord, since it is your wish, I will speak. Is not her ladyship, the Countess, at this moment in the vicinity of the small town of San Juan?"

"She is; but how do you know it, since, as you told me you have only been back to Saint Domingo for a few hours?"

"I presumed so, because on board the vessel in which I returned to Hispaniola, I heard something about an interview which the chief of the adventurers was to have in a few days in the neighbourhood of the Artibonite."

"Oh!" the Count exclaimed; "You lie, scoundrel!"

"For what object, my lord?" the spy answered, coolly.

"How do I know? through hatred, envy, perhaps."

"I," he said, with a shrug of his shoulders. "Nonsense, my lord. Men like me—spies, if things must be called by their proper name—are only led away by one passion—that of money."

"But what you tell me is impossible," the Count observed, with agitation.

"What prevents you from assuring yourself that I speak the truth, my lord?"

"I will do so, *¡Viva Dios!*" he exclaimed, stamping his foot furiously.

Then he walked up to the spy, who was standing calm and motionless in the centre of the room, and fixed on him a glance full of rage, but impossible to describe.

"Listen, villain!" he said in a hollow voice, half choked with passion; "If you have lied, you shall die!"

"Agreed, my lord," the spy replied, coldly; "but if I have spoken the truth?"

"If you have spoken the truth," he exclaimed, but suddenly broke off, "but no, it is impossible, I repeat!" and seeing a fugitive smile playing round the lips of his companion, he added, "well, be it so; if you have spoken the truth, you shall fix your own reward, and whatever it may be, on my word as a gentleman, you shall have it."

"Thanks, my lord," he replied, with a bow; "I hold you to your word."

The Count walked several times up and down the saloon, suffering from intense agitation, appearing to have completely forgotten the presence of the spy, muttering unconnected words, breaking out into passionate gestures, and in all probability revolving in his head sinister projects of vengeance. At length he stopped and addressed the spy again.

"Withdraw," he said to him, "but do not leave the palace; or, stay, wait a moment."

Seizing a bell on the table, he rang it violently.

A valet appeared.

"A corporal and four men," he said.

The spy shrugged his shoulders.

"Why all these precautions, my lord?" he asked; "is it not contrary to my interest to go away?"

The Count examined him for a moment attentively, and then made the valet a sign to withdraw.

"Very good," he then said, "I trust to you, Don Antonio de la Ronda. Await my orders, I shall soon have need of you."

"I shall not go away far, my lord."

And after bowing respectfully, he took his leave, and withdrew.

The Count, when left alone, gave way for some minutes to all the violence of a rage so long restrained, but he gradually regained his coolness and the power of reflection.

"Oh! I will avenge myself!" he exclaimed.

Then he gave, with feverish activity, the necessary orders that numerous bodies of troops should be sent off to different points, so as to completely invest the hatto del Rincón, to which spot two Fifties were sent, commanded by experienced and resolute officers.

These measures taken, the Count, wrapped in a large cloak, mounted his horse an hour after sunset, and followed by Don Antonio de la Ronda, who had not the slightest desire to leave him, and a few confidential officers, he left his palace incognito, rode through the town unrecognized, and reached the open country.

"Now, caballeros," he said in a hollow voice, "gallop your hardest, and do not be afraid of foundering your horses. Relays are prepared at regular distances along the road."

He dug his spurs into the flanks of his horse, which snorted with pain, and the party set out with the headlong speed of a whirlwind.

"Ah, Santiago! Santiago;" the Count exclaimed at times while urging on his steed, whose efforts were superhuman, "shall I arrive in time?"

CHAPTER XXIV.

PORT MARGOT.

We will now return to the filibustering flotilla, which we left sailing freely toward the great North Key, a rendezvous admirably selected, owing to its proximity to Saint Domingo, and exactly facing the island of the Tortoise.

According to their habit, whenever they undertook an expedition, the adventurers had only troubled themselves with laying in a stock of ammunition, and only took two days' provisions with them, as they intended to make descents on the islands which they knew they must pass, and pillage the Spanish colonists settled on them. This was exactly what happened. The filibusters left behind them a long train of fire and blood, murdering, without pity, the defenceless Spaniards, who were terrified at the sight of them, seizing on their cattle and firing their houses after they had plundered them.

The first vessel to anchor off the Great Key was the lugger with Montbarts on board, and commanded by Michael le Basque; on the next day the two brigantines arrived, a few hours after one another.

They came to anchor on the right and left of the admiral, about two cables' length from the coast.

At this period the Great Key was inhabited by red Caribs, expelled from St. Domingo by the cruelty of the Spaniards, and who had taken refuge on this island, where they lived rather comfortably, owing to the fertility of the soil, and the alliance they had contracted with the filibusters.

The three vessels had scarce cast anchor, ere they were surrounded by a great number of canoes, manned by Caribs, who brought them refreshments of every description.

The same evening the admiral went ashore with the greater part of his crew: the other captains imitated him, and only left behind the men absolutely necessary to guard the ships.

At a signal from the admiral, the crews arranged themselves in a semicircle round him; the captains standing in front of the first line.

Behind them were the Caribs, alarmed in their hearts at this formidable landing, whose motive they could not divine, anxiously awaiting what was going to happen, and not at all comprehending this display of strength.

Montbarts, holding in one hand the staff of a white flag, whose folds floated on the breeze above his head, and his long sword in the other, looked round at the men gathered before him.

Most of them were scarce clad, but all were well armed. They had weather-beaten complexions, vigorous limbs, huge muscles, energetic features, and a defiant glance. The adventurers thus collected around this man, who stood haughtily in front of them, with his head thrown back, quivering lips, and a flashing eye, offered a striking spectacle; their savage grandeur and rough gestures were not deficient in a certain majesty, which was rendered still more imposing by the primitive landscape that formed the background of the picture, and the picturesque group of Indians, whose anxious faces and characteristic poses added to the effect of the scene.

For some time the rustling of the crowd was audible, like the sound of the sea breaking on a beach, but gradually the noise died away, and a profound silence fell on all.

Montbarts then advanced a step, and in a firm and sonorous voice, whose manly accents soon captivated all these men who listened eagerly to his words, he revealed to them the purpose of the expedition, which up to this time was unknown to them.

"Brothers of the coast," he said; "messmates and friends, the moment has arrived to reveal to you what I await from your courage and your devotion to the common cause. You are not mercenaries, who, for scanty pay, let themselves be killed like brutes, ignorant for what or from whom they are fighting. No! You are picked men, who wish to know to what object you are advancing, and what profit you will derive from your efforts. Several of our most renowned comrades and myself have resolved to attack in the heart of their richest possessions these cowardly Spaniards, who believed they dishonoured us by branding us with the name of *ladrones*, and whom the merest sight of our smallest canoes puts to flight like a flock of startled seagulls. But in order that our vengeance may be certain, and that we succeed in seizing the wealth of our enemies, we must possess a point sufficiently near the centre of our operations, to enable us to rush upon them unawares, and so strong that the whole power of Castile may be broken against it in impotent efforts. St. Christopher is too remote. Moreover, the descent of Admiral Don Fernando of Toledo is a proof to us, that however brave we may be, we shall never succeed in fortifying ourselves strongly enough there to defy the rage of our enemies. It was, therefore, absolutely necessary to find a spot more favourable to our projects, a point which could easily be rendered impregnable. Our friends, and myself set to work. For a long time we sought with the perseverance of men resolved to succeed. Heaven has at length deigned to bless our efforts. We have found this refuge under the most fortunate conditions."

Here Montbarts made a pause for several seconds.

An electric quiver ran along the ranks of the adventurers; their eyes flashed fire, they grasped their fusils in their powerful hands, as if they were impatient to commence the struggle promised them.

A smile of satisfaction illumined for a moment the adventurer's pale face. Then, waving his hand to command attention, he resumed;—

"Brethren, before us is Saint Domingo;" and he stretched out his hand towards the sea. "Saint Domingo, the loveliest and wealthiest of all the isles possessed by Spain. On this island several of our brothers, who escaped the massacre of St. Christopher, have established themselves, and are contending energetically against the Spaniards, to hold the ground wrested from them. Unfortunately too few in number, in spite of their bravery, to resist for any length of time the enemy's troops, they would soon be forced to quit the island, if we did not go to their assistance. They have summoned us. We have responded to this appeal of our brothers, whom honour ordered us to succour in the hour of danger. While doing a good deed, we are carrying out the plan so long resolved by ourselves, and at last we have found the impregnable spot we have so long desired. You all know the island of Tortuga, brethren? Separated only by a narrow channel from Saint Domingo, it rises like an advanced sentry in the middle of the sea. It is the eagle's nest, whence we will laughingly brave the fury of the Spaniards. To Tortuga, brethren!"

"To the island of the Tortoise!" the adventurers shouted, brandishing their weapons enthusiastically.

"Good!" Montbarts continued. "I knew that you were men who would understand me, and that I could reckon upon you. Before seizing on Tortuga, however, which is only defended by an insignificant garrison of twenty soldiers, who will fly at the first blow, we must, by protecting our brethren at Saint Domingo, and securing them the territory they occupy, obtain for ourselves useful ports, advantageous outlets, and, before all, the means of easily injuring the Spaniards, and, if it be possible, expelling them entirely from the island, of which they have already lost a portion. Tomorrow, we will proceed to Port Margot, come to an understanding there with our brethren, and arrange our plans, so as to derive both honour and profit from our expedition. And now, brethren, let each crew go aboard. Tomorrow, at sunrise, we will set sail for Port Margot, and in a few days I promise you glorious fights, and a rich booty to divide among you all. Long live France, and death to Spain!"

"Long live France! Death to Spain! Long live Montbarts!" the adventurers exclaimed.

"Let us embark, brethren," Montbarts added. "Do not forget that the poor Indians of this island are our friends, and must be treated as such by you."

The adventurers then followed their officers, and embarked in the most perfect order.

At sunrise, the squadron raised anchor. We need not say that all the refreshments purchased of the Indians were scrupulously paid for, and that no one had reason to complain of their stay at the Great Key. A few hours later the flotilla entered the channel separating Saint Domingo from Tortuga, and anchored off Port Margot.

The Spanish island lay before them with its large mounds, tall cliffs, and its mountains, whose peaks seemed hidden in the clouds, while on the starboard, Tortuga, with its dense, verdant forests, seemed a basket of flowers rising from the bottom of the sea.

They had scarce landed ere a canoe, manned by four men, hailed the lugger. These four men were Lepoletais, whom we have already caught a glimpse of; one of his apprentices, L'Olonnais, and Omopoua, the Carib chief.

The Indian had nearly got rid of the European dress, and resumed that of his nation.

Montbarts went to meet his visitors, saluted them, and led them down to the cabin.

"You are welcome," he said to them. "In a few minutes the other leaders of the expedition will be here, and then we will talk. In the meanwhile, take some refreshment."

And he gave an engagé orders to bring in spirits.

Lepoletais and Omopoua sat down without pressing, but L'Olonnais remained modestly standing. In his quality of apprentice he dared not place himself on a footing of equality with the adventurers. At this moment Michael the Basque entered the cabin.

"Messmate," he said to Montbarts, "Captain Drake and David have just come aboard. They are waiting on deck."

"Tell them to come below. I want to talk with them.".

Michael went out. A few minutes after, he returned, accompanied by the two captains.

After the first compliments, the two officers drank a bumper, then took their seats, and awaited the communication which their chief was evidently about to make to them.

Montbarts knew the value of time, hence he did not put their patience to a long trial.

"Brothers," he said, "I present to you Lepoletais, whom you doubtless know already by reputation."

The adventurers bowed smilingly, and spontaneously offered their hand to the buccaneer.

The latter cordially returned the pressure, delighted in his heart at so frank a reception.

"Lepoletais," Montbarts continued, "is sent to me as a delegate by our brethren, the buccaneers of Port Margot and Port de Paix; I prefer to let him himself explain what he expects from us—in this manner we shall more easily arrive at an understanding. Speak, then, I pray, brother, we are listening."

Lepoletais first poured out a glass of rum, which he swallowed at a draught, no doubt for the purpose of clearing his ideas; then, after two or three sonorous "hums!" he resolved to speak.

"Brethren," he said, "whatever be the name given us—filibusters, buccaneers, or habitants—our origin is the same, is it not? And we are all adventurers. Hence, we are bound to assist and protect one another, like the free companions we are; but, in order that this protection may be efficient—that nothing may weaken in the future the alliance we contract today—we must, like yourselves, find some real profit in the alliance. Is not this the case?"

"Certainly," Michael said, to encourage him.

"This, then, is what is happening," Lepoletais continued; "we buccaneers and habitants are here something like the bird on the tree, continually pursued by the gavachos, who track us like wild beasts, wherever they surprise us, sustaining an unequal contest, in which we must eventually succumb, not knowing today if we shall be alive tomorrow, and gradually losing all the ground which we gained at the outset. This deplorable state of things could not go on much longer without entailing a catastrophe, which, with your aid, we hope not only to avert, but to prevent definitively; by seizing Tortuga, which is badly guarded, and will be badly defended, you procure us a sure shelter in case of danger, an ever open refuge in the event of a crisis. But this is not all; we must secure frontiers, so that tranquillity may prevail in our country, that merchant vessels may not fear to enter our ports, and that we may find an outlet for our hides, our boucaned meat, and our tallow. These frontiers can be easily secured; the only thing wanting is to seize on two points, one in the interior, which the Spaniards call the Great Savannah of San Juan, and which we have christened the Grand Fond. The town of San Juan is but poorly fortified, and merely inhabited by mulattos, or men of mixed blood, whom we could easily conquer."

"Is not the Grand Fond, as you call it, traversed by the Artibonite?" Montbarts asked, while exchanging a meaning glance with L'Olonnais, who was standing by his side.

"Yes," Lepoletais replied; "and in the centre is a hatto called the Rincón, belonging, I believe, to the Spanish Governor."

"It would be a master stroke to seize that man," Michael the Basque observed.

"Yes, but there is little probability of succeeding in capturing him, for he is at Saint Domingo," Lepoletais replied.

"It is possible; but go on."

"The other point is a port called Leogane, or, as the Spaniards term it, *la Iguana*, or the Lizard, from the shape of the tongue of land on which it is built; the possession of this port would render us masters of the whole western part of the island, and allow us to establish ourselves there securely."

"Is Leogane defended?" David inquired.

"No," Lepoletais answered, "the Spaniards let it fall into ruins, as they do, indeed, with nearly all the points they occupy; through the want of labourers, since the almost utter extinction of the Indian race of the island, they gradually abandon the old establishments, and retire to the East."

"Very good," said Montbarts; "is that all you desire?"

"Yes, all," Lepoletais answered.

"Now, what do you propose, brother?"

"This: we buccaneers will hunt for you wild oxen and boars, and provision your ships at a price agreed on between us, but which must never be higher than one-half the price we ask of foreign vessels that come to trade with us; in addition, we will defend you if attacked, and in great expeditions you will have the right to claim one man in five to accompany you, when you require it. The habitants will cultivate the land, and supply you with vegetables, tobacco, and wood to repair your vessels, on the same conditions as the provisions. This is what I am ordered to propose to you, brothers, in the name of the French habitants and buccaneers of Saint Domingo; if these conditions please you, and I consider them just and equitable, accept them, and you will have no cause to repent having negotiated with us."

These propositions the filibusters were already acquainted with, and had discussed their advantages; hence they did not take long to deliberate, for they had made up their mind beforehand, as their presence at Port Margot proved.

"We accept your propositions, brother," Montbarts answered—"here is my hand, in the name of the filibusters I represent."

"And here is mine," Lepoletais said, "in the name of the habitants and buccaneers."

There was no other treaty but this honest shake of the hand between the adventurers; thus was concluded an alliance, which remained up to the dying day of buccaneering, as fresh and lively as when first made between the adventurers.

"Now," Montbarts continued, "let us proceed orderly. How many brothers have you capable of fighting?"

"Seventy," Lepoletais answered.

"Very good; we will add to these one hundred and thirty more from the fleet, which will give us an effective strength of two hundred good fusils. And you, Chief, what can you do for us?"

Up to this moment Omopoua had remained silent, listening to what was said with Indian gravity and decorum, and patiently waiting till his turn to speak arrived.

"Omopoua will add two hundred Carib warriors, with long fusils, to the palefaces," he replied; "his sons are warned; they await the order of the Chief —L'Olonnais has seen them."

"Good! These four hundred men will be commanded by myself; as this expedition is the most difficult and dangerous, I will undertake it. Michel le Basque will accompany me. I have aboard a guide, who will conduct us to Grand Fond. You, Drake, and you, David, will attack Leogane with your ships, while Bowline, with only fifteen men, will seize on Tortuga. Let us combine our movements, brothers, so that our three attacks may be simultaneous, and the Spaniards, surprised on three points at once, may not be able to assist one another. Tomorrow you will sail, gentlemen, taking with you one hundred and eighty-five men, more than sufficient, I believe, to capture Leogane. As for you, Bowline, you will keep the lugger with the fifteen men left you, and remain here, while watching Tortuga closely. This is the fifth of the month, brothers; on the fifteenth we will attack, as ten days will be sufficient for all of us to reach our posts, and take all the necessary measures. Now, gentlemen, return aboard your vessels, and send ashore, under orders of their officers, the contingents I intend to take with me."

The two Captains bowed to the Admiral, left the cabin, and returned to their ships.

"As for you," Montbarts added, turning to Lepoletais, "this is what you will do, brother. You will go with Omopoua to the Grand Fond, as if hunting, but you will carefully watch the town of San Juan, and the hatto del Rincón; we must, if possible, make sure of the inhabitants of that hatto; they are rich and influential, and their capture may be of considerable importance to us. You will arrange with Omopoua on the subject of the allies he promises to bring us; perhaps it will be as well for the Chief to try and lead the Spaniards on to his track, and force them to quit their positions: by managing cleverly we might then be able to defeat them in detail. Have you understood me, brother?"

"Zounds!" Lepoletais answered, "I should be an ass if I did not. All right! I will manoeuvre as you wish."

Montbarts then turned to the engagé, and made him a sign.

L'Olonnais drew nearer.

"Go ashore with the Carib and Lepoletais," the Admiral whispered in his ear —"look at everything, hear everything, watch everything; in an hour you will receive through Bowline a letter, which you must deliver into the hands of Doña Clara de Bejar, who resides in the hatto on the Grand Fond."

"That is easy," L'Olonnais answered, "if it must be, I will hand it to her in the midst of all her servants, in the hatto itself."

"Do nothing of the sort; arrange it so that she must come and fetch the letter."

"Hang it! That is more difficult! Still, I will try to succeed."

"You must succeed!"

"Ah! In that case, on the word of a man, you may reckon on it—though, hang me if I know how I shall manage it!"

Lepoletais had risen.

"Farewell, brother," he said; "when you land tomorrow I shall be on my way to the Grand Fond; I shall, therefore, not see you again till we meet there; but do not be alarmed—you shall find everything in order when you arrive. Ah! By the way, shall I take my body of buccaneers with me?"

"Certainly; they will be of the greatest use to you in watching the enemy; but hide them carefully."

"All right," he said.

At this moment Michael the Basque rushed suddenly into the cabin, with his features distorted by passion.

"What is the matter, messmate? Come, recover yourself," Montbarts said coolly to him.

"A great misfortune has happened to us," Michael exclaimed, as he passionately pulled out a handful of hair.

"What is it? Come, speak like a man, messmate."

"That villain, Antonio de la Ronda—"

"Well?" Montbarts interrupted, with a nervous tremor.

"He has escaped!"

"Malediction!"

"Ten men have set out in pursuit."

"Stuff! It is all up now; they will not catch him. What is to be done?"

"What has happened?" Lepoletais asked.

"Our guide has escaped."

"Is it only that? I promise to find you another."

"Yes, but this one is probably the cleverest spy the Spaniards possess; he knows enough of our secrets to make our expedition fail."

"Heaven preserve us from it! Stuff!" the buccaneer added, carelessly—"Think no more about it, brother; what is done is done—let us go ahead all the same."

And he left the cabin, apparently quite unaffected by the news.

CHAPTER XXV.

FRAY ARSENIO.

Let us now tell the reader who these buccaneers were of whom we have several times spoken, and what was the origin of the name given them, and which they gave themselves.

The red Caribs of the Antilles were accustomed, when they made prisoners in the obstinate contests they waged with each other, or which they carried on against the whites, to cut their prisoners into small pieces, and lay them upon a species of small hurdles, under which they lit a fire.

These hurdles were called *barbacoas*, the spot where they were set up *boucans*, and the operation *boucaning*, to signify at the same time roasting and smoking.

It was from this that the French boucaniers (anglicised into buccaneers) derived their name, with this difference, that they did to animals what the others did to men.

The first buccaneers were Spanish settlers on the Caribbean islands, who lived on intimate terms with the Indians; hence when they turned their attention to the chase, they accustomed themselves without reflection to employ these Indian terms, which were certainly characteristic, and for which it would have been difficult to substitute any others.

The buccaneers carried on no other trade but hunting; they were divided into two classes, the first only hunting oxen to get their hides, the second killing boars, whose flesh they salted and sold to the planters.

These two varieties of buccaneers were accoutred nearly in the same way, and had the same mode of life.

The real buccaneers were those who pursued oxen, and they never called the others by any name but hunters.

Their equipage consisted of a pack of twenty-four dogs, among which were two bloodhounds, whose duty it was to discover the animal; the price of these dogs, settled among themselves, was thirty livres.

As we have said, their weapon was a long fusil, manufactured at Dieppe or Nantes; they always hunted together, two at the least, but sometimes more, and then everything was in common between them. As we advance in the history of these singular men, we shall enter into fuller details about their mode of life and strange habits.

When Don Sancho and the Major-domo left them, Lepoletais and L'Olonnais had for a long time looked with a mocking glance after the two Spaniards, and then went on building their ajoupa and preparing their boucan, as if nothing had happened. So soon as the boucan was arranged, the fire lit, and the meat laid on the barbacoas, L'Olonnais set about curing the hide he had brought with him, while Lepoletais did the same to that of the bull which he had killed an hour previously.

He stretched the hide out on the ground, with the hairy side up, fastened it down by sixty-four pegs, driven into the earth, and then rubbed it vigorously with a mixture of ashes and salt, to make it dry more quickly.

This duly accomplished, he turned his attention to supper, the preparations for which were neither long nor complicated. A piece of meat had been placed in a small cauldron, with water and salt, and soon boiled; L'Olonnais drew it out by means of a long pointed stick, and laid it on a palm leaf in lieu of a dish; then he collected the grease with a wooden spoon, and threw it into a calabash. Into this grease he squeezed the juice of a lemon, added a little pimento, stirred it all up, and the sauce, the famous *pimentado*, so liked by the buccaneers, was ready. Placing the meat in a pleasant spot in front of the ajoupa, with the calabash by its side, he called Lepoletais, and the men sitting down facing each other, armed themselves with their knife and a wooden spit instead of a fork, and began eating with a good appetite, carefully dipping each mouthful of meat in the pimentado, and surrounded by their dogs, which, though not daring to ask for anything, fixed greedy glances on the provisions spread out before them, and followed with eager eyes every morsel swallowed by the adventurers.

They had been eating this in silence for some time, when the bloodhounds raised their heads, inhaling the air restlessly, and then gave several hoarse growls; almost immediately the whole pack began barking furiously.

"Eh, eh!" Lepoletais said, after drinking a mouthful of brandy and water, and handing the gourd to the engagé, "What is the meaning of this?"

"Some traveller, no doubt," L'Olonnais answered carelessly.

"At this hour," the buccaneer went on, as he raised his eyes to the sky, and consulted the stars, "why hang it all, it is past eight o'clock at night."

"Zounds! I do not know what it is. But stay, I do not know whether I am mistaken, for I fancy I can hear a horse galloping."

"It is really true, my son, you are not mistaken," the buccaneer continued, "it is indeed a horse; come, quiet, you devils," he shouted, addressing the dogs, which had redoubled their barking, and seemed ready to rush forward, "quiet, lie down, you ruffians."

The dogs, doubtless accustomed for a long time to obey the imperious accents of this voice, immediately resumed their places, and ceased their deafening clamour, although they still continued to growl dully.

In the meanwhile the galloping horses which the dogs had heard a great distance off, rapidly drew nearer; it soon became perfectly distinct, and at the end of a few minutes a horseman emerged from the forest, and became visible, although owing to the darkness it was not yet possible to see who this man might be.

On turning into the savannah, he stopped his horse, seemed to look around him, with an air of indecision, for some minutes, then, loosening the rein again, he came up toward the boucan at a sharp trot.

On reaching the two men, who continued their supper quietly, while keeping an eye on him, he bowed, and addressed them in Spanish—

"Worthy friends," he said to them, "whoever you may be, I ask you, in the name of the Lord, to grant a traveller, who has lost his way, hospitality for this night."

"Here is fire, and here is meat," the buccaneer replied, laconically, in the same language the traveller had employed; "rest yourself, and eat."

"I thank you," he said.

He dismounted: in the movement he made to leave the saddle, his cloak flew open, and the buccaneers perceived that the man was dressed in a religious garb. This discovery surprised them, though they did not allow it to be seen.

On his side the stranger gave a start of terror, which was immediately suppressed, on perceiving that in his precipitation to seek a shelter for the night, he had come upon a boucan of French adventurers.

The latter, however, had made him a place by their side, and while he was hobbling his horse, and removing its bridle, so that it might graze on the tall close grass of the savannah, they had placed for him, on a palm leaf, a lump of meat sufficient to still the appetite of a man who had been fasting for four and twenty hours.

Somewhat reassured by the cordial manner of the adventurers, and, in his impossibility to do otherwise, bravely resolving to accept the awkward situation in which his awkwardness had placed him, the stranger sat down between his two hosts, and began to eat, while reflecting on the means of escaping from the difficult position in which he found himself.

The adventurers, who had almost completed their meal before his arrival, left off eating long before him; they gave their dogs the food they had been expecting with so much impatience, then lit their pipes, and began smoking, paying no further attention to their guest beyond handing him the things he required.

At length the stranger wiped his mouth, and, in order to prove to his hosts that he was quite as much at his ease as they, he produced a leaf of paper and tobacco, delicately rolled a cigarette, lit it, and smoked apparently as calmly as themselves.

"I thank you for your generous hospitality, señores," he said, presently, understanding that along silence might be interpreted to his disadvantage, "I had a great necessity to recruit my strength, for I have been fasting since the morning."

"That is very imprudent, señor," Lepoletais answered, "to embark thus without any biscuit, as we sailors say; the savannah is somewhat like the sea, you know when you start on it, but you never know when you will leave it again."

"What you say is perfectly true, señor; had it not been for you, I am afraid I should have passed a very bad night."

"Pray say no more about that, señor; we have only done for you what we should wish to be done for us under similar circumstances. Hospitality is a sacred duty, which no one has a right to avoid: besides, you are a palpable proof of it."

"How so?"

"Why, you are a Spaniard, if I am not mistaken, while we, on the contrary, are French. Well, we forget for the moment our hatred of your nation, to welcome you at our fireside, as every guest sent by Heaven has the right to be received."

"That is true, señor, and I thank you doubly, be assured."

"Good Heavens!" the buccaneer replied, "I assure you that you act wrongly in dwelling so much on this subject. What we are doing at this moment is as much for you as in behalf of our honour, hence I beg you, señor, not to say any more about it, for it is really not worth the trouble."

"Bless me, señor," L'Olonnais said with a laugh, "why, we are old acquaintances, though you little suspect it, I fancy."

"Old acquaintances!" the stranger exclaimed, in surprise; "I do not understand you, señor."

"And yet what I am saying is very clear."

"If you would deign to explain," the stranger replied, completely thrown on his beam ends, as Lepoletais would have said, "perhaps I shall understand, which, I assure you, will cause me great pleasure."

"I wish for nothing better than to explain myself, señor," L'Olonnais said, with a bantering air; "and in the first place, permit me to observe, that, though your cloak is so carefully buttoned, it is not sufficiently so to conceal the Franciscan garb you wear under it."

"I am indeed a monk of that order," the stranger answered, rather disconcerted; "but that does not prove that you know me."

"Granted, but I am certain that I shall bring back your recollection by a single word."

"I fancy you are mistaken, my dear señor, and that we never saw each other before."

"Are you quite sure of that?"

"Man, as you are aware, can never be sure of anything; still, it seems to me —"

"And yet, it is so long since we met; it is true that you possibly did not pay any great attention to me."

"On my honour, I know not what you mean," the monk remarked after attentively examining him for a minute or two.

"Come," the engagé said with a laugh, "I will take pity on your embarrassment; and, as I promised you, dissipate all your doubts by a single word; we saw each other on the island of Nevis. Do you remember me?"

At this revelation, the monk turned pale; he lost countenance, and for some minutes remained as if petrified; still the thought of denying the truth did not come to him for a second.

"Where," L'Olonnais added, "you had a long conversation with Montbarts."

"Still," the monk said with a hesitation that was not exempt from terror, "I do not understand—"

"How I knew everything," L'Olonnais interrupted him laughingly, "then, you have not got to the end of your astonishment."

"What, I am not at the end?"

"Bah, Señor Padre, do you fancy that I should have taken the trouble to bother you about such a trifle? I know a good deal more."

"What do you say?" the monk exclaimed, recoiling instinctively from this man whom he was not indisposed to regard as a sorcerer, the more so because he was a Frenchman, and a buccaneer to boot, two peremptory reasons why Satan should nearly be master of his soul, if by chance he possessed one, which the worthy monk greatly doubted.

"Zounds!" the engagé resumed, "You suppose, I think, that I do not know the motive of your journey, the spot where you have come from, where you are going, and more than that, the person you are about to see."

"Oh, come, that is impossible," the monk said with a startled look.

Lepoletais laughed inwardly at the ill-disguised terror of the Spaniard.

"Take care, father," he whispered mysteriously in Fray Arsenio's ear, "that man knows everything; between ourselves, I believe him to be possessed by the demon."

"Oh!" he exclaimed, rising hastily and crossing himself repeatedly, which caused the adventurers a still heartier laugh.

"Come, resume your seat and listen to me," L'Olonnais continued as he seized him by the arm, and obliged him to sit down again, "my friend and I are only joking."

"Excuse me, noble caballeros," the monk stammered, "I am in an extraordinary hurry, and must leave you at once, though most reluctantly."

"Nonsense! Where could you go alone at this hour? Fall into a bog. Eh?"

This far from pleasant prospect caused the monk to reflect; still, the terror he felt was the stronger.

"No matter," he said, "I must be gone."

"Nonsense, you will never find your road to the hatto del Rincón in this darkness."

This time the monk was fairly conquered, this new revelation literally benumbed him, he fancied himself suffering from a terrible nightmare, and did not attempt to continue an impossible struggle.

"There," the engagé resumed, "now, you are reasonable; rest yourself, I will not torment you any more, and in order to prove to you that I am not so wicked as you suppose me, I undertake to find you a guide."

"A guide," Fray Arsenio stammered, "Heaven guard me from accepting one at your hand."

"Reassure yourself, señor Padre, it will not be a demon, though he may possibly have some moral and physical resemblance with the evil spirit; the guide I refer to is very simply a Carib."

"Ah!" said the monk drawing a deep breath, as if a heavy weight had been removed from his chest, "If he is really a Carib."

"Zounds! Who the deuce would you have it be?" Fray Arsenio crossed himself devoutly.

"Excuse me," he said, "I did not wish to insult you."

"Come, come, have patience, I will go myself and fetch the promised guide, for I see that you are really in a hurry to part company."

L'Olonnais rose, took his fusil, whistled to a bloodhound, and went off at a rapid pace.

"You will now be able," said Lepoletais, "to continue your journey without fear of going astray."

"Has that worthy caballero really gone to fetch me a guide, as he promised?" Fray Arsenio asked, who did not dare to place full confidence in the engagé's word.

"Hang it! I know no other reason why he should leave the boucan."

"Then you are really a buccaneer, señor?"

"At your service, padre."

"Ah, ah! And do you often come to these parts?"

"Deuce take me if I do not believe you are questioning me, monk," Lepoletais said with a frown, and looking him in the face; "how does it concern you whether I come here or not?"

"Me? Not at all."

"That is true, but it may concern others, may it not? And you would not be sorry to know the truth."

"Oh? can you suppose such a thing?" Fray Arsenio hastily said.

"I do not suppose, by Heaven, I know exactly what I am saying, but, believe me, señor monk, you had better give up this habit of questioning, especially with buccaneers, people who through their character, do not like questions, or else you might some day run the risk of being played an ugly trick. It is only a simple piece of advice I venture to give you."

"Thank you, señor, I will bear it in mind, though in saying what I did, I had not the intention you suppose."

"All the better, but still profit by my hint."

Thus rebuffed, the monk shut himself up in a timid silence; and in order to give a turn to his thoughts which, we are bound to say, were anything but rosy colored at this moment, he took up the rosary hanging from his girdle, and began muttering prayers in a low voice.

Nearly an hour passed then without a word being exchanged between the two men; Lepoletais cut up tobacco, while humming a tune, and the monk prayed, or seemed to be doing so.

At length a slight noise was heard a short distance off, and a few minutes later the engagé appeared, followed by an Indian, who was no other than Omopoua, the Carib chief.

"Quick, quick, señor monk," L'Olonnais said gaily; "here is your guide, I answer for his fidelity; he will lead you in safety within two gun shots of the hatto."

The monk did not let the invitation be repeated, for anything seemed to him preferable to remaining any longer in the company of these two reprobates; besides, he thought that he had nothing to fear from an Indian.

He rose at one bound, and bridled his horse again, which had made an excellent supper, and had had all the time necessary to rest.

"Señores," he said, so soon as he was in the saddle, "I thank you for your generous hospitality, may the blessing of the Lord be upon you!"

"Thanks," the engagé replied with a laugh, "but one last hint before parting; on arriving at the hatto, do not forget to tell Doña Clara from me, that I shall expect her here tomorrow; do you hear?"

The monk uttered a cry of terror; without replying, he dug his spurs into his horse's flanks, and set off at a gallop, in the direction where the Carib was already going, with that quick, elastic step, with which a horse has a difficulty in keeping up.

The two buccaneers watched his flight with a hearty laugh, then, stretching out their feet to the fire, and laying their weapons within reach, they prepared to sleep, guarded by their dogs, vigilant sentries that would not let them be surprised.

CHAPTER XXVI.

THE CONSEQUENCES OF A MEETING.

Fray Arsenio followed his silent guide delightedly, although he was surrendered into the hands of an Indian, who must instinctively hate the Spaniards, those ferocious oppressors of his decimated and almost destroyed race. Still, the monk was glad at having escaped safe and sound from the clutches of the adventurers, whom he feared not only as ladrones, that is to say, men without faith and steeped in vice, but also as demons, or at the least sorcerers in regular connection with Satan, for such were the erroneous ideas which the most enlightened of the Spaniards entertained about the filibusters and buccaneers.

It had needed all the devotion which the monk professed for Doña Clara, and all the ascendancy that charming woman possessed over those who approached her, to make him consent to execute a plan so mad in his opinion, as that of entering into direct relation with one of the most renowned chiefs of the filibusters, and it was with a great tremor that he had accompanied his penitent to Nevis.

When we met him, he was proceeding to the hatto, to inform Doña Clara, as had been arranged between them, of the arrival of the filibustering squadron at Port Margot, and consequently of Montbart's presence in the island of Saint Domingo.

Unfortunately the monk, but little used to night journeys, across untrodden roads which he must guess at every step, lost himself on the savannah; overcome with terror, almost dead with hunger, and worn out by fatigue, the monk had seen the light of a fire flashing a short distance off; the sight of this had restored him hope, if not courage, and he had consequently ridden as fast as he could toward the fire, and tumbled headlong into a boucan of French adventurers.

In doing this, he unconsciously followed the example of the silly moth, which feels itself irresistibly attracted to the candle in which it singes its wings.

More fortunate than these insects, the monk had burned nothing at all; he had rested, eaten and drunk well, and, apart from a very honest terror at finding himself so unexpectedly in such company, he had escaped pretty well, or at least he supposed so, from this great danger, and had even succeeded in obtaining a guide. Everything, then, was for the best, the Lord had not ceased to watch over His servant, and the latter only needed to let himself be guarded by Him. Moreover the monk's confidence was augmented by the taciturn carelessness of his guide who, without uttering a syllable, or even appearing to trouble himself about him the least in the world, walked in front of his horse, crossing the savannah obliquely, making a way through the tall grass, and seemed to direct himself as surely amid the darkness that surrounded him, as if he had been lit by the dazzling sunbeams.

They went on thus for a long time following each other without the interchange of a word; like all the Spaniards, Fray Arsenio professed a profound contempt for the Indians, and it was much against his will that he ever entered into relations with them. For his part, the Carib was not at all anxious to carry on with this man, whom he regarded as a born foe of his race, a conversation which could only be an unimportant gossip.

They had reached the top of a small hill, from which could be seen gleaming in the distance, like so many luminous dots, the watch fires of the soldiers encamped round the hatto, when all at once, instead of descending the hill and continuing his advance, Omopoua stopped, and looked round him anxiously, while strongly inhaling the air, and ordering the Spaniard by a wave of his hand to halt.

The latter obeyed and remained motionless as an equestrian statue, while observing with a curiosity blended with a certain amount of discomfort, the manoeuvres of his guide.

The Carib had laid himself down and was listening with his ear to the ground.

At the end of a few minutes he rose again, though he did not cease listening.

"What is the matter?" the monk, whom this conduct was beginning seriously to alarm, asked.

"Horsemen are coming towards us at full speed."

"Horsemen at this hour of night on the savannah?" Fray Arsenio remarked incredulously; "It is impossible."

"Why, you are here?" the Indian said with a jeering smile.

"Hum! That is true," the monk muttered, struck by the logic of the answer; "who can they be!"

"I do not know, but I will soon tell you," the Carib answered.

And before the monk had the time to ask him what his scheme was, Omopoua glided through the tall grass and disappeared, leaving Fray Arsenio greatly disconcerted at this sudden flight, and extremely annoyed at finding himself thus left alone in the middle of the desert.

A few minutes elapsed, during which the monk tried, though in vain, to hear the sound which the Indian's sharp sense of hearing had caused him to catch long before, amid the confused rumours of the savannah.

The monk, believing himself decidedly deserted by his guide, was preparing to continue his journey, leaving to Providence the care of bringing him safely into port, when he heard a slight rustling in the bushes close to him, and the Indian reappeared.

"I have seen them," he said.

"Ah!" the monk replied; "And who are they?"

"White men like you."

"Spaniards in that case?"

"Yes, Spaniards."

"All the better," Fray Arsenio continued, whom the good news completely reassured; "are they numerous?"

"Five or six at least; they are proceeding like yourself, towards the hatto, where, as far as I could understand, they are very eager to arrive."

"That is famous; where are they at this moment?"

"Two stones' throw at the most. According to the direction they are following, they will pass the spot where you are now standing."

"Better still. In that case we have only to wait."

"You can do so, if you think proper; but I have no wish to meet them."

"That is true, my friend," the monk remarked, with a paternal air. "And possibly such a meeting would not be agreeable to you; so pray accept my thanks for the manner in which you have guided me hitherto."

"You are quite resolved on waiting for them, then? If you like, I can enable you to avoid them."

"I have no motive for concealing myself from men of my own colour. Whoever they may be, I feel sure that I shall find friends in them."

"Very good. Your affairs concern yourself, and I have nothing to do with them. But the sound is drawing nearer, and as they will speedily arrive, I will leave you, for it is unnecessary for them to find me here."

"Farewell."

"One last recommendation: if by chance they had a fancy to ask who served as your guide, do not tell them."

"It is not at all probable they will ask this."

"No matter. Promise me, if they do, to keep my secret."

"Very good. I will be silent, since you wish it; although I do not understand the motive for such a recommendation."

The monk had not finished the sentence, ere the Indian disappeared.

The horsemen were rapidly approaching. The galloping of their steeds echoed on the ground like the rolling of thunder. Suddenly several shadows, scarcely distinguishable in the obscurity, rose as it were in the midst of the darkness, and a sharp voice shouted—

"Who goes there?"

"A friend!" the monk answered.

"Tell your name, *¡sangre de Dios!*" the voice repeated, passionately, while the dry snap of a pistol being cocked, sounded disagreeably in the monk's ears. "At night there are friends in the desert!"

"I am a poor Franciscan monk, proceeding to the hatto del Rincón; and my name is Fray Arsenio Mendoza."

A hoarse cry replied to the monk's words—a cry whose meaning he had not the time to conjecture; that is to say, whether it was the result of pleasure or anger; for the horsemen came up with him like lightning, and surrounded him even before he could understand the reason of such a headlong speed to reach him.

"Why, señores," he exclaimed, in a voice trembling with emotion, "what is the meaning of this? Have I to do with the *ladrones?*"

"Good! Good! Calm yourself, Señor Padre," a rough voice answered, which he fancied he recognised. "We are not *ladrones*, but Spaniards like yourself; and nothing could cause us more pleasure than meeting you at this moment."

"I am delighted at what you say to me, caballero. I confess that at first the suddenness of your movements alarmed me; but now I am completely reassured."

"All the better," the stranger replied, ironically; "for I want to talk with you."

"Talk with me, señor?" he said, with surprise.

"The spot and the hour are badly chosen for an interview, I fancy. If you will wait till we reach the hatto, I will place myself at your disposal."

"Enough talking. Get off your horse," the stranger observed, roughly; "unless you wish me to drag you off."

The monk took a startled glance around him, but the horsemen looked at him savagely, and did not appear disposed to come to his help.

Fray Arsenio, through profession and temperament, was quite the opposite of a brave man. The way in which the adventure began was commencing seriously to alarm him. He did not yet know into what hands he had fallen, but everything led him to suppose that these individuals, whoever they might be, were not actuated by kindly feelings towards him. Still any resistance was impossible, and he resigned himself to obey; but it was not without a sigh of regret, intended for the Carib, whose judicious advice he had spurned, that he at length got off his horse, and placed himself in front of his stern questioner.

"Light a torch!" the strange horseman said. "I wish this man to recognise me, so that, knowing who I am, he may be aware that he cannot employ any subterfuge with me, and that frankness alone will save him from the fate that menaces him."

The monk understood less and less. He really believed himself suffering from an atrocious nightmare.

By the horseman's orders, however, one of his suite had lighted a torch of ocote wood.

So soon as the flame played over the stranger's feature, and illumined his face, the monk gave a start of surprise, and clasped his hands at the same time as his countenance suddenly reassumed its serenity.

"Heaven be praised!" he said, with an accent of beatitude impossible to render. "Is it possible that it can be you, Don. Stenio de Bejar? I was so far from believing that I should have the felicity of meeting you this night, Señor Conde, that, on my faith, I did not recognise you, and felt almost frightened."

The Count, for it was really he whom the monk had so unfortunately met, did not answer for the moment, but contented himself with smiling.

Don Stenio de Bejar, who had left Saint Domingo at full speed, for the purpose of going to the hatto del Rincón, in order to convince himself of the truth of the information given him by Don Antonio de la Ronda, thus found himself, by the greatest accident, just as he was reaching his destination, and when he least expected it, face to face with Fray Arsenio Mendoza; that is to say, with the only man capable of proving to him peremptorily the truth or falsehood of the assertions of the spy, who had denounced Doña Clara to her husband.

Fray Arsenio's reputation for poltroonery had long been current among his countrymen, and hence nothing seemed more easy than to obtain from him the truth in its fullest details.

The Count believed himself almost certain, by employing intimidation, to make Fray Arsenio confess what he knew: hence, so soon as the latter had mentioned his name, Don Stenio, warned by the spy, who rode at his side, resolved to terrify the monk, and thus render it impossible for him to resist the orders he might intimate to him.

We take pleasure in believing that in acting thus, the Count had not the slightest intention of treating the monk with a violence, which in any case would be deplorable, but dishonourable on the part of a man in his position. Unfortunately, through the unforeseen and incomprehensible resistance which, contrary to all probability, the monk offered him, the Count was led away by his passion, and gave orders against his better judgment, when harshness and even cruelty could in no case be justified.

After a silence of some seconds, Don Stenio fixed a piercing glance on the monk, as if he wished to read his very soul, and then seized him brutally by the arm.

"Where have you come from?" he asked him, in a rough voice. "Is it the custom for monks of your order to ramble about the country at this hour of the night?"

"My lord!" Fray Arsenio stammered, thrown off his guard by this question, which he was far from expecting.

"Come, come!" the Count continued; "Answer at once, and let us have no subterfuge or tergiversation."

"But, my lord, I do not at all understand this great anger which you appear to have with me. I am innocent, I vow!"

"Ah! ah!" he said, with an ironical laugh; "You are innocent! ¡*Viva Dios!* you make haste to defend yourself before you are accused; hence you feel yourself guilty."

Fray Arsenio was aware of the Count's jealousy, which he concealed so poorly, that, in spite of all his efforts, it was visible to everybody. Hence he understood that Doña Clara's secret had been revealed to her husband; and he foresaw the peril that menaced him for having acted as her accomplice. Still, he hoped that the Count had only learnt certain facts, while remaining ignorant of the details of the Countess' voyage; and hence, though he trembled at heart at the thought of the dangers to which he was doubtless exposed, alone and defenceless, in the hands of a man blinded by passion and the desire of avenging what he regarded as a stain on his honour, he resolved, whatever might happen, not to betray the confidence which a woman had unhappily placed in him.

He raised his head and replied with a firm voice, and with an accent at which he was himself astonished—

"My lord, you are governor of Saint Domingo; you have a right to exercise justice over those placed under your rule. You possess almost sovereign power, but you have no right, as far as I know, to ill treat me, either by word or deed, or to make me undergo an examination at your caprice. I have superiors on whom I am dependant; have me taken before them; hand me over to their justice, if I have committed any fault they will punish me, for they alone have the right of condemning or acquitting me."

The Count had listened to the monk's long answer, while biting his lips savagely and stamping his foot with passion. He had not thought to find such resistance in this man.

"So, then," he exclaimed, when Fray Arsenio at length ceased speaking, "you refuse to answer me?"

"I refuse, my lord," he coldly replied, "because you have no right to question me."

"You forget, however, Señor Padre, that if I have not the right, I have the might, at least, at this moment."

"You are at liberty, my lord, to abuse that might, by applying it to an unhappy and defenceless man. I am no soldier, and physical suffering frightens me. I do not know how I shall endure the tortures you will perhaps inflict on me, but there is one thing of which I am certain."

"What is it, may I ask, Señor Padre?"

"That I will die, my lord, before answering any of your questions."

"We shall see that," he said, sarcastically, "if you compel me to have recourse to violence."

"You will see," he replied, in a gentle but firm voice, which denoted an irrevocable determination.

"For the last time, I deign to warn you: take care—reflect."

"All my reflections are made, my lord; I am in your power. Abuse my weakness as you may think proper, I shall not even attempt a useless defence. I shall not be the first monk of my order who has fallen a martyr to duty: others have preceded me, and others will doubtless follow me in this painful track."

The Count stamped his foot savagely; the spectators, dumb and motionless, exchanged terrified glances, for they foresaw that this scene would soon have a terrible denouement, between two men, neither of whom would make concessions; while the first of them, blinded by rage, would soon not be in a condition to listen to the salutary counsels of reason.

"My lord," Don Antonio de la Ronda murmured, "the stars are beginning to turn pale, and the day will soon dawn; we are still far from the hatto, would it not be better to set out without further delay?"

"Silence!" the Count answered, with a smile of contempt. "Pedro," he added, addressing one of his domestics, "a match."

The valet dismounted and advanced with a long sulphured match in his hand.

"The two thumbs," the Count said, laconically.

The domestic approached the monk; the latter offered his hands without hesitation, although his face was fearfully pale, and his whole body trembled.

Pedro coolly rolled the match between his two thumbs, passing it several times under his nails, and then turned to the Count.

"For the last time, monk," the latter said, "will you speak?"

"I have nothing to say to you, my lord," Fray Arsenio replied, in a soft voice.

"Light it," the Count commanded, biting his lips till they bled.

The valet, with the passive obedience distinguishing men of this class, set fire to the match.

The monk fell on his knees and raised his eyes to Heaven. His face had assumed an earthy tint, a cold perspiration beaded on his temples, and his hair stood on end. The suffering he experienced must be horrible, for his chest heaved violently, although his parched lips remained dumb.

The Count watched him anxiously.

"Will you speak now, monk?" he said to him in a hollow voice.

Fray Arsenio turned toward him a face whose features were distorted by pain, and gave him a look full of ineffable gentleness.

"I thank you, my lord," he said, "for having taught me that pain does not exist for a man whose faith is lively."

"My curses on you, wretch!" the Count exclaimed, as he hurled him down with a blow on the chest. "To horse, señores, to horse, so that we may reach the hatto before sunrise."

The cavaliers remounted, and went off at full speed, leaving, without a glance of compassion, the poor monk, who, vanquished by pain, had rolled fainting on the ground.

CHAPTER XXVII.

THE ORGANIZATION OF THE COLONY.

A triple expedition, so serious as that conceived by Montbarts, demanded, for its success, extreme care and precautions.

The few points occupied by the buccaneers on the Spanish isles, did not at all resemble towns; they were agglomerations of houses built without order, according to the liking or caprice of the owner, and occupying a space twentyfold larger than they should have taken in accordance with the population. Hence, these points were spots almost impossible to defend against a well-combined attack of the Spaniards, if the thought occurred to the latter of finishing once for all with their formidable neighbours.

Port Margot, for instance, the most important point in the French possessions as a strategic position, was only a miserable hamlet, open to all comers, without police or organization, where every language was spoken, and which Spanish spies entered with the greatest facility without incurring a risk of discovery, and thus scented the plans of the filibusters.

Montbarts, before advancing and attacking the Spaniards, whom he correctly suspected of being already acquainted with the motive of his presence on the island, either through Don Antonio de la Ronda, or other spies, and not wishing, when he was preparing to surprise the enemy, to be himself surprised and see his retreat cut off by an unforeseen attack, resolved to shelter Port Margot from a *coup de main*.

The grand council of the filibusters was convened on board the admiral's lugger. In this way the resolutions formed by the council would not transpire outside, and not reach hostile ears, ever open to hear them.

Two days after the departure of Lepoletais, the council therefore assembled on the deck of the vessel, which had been prepared for the purpose, as the admiral's cabin had been judged too small to contain all those whom their wealth or their reputation authorized in being present at the meeting.

At ten in the morning, numerous skiffs left the shore and pulled alongside the lugger, boarding it on all sides simultaneously.

Montbarts received the delegates as they presented themselves, and led them beneath the awning prepared for them.

Ere long, all the delegates were assembled on board: they were forty in number; filibusters, buccaneers, and habitants, all adventurers who had lived for several years on the isles, and desperate enemies of the Spaniards. Their complexion, bronzed by the tropical sun, their energetic features, and flashing glances, made them resemble bandits rather than peaceful colonists; but their frank and decided manners allowed a guess at the prodigies of incredible daring which they had already accomplished, and were ready to accomplish again, when the moment for action arrived.

When all the members of the council were on board, Michael the Basque gave the skiffs orders to return ashore, and to come alongside again when they saw a large black and red flag hoisted at the mainmast of the lugger. A splendid lunch preceded the council, which, was held at table and during the dessert, so as to foil any indiscreet glances, which were doubtless watching what was going on aboard from the top of the cliffs.

When the repast was ended, and spirits, pipes, and tobacco had been laid on the table by the engagés, an order was given to remove the awning; the whole of the lugger's crew retired to the bows, and Montbarts, without leaving his seat, struck the table with his knife to request silence.

The delegates vaguely knew that grave interests were about to be discussed, hence they had only eaten and drunk for form's sake, and though the table offered all the appearances of a true filibustering orgy, their brains were perfectly clear, and their heads cool.

The road of Port Margot offered at this moment a strange spectacle, which was not deficient, however, in a certain picturesque and wild grandeur.

Thousands of canoes were lying on their oars, forming an immense circle, of which the filibustering squadron was the centre.

On shore, the cliffs and rocks were literally hidden by the confused and dense mass of spectators who had flocked from all the houses to watch, at a distance, this gigantic and Homeric feast, whose serious motive they were far from suspecting, beneath its frivolous appearance.

Montbarts, after calling his friends' attention in a few words, to the enormous crowd of spectators who surrounded them, and showing how correct he had been in taking his precautions in consequence, filled his glass, and rose, shouting in a sonorous voice—

"Brethren, the health of the king!"

"The health of the king!" the filibusters responded, as they rose, and clinked their glasses together.

At the same moment, all the guns of the lugger were discharged with a formidable noise; a loud clamour that rose from the beach proved that the spectators heartily joined in this patriotic toast.

"Now," the admiral continued, as he sat down, which movement was imitated by his companions, "let us talk of our business, and be careful in doing so, that our gestures may not allow a suspicion of what is occupying us, since our words cannot be overheard."

The council commenced its session. Montbarts, with the lofty views and clearness of expression he possessed, explained, in a few words, the critical position in which the colony would find it, unless energetic measures were taken, not only to place it in a position to defend itself, but also to hold out during the absence of the expedition.

"I can understand," he said in conclusion, "that so long as we merely purposed to hunt wild bulls, such precautions were unnecessary, for our breasts were a sure rampart for our habitations; but from today the position is changed, we wish to create for ourselves an impregnable refuge; we are going to attack the Spaniards in their homes, and must consequently expect terrible reprisals from enemies, who, from the way in which we act towards them, will soon comprehend that we wish to remain the sole possessors of this land, which they have accustomed themselves to regard as belonging to them legitimately; we must, therefore, be in a position, not alone to resist them, but to inflict on them such a chastisement for their audacity, that they will be for ever disgusted with any fresh attempts to regain the territory we have conquered. To effect this, we must build a real town, in the place of the temporary camp which has, up to the present, sufficed us; and, with the exception of the members of our association, no stranger must be allowed to introduce himself among us, for the sake of spying us, and repeating to our enemies our secrets, whatever their nature may be."

The filibusters warmly applauded these remarks, whose truth they recognized. They at length saw the necessity of setting order in their disorder, and entering the great human family, by themselves accepting some of those laws, from which they fancied they had enfranchised themselves for ever, and which are the sole condition of the vitality of society.

Under the omnipotent influence of Montbarts and the members of the association of the Twelve, who were scattered about the meeting, the urgent measures were immediately discussed and settled; but when everything was arranged, the council suddenly found itself stopped short by a difficulty of which it had not thought at all—who was to be entrusted with the duty of carrying out the measures, as no buccaneer had a recognized authority over the rest?

The difficulty was great; almost insurmountable. Still it was Montbarts who again smoothed down the difficulty to the general satisfaction.

"Nothing is more easy," he said, "than to find the man we want; this is an exceptional case, and we must act according to circumstances. Let us elect a chief, as for a dangerous expedition, let us choose one who is energetic and intelligent, which will be a trifle, as the only difficulty will be the choice among so many equally good. This chief will be elected by us, the first for a year, his successor for only six months, in order to guard against any abuse of power they might eventually be attempted to try. This chief will assume the title of governor, and in reality govern all civil matters, assisted by a council of seven members, chosen by the habitants, as well as by subaltern agents, nominated by himself. The laws he will employ exist, for they are those of our association; it is understood that the governor will watch, like a captain aboard his ship, over the safety of the colony, and, in the event of treachery, will be punishable with death. This proposition is, I believe, the only one that we can take into consideration; does it suit you, brothers? Do you accept it?"

The delegates replied by a universal affirmation,

"In that case let us at once proceed to the election."

"Pardon me, brothers," Belle Tête said, "with your permission, I have a few remarks to submit to the council."

"Speak, brother, we will hear you," Montbarts answered him.

"I offer myself," Belle Tête said frankly, "as governor, not through ambition, for that would be absurd, but because I believe that I am at this moment the best man for the place; you all know me, and hence I will not put forward my qualifications. Certain reasons urge me to try, if possible, to withdraw my promise, and not follow the expedition; to which, however, I feel convinced that I shall render great services, if you choose me as governor."

"You have heard, brethren," Montbarts said, "consult together, but fill your glasses first, you have ten minutes to reflect; at the end of that time all the glasses that have not been emptied will be considered as adverse votes."

"Ah, traitor," Michael the Basque said, leaning over to Belle Tête's ear, by whose side he was seated, "I know why you want to stop at Port Margot."

"You? Stuff," he answered with embarrassment.

"Zounds, it is not difficult to guess, you are caught, mate."

"Well, it is true, and you are right, that little devil of a woman I bought at St. Kitts has turned my head; she turns me round her little finger."

"Ah! love!" Michael said ironically.

"The deuce take love, and the woman too; a girl no bigger than that, whom I could smash with one blow."

"She is very pretty, you showed good taste; her name is Louise, is it not?"

"Yes, Louise; it was a bad bargain I made."

"Nonsense!" Michael said, with the utmost seriousness, "well, there is a way of arranging the matter."

"Do you think so?"

"Zounds, I am sure of it."

"I should like to know it, for I confess to you that she has completely upset my ideas; the confounded girl, with her bird's voice, and sly smile, turns me about like a whirligig: by Heaven, I am the most unfortunate of men—tell me your plan, brother."

"Why, sell her to me."

Belle Tête suddenly turned pale at this blunt offer, which, indeed, settled everything; but which, though he did not suspect it, Michael only made in a joke, and to try him; he frowned, and angrily replied in a voice trembling with emotion, and striking the table with his fist—

"Zounds, mate, that is a magnificent way you have found, but the fiend take me if I accept it; no, no, whatever sorrow the little witch causes me—have I not told you that she has bewitched me?—I love her! Blood and thunder, do you understand that?"

"Of course I understand it; but come, reassure yourself, I have not the slightest intention of depriving you of your Louise; what should I do with a wife? Besides, what I have seen of other men's love affairs, does not offer me the slightest inducement to try it on my own account."

"All right," Belle Tête replied, reassured by this frank declaration, "that is speaking like a man; and, after all, you are right, brother; although I would not consent for anything in the world to part with my Louise, still, after the experience I have of her, if the bargain was to be made again, hang me if I would purchase her."

"Stuff!" said Michael, with a shrug of his shoulders, "Men always say that, and when the moment arrives, they never fail to begin the same folly over again."

Belle Tête reflected for a moment, and then tapped Michael amicably on the shoulder, at the same time saying with a laugh—

"On my word that is true, brother; you are right, I believe that I should really behave as you say."

"I am certain of it," Michael replied, with another shrug of his shoulders.

During this aside, between the two adventurers, the ten minutes had elapsed.

"Brethren," said Montbarts, "we are about to proceed to an examination of the votes."

He looked: all the glasses were empty.

"You are unanimous," he said, "and that is well. Brother Belle Tête, you are elected governor of Port Margot."

"Brethren," the latter said, bowing all round, "I thank you for having given me your votes. I shall not deceive your expectations; our colony, even though I was obliged to bury myself beneath its ruins, shall never fall into the hands of the Spaniards, and you know me well enough not to doubt my oath. I intend to set to work this very day; for, as our admiral has very justly said, we have not a moment to lose. Confide the duty of guarding your interests to me."

"Before we separate," said Montbarts, "it would be as well, I fancy, to agree to keep our deliberations secret for a few days."

"You may divulge them tomorrow without danger," Belle Tête continued; "but allow me, brethren, to choose from among you the few assistants I shall require."

"Do so," the filibusters answered.

Belle Tête named eight adventurers, whose blind bravery he knew, and then addressed the delegates for the last time, who were already rising and preparing to leave the ship.

"You remember, I trust that I am considered by you the leader of an expedition."

"Yes," they replied.

"Consequently you owe me the most perfect obedience to all the orders I shall give you in the common interest."

"Yes," they repeated.

"You swear, then, to obey me without any hesitation or murmuring?"

"We do."

"Very good; now farewell for the present, brothers."

The boats had been recalled by a flag hoisted at the main yard, and a few minutes after all the delegates had left the ship, except Belle Tête and the eight officers chosen by him.

Montbarts and Belle Tête remained shut up for some hours, doubtless settling the measures which must be adopted in order to obtain the desired result as soon as possible; then, a little before sunset, the new Governor took leave of the Admiral, entered a boat prepared expressly for him, and returned ashore, followed by his officers.

About eleven o'clock in the evening, when the town appeared completely asleep, when all doors were shut, and lights extinguished, an observer in a position to see what was going on, would have noticed a strange spectacle.

Armed men glided gently out of the houses, casting inquiring glances to the right and left, that seemed trying to pierce the profound darkness by which they were surrounded. They proceeded separately on tiptoe to the principal square, where they joined other men armed like themselves, who, having arrived first, were waiting.

Ere long the number of these men, which was augmented every moment, became considerable; at an order, given in a low voice, they broke up into several parties, left the square by different outlets, went out of the town, and formed a wide circle all round it.

One last band of about forty men had remained in the square, however; this party was broken up in its turn, but, instead of also leaving the town, platoons, composed of ten men each, went from the square in four different directions, and entered the streets.

The latter were proceeding to pay domiciliary visits; no house escaped their vigilance, they entered all, searching them with the most scrupulous exactness, sounding the walls and flooring, and even opening cupboards and chests.

Such minute researches necessarily occupied a long time, and did not terminate till sunrise.

Eight Spanish spies had been discovered in the houses, and three arrested by the sentries at the moment when they attempted flight, or eleven in all.

The Governor had them temporarily put in irons aboard the lugger, so that they could not escape.

At sunrise, buccaneers, habitants, engagés, and filibusters, all armed with spades, pickaxes, and hatchets, set about digging a trench round the town.

This job, which was performed with extraordinary ardor, lasted three days; the trench was twelve feet wide, by fifteen deep, and the earth was thrown up on the side of the town; on this *talus* stakes were planted, bound together with strong iron bands, embrasures being left to place guns, and for loopholes.

While the entire population thus laboured with the feverish ardor that accomplishes prodigies, large clearings had been effected in the woods surrounding the port; then the forest was fired, care being taken that the fire should not extend beyond a demi-league in all directions.

These gigantic works, which, in ordinary times, would demand a lengthened period, were finished at the end of ten days, which would seem incredible were not the fact stated in several records worthy of belief.

Port Margot was thus, thanks to the energy of its Governor, and the passive obedience with which the filibusters executed his orders, not only protected against a *coup de main*, but also rendered capable of resisting a regular siege. And this had been effected with such secrecy, that nothing had transpired abroad; and owing to the precautions taken at the outset, the Spaniards had no suspicion of the change so menacing to them, and which presaged an internecine war.

When the fortifications were finished, the Governor had eleven gallows erected, at a certain distance from each other, on the glacis. The unhappy Spanish spies were suspended from them, and their bodies were fastened to the gallows by iron chains, so that, as Belle Tête said, with an ill-omened smile, the sight of the corpses might terrify those of their compatriots, who might be tempted to follow their example, and introduce themselves into the town.

All the habitants were then convoked in the chief square, and Belle Tête mounted a platform erected for the purpose, and announced to them the determinations formed aboard the lugger, his nomination to the post of Governor, the measures he had thought it his duty to take for the general welfare, and ended by asking their approbation.

This approbation the inhabitants most willingly granted, because they found themselves in presence of accomplished facts, which did not in any way injure them.

The Governor, thus finding his undertakings sanctioned, invited the inhabitants to nominate a council of seven members chosen from among themselves; and this proposition they joyfully accepted, because they justly anticipated that these councillors would defend their interests.

The seven municipal councillors were therefore elected at once, and, by the Governor's invitation, took their seat by his side on the platform.

Then the Governor informed his audience that nothing was changed in the colony, which would continue to be governed by the laws in force among the filibusters, that everyone would live in the same liberty as in the past, and that the measures taken were solely intended to protect the interests of all, and in no way to annoy the colonists, or subject them to a humiliating yoke.

This final assurance produced the best effect on the crowd, and the Governor retired, amid shouts and the warmest protestations of devotion.

Although Montbarts had chosen to remain obstinately in the background, all these ameliorations were solely due to him; Belle Tête had merely been a passive and submissive agent in his hands.

When the Admiral, saw matters in the state he desired, he resolved to depart, and after a final interview with the Governor, he placed himself at the head of his filibusters, and left the town.

Michael the Basque had departed several hours previously, entrusted with a secret mission, and accompanied by ninety resolute men.

From this moment the expedition commenced; but what its result would be no one could as yet foretell.

CHAPTER XXVIII.

THE FLIGHT FROM THE HATTO.

Without taking the time to peruse the letters that were handed him, Don Sancho concealed them in his doublet, and proceeded hastily to his sister's apartment.

She was anxiously awaiting him.

"Here you are at last, brother," she exclaimed on perceiving him.

"What," the young man replied, as he kissed her hand, "were you expecting me?"

"Oh, yes, that I was; but you are very late—what has kept you so long?" she asked, in agitation.

"Where have I been? Why, s'death! I have been hunting, the only pleasure allowed a gentleman in this horrible country."

"What, at this hour?"

"Zounds, my dear Clara, a man gets home when he can, especially in this country, where we ought to feel very happy at reaching home again at all."

"You are speaking in enigmas, brother, and I do not at all understand you; be kind enough, therefore, to explain yourself clearly—have you fallen into bad company?"

"Yes, and very bad, too; but forgive me, my dear Clara, if you have no objection, let us proceed regularly. You desired to see me immediately on my return, and here I am at your orders; be kind enough, therefore, to tell me how I can possibly be of service to you, and then I will narrate the series of singular events with which my today's sport has been diversified. I will not hide from you that I have certain questions to ask of you, and certain explanations, which I feel sure you will not refuse to give me."

"What do you mean, Sancho?"

"Nothing at present; do you speak first, sister."

"Well, if you insist on it—"

"I do not insist at all, sister—I only request it."

"Very good, I yield to your request; I have received several letters."

"So I have; but I confess that I have not read them yet, and do not think they are of any great importance."

"I have read mine, and do you know what they tell me beside other news?"

"Indeed, no, unless it be my appointment to the post of Alcade Mayor of Hispaniola, which, I allow, would greatly surprise me," he said, laughingly.

"Do not jest so, Sancho; the matter is very serious."

"Really? In that case speak, little sister. You see I have as solemn a face as your dear husband."

"It is exactly to him I refer."

"Stuff! My brother-in-law? Has any accident happened to him in the performance of his noble and wearisome duties?"

"No, on the contrary, he is in better health than usual."

"In that case, all the better for him; I wish him no harm, though he is the most fastidious gentleman of my acquaintance."

"Will you listen to me—yes or no?" she asked, impatiently.

"Why, I am doing so, dear sister."

"You are really insupportable."

"Come, do not be angry—I have done; I will not laugh anymore."

"Have you seen the two Fifties encamped in front of the hatto?"

"Yes, and I must allow that I was greatly surprised to see them."

"You will be much more surprised on hearing that my husband is coming here."

"He? Impossible, sister! He did not say a word to me about the journey."

"Because it is secret."

"Ah, ah!" the young man remarked, with a frown; "And are you sure that he is coming?"

"Certain. The person who writes me so was present at his departure, which no one suspects; the courier who brought me the news, and to whom the greatest diligence was recommended, is only a few hours ahead of him."

"This is, indeed, serious," the young man muttered.

"What is to be done?"

"S'death!" the young man replied, carelessly, but gazing fixedly at Doña Clara—"Welcome him."

"Oh!" the lady exclaimed, twisting her hands despairingly, "I have been betrayed—he is coming to avenge himself!"

"Avenge himself? For what, sister?"

She gave him a look of strange significance, and then bent over him.

"I am ruined, brother," she said, in a hollow voice, "for this man knows everything, and will kill me."

Don Sancho, in spite of himself, was affected by this sorrow; he adored his sister, and felt ashamed of the part he was playing at this moment before her.

"And I, too, Clara," he said to her, "know everything."

"You! Oh, you are jesting, brother."

"No, I am not; I love you, and wish to save you, even if I gave my life to do so: hence, reassure yourself, and do not fix upon me eyes haggard with grief."

"What do you know, in heaven's name?"

"I know that which probably a traitor, as you called him, has sold to your husband, that is to say, that you left the hatto, went aboard a vessel, which conveyed you to Nevis, and there—"

"Oh! Not a word more, brother," she exclaimed as she fell into his arms; "you are really well informed, but I swear to you, brother, in the name of what is most sacred in the world, that, although appearances condemn me, I am innocent."

"I know it, sister, and never doubted it; what is your intention, will you await your husband here?"

"Never, never! Did I not tell you he would kill me?"

"What is to be done then?"

"Fly, fly without delay; at once."

"But where shall we go?"

"How do I know? To the cliff or the forest, live among the wild beasts sooner than remain any longer here."

"Very good, we will go, I know where to take you."

"You?"

"Yes, did I not tell you that sundry accidents happened to me today while hunting?"

"So you did; but what has that to do with it?"

"A great deal," he interrupted; "the Major-domo, who accompanied me, and I tumbled over an encampment of filibusters."

"Ah," she said, turning paler than she had been before.

"Yes, and I intend to conduct you to that encampment; besides, one of the buccaneers entrusted me with a message for you."

"What do you mean?"

"Exactly what I am saying, sister."

She appeared to reflect for an instant, and then turned resolutely to the young man.

"Well, be it so, brother, let us go to those men, though they are represented as so cruel; perhaps every human feeling has not been extinguished in their hearts, and they will take pity on me."

"When shall we go?"

"As speedily as possible."

"That is true, but the hatto is probably watched and the soldiers have doubtless secret orders, you may be a prisoner without suspecting it, my poor sister; for what other reason would the two Fifties be here?"

"Oh! In that case I am lost."

"Perhaps there is one way, and the orders given doubtless only affect you; but unfortunately the journey will be long, fatiguing, and beset with numberless perils."

"What matter, brother? I am strong, do not be anxious about me."

"Very good, we will try; you are absolutely determined on flight?"

"Yes, whatever may befall me."

"Well then, we will put our trust in heaven, wait for me a moment."

The young man left the room and returned a few minutes later, bearing a rather large bundle under his arm.

"Here are my page's clothes, I do not know how they happen to be in my possession, but my valet probably placed them in my portmanteau by mistake, for they are new, and I remember that the tailor brought them home a few minutes before my departure from Saint Domingo, but I thank accident for causing it to be so. Dress yourself, wrap yourself up in a cloak, put this hat on your head, I will answer for everything. Besides, this costume is preferable to your woman's clothes for crossing the savannah; mind and not forget to place these pistols and this dagger in your belt, for there is no knowing what may happen."

"Thanks brother! I shall be ready in a quarter of an hour."

"Good; during that time I will go and reconnoitre; do not open the door to anyone but me."

"You may depend upon me."

The young man lit a cigarette and left the apartment with the most careless air he could assume.

On entering the zaguán, the Count found himself face to face with the Majordomo. Señor Birbomono had such an anxious look that it did not escape Don Sancho; still he continued to advance, pretending not to notice it.

But the Major-domo came straight up to him.

"I am glad to meet you, Excellency," he said, "if you had not come within ten minutes, I should have knocked at the door of your apartment."

"Ah!" Don Sancho observed, "What pressing motive was there to urge you to such a step?"

"Is your Excellency aware of what is taking place?" the Major-domo continued, without appearing to notice the young man's ironical tone.

"What! Is there really anything happening?"

"Does not your Excellency know it?"

"Probably not, as I ask you; after all, as the news, I am sure, interests me but very slightly, you are quite at liberty not to tell it to me."

"On the contrary, Excellency, it interests you as well as all the inhabitants of the hatto."

"Oh! oh! What is it then?"

"It appears that the commander of the two Fifties, has placed sentries all round the hatto."

"Very good, in that case, we need not fear being attacked by the buccaneers, of whom you are so afraid, and I will thank the commandant for it."

"You are at liberty to do so, Excellency, but I fancy you will find it difficult."

"Why so?"

"Because orders are given to let anyone enter the hatto but nobody leave it."

A shudder ran through the young man's veins on hearing this; he turned frightfully pale, but recovering himself almost immediately, remarked carelessly,

"Stuff! that order cannot affect me."

"Pardon me, Excellency, it is general."

"In that case, you think that, if I tried to go out—"

"You would be stopped."

"Confound it, that is very annoying, not that I have any intention of going out, but as by my character, I am very fond of doing things which are prohibited—"

"You would like to take a walk, I suppose, Excellency?"

Don Sancho looked at Birbomono, as if trying to read his thoughts.

"And suppose such were my intention?" he resumed presently.

"I would undertake to get you out."

"You?"

"Yes, I; am I not the Major-domo of the hatto?"

"That is true; thus, the prohibition does not extend to you?"

"To me, as to the rest, Excellency; but the soldiers do not know the hatto as I know; I could Slip between their fingers, whenever I liked."

"I have strong inclination to try it."

"Do so, Excellency; I have three horses at a spot where no one but myself could find them."

"Why, three horses?" the young man asked, pricking up his ears.

"Because, doubtless, you do not wish to ride with me only, but will take someone with you."

Don Sancho, understanding that the Major-domo had penetrated his thoughts, made up his mind at once.

"Let us play fairly," he said, "can you be faithful."

"I am so, and devoted too, Excellency, as you have a proof."

"What assures me that you are not laying a trap for me?"

"With what object?"

"That of obtaining a reward from the Count."

"No, Excellency, no reward would induce me to betray my mistress; I may be anything you please, but I love Doña Clara, who has always been kind to me, and has often protected me."

"I am willing to believe you, and indeed have no time to discuss the point, but here are my conditions: a bullet through the head if you betray me, a thousand piastres if you are faithful; do you accept them?"

"I do, Excellency, the thousand piastres are gained."

"You know that I do not threaten in vain."

"I know you."

"Very good, what must we do?"

"Follow me, that is all; our flight will be most easy, for I prepared everything on my return; I had my suspicions on seeing those demons of soldiers, suspicions which were soon changed into certainty, after some skilful inquiries here and there; my devotion to my mistress rendered me clear sighted, and you see that I acted wisely in taking my precautions."

The accent with which the Major-domo pronounced these words, had such a stamp of truth, his face was so frank and open, that the young Count's last suspicions were dissipated.

"Wait for me," he said, "I will go and fetch my sister."

And he hurried away.

"Oh!" said Birbomono, with a grin, so soon as he was alone, "I do not know whether Señor don Stenio de Bejar will be pleased at seeing his wife escape in this way, when he felt so certain of holding her; poor señora! She is so good to us all, that it would be infamous to betray her, and then, after all, this is a good deed which brings me one thousand piastres," he added, rubbing his hands, "that is a very decent amount."

It was about eleven o'clock at night, all the lights in the hatto were extinguished by orders of the Major-domo, who had provided for everything; the slaves had been dismissed to their huts, and a solemn silence brooded over the landscape, a silence solely interrupted at regular intervals, by the sentries who challenged each other in a monotonous voice.

Don Sancho soon returned, accompanied by his sister, wrapped up like himself, in a long mantle.

Doña Clara did not speak, but on joining the Major-domo, she gracefully held out her right hand to him, on which he respectfully impressed his lips.

Although the officers had told the soldiers to keep a good guard, and watch carefully, not only the hatto, but its environs, the latter, slightly reassured by the darkness on one hand, and on the other, by the gloomy and mysterious depths of the forests that surrounded them, stood motionless behind the trees, contenting themselves with responding to the challenge, every half hour, but not venturing to go even a few yards from the shelter they had chosen.

The reasons for this apparent cowardice, were simple, and although we have explained them, we will repeat them here, for the sake of greater clearness.

In the early times of the buccaneers landing on Saint Domingo, the Fifties sent by the governor in pursuit of them, were armed with muskets; but after several encounters with the French, in which the latter gave them an awful thrashing, their terror of the adventurers became so great that, whenever they were sent on an expedition against these men, whom they almost regarded as demons, no sooner did they enter the forests, or the mountain gorges, or even the savannahs, where they might suppose the buccaneers to be ambushed, than they began to fire their pieces right and left, for the purpose of warning the enemies, and inducing them to withdraw.

The result of this clever manoeuvre was that the adventurers, thus warned, decamped in reality, and thus became intangible; the governor noticing this result, eventually guessed its cause, and hence, in order to avoid such a thing in future, he took the muskets away from the soldiers and substituted lances. This change, let us hasten to add, was not at all to the liking of these brave soldiers, who thus saw their ingenious scheme foiled, and were even more exposed to the blows of their formidable enemies.

It was almost without being obliged to take any other precaution than that of walking noiselessly and not speaking, that the Major-domo and the two persons he served as guide, succeeded in quitting the hatto on the opposite side to that on which the Fifties had established their bivouac.

Once the line of sentries was passed, the fugitives hurried on more rapidly, and soon reached a thicket in the midst of which three fully accoutred horses were so thoroughly hidden that unless known to be there, it would have been impossible to find them; for a greater precaution, and to prevent them from neighing, the Major-domo had fastened a cord round their nostrils.

So soon as the three were mounted, and before starting, Birbomono turned to Don Sancho,—

"Where are we going, Excellency?" he asked.

"Do you know the spot where the buccaneers we met today are bivouacked?" the young man replied.

"Yes, Excellency."

"Do you think you could succeed in finding the bivouac in the midst of the darkness?"

The Major-domo smiled.

"Nothing is more easy," he said.

"In that case lead us to those men."

"Very good; but, Excellency, be good enough not press your horse on at present, for we are still near the house, and the slightest imprudence would be sufficient to give an alarm."

"Do you think, then, that they would venture to pursue us?"

"Separately, certainly not; but as they are so numerous, they would not hesitate; the less so, because from what I heard them say, they feel certain that the buccaneers have never come into these parts. This redoubles their bravery, and they would perhaps not be sorry to furnish a proof of it at our expense."

"Excellent reasoning; regulate our pace, therefore, as you think proper, and we will only act in accordance with your judgment."

They set out; with the exception of the precautions they were obliged to take not to be discovered, the journey had nothing disagreeable about it, on a bright and perfumed night, beneath a sky studded with brilliant stars, and in the midst of a most delightful scenery, whose slightest diversities the transparency of the atmosphere allowed to be seen.

After an hour spent in a moderate trot, their pace became insensibly more rapid, and the horses growing gradually more excited, eventually broke into a gallop, at which their riders kept them for a considerable period.

Doña Clara bent over her horse's neck, and with her eyes eagerly fixed ahead, seemed to upbraid the slowness of this ride, which, however, had assumed the headlong speed of a pursuit: at times she leant over to her brother, who constantly kept by her side, and asked him in a choking voice—

"Shall we soon arrive?"

"Yes, have patience, sister," the young man said, suppressing a sigh of pity for the agony which preyed on his sister's heart.

And their pace grew more rapid than ever.

The stars were already expiring in the heavens, the atmosphere was growing refreshed, the horizon was striped by long mother-o'-pearl coloured bands, a light sea breeze brought up to the travellers its alkaline odours, and the night had passed. Suddenly, at the moment when the three riders were about to emerge from a thick wood, in which they had been following a track made by the wild cattle for nearly an hour, the Major-domo, who was a few yards ahead, pulled up his horse and leant back.

"Stop, in Heaven's name!" he exclaimed, in a low voice.

The young couple obeyed, though they did not comprehend this order.

The Major-domo went up to them.

"Look!" he muttered, and stretched out his arm toward the savannah.

A rapid gallop, that drew nearer every second, but which the noise of their own march had prevented them from hearing, now smote their ears, and almost at the same moment they saw through the screen of foliage which hid them from sight, several horsemen pass as if borne along by a hurricane.

A branch struck off the hat of one of the riders as he passed.

"Don Stenio!" Doña Clara exclaimed in horror.

"Zounds!" Don Sancho said, "We were just in time."

CHAPTER XXIX.

EVENTS ACCUMULATE.

The horsemen had continued their wild course without perceiving the fugitives: one of them, indeed, at the cry uttered by Doña Clara, had made a gesture as if to stop his steed, but doubtless supposing that he had been mistaken, he followed his companions after a moment's hesitation, which was very fortunate for him, as Don Sancho had already drawn a pistol, with the resolution of blowing out his brains.

For some minutes the fugitives remained motionless, anxiously listening to the galloping of the horses, whose sound rapidly retired, and was soon lost in the distance, when it became confounded with the other noises of the night.

Then they breathed again, and Don Sancho put back in his holster the pistol which he had held in his hand up to this moment.

"Hum!" he muttered; "Only the thickness of a bush saved us from being discovered."

"Heaven be thanked!" Doña Clara said; "We are saved!"

"That is to say, my little sister, we are not caught," the young man replied, incapable of maintaining his seriousness for five minutes, however grave circumstances might be.

"They are going at a tremendous pace," the Major-domo now remarked; "we have nothing more to fear from them."

"In that case, let us be off," Don Sancho replied.

"Yes, yes, let us go," Doña Clara murmured.

They dashed out of the thicket which had offered them so sure a protection, and entered the plain.

The sky became lighter every moment; and although the sun was still beneath the horizon, its influence was beginning to be felt. Nature appeared to shake off her nocturnal sleep; some birds were already awake under the soft leaves, and preluding, by soft twittering, their matin chant; the dark outlines of savage animals bounded through the tall dew-laden grass; and the birds of prey, expanding their mighty wings, rose high in æther, as if they wished to go and meet the sun, and salute its advent: in a word, it was no longer night, without being fully day.

"Ah! What I do see at the foot of that mound?" Don Sancho suddenly said.

"Where?" Birbomono asked.

"There, straight in front of us."

The Major-domo placed his hands over his eyes, and looked attentively.

"¡*Viva Dios!*" he exclaimed, at the end of a moment, "It is a man!"

"A man?"

"On my word, yes, Excellency; and, as far as I can distinguish at this distance, a Carib savage."

"Zounds! What is he doing on that mound?"

"We shall be able to assure ourselves of that more easily directly, unless he thinks proper to keep out of our way."

"Well, let us go to him, in Heaven's name."

"Brother," Doña Clara objected, "what is the use of lengthening our journey, when we are so hurried?"

"That is true," the young man said.

"Reassure yourself, señora," the Major-domo observed; "that hillock is exactly on the road we must follow, and we cannot help passing it."

Doña Clara said no more, and the trio set out again.

They soon reached the mound, which they ascended at a gallop.

The Carib had not quitted the spot, but the riders stopped in stupor on perceiving that he was not alone.

The Indian, kneeling on the ground, appearing to be attending to a man stretched out before him, and who was beginning to regain his senses.

"Fray Arsenio!" Doña Clara exclaimed at the sight of this man. "Great Heavens! He is dead!"

"No," the Indian answered in a gentle voice, as he turned to her, "but he has been most horribly tortured."

"He! Tortured?" his hearers exclaimed, unanimously.

"Look at his hands," the Carib continued.

The Spaniards uttered a cry of horror and pity at the sight of the poor monk's bleeding and swollen thumbs.

"Oh, it is frightful!" they murmured, sadly.

"Wretch," Don Sancho said in his indignation, "you have brought him to this state!"

The Carib shrugged his shoulders disdainfully.

"The paleface is mad!" he replied; "My brothers do not torture the chiefs of prayer—they respect them. White men, like himself, have inflicted this atrocious punishment upon him."

"Explain yourself, in Heaven's name," Doña Clara continued; "how is it that we find this worthy monk here in such a pitiable state?"

"It will be better to let him explain himself when he has regained his senses. Omopoua knows but little."

"That is true," Doña Clara said, as she dismounted and knelt by the side of the wounded man. "Poor fellow! What frightful suffering he must be enduring."

"Can you not tell us anything, then?" Don Sancho asked.

"Almost nothing," the chief replied, "this is all that I know."

And he narrated in what way the monk had been confided to him, and how he had served as his guide, till they met the white men, when the monk discharged him for the purpose of joining them.

"But," he added, "I know not why, some secret foreboding seemed to warn me not to leave him: hence, instead of going away I hid myself in the shrubs, and witnessed, unseen, the tortures they had him undergo, while insisting on his revealing to them a secret, which he refused to divulge. Conquered by his constancy, they at length abandoned him half dead. Then I rushed from my hiding place, and flew to his help. That is all I know; I am a chief, I have no forked tongue, and a falsehood has never sullied the lips of Omopoua."

"Forgive me, Chief, the improper language I used at the first moment; I was blinded by anger and sorrow," said Don Sancho, holding out his hand.

"The paleface is young," the chief replied with a smile; "his tongue moves more quickly than his heart;" then he took the hand so frankly offered him, and pressed it cordially.

"Oh, oh!" the Major-domo said, with a shake of his head, and leaning over to Don Sancho's ear, "If I am not greatly mistaken, Don Stenio is mixed up in this affair."

"It is not possible," Don Sancho replied, with horror.

"You do not know your brother-in-law, Excellency; his is a weak nature, and all such are cruel; believe me, I am certain of what I state."

"No, no, it would be too frightful."

"Good Heaven," Doña Clara said, at this moment, "we cannot remain here any longer, and yet I should not like to abandon the poor man."

"Let us take him with us," Don Sancho quickly remarked.

"But will his wounds permit him to endure the fatigue of a long ride?"

"We are almost at our journey's end," the Major-domo said, and then, turning to the Carib, added—

"We are going to the bivouac of the two buccaneers, who were hunting on the savannah yesterday."

"Very good;" said the chief, "I will lead the palefaces by a narrow road, and they will arrive ere the sun reaches the edges of the horizon."

Doña Clara and her brother remounted. The monk was cautiously placed in front of the Major-domo, and the small party set out again at a foot pace, under the guidance of the Carib chief.

Poor Fray Arsenio gave no other signs of existence but deep sighs, which at intervals heaved his chest, and stifled groans torn from him by suffering.

At the end of three quarters of an hour they reached the boucan, by the near cut, which Omopoua indicated to them.

It was empty, but not deserted, as was proved by the bull hides, still stretched out on the ground, and held down by pegs, and the boucaned meat suspended from the forks of the branches.

The adventurers were probably away, hunting.

The travellers were considerably annoyed by this contretemps, but Omopoua relieved them of their embarrassment.

"The palefaces need not be anxious," he said, "the chief will warn his friends, the white *franiis*—in their absence the paler faces can use, without fear, everything they find here."

And, joining example to precept, the Carib prepared a bed of dry leaves, which he covered with skins, and, with the Major-domo's aid, carefully laid the wounded man upon it; then he lit a fire, and after, for the last time repeating to the fugitives the assurance that they had nothing to fear, he went off, gliding like a snake through the tall grass.

The Major-domo, who was tolerably well acquainted with the manners of the adventurers, with whom he had had some relations, though always against his will, for, brave though he was, or boasted of being, they inspired him with a superstitious terror—reassured the others as to their position, by declaring to them, that hospitality was so sacred with the buccaneers, that, if they were their most inveterate foes instead of quasi guests, as they had only come on their formal invitation, they would have nothing to apprehend from them.

In the meanwhile, thanks to the attention which Doña Clara had not ceased to bestow on him, the poor monk had returned to his senses. Although very weak at first, he gradually regained sufficient strength to impart to Doña Clara all that happened to him since their separation. This narration, whose conclusion coincided in the minutest details with that previously made by the Carib, plunged Doña Clara into a state of stupefaction, which soon changed into horror, when she reflected on the terrible dangers that menaced her.

In truth, what help could she expect? Who would dare to protect her against her husband, whose high position and omnipotence would annihilate every effort she might make to escape from his vengeance.

"Courage," the monk murmured, with a tender commiseration, "courage, my daughter, above man there is God. Have confidence in Him; He will not abandon you: and if everything fail you, He will come to your assistance, and interfere in your favour."

Doña Clara, in spite of her perfect faith in the power of Providence, only replied to this consolation by tears and sobs; she felt herself condemned.

Don Sancho was hurriedly walking up and down in the front of the ajoupa, twisting his moustache, stamping his foot passionately, and revolving in his head the maddest projects.

"Bah," he muttered, at last, "if that demon will not listen to reason, I will blow out his brains, and that will settle everything."

And highly pleased at having, after so many vain researches, discovered this expeditious mode of saving his sister from the violence, which the desire of vengeance would probably suggest to Don Stenio, the young man lit a cigarette, and patiently awaited the return of the buccaneers, feeling now quite calm and perfectly reassured about the future.

The Major-domo, who was almost indifferent as to what was going on around him, and delighted with the hope of the promised thousand piastres, had turned the time to a good use. Reflecting that on their return, the buccaneers, doubtless, would not be sorry to find their breakfast ready, he had placed in front of the fire an iron pot, in which he placed an enormous lump of meat, to boil, with a reasonable quantity of water; in lieu of bread, he had thrust several ignamas under the ashes, and then busied himself with preparing the pimentado, that absolutely necessary sauce for every buccaneer meal.

The fugitives had held possession of the boucan for nearly an hour and a half, when they heard furious barking, and some twenty dogs rushed howling toward them: but a sharp, though still distant whistle recalled them, and they went off again as quickly as they had come.

A few minutes later, the Spaniards perceived the two buccaneers; they were running up with a surprising speed, although both bore a load weighing upwards of a hundredweight, and were in addition embarrassed by their weapons and hunting equipment.

Their first care, on arriving at the boucan, was to throw on the ground the eight or ten fresh bull hides, till reeking with blood and grease, which they brought, and they then advanced toward the strangers, who, on their side, had risen to receive them.

The dogs, as if they had understood that they must maintain a strict neutrality, were lying on the grass, but kept their flashing eyes fixed on the Spaniards, probably ready to spring at their throat upon the first signal.

"You are welcome at the ajoupa," Lepoletais said, doffing his hat with a politeness that could hardly have been expected on seeing his rough appearance. "So long as you like to remain here, you will be regarded as our brothers; whatever we possess is yours, dispose of it as you think proper, as well as of our arms, should an occasion offer for you to demand our help."

"I thank you in the name of my companions, caballero, and accept your kind proposal," Doña Clara answered.

"A woman!" Lepoletais exclaimed, in surprise, "Pardon me, Madam, for not recognizing you at once."

"I am, caballero, Doña Clara de Bejar, to whom, as I was informed, you have a letter to deliver."

"In that case doubly welcome, madam; as for the note in question, I have not the charge of it, but my comrade."

"Zounds," L'Olonnais exclaimed, who had gone up to the wounded man, "Omopoua certainly told us that this poor devil of a monk had been almost dismasted, but I did not expect to find him in so pitiable a state."

"Well," Lepoletais remarked with a frown, "I am not a very religious man, but hang me if I should not hesitate to treat a monk in this way; only a pagan is capable of committing such a crime."

Then, with a truly filial attention, which the Spaniards admired, the rude adventurer set to work, offering some relief to the wounded man's intolerable sufferings, in which he entirely succeeded, owing to a long practice in treating wounds of every description, and Fray Arsenio soon fell into an invigorating sleep.

During this time L'Olonnais had handed to Doña Clara the letter which Montbarts had entrusted to him for her, and the young lady had withdrawn a little for the purpose of reading it.

"Come, come," L'Olonnais said gaily, as he tapped the Major-domo's shoulder, "that is what I call a sensible lad, he has thought of the substantials; breakfast is ready."

"If that be the case," Lepoletais said, with a significant wink to his comrade; "we will eat double tides, for we shall have work before long."

"Shall we not wait the return of the Indian chief?" Don Sancho asked.

"For what purpose?" L'Olonnais said, with a laugh. "Do not trouble yourself about him, my gentleman: he is a long way off if he is still running. Each of us has his work cut out for him."

"I don't care!" Lepoletais remarked. "You had a deuced fine scent, Señor, in responding to our invitation so quickly!"

"Why so?"

"You will soon know. But now take my advice—recruit your strength by eating."

At this moment Doña Clara rejoined the party. Her demeanour was firmer, and her face almost gay.

The table was soon laid—leaves serving for plates. They sat down to it, that is to say, they formed a circle on the ground, and bravely assailed the provisions.

Don Sancho had resumed all his gaiety. This life appeared to him delightful, and he laughed heartily, while eating with a good appetite. Doña Clara herself, in spite of her inward preoccupation, did honour to this improvised banquet.

"Up! my darlings," Lepoletais had said to his dogs. "Tally ho! No idleness, but go and watch the approaches while we are breakfasting. Your share shall be kept."

The dogs had risen with admirable obedience, and turning their backs on the boucans, scattered in all directions, and speedily disappeared.

"Yours are first-rate dogs," said Don Sancho.

"You Spaniards are good judges of that," the buccaneer replied, mockingly.

The gentleman felt the sting, and did not deem it advisable to dwell on the subject. In fact, it was at Saint Domingo that the Spaniards inaugurated the frightful custom of training bloodhounds to hunt the Indians, and employing them as auxiliaries in their wars.

The breakfast was concluded without any fresh incident worthy of remark, and the most perfect cordiality prevailed during the repast.

When the masters had finished, it was the turn of the servants; that is to say, L'Olonnais whistled up the dogs, which in an instant were collected round him, and gave them their share in equal portions.

The buccaneers, leaving their guests, and at liberty to employ their time as they thought proper, were soon actively busied in preparing their hides.

Several hours passed in this way. About three in the afternoon a dog barked, and then held its tongue.

We have forgotten to state that, after their meal, the dogs returned to their posts at a signal from the engagé.

The two buccaneers exchanged a glance.

"One!" said L'Olonnais.

"Two!" Lepoletais almost immediately answered on a second bark, which broke out in a different direction.

Ere long, like an electric current, the challenges of the hounds succeeded each other with extreme rapidity, raised in all directions.

Still, nothing seemed to justify these warnings given by the sentries. No suspicious sound could be heard, and the savannah seemed to be plunged into the most perfect solitude.

"I beg your pardon, caballero," Don Sancho said to Lepoletais, who continued his task with the same ardor, while laughing merrily with his comrade; "but will you permit me to ask you a question?"

"Do so, do so, my good gentleman. It is at times well to ask questions: besides, if the question does not suit me, I shall be at liberty not to answer it, I suppose?"

"Oh! Of course."

"In that case, speak without fear."

"For some minutes past your dogs seem to have been giving you signals—or, at least, I suppose so?"

"You suppose right, caballero. They are really signals."

"And would there be any indiscretion in asking you the meaning of the signals?"

"Not the least in the world, señor, especially as they interest you quite as much as us."

"I do not understand you."

"You will soon do so. These signals signify that the savannah is at this moment invaded by several Fifties, which are manoeuvring to surround us."

"¡Diablos!" the young man exclaimed, with a start of surprise: "And you do not feel more affected than that?"

"Why anticipate anxiety? My comrade and I had a pressing job which we were obliged to finish. Now that it is done, we are going to turn our attention to the señores."

"But we cannot possibly resist so many enemies?"

"Ah! Ah! Do you really feel inclined for a brush?"

"S'death! My sister and I are incurring quite as much danger as you, and we have not a minute to lose in attempting flight."

"Flight?" the buccaneer said, with a grin; "Nonsense! You must be laughing, my gentleman: we are enclosed in an impassable circle—or what looks so."

"In that case, we are lost."

"How you go on! On the contrary, they are lost."

"They? Why, we are only four against a hundred."

"You are mistaken. There are two hundred; and that makes fifty for each of us. Call in the dogs, L'Olonnais; they are now useless. Stay! Look there; can you see them?"

And he stretched his arm out straight ahead.

In fact, the long lances of the Spanish soldiers appeared above the tall grass. Lepoletais had told the truth. These lances formed a circle, which was being more and more contracted round the boucan.

"Come! That is rather neat," the buccaneer added, as he affectionately tapped the butt of his long fusil.

"Señora," he added, "keep by the side of the wounded man."

"Oh! Let me give myself up," she exclaimed, frantically. "It is on my account that this terrible danger menaces you."

"Señora," the buccaneer replied, as he struck his chest with a gesture of supreme majesty; "you are under the safeguard of my honour, and I swear by Heaven, that no one, so long as I live, shall dare to lay a finger upon you! Go to the wounded man."

Involuntarily subdued by the accent with which the buccaneer uttered these words, Doña Clara bowed without replying, and pensively seated herself inside the ajoupa, by the side of Fray Arsenio, who was still asleep.

"Now, caballero," Lepoletais said to Don Sancho, "if you have never been present at a buccaneering expedition, I promise you you are going to see some fun, and enjoy yourself."

"Well," the young man replied, recklessly; "I will fight, if I must. It is a glorious death for a gentleman, to die sword in hand!"

"Come," said the buccaneer, as he gave him a friendly tap on the shoulder; "you are a fine lad. Something can be made of you."

The Fifties still approached, and the circle grew more and more contracted.

CHAPTER XXX.

THE EXTERMINATOR.

For some minutes a mournful silence—a complete calm, which, however, was loaded with menace, hung heavily over the savannah.

At a whistle from the engagé, the dogs ranged themselves behind their masters, with heads down, lips drawn back to display their sharp teeth, and flashing eyes, they awaited the order to rush forward, though without giving the slightest bark or growl.

L'Olonnais, leaning on his long fusil, was smoking his pipe quietly, while casting sarcastic glances around.

Lepoletais occupied himself with the utmost order in arranging various articles which had been deranged during his morning's operations.

The Major-domo, though in his heart he felt very anxious as to the result of this apparently so disproportionate combat, was obliged to grin and bear it—to use a familiar expression; for he was aware that if he fell into the hands of his master, he had no mercy to expect from him, after the manner in which he had thwarted his projects, by favouring the flight of the Countess.

Don Sancho de Peñaflor, in spite of his natural levity and warlike character, was not without anxiety either, for, as an officer of the Spanish army, his place was not in the ranks of the buccaneers, but with the soldiers who were preparing to attack them.

Doña Clara, kneeling by the side of the monk, with clasped hands, eyes raised to heaven, and face inundated with tears, was fervently imploring the protection of the Almighty.

As for Fray Arsenio, he was quietly sleeping.

Such was the picturesque aspect, imposing in its simplicity, offered at this moment by the camp of the adventurers. Four men were preparing coolly, and as if for the mere fun of the thing, to contend against upwards of two hundred regular troops, from whom they knew that they had no quarter to expect, but whom their insane resistance would probably exasperate, and urge to measures of cruel violence.

In the meanwhile the circle was more and more contracted, and the heads of the soldiers were already beginning to appear above the tall grass.

"Ah, ah!" said Lepoletais, rubbing his horney hands together with an air of triumph—"I fancy it is time to open the ball; what do you say, my boy?"

"Yes, this is the right moment," the engagé replied, as he went to fetch a log from the fire.

"Mind not to stir from the spot where you are," Lepoletais recommended the two Spaniards: "zounds! pay attention to this, or you will run a risk of having your goose cooked," and he laid a stress on the last words, with an evidently sarcastic meaning.

The buccaneers, before establishing their bivouac, had pulled up the grass for a distance of about thirty paces all around the ajoupa; this grass, dried and calcined by the heat of the sun, had been piled up at the border of the cleared ground.

The engagé laid down his fusil, walked straight to this grass, set it on fire, and then slowly returned to rejoin his companions.

The effect of this manoeuvre was instantaneous, a jet of flame suddenly burst out, spread in all directions, and soon a large portion of the savannah presented the appearance of a vast furnace.

The buccaneers laughed heartily at what they considered an excellent joke.

The Spaniards, taken unawares, uttered cries of terror, and rapidly recoiled, pursued by the flame, which constantly spread, and continually advanced toward them.

Still, it was evident that the adventurers had no intention of burning the unfortunate Spaniards alive; the fire lit by them had not sufficient consistency for that; the grass burned and went out again with extreme rapidity. Doubtless the sole result that the buccaneers had wished to obtain, was to cause a panic terror to their enemies, and cast disorder among them; and in this they had been perfectly successful.

The soldiers, half roasted by the flames, fled, uttering cries of terror before this sea of fire, which seemed incessantly to pursue them, without thinking of looking back, or obeying their officers, and having but one thought, escaping the terrible danger that menaced them.

While this was going on Lepoletais coolly explained to Don Sancho the probable results of the expedient he had employed.

"You see, Señor," he said, "this blaze is nothing; it is an almost inoffensive straw fire; in a few minutes, or half an hour at the latest, it will be extinguished. If these men are cowards we shall have got rid of them, if not, they will return, and then the affair will be serious."

"But, as you recognize the inefficiency of this means, why did you employ it? In my opinion it is more injurious than usual to our defence."

The buccaneer shook his head several times.

"You do not understand," he said; "I had several motives for acting thus. In the first place, however brave you may suppose your countrymen to be, they are now demoralised, and it will be very difficult to restore them the courage they no longer possess; on the other hand, I was not sorry to see clearly around me, and sweep the savannah a little, and lastly," he added, with a cunning look, "who told you that the fire I lighted was not a signal?"

"A signal?" Don Sancho exclaimed; "Then you have friends near here?"

"Who knows? Señor, my companions are very active, and are frequently met with when least expected."

"I confess that I do not understand a word of what you are saying to me."

"Patience, Señor, patience! You will soon understand, I assure you, and will not require any great effort of the intellect to do so. L'Olonnais," he added, turning to his comrade, "I think you had better go down there now."

"That is true," L'Olonnais replied, as he carelessly threw his fusil over his shoulder, "he will be expecting me."

"Take some of the dogs with you."

"What for?"

"To guide you, my lad; it is not easy now to find one's way through the ashes, for all the trails are covered."

The engagé called several dogs by their name, and went off without replying, followed by a portion of the pack.

"There," Lepoletais continued, pointing to the engagé, who seemed to be running, as he went at such a pace, "just look at that fellow, he is a fine chap, eh? And how he behaves, though he has not been more than two months in America; in three years from this time I predict to you that he will be one of our most celebrated adventurers."

"Did you buy him?" Don Sancho asked, though but little interested in details which had no importance for him.

"Unluckily, no, he has only been lent to me for a few days; he is the engagé of Montbarts the Exterminator: I offered him two hundred piastres for him, but he refused to sell him."

"What?" the young man exclaimed—"Montbarts, the celebrated filibuster?"

"The very man; he is a friend of mine."

"In that case he is close at hand?"

"That, Señor, is one of the things which you will learn shortly."

As the buccaneer had foreseen, the fire went out almost as quickly as it blazed up, for want of aliment on this savannah, where only grass and a few insignificant shrubs grew.

The Spaniards had sought shelter on the banks of the stream, whose barren sand preserved them from contact with the fire. The forests, too remote from the scene of the fire, had not caught, although a few tongues of flame had played round their edge.

From the boucan it was easy to perceive the Spanish officers striving to restore some degree of order among their troops, doubtless for the purpose of attempting a new attack, although Lepoletais did not appear at all alarmed. Among the officers one was especially remarkable; he was on horseback, and was taking immense trouble to form the ranks, and the other officers came up in turn to receive his orders.

This officer Don Sancho recognized at the first glance.

"This is what I feared," he muttered; "the Count has placed himself at the head of the expedition, and we are lost."

In truth, it was Don Stenio de Bejar, who, on arriving at the hatto at daybreak, and learning the flight of the Countess, resolved to command the expedition.

The position of the adventurers was critical, reduced as they were to three, encamped in the middle of a bare plain, and without entrenchments of any description. Still, the confidence of the buccaneer did not seem diminished, and it was with an ironical air that he examined the preparations the enemy was making against him.

The Spaniards, formed again with great difficulty by the energy of their officers, at last started, and proceeded once more toward the boucan, while taking the same precautions as before, that is to say, being careful to extend their front, so as to form a complete circle, and entirely surround the encampment.

But the march of the Fifties was slow and measured; it was only with extreme caution that the soldiers ventured on this scarcely cooled ground, which might conceal fresh snares.

The Count, pointing to the boucan with his sword, in vain excited his troops to press on, and finish with this handful of scoundrels who dared to oppose His Majesty's troops; the soldiers would not listen, and only advanced with greater caution, for the calmness and apparent negligence of their enemies frightened them more than a hostile demonstration, and must, in their opinion, be owing to some terrible trap laid for them.

At this moment the situation was complicated by a strange episode; a canoe crossed the stream, and ran ashore exactly at the spot which the Spaniards had quitted only a few minutes previously.

This canoe contained five persons, three adventurers, and two Spaniards.

The adventurers stepped ashore as calmly as if they; were quite alone, and pushing the two Spaniards before them, advanced resolutely toward the soldiers.

The latter, astonished, confounded at such audacity, watched them coming without daring to make a movement to oppose them.

These three adventurers were Montbarts, Michael the Basque, and L'Olonnais, and seven or eight dogs followed them. The two Spaniards walked unarmed in front of them, being alarmed about their fate, as was proved by the pallor of their faces, and the startled glances which they threw around them.

The Count, on perceiving the adventurers, uttered a cry of rage, and bounded with uplifted sword to meet them.

"Down with the ladrones!" he cried.

The soldiers, ashamed of being held in check by three men, wheeled round, and boldly advanced.

The adventurers were surrounded in an instant; but, without displaying the slightest surprise at this manoeuvre, they also halted, and standing shoulder to shoulder, faced all sides at once.

The soldiers instinctively stopped.

"Death!" the Count cried; "No mercy for the ladrones!"

"Silence," Montbarts replied; "before menacing, listen to the news these two couriers bring you."

"Seize these villains!" the Count yelled again. "Kill them like dogs!"

"Nonsense," Montbarts remarked, ironically; "you are mad, my worthy sir. Seize us! Why, I defy you to do it."

The three adventurers then emptied their powder flasks into their caps, and placed their bullets on the top of it; then, holding in one hand their caps thus converted into grenades, and in the other their lighted pipes, they waited for the signal.

"Attention, brothers," Montbarts said; "and you scoundrels, make way, there, unless you wish us to blow you all up."

And with a firm and measured step the three adventurers advanced toward the Spaniards, who were struck with terror, and really opened their ranks to make a passage for them.

"Oh!" Montbarts added, with a laugh, "Do not fear that we shall attempt to fly; we only want to join our comrades."

Then was witnessed the extraordinary scene of two hundred men timidly following at a respectful distance three filibusters, who, while walking and smoking to keep their pipes from going out, did not cease from jeering them for their cowardice.

Lepoletais was quite wild with delight: as for Don Sancho, he did not know whether to feel most astonished at the mad temerity of the French, or the cowardice of his countrymen.

The three adventurers thus most easily effected their junction with their companions without having been once disturbed by the Spaniards during a rather long walk. In spite of the prayers and exhortations of the Count to his soldiers, the only thing he obtained from them was, that they continued to advance instead of retreating, as they had a manifest intention of doing.

But, while the adventurers thus drew the soldiers after them, and concentrated their entire attention, a thing was happening which the Count perceived when too late, and which began to cause him serious alarm as to the result of his expedition.

In the rear of the centre formed by the Spanish soldiers, another circle had been drawn up as if by enchantment, but the latter was composed of buccaneers and red Caribs, at whose head Omopoua made himself remarkable.

The adventurers and Indians had manoeuvred with so much intelligence, vivacity, and silence, that the Spaniards were enveloped in a network of steel, even before they had suspected the danger that menaced them.

The Count uttered an exclamation of rage, to which the soldiers responded by a cry of terror.

The situation was, in fact, extremely critical for the unhappy Spaniards, and unless a miracle occurred, it was literally impossible for them to escape death.

In fact they had no longer to contend against a few men, resolute, it is true, but whom numbers must eventually conquer, even at a sacrifice; the filibusters were at least two hundred, and with their allies the Caribs, formed an effective strength of five hundred men, all as brave lions, and three hundred more than the Spaniards; the latter understood that they were lost.

On arriving at the boucan, directly that he had squeezed Lepoletais' hand and complimented him on the way in which he had contrived to gain time, Montbarts gravely occupied himself with his comrades, in restoring the powder and bullets to their respective receptacles, as he probably judged that their caps might now be used for their legitimate purpose.

While the filibuster was engaged in this occupation, Doña Clara, pale as a corpse, fixed on him burning glances, though she did not venture to approach him. At length she took courage, advanced a few paces and murmured with an effort in a trembling voice and with clasped hands,—

"I am here, sir."

Montbarts trembled at the sound of this voice, and turned pale; but he made an effort over himself and softened the rather hard expression of his eye.

"I have come solely on your account, Madam," he replied with a polite bow; "I shall have the honour of placing myself at your orders in a moment; permit me first to make sure that our interview will be uninterrupted."

Doña Clara hung her head and returned to her seat by the wounded man.

The adventurers had continued to advance and were soon scarce ten paces from the Spaniards, whose terror was augmented by this disagreeable vicinity.

"Hola, brothers!" Montbarts shouted in a powerful voice; "Halt, if you please."

The filibusters instantaneously became motionless.

"And now, you fellows," the Admiral continued, addressing the soldiers; "throw down your arms, unless you wish to be immediately shot."

All the lances and swords fell on the ground with a unanimity which proved the desire of the soldiers not to have the menace carried into effect.

"Surrender your sword, sir," Montbarts said to the Count.

"Never!" the latter exclaimed, as he made his horse curvet, and advanced with upraised blade on the adventurer, from whom he was only three paces distant.

At the same instant a fusil was discharged and the sword blade, struck within an inch of the guard, was shivered; the Count found himself disarmed. With a sudden movement Montbarts seized the horse's bridle with one hand, and with the other hurled the Count from the saddle and laid him prostrate on the ground.

"Patatras!" Lepoletais said laughingly, while reloading his fusil; "What a deuced funny idea to try alone to resist five hundred men."

The Count rose quite confused by his fall; a livid pallor covered his face, and his features were contracted by anger; all at once his eyes fell upon the Countess.

"Ah!" He yelled with the cry of a tiger, as he darted towards her, "At least I shall avenge myself."

But Montbarts seized him by the arm and rendered him motionless.

"One word, one gesture, and I blow out your brains like the wild beast you are," he said to him.

There was such an accent of menace in the filibuster's words; his interference had been so rapid that the Count, involuntarily cowed, fell back with his arms folded on his chest and remained apparently calm, although a volcano was at work in his heart, and his eyes were obstinately fixed on the Countess.

Montbarts gazed for a moment at his enemy with an expression of pity and contempt.

"You have desired, sir," he at length said to him ironically; "to try your strength with the filibusters and will soon learn the cost; while impelled by a mad desire of vengeance and inspired by an imaginary jealousy, you were virulently pursuing a lady whose noble heart and brilliant virtues you are incapable of appreciating, one half of the island of which you are the governor has been torn forever from the power of your sovereign, by my companions and myself; Tortuga, Leogane, San Juan de Goava, and your hatto del Rincón, suddenly surprised, have fallen without a blow."

The Count drew himself up, a feverish flush covered his face, he advanced a step and cried in a voice choking with passion,—

"You lie, villain; however great your audacity may be, it is impossible that you have succeeded in seizing the places you mention."

Montbarts shrugged his shoulders.

"An insult coming from lips like yours has no effect," he said, "you shall soon have the confirmation of what I assert; but enough of this subject; I wished to have you in my power in order that you may be witness of what I have to say to this lady. Come," he added, addressing Doña Clara; "come, madam, and forgive me for not wishing to see you except in the presence of the man you call your husband."

On hearing the appeal, Doña Clara rose trembling, and tottered forward.

There was a momentary silence; Montbarts, with his head hanging on his chest, seemed plunged in bitter thoughts; at length he drew himself up, passed his hand over his forehead as if to drive away the mist that obscured his reason, turned to Doña Clara, and said to her in a gentle voice,—

"You desired to see me, madam, in order to remind me of a time forever past, and to confide a secret to me. This secret I have no right to know; the Count de Barmont is dead, dead to everybody, to you before all, who did not blush to renounce him, and though you belonged to him by legitimate ties, and before all by the more legitimate one of a powerful love, cowardly permitted yourself to be chained to another; this is a crime, madam, which no forgiveness can efface, either in the present or past."

"Pity me, sir," the unhappy lady said, as she writhed beneath this curse and burst into tears; "pity me, in the name of my remorse and my sufferings!"

"What are you doing, madam?" the Count exclaimed, "Rise at once."

"Silence," Montbarts said in a harsh voice, "Allow this culprit to be bowed beneath the weight of her repentance; you, who have been her executioner, have less right than anyone else to protect her."

Don Sancho had rushed toward his sister and, roughly repulsing the Count, raised her in his arms. Montbarts continued.

"I will only add one word, madam; the Count de Barmont had a child; on the day when that child comes to ask his mother's pardon of me, I will grant it—perhaps," he added in a faint voice.

"Oh!" the young lady exclaimed with a feverish energy, as she seized the hand which the filibuster had not the courage to withdraw from her, "Oh sir! You are great and noble, this promise restores me all my hope and courage; oh! I swear to you, sir, I will find my child again."

"Enough, madam," Montbarts continued with ill suppressed emotion; "this interview has lasted too long; here is your brother, he loves you, and will be able to protect you; there is another person whom I regret not to see here, for he would have advised and sustained you, in your affliction."

"To whom do you allude?" Don Sancho asked.

"To the confessor of your sister."

The young man turned away without answering.

"Why, brother," Lepoletais here observed, "here he is half dead, look at his burnt hands."

"Oh!" Montbarts exclaimed, "It is really he, who is the monster that has dared—"

"Here he is!" the buccaneer replied, as he tapped the shoulder of the Count, who was dumb with stupor and horror, for only at this moment did he notice his victim.

Two flashes of flame started from Montbart's eyes.

"Villain," he exclaimed, "what, torture an inoffensive man! Oh, Spaniards, race of vipers! What sufficiently horrible punishment could I inflict on you!"

All his hearers trembled at this passion so long restrained, which had at length burst its bonds and now overflowed with irresistible violence.

"By Heaven!" the filibuster exclaimed in a terrible voice, "It is the worse for you, butcher, that you remind me I am Montbarts the exterminator. L'Olonnais, prepare the fire under the barbacoas of the boucan."

An indescribable terror seized on all the hearers of this order, which clearly expressed to what a horrible punishment the Count was condemned; Don Stenio himself, in spite of his indomitable pride, felt a chill at his heart.

But at this moment, the monk, who had hitherto remained motionless on his couch, and apparently insensible to what was going on, rose with a painful effort, and leaning on the shoulders of Doña Clara and her brother, tottered forward, and knelt with them to the filibuster.

"Pity," he exclaimed, "pity, in Heaven's name!"

"No," Montbarts replied harshly, "This man is condemned."

"I implore you, brother, be merciful," the monk went on to urge him.

All at once the Count drew two pistols from his doublet, and pointed one at Doña Clara, while he placed the other against his own forehead.

"Of what use is it to implore a tiger," he said, "I die, but by my own hands, and I die avenged," and he pulled the trigger.

The double detonation was blended in one.

The Count fell dead on the ground; the second shot badly aimed did not strike Doña Clara, but Fray Arsenio, and laid him dying at the foot of his assassin. The last word of the poor monk was, "pity!"

And he expired with his eyes fixed on heaven, as if with a last prayer addressed in favour of his murderer.

At sunset the savannah had returned to its habitual solitude; Montbarts, after having the victim and the assassin interred in the same grave, doubtless that the just man might protect the culprit in the presence of the Most High, set out for Port Margot, at the head of the filibusters and Caribs.

Doña Clara and her brother returned to the hatto del Rincón, accompanied by the Spanish soldiers, to whom Montbarts had consented to restore their liberty, through consideration for the two young people.